There are secrets no one tells . . .

JOURNEY

Also by Danielle Steel

DANIELLE STEEL

JOURNEY

A Dell Book

JOURNEY
A Dell Book

PUBLISHING HISTORY
Delacorte Press hardcover edition published November 2000
Dell mass market edition published November 2001
Dell mass market reissue / August 2006

Published by Bantam Dell
A Division of Random House, Inc.
New York, New York

Excerpt from "Journey" by Edna St. Vincent Millay from *Collected
Poems*, HarperCollins Copyright © 1921, 1948 by Edna St. Vincent
Millay

Library of Congress Catalog Card Number: 00031512

ISBN-13: 978-0-440-24376-2
ISBN-10: 0-440-24376-9

Printed in the United States of America
Published simultaneously in the United States and Canada

www.bantamdell.com

OPM   10 9 8 7 6 5 4 3 2 1

To my children,
Beatie, Trevor, Todd, Sam,
Victoria, Vanessa, Maxx, and Zara,
who have traveled far with me,
with faith and good humor and so much love.

And to Nick,
who is safely in God's loving hands.

with all my love,

d.s.

JOURNEY

My journey has been long. I do not regret it. At times, it has been dark, a perilous course. At other times, joyous, dappled with sunlight. It has been hard more often than easy.

The road was fraught with dangers for me from the beginning, the forest thick, the mountains high, the darkness terrifying. And through it all, even in the mists, a small pinpoint of light, a tiny star to guide me.

I have been both wise and foolish. I have been loved, and betrayed, and abandoned. And much to my despair, I have unwittingly wounded others, and humbly beg their forgiveness. I have forgiven those who have hurt me, as I pray they will forgive me for allowing them to hurt me. I have loved much, and given of my whole heart and soul. And even when badly wounded, have continued on the path, with faith, and hope, and even blind belief, toward love and freedom. The journey continues, easier than it has been.

For those of you still lost in the darkness, may your traveling companions treat you well. May you find safe havens when you need them, and clearings in the forest. May you find cool waters where you can safely drink, quench your thirst, and bathe your wounds. And may you one day find healing.

When we meet, our hands will join, and we will know each other. The light is there, waiting for us. We must each, in our own way, journey on until we find it. To reach it, we will need determination, strength and courage, gratitude and patience. And after all that, wisdom. And at journey's end, we will find ourselves, we will find peace, and the love that, until now, we have only dreamed of.

May God speed you on your journey, and protect you.

d.s.

"Journey"

". . . All my life long
Over my shoulder have I looked at peace;
And now I fain would lie in this long grass
And close my eyes."

EDNA ST. VINCENT MILLAY

Chapter 1

THE LONG BLACK LIMOUSINE pulled up slowly, and came to a stop, in a long line of cars just like it. It was a balmy evening in early June, and two Marines stepped forward in practiced unison, as Madeleine Hunter emerged gracefully from the car in front of the east entrance to the White House. A brightly lit flag was fluttering in the summer breeze, and she smiled at one of the Marines as he saluted. She was tall and thin, in a white evening gown that draped elegantly from one shoulder. Her hair was dark and swept up in a neat French twist which showed off her long neck and single bare shoulder to perfection.

Her skin was creamy, her eyes blue, and she moved with enormous poise and grace in high-heeled silver sandals. Her eyes danced as she smiled, and stepped aside as a photographer flashed her picture. And then another, as her husband stepped out of the car and took his place beside her. Jack Hunter was powerfully built, a man of forty-five, he had made his first fortune in the course of a career in pro football, invested it brilliantly, and in time had traded and sold and bought first a radio station, then added television to it, and by forty owned one of the major cable networks. Jack Hunter had long since turned his good fortune into big business. And he was very big business.

The photographer snapped their photograph again, and then they swiftly disappeared into the White House. They made a striking couple, and had for seven years. Madeleine was thirty-four, and had been twenty-five when he discovered her in Knoxville. Her drawl had long since disappeared, as had his. Jack was from Dallas, and he spoke in powerful, clipped tones that convinced the listener instantly that he knew exactly what he was doing. He had dark eyes that pursued his quarry to all corners of the room, and he had a way of listening to several conversations at once, while still managing to seem intent on the person to whom he was speaking. There were times, people who knew him well said, when his eyes seemed to bore right through you, and other times when you felt he was about to caress you. There was something powerful and almost hypnotizing about him. Just looking at him, sleekly put together in his dinner jacket and perfectly starched shirt, his dark hair smoothly combed, he was someone one wanted to get to know and be close to.

He had had the same effect on Madeleine when they met, when she was barely more than a girl in Knoxville. She had had a Tennessee drawl then, she had come to Knoxville from Chattanooga. She'd been a receptionist at the television station where she worked, until a strike forced her into doing first weather, and then news, on camera. She was awkward and shy, but so beautiful that the viewers who saw her sat mesmerized as they stared at her. She looked more like a model or a movie star, but she had a girl-next-door quality about her that everyone loved, and a breathtaking ability to get right to the heart of a story. And Jack was bowled over when he first saw her. Her words as well as her eyes were searing.

"What do you do here, pretty girl? Break all the boys' hearts, I'll bet," he'd said to her. She didn't look a minute over twenty, though she was nearly five years older. He had stopped to talk to her when she came off the air.

"Not likely," she laughed. He was negotiating to buy the station. And he had, two months later. And as soon as he did, he made her co-anchor, and sent her to New York to teach her first everything she needed to learn about network news, and then how to do her hair and makeup. And the effect, when he saw her on the air again, was impressive. Within months, her career was off and running.

It was Jack who helped extricate her from the nightmare she had been living, with a husband she'd been married to since she was seventeen, who had committed every possible kind of abuse on her. It was no different from what she had seen happen in Chattanooga as a child, between her parents. Bobby Joe had been her high school sweetheart, and they'd been married for eight years when Jack Hunter bought the cable network in Washington, D.C., and made her an irresistible offer. He wanted her as his prime-time anchor, and promised her that if she came, he'd help her sort her life out, and cover all the most important stories.

He came to Knoxville himself in a limousine. She

met him at the Greyhound bus station, with one small Samsonite bag and a look of terror. She got into the car with him without a sound, and they drove all the way to Washington together. It took Bobby Joe months to figure out where she was, and by then she had filed for divorce, with Jack's help, and a year later, they were married. She had been Mrs. Jack Hunter for seven years, and Bobby Joe and his unthinkable abuse on her were a dim nightmare. She was a star now. She led a fairy-tale life. She was known and respected and adored all across the country. And Jack treated her like a princess. As they walked into the White House arm in arm, and stood in the reception line, she looked relaxed and happy. Madeleine Hunter had no worries. She was married to an important, powerful man, who loved her, and she knew it. She knew that nothing bad would ever happen to her again. Jack Hunter wouldn't let it. She was safe now.

The President and First Lady shook hands with them in the East Room, and the President said in an undervoice to Jack that he wanted to catch a private moment with him later. Jack nodded, and smiled at him, as Madeleine chatted with the First Lady. They knew each other well. Maddy had interviewed her several times, and the Hunters were invited to the White House often. And as Madeleine drifted into the room on her husband's arm, heads turned, people smiled and nodded, everyone recognized her. It was a long, long way from Knoxville. She didn't know where Bobby Joe was now, and no longer cared. The life she had known with him seemed entirely unreal now. This was her reality, a world of power and important people, and she was a bright star among them.

They mingled with the other guests, and the French Ambassador chatted with Madeleine amiably and introduced her to his wife, while Jack moved away to speak to a Senator who was the head of the Senate Ethics Committee. There was a matter before them that Jack had been wanting to discuss with him. Madeleine saw them out of the corner of her eye, as the Brazilian Ambassador approached her, with an attractive Congresswoman from Mississippi. It was, as always, an interesting evening.

Her dinner partners, when they moved into the State Dining Room, were a Senator from Illinois and a Congressman from California, both of whom she had met before, and who vied all evening for her attention. Jack was sitting between the First Lady and Barbara Walters. It was late in the evening before he joined his wife again, and they moved smoothly onto the dance floor.

"How was it?" he asked casually, watching several key players as he danced with her. Jack rarely lost track of the people around him, and he usually had an agenda, of those he wanted to see, and meet, and touch base with again, either about a story or a matter of business. He rarely, if ever, missed opportunities, and never simply spent an evening without some plan to what he was doing. He had spent a few minutes in a quiet aside with the President, and then President Armstrong had invited him to Camp David for lunch that weekend to continue the conversation. But Jack was concentrating on his wife now.

"So how was Senator Smith? What did he have to say for himself?"

"The usual. We talked about the new tax bill," she

smiled at her handsome husband. She was a worldly woman now, of considerable sophistication and enormous polish. She was, as Jack liked to say, a creature entirely of his making. He took full credit for how far she had come, and the enormous success she enjoyed on his network, and he loved to tease her about it.

"That sounds pretty sexy," he said, referring to the tax bill. The Republicans were having a fit over it, but Jack thought the Democrats would win this one, particularly with the President behind them, which he was squarely. "What about Congressman Wooley?"

"He's so cute," she said, smiling up at Jack again, as always, still a little dazzled by his presence. There was something about her husband's looks, his charisma, the aura that surrounded him, that still impressed her. "He talked about his dog and his grandchildren. He always does." She liked that about him, and he was crazy about the woman he had been married to for nearly sixty years now.

"It's a wonder he still gets elected," Jack said as the music ended.

"I think everyone loves him." The warm heart of the girl next door from Chattanooga hadn't left her, despite her good fortune. She never lost sight of where she'd come from, and there was still a certain ingenuousness about her, unlike her husband, who was sharply honed, and on occasion somewhat abrasive and aggressive. But she liked talking to people about their kids. She had none of her own, and Jack had two sons in college in Texas, though he rarely saw them, but they were fond of Maddy. And despite his vast success, their mother had few good things to say about their father, or Maddy.

They had been divorced for fifteen years, and the word she used most often to describe him was *ruthless*.

"Ready to call it a night?" Jack asked, as he assessed the room again, and decided that he had already touched base with everyone that mattered, and the party was nearly over. The President and First Lady had just left, and their guests were free to go now. Jack saw no reason to stay any longer. And Maddy was happy to go home, she had to be in the newsroom early the next morning.

They left the party quietly, and their driver was waiting for them near the door, as they made a graceful exit. And Maddy settled comfortably into the limousine beside her husband. It was a long way from Bobby Joe's old Chevy truck, the parties they had gone to at the local bar, and the friends they had visited in trailers. Sometimes she still had trouble believing that her two very different lives were part of one lifetime. This was all so different. She moved in the world of Presidents and Kings and Queens, politicians and princes and tycoons like her husband.

"What did you and the President talk about tonight?" she asked, stifling a yawn. She looked as lovely and as beautifully put together as she had at the beginning of the evening. And more than she realized, she was an incredible asset to her husband. Rather than being recognized as the man who had invented her, he was seen now as Madeleine Hunter's husband, and if he knew it, he never acknowledged it to Maddy.

"The President and I discussed something very interesting," Jack said, looking vague, "I'll tell you about it when I'm free to talk about it."

"When will that be?" she asked with renewed interest.

She was not only his wife, but had become a skilled reporter, and she loved what she did, the people she worked with, and the newsroom. She felt as though she had her fingers on the pulse of the nation.

"I'm not sure yet. I'm having lunch with him on Saturday at Camp David."

"It must be important." But it all was. Anything that involved the President was potentially a big story.

They drove the short distance to R Street, chatting about the party. And Jack asked her if she'd seen Bill Alexander.

"Only from a distance. I didn't realize he was back in Washington." He had been in seclusion for the past six months, after the death of his wife in Colombia the year before. It had been a terrible story, which Maddy remembered all too clearly. She had been kidnapped by terrorists, and Ambassador Alexander had handled the negotiations himself, awkwardly apparently. After collecting the ransom, the terrorists had panicked and killed her. And the Ambassador had resigned shortly after.

"He's a fool," Jack said without preamble or pity for him. "He never should have tried to handle it himself. Anyone could have predicted that would happen."

"I don't suppose he believed that," Maddy said quietly, glancing out the window.

And a moment later, they were home, and she and Jack walked up the stairs as he took his tie off.

"I have to be in the office early tomorrow," she said, as he unbuttoned his shirt in their bedroom, and she slipped her dress off and stood before him in nothing more than pantyhose and her high-heeled silver sandals. She had a spectacular body which was never wasted on him, nor had it been in her previous life, though the two men she had been married to were extraordinarily different. The one brutal and unkind and rough with her, indifferent to her feelings, or cries of pain when he hurt her, the other so smooth, so careful, so seemingly respectful of her. Bobby Joe had once broken her arms, and she had broken her leg when he pushed her down the stairs. That had been right after she had met Jack, and he had been in a jealous rage about him. She had sworn to him that she wasn't involved with Jack, and she hadn't been then. He was her employer and they were just friends, the rest had come later, after she left Knoxville and moved to Washington to work for him at his cable network. Within a month of her arrival in Washington she and Jack had become lovers, but her divorce was already in the works then.

"Why are you going in early?" Jack asked over his shoulder as he disappeared into his black marble bathroom. They had bought the house five years before, from a wealthy Arab diplomat. There was a full gym and a swimming pool downstairs, beautiful reception rooms Jack liked to use to entertain, and all six of the house's bathrooms were marble. The house had four bedrooms, a master, and three guest rooms.

There was no plan to turn any of the guest rooms into a nursery. Jack had made it very clear to her right from the beginning that he didn't want children. He hadn't enjoyed the two he had when they were growing up, and he had no desire to have more, in fact he absolutely forbade it. And after a brief period of mourning for the babies she would never have, at Jack's insistence, Maddy had had her tubes tied. She thought it was better in some ways, she had had half a dozen abortions during her years with Bobby Joe, and she wasn't even sure anymore if she could have a normal baby. It seemed easier to give in to Jack's wishes and not take any chances. He had given her so much, and wanted such great things for her, she could see his point that children would only be an obstacle she'd have to overcome, and a burden on her career. But there were still times when she regretted the irreversibility of her decision. At thirty-four, a lot of her friends were still having babies, and all she had was Jack now. She wondered if she'd regret it even more when she grew older and had no grandchildren, or children of her own. But it was a small price to pay for the life she shared with Jack Hunter. And it had been so important to Jack. He had insisted on it.

They met again in their large comfortable bed, and Jack pulled her close, as she cuddled up to him, and rested her head on his shoulder. They often lay there for a while before they went to sleep, talking about what had happened that day, the places they'd been, the people they'd met with, the parties they'd been to. As they did now, and Maddy tried to guess what the President was up to.

"I told you, I'll tell you when I can, stop guessing."

"Secrets drive me crazy," she giggled.

"You drive me crazy," he said, turning her gently toward him, and feeling the satin of her flesh beneath the silky nightgown. He never tired of her, she never bored him, in bed or out, and he took pleasure in knowing that she was his, body and soul, not only at the network, but in their bedroom. Most particularly there, he had an insatiable appetite for her, and at times she felt as though he were going to devour her. He loved everything about her, knew everything she did, liked knowing where she was every moment of the day, and what she was doing. And he had a lot to say about it. But all he could think of now was the body he could never get enough of, and as he kissed her and grabbed her hard, she moaned softly. She never resented or objected to the way he took her, or how often. She loved the fact that he wanted her so much, and it pleased her to know that she still excited him so intensely. It was all so different than it had been with Bobby Joe. Bobby had wanted nothing more than to use her and to hurt her. What excited Jack was beauty and power. Having "created" Maddy made him feel powerful, and "possessing" Maddy in bed nearly drove him out of his senses.

Chapter 2

As she always did, Maddy got up at six o'clock, and slipped quietly into her bathroom. She showered and dressed, knowing that they would do her hair and makeup, as they did every day, at the network. And when Jack came down to the kitchen at seven-thirty, freshly combed and shaven, in a dark gray suit and starched white shirt, he found her fresh-faced, in a dark blue pantsuit, drinking coffee and reading the morning paper.

She looked up, when she heard him come in, and commented on the latest scandal on the Hill. One of the Congressmen had been arrested the night before, for consorting with a hooker. "You'd think they'd know better," she said, handing him the *Post*, and reaching for *The Wall Street Journal*. She liked reading the papers before she got to the newsroom. She usually read *The New York Times* on the way to work, and if she had time, the *Herald Tribune*.

They left for work together at eight o'clock, and Jack

asked her if she was working on a story that was taking her in so early. Sometimes she didn't go in till ten. She usually worked on stories all day, and taped interviews during lunch. She didn't go on the air until five o'clock, and then again at seven-thirty. She was through by eight, and when they were going out for the evening, she changed in her dressing room at the network. It was a long day for both of them, but they liked it.

"Greg and I are working on a series of interviews of women on the Hill. We want to figure out who's doing who, and when. We already have five women lined up. I think it'll be a good story." Greg Morris was her co-anchor, a young black reporter from New York, who had worked with her for the past two years, and they were fond of each other, and loved working together.

"Don't you think you should do the story on your own? Why do you need Greg to do it with you?"

"It keeps things interesting," she said coolly, "the male perspective." She had her own ideas about the show, which often differed from her husband's, and sometimes she didn't like telling him too much about what she was doing. She didn't want him to interfere with her stories. Sometimes, it was a challenge being married to the head of the network.

"Did the First Lady talk to you last night about your being on her Commission on Violence Against Women?" Jack asked casually, as Maddy shook her head. She had heard vague rumors about the commission the First Lady was forming, but she hadn't mentioned it to Maddy.

"No, she didn't."

"She will," Jack said smoothly. "I told her I thought you'd love to be on it."

"I would, if I have time. It depends how much of a commitment it involves."

"I told her you'd do it," Jack said bluntly. "It's good for your image."

Maddy was silent for a moment, as she stared out the window. They were being driven to work by Jack's driver, he had been with Jack for years, and they both trusted him completely. "I'd like a chance to make that decision for myself," she said quietly. "Why did you tell her I'd do it?" It made her feel like a kid when he did that. He was only eleven years older than she, but sometimes he treated her as though she were a child, and he the father.

"I told you. It will be good for you. Consider it an executive decision by the head of the network." Like so many others. She hated it when he did that, and he knew it. It truly annoyed her. "Besides, you just said you'd like to."

"*If* I have time. Let me decide that." But they were at the network by then, and Charles was opening the car door for them. There was no time to pursue the conversation further. And Jack didn't look as though he intended to anyway. He had obviously made his mind up. He gave her a quick kiss as they said good-bye. He disappeared into his private elevator, and after passing through security and the metal detector, Maddy took the elevator up to the newsroom.

She had a glassed-in office there, a secretary and research assistant, and Greg Morris had a slightly smaller office very near her. He waved as he saw her walking swiftly into her office, and he came in with a mug of coffee in his hand a minute later.

"Good morning . . . or is it?" He looked her over

carefully, and thought he detected something as she glanced at him. Though it was hard to see it unless you knew her well, inside she was seething. Maddy didn't like to get angry. In her past life, anger had meant danger, and she never forgot that.

"My husband just made an 'executive decision.'" She glanced at Greg with unveiled annoyance. He was like a brother to her.

"Uh-oh. Am I getting fired?" He was teasing, his ratings were nearly as high as hers, but you were never entirely sure where you stood with Jack. He was capable of making sudden, seemingly irrational, nonnegotiable decisions. But as far as Greg knew, Jack liked him.

"Nothing that dramatic, thank you." Maddy was quick to put his mind to rest. "He told the First Lady I'd be on her new Commission on Violence Against Women, without even asking me about it."

"I thought you liked that kind of thing," Greg said, sprawling in the chair across her desk from her, as she sat down primly in her seat.

"That's beside the point, Greg. I like to be asked. I'm a grown-up."

"He probably figured you'd want to do it. You know how dumb men are. They forget to go through all the steps between A and Z, and just make assumptions."

"He knows how much I hate that." But they both also knew that Jack made a lot of decisions for her. It was the way things had always been between them. He said he knew what was best for her.

"I hate to be the one to tell you, but we just got word of another 'executive decision' he must have made yesterday. It just filtered down from Mount Olympus before you got here." Greg looked less than pleased as he said it. He was a good-looking African-American man with a casual style, and long, graceful limbs. As a kid, he had wanted to be a dancer, but had wound up in news instead, and loved it.

"What are you talking about?" Maddy looked worried.

"He took a whole segment out of the show. Our political commentary on the seven-thirty."

"He did *what*? Why? People love that. And we like to do it."

"He wants more hard news on the seven-thirty. They said it was a ratings-based decision. They want us to try it this way."

"Why didn't he talk to us about it?"

"When does he ever ask us, Maddy? Come on, kiddo, you know him a lot better than I do. Jack Hunter makes his own decisions, without consultation from the on-air talent. That's hardly a news flash."

"Shit." She looked angry as she poured herself a cup of coffee. "That's nice. So no editorials at all now? That's just plain stupid."

"I thought so too, but Father Knows Best. They said they might put it back in on the five o'clock if people complain about it. But not for the moment."

"Great. Christ, you'd think he would have warned me."

"The way he usually does, right, Pocahontas? Give me a break. Let's face it, we just work here."

"Yeah, I guess so." She steamed silently about it for a minute and then got down to work with Greg, figuring out who they were going to interview first, among the list of Congresswomen they had already selected. It was nearly eleven before they finished, and Maddy went out to do some errands and grab a sandwich. She was back at her desk at one, working on the Congressional interviews again. She stayed at her desk all afternoon, and at four she walked into hair and makeup and met Greg there, and they chatted about the stories that had broken that afternoon. So far, there was nothing important.

"Have you ripped Jack's head off yet about our editorials?" He grinned at her.

"No, but I will later, when I see him." She never saw him in the course of the day, although they usually left work together, unless he had somewhere to go after work that didn't include her, and then she went home alone, and waited for him.

The five o'clock news went well, and she and Greg hung out and talked, as they always did, while waiting to go back on at seven-thirty. At eight o'clock they were finished, and Jack appeared as she came off the set. She said goodnight to Greg, took off her mike, picked up her handbag, and left with Jack a minute later. They had promised to drop by at a cocktail party in Georgetown.

"What the hell happened to our editorials?" she asked him as they sped toward Georgetown.

"The ratings showed that people were tired of them."

"Bullshit, Jack, they love them."

"That's not what we heard," he said firmly, unmoved by her comment.

"Why didn't you say something to me about it this morning?" She still looked annoyed as she talked about it.

"It had to go through channels."

"You never even asked me. It would have been nice

to know. I think you really made the wrong decision on that one."

"Let's see what the ratings tell us." They were at the party in Georgetown by then, and lost each other in the crowd for a while. She didn't see Jack again until he came to find her two hours later, and asked if she was ready to leave. They both were, it had been a long day and they'd been up late the night before, at the White House.

They didn't talk much on the way home, and he reminded her that he was going to Camp David for lunch with the President the next morning. "I'll meet you at the plane at two-thirty," he said, looking distracted. They went to Virginia every weekend. Jack had bought a farm there the year before he met Maddy, and it was a place he loved, and she had gotten used to. It had a rambling, comfortable house, and miles of land around it. He kept stables, and some Thoroughbreds. But in spite of the pleasant scenery, Maddy was always bored there.

"Do you want to just stay in town this weekend?" she asked hopefully, as she followed him into the house after Charles dropped them off.

"We can't. I invited Senator McCutchins and his wife for the weekend." He hadn't told her that either.

"Was that a secret too?" Maddy asked, looking irritated. She hated it when he didn't ask her about things like that, or at least warn her.

"I'm sorry, Maddy, I've been busy. I have a lot on my mind this week. There's some complicated stuff going on at the office." She suspected he was distracted by the meeting at Camp David. But he still could have told her about the McCutchinses coming for the weekend. He smiled at her gently as he said it. "That was thoughtless of me. I'm sorry, baby." It was hard to stay angry at him when he said it like that. He had an endearing way about him, and just as she started getting angry at him, she always found she couldn't.

"It's okay. I just would have liked to know." She didn't bother telling him that she couldn't stand Paul McCutchins. Jack knew it. He was fat, overbearing, and arrogant, and his wife always looked terrified of him. She was too nervous to say more than two words whenever Maddy saw her, and she looked as though she were scared of her own shadow. Even their kids looked nervous. "Are they bringing their kids?" They had three pale, whiny children, whose company Maddy never enjoyed, although she generally liked children. Just not the McCutchinses'.

"I told them they couldn't," Jack said with a grin. "I know you can't stand them, and I don't blame you. Besides, they scare the horses."

"That's something at least," Maddy said as they went inside. It had been a long week for both of them, and she was tired. She fell asleep in Jack's arms that night, and she didn't even hear him get up the next morning. He was up and dressed and reading the paper by the time she came down for breakfast.

Jack gave her a quick kiss and a few minutes later, he left for the White House, where he was meeting the Presidential helicopter to take him to Camp David.

"Have fun," she smiled at him, as she poured herself a cup of coffee. He looked as though he were in high spirits. Nothing excited Jack more than power. It was addictive.

And when she saw him at the airport that afternoon,

he was positively glowing. He looked as though he'd had a great time with Jim Armstrong.

"So, did you solve all the problems in the Middle East, or plan a small war somewhere?" she asked with a look of mischief. Just looking at him in the June sunshine, she fell in love with him all over again. He was so damn attractive, and so handsome.

"Something like that," he smiled mysteriously, as he followed her onto the plane he had bought that winter. It was a Gulfstream and he was happy with it. They used it every weekend, and he used it for business.

"Can you tell me about it?" She was dying of curiosity, but he shook his head and laughed at her. He loved teasing her with something he knew and she didn't.

"Not yet. Soon though."

There were two pilots and they took off twenty minutes later, as Jack and Maddy chatted in the comfortable chairs at the back of the plane, and they headed south to their farm in Virginia. And much to Maddy's chagrin, the McCutchinses were already waiting for them when they got there. They had driven down from Washington that morning.

Predictably, Paul McCutchins slapped Jack resoundingly on the back, and squeezed Maddy far too close when he embraced her, and his wife Janet said nothing. Her eyes only met Maddy's for an instant. It was as though she were afraid Maddy would see some dark secret in her, if she allowed her to look into her eyes for any longer. Something about Janet had always made Maddy uncomfortable, although she had never known what it was, and didn't care enough to think about it.

But Jack wanted some time to talk to Paul about a

bill he was endorsing. It had to do with gun control, an ever-sensitive issue, and eternally newsworthy.

The two men wandered off to the stables almost as soon as Jack and Maddy arrived, which left Maddy stuck with Janet. She suggested they go inside, and offered her fresh lemonade and cookies, the cook at the farm had made them. She was a wonderful Italian woman who had worked for them for years. Jack had actually hired her before he married Maddy. The farm always seemed more his than theirs, and he enjoyed it far more than she did. It was remote, and isolated, and Maddy had never been crazy about horses. Jack used it often to entertain people he needed to see for business, like Paul McCutchins.

Maddy asked about Janet's kids as they sat down in the living room, and when they finished the lemonade, she suggested they go for a walk in the garden. It seemed like an eternity waiting for Jack and Paul to come back from the stables. And Maddy chatted meaninglessly about the weather, the farm, its history, and the new rosebushes the gardener had planted. And she was startled when she glanced at Janet, and saw that she was crying. She wasn't an attractive woman, she was overweight, pale, and there was something infinitely sad about her. Now more than ever. As the tears coursed down her cheeks uncontrollably, she looked totally pathetic.

"Are you all right?" Maddy asked uncomfortably. But obviously, Janet wasn't. "Is there anything I can do?" Janet McCutchins shook her head and only cried harder.

"I'm sorry" was all she could manage.

"Don't be," Maddy said soothingly, stopping at a

garden chair, so the woman could sit down and regain her composure. "Would you like a glass of water?" Janet shook her head, as Maddy tried not to stare at her, and she blew her nose, and looked at Maddy. There was suddenly something very compelling about her, as their eyes met.

"I don't know what to do," she said in a quavering voice, which actually touched Maddy.

"Can I help in some way?" She wondered if the woman was ill, or if something was wrong with one of her children, she seemed so distraught, and so profoundly unhappy. Maddy couldn't even imagine what it could be.

"There's nothing anyone can do." She sounded desperate and hopeless. "I don't know what to do," she repeated. "It's Paul. He hates me."

"Of course he doesn't, I'm sure he doesn't," Maddy said, feeling stupid, with no knowledge whatsoever of the situation. For all she knew, he did hate her. "Why would he?"

"He has for years. He tortures me. He had to marry me because I got pregnant."

"In this day and age, he wouldn't still be there if he didn't want to be." Their oldest child was twelve, and they'd had two children since then. Although Maddy had to admit she had never seen Paul be pleasant to her. It was one of the things she disliked about him.

"We can't afford to get a divorce, and Paul says it would hurt him politically." It was a possibility, certainly, but other politicians had survived it. And then, Janet took her breath away with her next statement. "He beats me." Something in Maddy's blood ran cold as she heard the other woman say it. And with that, Janet gingerly pulled up her sleeve, and Maddy could see ugly bruises. She had heard unpleasant stories about his violent temper and arrogant attitude over the years, and now this confirmed it to her.

"I'm so sorry, Janet." She didn't know what to say, but her heart went out to her and all she wanted to do was hug her. "Don't stay," Maddy said softly. "Don't let him do that. I was married to a man like that for nine years." She knew all too well what it was like, although she had spent the last eight years trying to forget him.

"How did you get out?" They were suddenly like two prisoners of the same war, whispering in the garden.

"I ran away," Maddy said, sounding braver than she'd been at the time, and she wanted to be honest with this woman. "I was terrified. Jack helped me." But this woman had no Jack Hunter. She wasn't young or beautiful, she had no hope, no career, no way out, and she had three children to take with her. It was very different.

"He says he'll kill me if I go and take the kids. And he says if I tell anyone, he'll put me in a mental institution. He did that once, after my little girl was born. They gave me electric shock treatment." Maddy thought they should have given it to him, in places that would have really mattered to him, but she didn't say that to Janet. Just thinking of what the woman was going through and seeing her bruises made Maddy feel heartsick for her.

"You have to get help. Why don't you go to a safe house?" Maddy suggested.

"I know he'll find me. He'll kill me." Janet sobbed as she said it.

"I'll help you." Maddy volunteered without hesitating. She had to do something for this woman. She felt guiltier than ever for never having liked her. But she needed help now, and as a survivor of the same agony, she felt she owed it to her to help her. "I'll find out about some places for you to go with the kids."

"It'll wind up in the papers," Janet said, still crying, and feeling helpless.

"It'll wind up in the papers if he kills you," Maddy said firmly. "Promise me you'll do something. Does he hurt the children?" Janet shook her head, but Maddy knew it was more complicated than that. Even if he didn't touch them, he was distorting their minds and terrifying them, and one day the girls would marry men like their father, just as Maddy had, and maybe their son would think it was acceptable to beat his women. No one emerged unscathed from a home where their mother was beaten. It had led Maddy straight into the arms of Bobby Joe, and led her to believe that he had a right to do it.

And as Maddy took Janet's hand in her own, they heard the men approaching, and Janet quickly withdrew it, and within an instant, she was stone-faced. It was as though the conversation had never taken place, as the two men walked into the garden.

That night when they were alone, Maddy told Jack what had happened.

"He beats her," she said, still feeling sick about it.

"Paul?" Jack looked surprised. "I doubt that. He's kind of a gruff guy, but I don't think he'd do a thing like that. How do you know?"

"Janet told me," Maddy said, staunchly her friend now. They finally had something in common.

"I wouldn't take that too seriously," Jack said quietly. "Paul told me years ago, she has mental problems."

"I saw the bruises," Maddy said, looking angry. "I believe her, Jack. I've been there."

"I know you have. You don't know how she got the bruises. She may have just made that up to make him look bad. I know he's been seeing someone for a while. Janet is probably trying to get even with him, by saying ugly things about him." He was looking worse by the minute to Maddy, and she didn't doubt Janet's story for an instant. She hated Paul just thinking of it.

"Why don't you believe her?" Maddy asked angrily. "I don't understand that."

"I know Paul. He just wouldn't do that." It made Maddy want to scream as she listened. They argued about it until they went to bed, and she was so angry at Jack for not believing her that she was relieved they didn't make love that night. She felt far closer to Janet McCutchins, and had more in common with her, than with her own husband. But he didn't seem to notice how upset his wife was.

And before they left the next day, Maddy reminded her that she'd be in touch with information for her. But Janet looked blank as she said it. She was too afraid that Paul would hear them. She just nodded and got in the car, and they drove away a few minutes later. But as Maddy and Jack flew back to Washington that night, Maddy was staring out the window at the scenery below in silence. All she could think about was Bobby Joe and the desperation she had felt in those lonely years in Knoxville. And then she thought of Janet and the bruises she had shown her. It was as though Janet were being held prisoner, and she didn't have the courage or the energy to escape him. In fact, she was convinced she couldn't. And as they touched down in Washington, Maddy made a silent vow to do everything she could to help her.

Chapter 3

WHEN MADDY WENT TO WORK ON Monday morning, she ran into Greg as soon as she got to the office, followed him into his cubicle, and poured herself a cup of coffee.

"How was the weekend of Washington's most glamorous award-winning anchorwoman?" He liked to tease her about the life they led, and the fact that she and Jack were often at the White House. "Did you spend the weekend with our President, or just go shopping with the First Lady?"

"Very funny, smart-ass," she said, and took a sip of the steaming coffee. She was still haunted by the confessions of Janet McCutchins. "Actually, Jack had lunch with him on Saturday at Camp David."

"Thank God, you never let me down. It would kill me if I thought you were lining up at the car wash like the rest of us. I live vicariously through you. I hope you know that. We all do."

"Believe me, it's not that exciting." She never really

felt it was her life anyway, she always felt as though she were living in the spotlight she borrowed from her husband. "We had the McCutchinses down to Virginia for the weekend. God, he's disgusting."

"Handsome guy, the Senator. Very distinguished." Greg grinned at her.

Maddy was silent for a long moment, and then decided to take Greg into her confidence. They had become very close since they started working together, like brother and sister. She didn't have that many friends in Washington, she'd never had time to make them and those she had made, Jack never liked, and eventually pressured her not to see them. She never objected because Jack kept her so busy, she was always working. In the beginning, when she'd met women she liked, Jack always had some objection to them, they were fat, or ugly, or inappropriate, or indiscreet, or he thought they were jealous of her. He kept Madeleine carefully guarded, and inadvertently isolated. The only people she really had a chance to get close to were at the office. She knew he meant well in protecting her, and she didn't mind, but it meant that the person she was closest to was Jack, and in recent years, Greg Morris.

"Something awful happened this weekend." She started cautiously, still feeling a little awkward about divulging Janet's secret. Maddy knew she wouldn't want people talking about it.

"You broke a nail?" he needled her, and she usually laughed at him, but she looked serious this time.

"It was Janet."

"She looks pretty colorless and drab. I've only seen her a couple of times at Senate parties."

Maddy sighed, and decided to take the plunge. She trusted Greg completely. "He beats her."

"What? The Senator? Are you sure? That's pretty heavy."

"Very heavy. I believe her. She showed me the bruises."

"Hasn't she had mental problems?" Greg asked skeptically. It was the same reaction Jack had had, and it annoyed her.

"Why do men always say things like that about abused women? What if I had told you she had hit him with a golf club? Would you believe me? Or would you tell me that fat bastard was lying about it?"

"I'd probably believe him, I'm sorry to say. Because men don't lie about things like that. It's pretty unusual when a man is abused by a woman."

"Women don't lie either. But people like you, and my husband, make them feel like it's their fault, and they have to keep it a secret. And yes, she was in a mental hospital, but she doesn't look crazy to me, and those bruises were no figment of her imagination. She's terrified of him. I've always heard he was a son of a bitch to his staff, but I never knew he was an abuser." She had never spoken openly about her past to Greg. Like other women in the same situation, she felt it was somehow her fault, and kept it a dark secret. "I told her I'd help her find a safe house. Any ideas where I start?"

"What about the Coalition for Women? I have a friend who runs it. And I'm sorry about what I said. I should know better." He looked contrite as he said it.

"Yeah, you should. But thanks, I'll call her." He jotted down a name for her, and Maddy glanced at it. Fernanda Lopez. She vaguely remembered doing a

story about her when she first came to the network. It
had been a good five or six years before, but she remembered being impressed by her. But when Maddy
called from her own office, they told her Ms. Lopez was
on sabbatical, and her replacement had just left on ma-
ternity leave. The new woman in charge wasn't coming
in for two more weeks, and they'd have her call as soon
as she got there. They gave Maddy a few names to call
when she told them what she wanted. She tried but the
numbers were all answered by answering machines,
and when she called the Abused Women's Hotline, it
was busy. She'd have to call back later. And then she got
busy with Greg, and forgot about it until she went on
the air at five o'clock, and promised herself she'd try
again in the morning. If Janet had lived with it this long,
she would certainly survive until the next morning, but
Maddy did want to do something about it. It was obvious that Janet was too paralyzed by fear to help herself,
which wasn't unusual either.

When Greg and Maddy went on the air at five, they
covered the usual assortment of local, political, national, and international stories, and a plane crash at
JFK ate up most of the seven-thirty.

She went home in Jack's car alone that night, he had
another meeting with the President, and she couldn't
help wondering what was keeping them both so busy.
But she was thinking of Janet again when she got home,
and wondered if she should call her. But Maddy was
afraid that Paul might be listening to Janet's calls and
decided not to.

Maddy read a stack of articles she'd been meaning to
get to, and skimmed through a new book about the latest state of the art techniques in dealing with breast

cancer, to see if she wanted to interview the author as part of a news story. She did her nails, and went to bed early. And she heard Jack come in around midnight. But she was too tired to talk to him, and she fell back to sleep before he could join her. It was morning before she woke again, and she heard him walk into his bathroom and turn on the shower.

He was in the kitchen reading *The Wall Street Journal* when she came downstairs, and he looked up at her with a smile. She was wearing jeans, a red sweater, and bright red Gucci loafers. She looked fresh and young and sexy.

"You make me sorry I didn't wake you last night," he said with a smile, and she laughed at him, as she poured herself a cup of coffee and picked up the paper.

"You and the President must be up to some real mischief these days, with all those meetings. It better turn out to be something more interesting than a cabinet reshuffle."

"Maybe so," he said noncommittally, as they both turned back to their papers, and suddenly he heard Maddy gasp and glanced over at her. "What is it?" She couldn't speak for a moment as tears filled her eyes and she continued to try to read the article, but she was blinded by tears as she turned to her husband.

"Janet McCutchins committed suicide last night. She slashed her wrists in their house in Georgetown, one of her children found her and called 911, but she was already dead when they got there. They said she had bruises on her arms and legs, and they feared foul play initially, but her husband explained that she had fallen down the stairs the night before, over one of her son's skateboards. The son of a bitch . . . he killed her. . . ." She sounded choked and nearly breathless and she could feel her whole body tense as she thought about it.

"He didn't kill her, Maddy," Jack said quietly, "she killed herself. You said so."

"She thought she didn't have any other way out," Maddy said in a strangled voice, remembering the feeling all too vividly as she looked at her husband. "I could have done the same thing, if you hadn't gotten me out of Knoxville."

"That's bullshit and you know it. You'd have killed him first. She was disturbed, she had a history of mental problems. There were probably plenty of other reasons for her to do it."

"How the hell can you say that? Why don't you want to believe that that fat bastard abused her? Is that so incredible? Does he look all that nice to you? Why isn't it possible she was telling the truth? Because she's a woman?"

It made her furious listening to him, and even Greg had doubted the story when she told him. "Why is the woman always lying?"

"Maybe she wasn't. But the fact that she killed herself supports the theory that she was unbalanced."

"It supports the theory that she thought she had no other way out and she was desperate. Desperate enough to leave her kids motherless, and even risk having one of them find her." She was crying openly as she spoke to him, and her breath was coming in little staccato gasps of terror. She knew what it felt like to be so tortured, so terrified, so cornered that there seemed to be no escape route. If she hadn't been young and beautiful and Jack hadn't wanted her for the network, she might easily have met the same fate as Janet

McCutchins. And she wasn't so sure Jack was right that she would have killed Bobby Joe first. She had thought of suicide herself, more than once, on dark nights when he was drunk and her lips and eyes were swollen from his latest acts of vengeance. It was all too easy to understand what Janet had been feeling. And then she remembered the calls she had made the day before, on her behalf, from her office. "I called the Coalition for Women for her yesterday, and a hotline. Shit, I wish I had called her last night. But I was afraid to, I was afraid Paul would intercept the call and I'd get her in trouble."

"She was beyond your help, Mad. Don't beat yourself up over it. This proves it."

"This proves nothing, goddammit, Jack. She wasn't crazy. She was terrified. And how do you know where he was, or what he had done to her before she did it?"

"He's an asshole, not a murderer. I'd stake my life on it," he said calmly, as Maddy got ever more heated about it.

"Since when are you two such big pals? How the hell do you know what he did to her? You have no concept what that's like." She was shaking with sobs as she sat at their kitchen table and cried for a woman she scarcely knew, but she had once walked the same path she had, and she knew that she was one of the fortunate survivors. Janet hadn't been as lucky.

"I do know what it's like," he said quietly. "When I married you, you had terrible nightmares, and you slept in the fetal position with your arms over your head. I know, baby, I know . . . I saved you. . . ."

"I know you did," she said, blowing her nose, and looking at him sadly, "I never forget that. . . . I just feel so sorry for her. . . . Think of how she must have felt when she did it. Her life must have been an agony of terror."

"I suppose it was," he said coolly, "and I'm sorry for Paul and her kids. This is going to be rough for all of them. I just hope the media don't have a heyday with it."

"I hope some hotshot young reporter does an investigative piece on it, and exposes what he was doing to her. Not just for her sake, but all the other women who are still alive and in the same position."

"It's hard to understand why she didn't leave if it was that bad. She could have left. She didn't have to kill herself."

"Maybe she thought she did," Maddy said sympathetically, but Jack was unmoved by it.

"You got out, Maddy. She could have too!" he said firmly.

"It took me eight years to do it, and you helped me. Not everyone is that lucky. And I just got out by the grace of God and the skin of my teeth. Maybe in another year, he might have killed me."

"You wouldn't have let that happen." Jack sounded certain, but Maddy was less so.

"I let it happen for a hell of a long time until you came along. And my mother let it happen until my dad died. And I swear she missed it, and him until she died. Relationships like that are a lot sicker than people realize, for both the abused and the abuser."

"That's an interesting perspective," he said, looking skeptical again. "I think some people just ask for it, or expect it, or let it happen, because they're too weak to do anything else."

"You don't know anything about it, Jack," she said in a tense voice as she walked out of the kitchen, and went upstairs to get her bag and a jacket. She came down carrying a well-cut dark navy blazer, and she had put on small diamond earrings. She was always beautifully groomed and dressed, at home or at work, she never knew who she'd run into, and people recognized her everywhere she went.

They rode to work together that morning in silence. She was annoyed at some of the things Jack had said, and she didn't want to get in an argument with him about it. But Greg was waiting for her at work, he had seen the story, and he looked anguished.

"I'm sorry, Maddy, you must feel like shit. I know you wanted to help her. Maybe you couldn't have anyway." He tried to reassure her, but she turned and snapped at him as soon as he spoke.

"Why? Because she was psychotic, like all other abused women, and she *wanted* to slit her wrists? Is that what you think?"

"All I meant was that she may have been too scared to get out anyway, like someone shell-shocked in a war zone." Then he couldn't help adding, "Why do you think she did it? Just because he was abusing her, or do you think she was psychotic?" Maddy looked infuriated by the question.

"That's what Jack thinks, that's what most people think, that women in these situations are basically crazy anyway, regardless of what their husbands are doing to them. No one can understand why women don't leave. Well, some of them just can't . . . they just can't . . . ," she said, as she broke into sobs and Greg put his arms around her.

"I know, baby, I know. . . . I'm sorry . . . maybe you just couldn't save this one." He spoke in soothing tones and she was grateful for his arms around her.

"I wanted . . . to . . . help . . . her." She was wracked by sobs as she thought of the pain Janet must have been in to make her do it, and the agony her children must be in now, having lost their mother.

"How are we going to cover it?" Greg asked when she regained her composure.

"I'd like to do an editorial about abused women," she said thoughtfully, as Greg handed her a cup of coffee.

"That's been cut out of our format. Remember?"

"I'm going to tell Jack I want to do one anyway," she said firmly, and Greg shook his head. "I wish I could blow that bastard McCutchins right out of the water."

"I wouldn't do that if I were you. And Jack won't let you do an editorial. I don't care if you do sleep with him every night, we got the word from the top. No editorials, no social or political commentaries, straight news only. We tell it like it happened, with no add-ons from us."

"What's he going to do? Fire me? Besides, this is straight news. A senator's wife committed suicide, after being abused by her husband."

"Jack still won't let you say that, or do an editorial on it, if I know him, unless you take over the station at gunpoint. And I honestly don't think he'd like that, Maddy."

"No kidding. But I'm going to do it anyway. We're live, for chrissake, they can't knock me off the air, without creating a riot or a scandal. So we do one more editorial, and then apologize for it afterward. If he gets pissed, I can live with that."

"You're a brave woman," Greg said with the broad

ivory smile that dazzled the women he went out with. He was one of the most sought-after bachelors in Washington, and with good reason. He was smart, handsome, nice, and successful, a rare and highly desirable combination, and Maddy was crazy about him, in a purely wholesome sense, she loved working with him. "I'm not sure I'd like to be the one to challenge Jack Hunter and go against one of his edicts."

"I have connections," she said with the first smile she'd shown since she'd read about Janet McCutchins.

"Yeah, and the best legs at the network. That doesn't hurt either," he teased.

But at five o'clock, when she and Greg went on the air for the first time that day, Maddy was nervous. She looked as cool and impeccable as ever, in her red sweater, immaculately groomed hair, and simple diamond stud earrings. But Greg knew her well enough to see how anxious she was during the countdown to airtime.

"You gonna go for it?" he whispered as they got closer to airtime. She nodded to him, and then smiled as the camera zoomed in on her, and she introduced herself and her co-anchor. They worked their way through the news as they always did, working in perfect harmony, alternating stories, and then, Greg rolled his chair away, knowing what was coming, and Maddy's face was instantly serious as she faced the cameras on her own.

"There is a story in today's news, which affects each of us, some of us more than others. It's the story of Janet Scarbrough McCutchins's suicide in her Georgetown home, leaving her three children without a mother. It's a tragedy certainly, and who can say what sorrows forced Mrs. McCutchins to take her own life, but there are questions that can't be ignored, and may well never be answered. Why did she do it? What great pain was she in at that moment, and before? And why did no one listen, or see what must have been her desperation? In a recent conversation, Janet McCutchins told me that she'd been hospitalized briefly once, for depression. But a source close to Mrs. McCutchins said that there could be an issue of abuse here, which led to her suicide. If so, Janet McCutchins would not be the first woman to take her own life, rather than flee an abusive situation. Tragedies like this happen far too often. It is possible that Janet McCutchins had other reasons to take her own life. Perhaps her family knows why she did it, or her husband, or her closest friends, or her children. But it brings into sharper focus, for all of us, the issues that some women face about pain, about fear, and desperation. I cannot tell you why Janet McCutchins died. It is not my place to guess. We have been told that she left a letter to her children, and I'm sure we will never see it.

"But we cannot help but wonder, why it is that when a woman cries, the world turns a deaf ear, and too many of us say, 'There must be something wrong with *her* . . . maybe *she's* crazy.' But what if she isn't? Women die every day, by their own hand, and at the hands of their abusers. And too often we do not believe them when they tell us of the pain they're in, or we simply dismiss it. Perhaps it is too painful for us to listen.

"Women who do this are not crazy, most of them, not disturbed, they weren't too lazy or too stupid to leave. They were afraid to. They couldn't do it. Sometimes these women prefer to die at their own hands. Or they stay too long, and let their husbands kill them. It happens. It's real. We cannot turn our backs on these women. We must help them find a way out.

"I ask you now to remember Janet McCutchins. And the next time we hear of a death like this, ask yourself why? And when you do, be very silent, and listen to the answer, however frightening it may be.

"Goodnight. This is Maddy Hunter." They went straight to commercial, and everyone in the studio went crazy. No one had dared to stop her, and mesmerized by what she was saying, they hadn't cut to commercial early. Greg just stood by grinning and gave her the high five as she beamed at him. "How was it?" she asked in a choked whisper.

"Dynamite. I'd say we're going to be getting a visit from your husband in about four seconds."

It was two, as he exploded into the studio like a tornado, and was shaking with fury as he strode toward her. "Are you out of your fucking mind? Paul McCutchins is going to put me out of business!" He stood inches from her, and shouted right into her face. Maddy grew pale, but she never made a move backward. She held her ground, although she too was shaking. It terrified her when he, or anyone else, got angry, but this time she thought it was worth it.

"I said a source close to her said there *could* be an issue of abuse. Hell, Jack, I *saw* her bruises. She *told* me he beat her. What conclusion do you draw from that, when she commits suicide a day later? All I did was ask people to think about women who commit suicide. He can't touch us legally. I can testify to what she said to me, if I have to."

"And you damn well probably will have to. Are you

deaf, can't you read? I said no editorials, and I fucking meant it!"

"I'm sorry, Jack. I had to, I owed it to her, and other women in her position."

"Oh, for chrissake . . ." He ran a frantic hand through his hair, unable to believe what she'd done to him, and that the studio jocks had let her. They could have cut her off, but they hadn't. They liked what she had said about abused women. And Paul McCutchins had a reputation as a verbally abusive person and employer, and as a younger man, he had gotten into an inordinate amount of bar fights. He was one of the most hated Senators in Washington and had a violent temper that manifested itself often. No one had been anxious to defend him, and it seemed perfectly plausible to them, although Maddy never spelled it out, that he might have abused her. Jack was still storming around the studio shouting at everyone when Rafe Thompson, the producer, came to tell him that Senator McCutchins was on the phone for him. "Shit!" he shouted at his wife, "and how much would you like to bet that he's going to sue me?"

"I'm sorry, Jack," she said quietly, but without remorse, as the assistant producer came to tell her that the First Lady was calling. They each disappeared to separate phones, to very different conversations. Maddy recognized Phyllis Armstrong's voice instantly, and was filled with trepidation as she listened.

"I'm so proud of you, Madeleine," the warm voice of the older woman came across the line crisply. "That was a very brave thing you did, and very necessary. It was a wonderful broadcast, Maddy."

"Thank you, Mrs. Armstrong," Maddy said, sounding

calmer than she felt. She didn't tell her that Jack was enraged about it.

"I've been meaning to call you about the Commission on Violence Against Women. Actually, I asked Jack to tell you about it."

"He did. I'm very interested in it."

"Of course, he told me you'd love to do it, but I wanted to hear that from you myself. Our husbands have a way of volunteering us for what we least want to do. Mine is no exception." Maddy smiled as she listened, and it made her feel better about Jack volunteering her time so freely. He was so often overpowering and so liberal about voicing opinions and decisions for her; sometimes it seemed like a lack of respect to her.

"In this case, he was right. I would love to."

"I'm glad to hear it. We're meeting for the first time this Friday. At the White House, this time, in my private offices. We'll figure out a more appropriate location later. We're still pretty small, there are only a dozen of us. We're trying to figure out how to make an impact on the public, a real one, about violence committed against women. And I think you just took the first swing for us. Congratulations!"

"Thank you again, Mrs. Armstrong," Maddy said breathlessly, and she beamed at Greg as she hung up.

"Sounds like you were number one in the Armstrong ratings," he said proudly. He had loved how she'd done it. It took a lot of courage even if the head of the network was her husband. Now she'd have to go home and live with the fallout. And as everyone knew, Jack Hunter wasn't always a sweetheart, especially when someone crossed him. And Maddy wasn't any more exempt than anyone else.

As Maddy started to tell Greg what Mrs. Armstrong had said, Jack strode over to them with a look of fury. He was in a rage.

"Did you know about this?" Jack shot at Greg, desperate to blame someone, anyone, everyone, he looked as though he wanted to strangle Maddy.

"Not exactly, but close enough. I knew she was going to say something," Greg said honestly. He wasn't afraid of Jack, and although it was a well-kept secret, and he never said anything to Maddy about it, he didn't like Jack Hunter. He thought he was arrogant and overbearing and he didn't like the way he ran Maddy around, though he didn't comment on it to her. She had enough to deal with, without having to defend her husband.

"You could have stopped her," Jack accused him, "you could have talked right over her, and ended it before it started."

"I have too much respect for her to do that, Mr. Hunter. Besides, I agree with what she said. I didn't believe her when she told me about Janet McCutchins on Monday. This was a wake-up call to those of us who don't want to have to think about how desperate some women feel in abusive situations. It happens every day all around us. We just don't want to see it or hear it. But because of who she was married to, Janet McCutchins made us hear her. Maybe if enough people heard Maddy tonight, Janet McCutchins's death will mean something, and help someone. With all due respect, I think Maddy did the right thing." His voice quavered as he said the last words, and Jack Hunter glared at him.

"I'm sure our sponsors are going to love us if we get sued."

"Is that what McCutchins said on the phone?" Maddy asked with a look of concern. She wasn't sorry, but she hated causing Jack such distress. But in her mind, it had to be done. She had seen with her own eyes what McCutchins had already done to his wife, and she was willing to testify to it, if she had to. She had taken matters into her own hands on the air, whatever the potential cost to her or the network. To Maddy, it seemed worth it.

"He was making veiled threats, but the veil was very thin. He said he was calling his attorneys as soon as he hung up," Jack said to her harshly.

"I don't think he'll get too far," Greg said thoughtfully. "The evidence was apparently pretty damning. And Janet McCutchins spoke directly to Maddy. That should cover our asses."

"'Our' asses, how noble of you, Greg," Jack snapped at him. "As far as I know, mine is the only one on the line here. It was a goddamn stupid, irresponsible thing to do." And with that, he stalked across the studio again, and went back upstairs to his own quarters.

"Are you okay?" Greg looked at Maddy with concern, and she nodded at him.

"I knew he'd be upset, but I hope we don't get sued." She looked worried as she said it. She was hoping that McCutchins wouldn't dare sue them, and risk exposing himself.

"Did you tell him about the call from Phyllis Armstrong?"

"I didn't have time," she confessed. "I'll tell him when we get home."

But Maddy went home alone that night. Jack had

called his attorneys in to review the tape and discuss it with them, and it was one o'clock in the morning when he got home to Georgetown. Maddy was still awake, but he didn't say a word to her as he walked purposefully across their bedroom to his bathroom.

"How did it go?" she asked cautiously, as he turned and glared at her.

"I can't believe you'd do that to me. It was such a fucking stupid thing to do." He might as well have slapped her. But all Jack did was hit her with angry looks and words. It was obvious that he felt she had betrayed him.

"The First Lady called just after we went off the air, she was very excited about the broadcast, and thought it was a brave thing to do. I'm going on her commission this week," she said apologetically. She wasn't sure how she was going to make this up to him, but she would have to try now. She didn't want him to hate her over issues that came up at work.

"I already made that decision for you," he said, looking daggers at her as she mentioned the Commission on Violence Against Women.

"I made it for myself," she said quietly. "I have a right to do that, Jack."

"Are you lobbying for women's rights now too, as well as the abused? Do I have an editorial about that to look forward to? Why don't we just get you your own goddamn show, you can talk your head off all day long, and forget the news."

"If the First Lady liked it, how bad could it be?"

"Pretty goddamn bad, if McCutchins's lawyers say it is."

"Maybe it'll calm down in a few days," she said hopefully, as he walked slowly toward the bed, and stopped finally, to look down at her in thinly concealed fury. His anger hadn't dissipated or dimmed.

"If you ever do that again, I don't care if you are my wife, I'll fire you on the spot. Is that clear?" She nodded silently, feeling suddenly as though she had not done a good thing, but betrayed him. He had never in their nine years together been as angry at her, and she was wondering if he would ever forgive her for it, particularly if the network got sued.

"I thought it was an important thing to do."

"I don't give a damn what you think. I don't pay you to think. I pay you to look good and read the news off a TelePrompTer. That's all I want from you." And with that, he walked into his bathroom, and slammed the door behind him, as she burst into tears in their bedroom. It had been a stressful night for both of them. But in her heart of hearts, she still believed she'd done the right thing, whatever it cost her. And for the moment at least, it looked like it was going to cost her dearly.

When Jack came out of the bathroom, he got into bed without saying a word to her. He turned off the light, turned his back to her, and there was not a sound between them until she heard him snoring. But for the first time in years, she felt a ripple of terror inside her. His anger, however controlled, brought back old memories and was terrifying to her. And that night, for the first time in a long time, she had nightmares.

Jack said not a word to her over breakfast the next morning, and he left for work alone with his driver.

"How am I supposed to get to work?" she asked, looking dumbstruck, as he left her on the sidewalk.

He looked her right in the eye, slammed the door of the car, and spoke to her as he would have a stranger. "Take a cab."

Chapter 4

JANET MCCUTCHINS'S FUNERAL WAS on Friday morning, and Jack sent Maddy a message via his secretary that he was planning to go with her. They left the office in his car, he in a dark suit and striped black tie, she in a black linen Chanel suit and dark glasses, as they were driven to St. John's Church, across Lafayette Park from the White House. The service was long and agonizing, it was a high mass, with the choir singing the Ave Maria, and the front pew was full of Janet's nieces, and nephews and children. Even the Senator cried, and every important politician in the city seemed to be there. Maddy found herself staring at the Senator in disbelief, watching him cry, and her heart went out to the children. And without thinking, at the end of the service, she slipped her hand into Jack's arm. He glanced at her, and then pulled away from her just as quickly. He was still furious with her, and had barely spoken to her since Tuesday night.

They joined the others on the steps as the casket was

carried to the hearse, and the family got into limousines to go to the cemetery. The Hunters knew there was a luncheon at the McCutchinses' afterward, but neither of them wanted to go, as they weren't that close to them. And they rode back to the office in stony silence, side by side.

"How long is this going to go on, Jack?" she asked finally in the car, unable to stand it any longer.

"As long as I feel this way about you," he said bluntly. "You let me down, Maddy. No, to be accurate, you screwed me."

"It was bigger than that, Jack. A woman who had been abused killed herself, and was going to go down in history as a nutcase. It was about giving her, and her kids, a fair shake. And shining the spotlight on her abuser, even for a minute."

"And fucking me over in the process. Nothing you did changed the fact that she'll go down in history as a nutcase. The facts are there. She was in a mental hospital and had electric shock treatments for six months. How normal do you think she was, Mad? And was she worth making me an easy target for a lawsuit?"

"I'm sorry, Jack. I had to do it." She still believed she'd been right.

"You're as crazy as she was," he said with a look of disgust, glancing out the window. It was a nasty thing to say, and his tone stung, just as it had for the past three days.

"Can we call a truce for the weekend?" It was going to be grim in Virginia if he was going to continue to do this, and she was thinking of not going with him.

"I don't think so," he said coldly. "Besides, I have things to do here. I have some meetings at the

Pentagon. You can do whatever you want. I won't have time to spend with you."

"This is ridiculous, Jack. That was business. This is our life."

"The two stand pretty well intertwined in our case. You should have thought of that, before you shot off your mouth."

"Fine. Punish me then. But this is getting childish."

"If McCutchins sues me, believe me, the amount won't be 'childish.'"

"I'm not so sure he's going to do that, particularly with the First Lady applauding the broadcast. Besides, he can't defend himself. If there is an investigation, the coroner's report must show her bruises."

"He may not be as impressed with the First Lady as you are."

"Why don't you just give it a rest for a while, Jack? I can't unring the bell, and I wouldn't anyway. So why don't we just try to put it behind us?"

But as she said it, he turned to her with narrowed eyes, and the look in them was icy. "Maybe you'd like to refresh your memory a little bit, Joan of Arc, and recall that before you took up the crusades for the underdog, you were no one and nothing when I found you. You were nothing, Mad. Zero. You were a hick from nowhere going straight to a lifetime of beer cans and abuse in a trailer park. Whatever the hell it is you think you are now, keep in mind that I made you. And you owe me. I'm sick of this idealistic bullshit and a lot of whining and moaning about a fat, unattractive piece of shit like Janet McCutchins. She wasn't worth putting my ass on the line for, or yours, or the network's."

She looked at her husband suddenly as though he

were a stranger, and maybe he was, and she had just never noticed. "You're making me sick," she said, leaning forward and tapping the driver on the shoulder. "Stop the car. I'm getting out here."

Jack looked instantly startled. "I thought you were going back to the office."

"I am, I think I'd rather walk than sit here and listen to you talk to me like that. I get the message, Jack. You made me, and I owe you. How much? My life? My principles? My dignity? What's the price for saving someone from being poor white trash for the rest of her life? Let me know, when you figure it out. I want to be sure not to shortchange you." And with that, she got out of the car, and strode quickly away toward their office. Jack said nothing, and silently rolled up the window. And when he got back to his own office, he didn't call her. She was only five floors away, eating a sandwich with Greg.

"How was the funeral?" he asked with a look of concern for her. He thought she looked strained and exhausted.

"Depressing. That asshole cried through the whole service."

"The Senator?" She nodded, with her mouth full. "Maybe he feels guilty."

"He should. He might as well have killed her. Jack is still convinced that she was psychotic." And he was making her feel that way herself with the way he was behaving.

"Is Jack still pissed?" Greg asked cautiously, handing her his pickle, he knew she loved them.

"That doesn't begin to describe it. He's convinced I did it to spite him."

"He'll get over it," Greg said, sprawling back in his chair and looking at her. She was so damn smart and decent and incredible looking. Greg loved the fact that she was always willing to fight for what she believed in, but she seemed worried and unhappy. She hated it when Jack was angry at her, and he had never, in his seven years of marriage to her, been this angry before.

"What makes you think he'll get over it?" She wasn't as sure now, and for the first time ever felt her marriage in jeopardy, and in truth, that terrified her.

"He'll get over it because he loves you," Greg said firmly. "And he needs you. You're one of the best anchorwomen in the country, if not the best. He's not crazy."

"I'm not sure that's a valid reason to love me. I could think of other reasons that would mean more to me."

"Be grateful for what you've got, kid. He'll calm down. Probably over the weekend."

"He's having meetings at the Pentagon over the weekend."

"Something big must be brewing," Greg said with interest.

"Has been for a while, I think. He hasn't said anything, but he's met with the President a few times."

"Maybe we're going to drop a bomb on Russia," Greg said with a smile, neither of them believed that.

"That's a little passé, isn't it?" Maddy smiled back at him. "I guess they'll tell us sooner or later." And with that, she looked at her watch and stood up. "I have to get to the First Lady's commission. My meeting is at two. I'll be back in time to do makeup for the five o'clock."

"You'd be fine without it," he said smoothly, "have

fun. Give my love to the First Lady." Maddy grinned and waved at him as she left the office and went downstairs to hail a cab. It was a five-minute ride to the White House, and the First Lady had just arrived in a motorcade from the McCutchinses' house when Maddy got there, and they walked inside together, with members of the Secret Service all around them. Mrs. Armstrong inquired if Maddy had gone to the funeral, and when she said she had, Mrs. Armstrong commented on how tragic it had been to see the McCutchinses' children.

"Paul seemed very upset too," the First Lady said sympathetically, and then spoke to Maddy quietly as they rode the elevator to the private quarters. "Do you really believe he abused her?" She didn't question Maddy about her sources for the story.

Maddy hesitated but knew from past experience that she could trust her discretion. "Yes, I do believe it. She told me herself that he beat her, and she was terrified of him. She showed me the bruises on her arms last weekend. I know from what she said that she was telling me the truth, and I think Paul McCutchins knows that. He's going to want everyone to forget what I said," which was why she personally did not believe he would sue the network. The First Lady shook her head in dismay, and sighed as they stepped off the elevator to be met by her secretary and more Secret Service.

"I'm sorry to hear that." She didn't doubt for a minute what Maddy told her, unlike Greg and Jack. As a woman, she was willing to accept it. And she had never liked Paul McCutchins either; he seemed like a bully to her. "I guess that's why we're here today, isn't it? What a perfect example of an unpunished act of violence against a woman. I'm so glad you did that editorial, Maddy. Has there been much reaction to it?" Maddy smiled at the question.

"We got thousands of letters from female viewers, applauding it. Almost none from men. And my husband is about ready to divorce me."

"Jack? How limited of him. I'm surprised to hear it." Phyllis Armstrong looked genuinely surprised. Like her husband, she had always been fond of Jack Hunter.

"He's afraid the Senator is going to sue him," Maddy explained to her.

"I don't think he'll dare if it's true," Phyllis Armstrong said practically, as they entered the room where the other members of the newly formed commission were waiting for them. "Particularly if it's true. He won't want to take a chance that you can prove it. Did she leave a note, by the way?"

"There was supposedly a letter to her kids, but I don't know who, if anyone, read it. The police gave it to Paul when they found it."

"My bet is that nothing more will come of it. Tell Jack to relax. It was a good thing to do. It shone a bright light on the dark area of abuse, and violence committed against women."

"I'll tell him you said so," Maddy said with a smile, as her eyes swept the room. There were eight women and four men, and she herself was the eighth woman. She recognized two federal judges among the men, a justice of the court of appeals among the women, and another member of the press. The First Lady introduced the other women and explained that they were two teachers, an attorney, a psychiatrist, and a physician. The third man was a physician too, and the last man Maddy was introduced to in the group was Bill Alexander, the former Ambassador to Colombia who had lost his wife to terrorists. The First Lady said he was taking some time off after leaving the State Department, and writing a book now. They were an interesting, eclectic group, Asian, African-American, and Caucasian, some young, some old, all professional, several well known, and Maddy was by half a dozen years the youngest among them, and possibly the most famous, with the exception of the First Lady.

Phyllis Armstrong called the meeting to order rapidly and succinctly, and her secretary sat in the room to take notes. She had left the Secret Service outside, and the members of the commission were sitting in a comfortable living room, with a large silver tray, with coffee and tea and a plate of cookies, on a handsome antique English table. She chatted with each person by name and looked around the room with a motherly expression. She had already told them about Maddy's brave editorial on Tuesday night, about Janet McCutchins, although several of them had heard it, and heartily approved of it.

"Do you know for a fact that she was abused?" one of the women asked her and Maddy hesitated before she answered.

"I'm not sure how to answer that. I believe she was, although I couldn't prove it in a court of law. It was hearsay. She told me." Maddy turned to the First Lady with a questioning look. "I assume that what we say here is privileged and confidential." It was often that way with Presidential commissions.

"Yes, it is," Phyllis Armstrong reassured her.

"I believed her, although the first two people I told

did not believe me. They were both men, one is my co-anchor on the show, the other is my husband, and both should know better."

"We're here today, to discuss what we can do about the problem of crimes committed against women," Mrs. Armstrong said as she opened the meeting. "Is it a question of legislation, addressing the public perception of abuse? How can we deal with this most effectively? And then, I'd like to see what we can do about it. I believe we all would." Everyone around the room nodded. "I'd like to do something a little unusual today. I'd like each of us to say why we're here, either for professional reasons, or personal ones, if you feel comfortable talking about it. My secretary won't take notes, and if you don't want to speak, you don't have to. But I think it could be interesting for us," and although she didn't say it, she knew it would form an instant bond between them. "I'm willing to go first, if you'd prefer it." Everyone waited respectfully for her to speak, and she told them something none of them had known about her.

"My father was an alcoholic, and he beat my mother every weekend without fail, after he got paid on Friday. They were married for forty-nine years, until she finally died of cancer. His beating her was something of a ritual for all of us, I had three brothers and a sister. And we all accepted it as something inevitable like church on Sunday. I used to hide in my room so I wouldn't have to hear it, but I did anyway. And afterward, I would hear her sobbing in her bedroom. But she never left him, never stopped him, never hit him back. We all hated it, and when they were old enough, my brothers went out and got drunk themselves. One of them was abusive to his wife when he grew up, he was the oldest, my next brother was a teetotaler and became a minister, and my baby brother died an alcoholic at thirty. And no, I don't have a problem with alcohol myself, in case you're wondering. I don't like it much, and drink very little, and it hasn't been a problem for me. What has been a problem for me all my life is the idea, the reality, of women being abused all over the world, more often than not by their husbands, and no one doing anything about it. I've always promised myself I would get involved one day, and I'd like to do something, anything, to effect a change now. Every day, women are being mugged on the streets, sexually assaulted and harassed, date-raped, and beaten and killed by their partners and husbands, and for some reason, we accept it. We don't like it, we don't approve of it, we cry when we hear about it, particularly if we know the victim. But we don't stop it, we don't reach out and take the gun away, or the knife, or the hand, just as I never stopped my father. Maybe we don't know how, maybe we just don't care enough. But I think we do care. I think we just don't like to think about it. But I want people to start thinking, and to stand up and do something about it. I think it's time, it's long overdue. I want you to help me stop the violence against women, for my sake, for your sake, for my mother's sake, for our daughters and sisters and friends. I want to thank you all for being here, and for caring enough to help me." There were tears in her eyes when she stopped talking, and for an instant, everyone stared at her. It was not an unusual story. But it made Phyllis Armstrong much more real to them.

The psychiatrist who had grown up in Detroit told a similar story, except that her father had killed her

mother, and gone to prison for it. She said that she herself was gay, and she had been raped and beaten at fifteen by a boy she had grown up with. She had lived
with the same woman now for fourteen years, and said
that she felt she had recovered from the early abuses in
her life, but she was concerned about the increasing
trend of violent crimes against women, even in the gay
community, and our ability to look the other way while
they happened.

Some of the others had no firsthand personal experience with violence, but both federal judges said they
had had abusive fathers who had slapped their mothers
around, and until they grew up and learned otherwise,
they thought it was normal. And then it was Maddy's
turn, and she hesitated for a moment. She had never
before told her story to anyone in public, and she felt
naked now as she thought about it.

"I guess my story isn't all that different from the others," she started. "I grew up in Chattanooga, Tennessee,
and my father always hit my mother. Sometimes she hit
him back, most of the time, she didn't. Sometimes he
was drunk when he did it, sometimes he just did it because he was mad at her, or at someone else, or at
something that had happened that day. We were dirt
poor, and he never seemed to be able to keep a job, so
he hit my mother about that too. Everything that happened to him was always her fault. And when she wasn't
around, he hit me, but not very often. Their fighting
was kind of the background music to my childhood, a
familiar theme I grew up with." She felt a little breathless as she said it, and for the first time in years, you
could hear the remnants of her Southern accent as she
continued. "And all I wanted to do was get away from it.

I hated my house, and my parents, and the way they treated each other. So I married my high school sweetheart at seventeen, and as soon as we were married, he started to beat me up. He drank too much, and didn't work a lot. His name was Bobby Joe, and I believed him when he said that it was all my fault, if I weren't such a pain in the ass and such a bad wife, and so stupid and careless and just plain dumb, he wouldn't 'have' to hit me. But he had to. He broke both my arms once, and he pushed me down the stairs once, and I broke my leg. I was working at a television station in Knoxville then, and it got sold to a man from Texas, who eventually bought a cable TV network in Washington, and took me with him. I guess most of you know that part. It was Jack Hunter. I left my wedding ring and a note on my kitchen table in Knoxville, and met Jack at the Greyhound bus station with a Samsonite suitcase with two dresses in it, and I ran like hell, all the way to Washington to work for him. I got a divorce, and married Jack a year after that, and no one's ever laid a hand on me since then. I wouldn't let them. I know better now. If anyone even looks cross-eyed at me, I run like hell. I don't know why I got lucky, but I did. Jack saved my life. He made me everything I am today. Without him, I'd probably be dead by now. I think Bobby Joe would have probably killed me one night, pushing me down the stairs till I broke my neck, or kicking me in the stomach. Or maybe just because I'd want to die finally. I've never said anything about any of this because I was ashamed of it, but now I want to help women like me, women who aren't as lucky as I've been, women who think they're trapped, and don't have a Jack Hunter waiting for them with a limousine to take them to another city. I want to reach out to these women and help them. They need us," she said, as tears filled her eyes, "we owe it to them."

"Thank you, Maddy," Phyllis Armstrong said softly. They all shared a common bond, or most of them, lawyers and doctors and judges and even a First Lady, histories of violence and abuse, and only by sheer luck and grit had they survived it. And they were all acutely aware that there were countless others who weren't as lucky, and needed their help. The group sitting in the First Lady's private quarters was anxious to help them.

Bill Alexander was the last to speak, and his story was the most unusual, as Maddy suspected it would be. He had grown up in a good home in New England, with parents who loved him and each other. And he had met and married his wife when she was at Wellesley, and he was at Harvard. He had a doctorate in foreign policy and political science, and had taught at Dartmouth for several years, and then Princeton, and was teaching a class at Harvard when he was made Ambassador to Kenya at fifty. His next post was in Madrid, and from there he was sent to Colombia. He said that he had three grown children who were respectively, a doctor, a lawyer, and a banker. All very respectable and academically impressive. His had been a quiet, "normal" life, in fact, he said with a smile, a fairly boring, but satisfying existence.

Colombia had been an interesting challenge for him, the political situation there had been delicate, and the drug trade pervaded everything in the country. It was intricately interwoven into all forms of business, tainted politics, and corruption was rampant. He had been fascinated by what he had to do there, and felt equal to the task until his wife was kidnapped. His voice quavered as he said it. She was held prisoner for seven months, he said, fighting back tears, and then finally gave in to them, as the psychiatrist sitting next to him gently reached out to touch his arm, as though to steady him, and he smiled at her. They were all friends now, and knew each other's most intimate, and best-hidden secrets.

"We tried everything to get her back," he explained in a deep, troubled voice. Maddy had calculated from the time he'd spent in his three diplomatic posts that he was sixty. He had white hair, and blue eyes, and a youthful face, and he looked strong and athletic. "The State Department sent special negotiators to talk to representatives from the terrorist group that was holding her hostage. They wanted a prisoner exchange, trading her for one hundred political prisoners, and the State Department wouldn't agree to it. I understand the reasons for it, but I didn't want to lose her. The CIA tried too, and they tried to kidnap her back, but they fumbled the attempt, and she was moved into the mountains and after that we couldn't find her. Eventually, I personally paid the ransom they wanted, and then I did a very foolish thing." His voice shook again as he continued to tell the story, and Maddy's heart went out to him, as did everyone's, as they listened. "I tried to negotiate with them myself. I did everything I could. I almost went crazy trying to get her back. But they were too smart, too quick, too evil to beat. We paid the ransom, and three days later, they killed her. They dumped her body on the steps of the Embassy," he said, choking on the words and giving in to tears now, "and they had cut her hands off." He sat there sobbing for a moment, and no one moved, and then Phyllis Armstrong reached out and touched him, and he took a deep breath, as the others murmured their sympathy to him. It was a horrifying story, and a trauma everyone wondered how he had lived through. "I felt entirely responsible for making a botch of it. I should never have tried to negotiate with them myself, it just seemed to make them madder. I thought I could help, but I suspect that if I had left it alone and let the experts handle it, they'd have kept her for a year or two, as they had with others, and then released her. But by doing it myself, I more or less killed her."

"That's nonsense, Bill," Phyllis said firmly, "I hope you know that. You can't guess what might have happened. Those people are ruthless and immoral, a life means nothing to them. They might very well have killed her anyway. In fact, I'm sure they probably would have."

"I think I'll always feel as though I did," Bill said mournfully, "the press more or less said that." And suddenly, as she listened, Maddy remembered Jack telling her that Bill Alexander was a fool, and she wondered how he could be so heartless, now that she knew the story.

"The press likes to make a sensation of things. They don't know what they're talking about most of the time," Maddy added for good measure, as he glanced up at her with eyes full of sorrow. She had never seen so much pain in her life and she wanted to reach out and touch him but she was sitting too far away from him. "They just want to sell a story. I can tell you that from experience, Ambassador. I'm so sorry all of that happened to you," Maddy said kindly.

"So am I. Thank you, Mrs. Hunter," he said, and blew his nose in the clean handkerchief he took from his pocket.

"We all have tough stories. That's why we're here. That's not why I asked you to be here," Phyllis Armstrong brought them slowly to order. "I didn't know most of these histories when I asked you to come here. I asked you because you're intelligent, caring people. That's why you came, and why you want to help the commission. We've all learned from experience, the hard way, or most of us at least. We know what we're talking about, and what it feels like. What we need to do now is figure out what to do about it, how to help the people who are still out there. We're survivors, all of us, but they may not be. We have to get to them soon, and to the media, and the public. The clock is ticking, and we have to get to them before we lose them. Women die every day, murdered by their husbands, raped in the streets, kidnapped and tortured by strangers, but most women are killed by men, men they know, and more often than not, their spouses and boyfriends. We need to educate the public, and show the women where to go to get help before it is too late for them. We have to change the laws, and make them tougher. We have to make the prison sentences match the crime, and make it too costly to commit an act of violence on a woman, or anyone for that matter. It's a war of sorts, a war we have to fight and win. And I want each of you to go home and think about what we can do to change things. I suggest we meet again in two weeks, before most of you go away for the summer, and let's try to come up with some solutions. Today, I mostly wanted you to get to know each other. I know each of you, some

of you fairly well in fact, but now you know who you'll
be working with and why they're here. We're all here
for the same reason essentially, and some of us may
have suffered, but all of us want to make a difference,
and we can do it. Individually, we're all capable of it,
collectively we will provide a force that cannot be resis-
ted. I'm putting all of my confidence in you, and I want
to do some thinking about this myself before we meet
again." She stood up then, with a warm smile that enveloped each of them. "Thank you for coming here
today. Feel free to stay and chat for a while.
Unfortunately, I have to move on to my next appointment."

It was nearly four o'clock and Maddy couldn't believe how much she'd heard in two hours. It had been
so emotional for all of them that she felt as though she
had spent days with them. And she made a point of going over to Bill Alexander and talking to him before she
left. He looked like a kind man, and his story was so
tragic. He looked as though he still hadn't recovered
from it, and that hardly surprised her, given the trauma
he'd been through, and it had happened only seven
months before. She was surprised he was coherent.

"I'm so sorry, Ambassador," she said gently. "I remember the story, but it's different hearing it from you.
What a nightmare to go through."

"I'm not sure I'll ever recover," he said honestly. "I
still dream about it." He told her he had recurring
nightmares, and the psychiatrist asked if he was in therapy, and he said he had been for several months, but
was getting by on his own now. He certainly looked sane
and normal, and was obviously extremely intelligent,
but Maddy couldn't help wondering how he could

survive an experience like that and still be functioning sensibly and calmly. He was clearly an extraordinary person. "I look forward to working with you," Maddy said with a smile.

"Thank you, Mrs. Hunter," he said smiling back at her.

"Call me Maddy, please."

"I'm Bill, and I saw your story the other night, about Janet McCutchins. It was very disturbing, as it should be."

She smiled ruefully at the compliment and thanked him. "My husband has yet to forgive me. He was very upset about the implications for the network."

"You have to be brave and just do the right thing sometimes. You know that as well as I do. You have to listen to your heart as well as your advisers. I'm sure he understands that. It was the right thing to do, and you did it."

"I don't think he'd agree with you, but I'm glad I did it," she admitted.

"People need to hear it," he said firmly, the strength coming back into his voice. And he looked younger as he chatted with her. She was very impressed by him, both by his presence and the way he had handled himself at their first meeting. She could see why Phyllis had asked him.

"I think they do need to hear it," Maddy said, and then glanced at her watch. It was after four and she had to get to the studio for hair and makeup. "I'm afraid I've got a five o'clock show to do. I'll see you at the next meeting." Maddy shook hands with several people before she left the room, and then she left the White House as quickly as she could, and caught a cab back to the network.

Greg was already in the chair getting his makeup done when she got there. "So how was it?" he asked conversationally. He was intrigued by the commission being organized by the First Lady, and thought it would make a great story.

"Very interesting. I loved it. I met Bill Alexander there, the ex-Ambassador to Colombia whose wife was killed by terrorists last year. What an awful story."

"I remember it vaguely. I saw a clip of him, he was an absolute mess when they brought her body back to the Embassy, not that I blame him. Poor guy, how is he?"

"He seems fine, though I guess he's still pretty shaken. He's writing a book about it."

"Sounds like a good story. Who else was there?" She reeled off a few names, but told him none of the personal stories that had been told, she knew she had an obligation not to, and she respected it. And as soon as her makeup was done, she walked into the studio and looked at the stories they'd be covering. There was nothing startling or terrific, it was all fairly run of the mill, and once they were on the air, they ran through it smoothly, and then she went back to her office. There were some stories she wanted to read about, and some research she had to do before the seven-thirty show. And at eight o'clock, she was finished. It had been a long day, and as she got ready to leave the office, she called Jack. He was still upstairs, finishing a meeting.

"Am I getting a ride, or do you want me to walk home?" she asked him and he smiled at the question, in spite of himself. He was still angry at her, but he knew it couldn't go on forever.

"I'm going to have you run behind the car for the

next six months, to atone for your sins, and what you may cost me."

"Phyllis Armstrong doesn't think he'll sue us."

"I hope she's right. If she isn't, will the President foot the bill? It'll be a big one."

"Let's hope it never happens," she said quietly. "The commission was terrific by the way. There are some great people on it." It was the first real conversation they'd had since Tuesday, and she was glad he was finally unbending a little.

"I'll meet you downstairs in ten minutes," he said quickly. "I have to wind some things up here."

And when he came downstairs to the lobby ten minutes later, he didn't look happy to see her, but he looked less ferocious than he had for the past three days, since her "transgression." And they were both careful not to mention it on the way home. They stopped for a pizza, while she told him about the commission meeting that afternoon. But she didn't give him the personal details either, just the rough form, and what they hoped to do. She felt protective of the people she had met there.

"Is there a common bond among you, or are you all just smart and interested in the topic?"

"Both. It's amazing how violence touches everyone's life at one time. Everyone was very honest about it." It was all she could tell him, or would.

"You didn't tell them your story, did you?" He looked concerned, as he watched her face.

"Yes, I did, as a matter of fact. We were all pretty candid."

"That's stupid, Mad," he said bluntly. He was still annoyed at her, and wasn't pulling any punches. "What if someone feeds that to the press? Is that the image you want out there? Bobby Joe kicking your ass down the stairs in Knoxville?" He sounded critical, and she didn't like it, but she didn't comment on what he'd said.

"Maybe that's okay, if it helps someone else realize that abuse happens to people like me too. Maybe that's worth a little exposure if it saves someone's life, or gives them hope that they can escape."

"All it'll give you is a headache, and a trailer park image I've invested a fortune to get rid of. I don't understand how you could be so stupid."

"I was honest. So was everyone there. Some of the stories were a lot worse than mine." The First Lady's certainly wasn't pretty and she hadn't held back either. They had all been very open, which was the beauty of what they had shared. "Bill Alexander is on the commission too. He told us about his wife getting kidnapped." It was public knowledge so she could say that much to Jack, but he just shrugged his shoulders in response, and was clearly unsympathetic.

"He might as well have killed her himself. It was a damn stupid thing to do, trying to negotiate for her himself. The whole damn State Department told him that, but he refused to listen."

"He was desperate, and probably not all that rational. She was held hostage for seven months before they killed her. He must have gone crazy, waiting." She still felt sorry for him when she thought of it, but Jack was unmoved, which annoyed her. He seemed to have a total disregard for the man's feelings and what he'd been through. "What do you have against him? I get the feeling you don't like him."

"He was one of the President's advisers for a short time, after he taught at Harvard. His ideas go right back to the Middle Ages, and he's a stickler for principles and morality. The original pilgrim." It was an unkind way of describing him, and it irked Maddy as she listened.

"I think there's more to him than that. He seems very sensible, and intelligent, and a very decent person."

"I guess I just don't like him. Not enough life to the guy, or sex appeal or something." It was an odd thing for him to say because Bill was a handsome man, but there was something very straight arrow and sincere about him. He was the exact opposite of the jazzier crowd Jack Hunter liked to hang out with, but Maddy wasn't sure she minded Bill's style and ideas. Although he didn't seem glamorous enough to her husband.

They were home by ten o'clock, and out of habit, she turned on the news and then stopped dead in her tracks when she saw that U.S. troops had led another invasion on Iraq. She turned toward Jack, and saw something odd in his eyes as he watched the broadcast.

"You knew about this, didn't you?" she asked him directly.

"I don't advise the President on his wars, Mad. Just about media issues."

"Bullshit. You knew. That's why you went to Camp David last week, isn't it? And why you're going to the Pentagon this weekend. Why didn't you tell me?" There had been times when he shared top secret information with her, but this time he hadn't. For the first time, she felt as though he didn't trust her, and she was hurt by it.

"This was too sensitive, and too important."

"We're going to lose a lot of boys over there, Jack," she said, sounding worried. Her mind was whirling. It was going to be an important story for her too, on Monday.

"Sometimes that's a sacrifice you have to make," he said coolly. He thought the President had made the right decision. He and Maddy had differed on that subject before, and she wasn't as convinced as her husband.

They watched the last of the news as the anchor said that nineteen marines had been killed that morning in an exchange with Iraqi soldiers. Then Jack switched off the set, and she followed him into their bedroom. "It's interesting that President Armstrong let you in on it. Why, Jack?" She looked suspicious as she asked him.

"Why shouldn't he? He trusts me."

"He trusts you, or he's using you as a spin doctor, to make the American public swallow this without hurting his image?"

"He has a right to get advice on how to handle the media. There's no crime in that."

"No crime, but maybe not very honest either, to sell the public something that might be a very bad idea in the long run."

"Spare me your political opinions, Mad. The President knows what he's doing." He dismissed her summarily, which annoyed her, and it intrigued her that Jack was developing such a position of importance with the current administration. She wondered if that was partly behind his fury over her story about Janet McCutchins on Tuesday. Maybe he was afraid of some embarrassment that could upset the delicate balance of power for him. Jack always kept his eye on the ball, and what it could potentially cost him. He made calculations about everything he touched and even more so about the things that might touch him. But when he climbed into bed with her that night, he was warmer to her than he had been in days, and when he reached out and pulled her closer, she could sense that he was hungry for her.

"I'm sorry it's been such a bad week for us," she said gently, as he held her.

"Don't do it again, Mad. I won't forgive you next time, and do you know what would happen if I ever fired you?" His voice sounded hard and cold. "You'd be dead in the water the next day. You'd be finished, Mad. Your career depends on me, and don't you ever forget it. Don't fuck with me, Maddy. I could snuff out your career like a candle. You're not the star you like to think you are. It's all because you're married to me." The way he said it made her feel sick and sad, not for what she might lose if he threw her out, but for the way he said it to her. She didn't say anything in response, and he pinched her nipples hard, too hard, and then without another word, he grabbed her, and showed her who was in control. It was never Maddy, always Jack. She was beginning to think that power and control were all that mattered to him.

Chapter 5

ON SATURDAY, WHEN MADDY GOT UP, Jack was already dressed and about to leave for his meeting. He told her he'd be at the Pentagon all day, and not to expect to see him until dinnertime. "Why are you going there?" she asked, as she watched him from their bed. He looked handsome and well dressed, in a pair of slacks and a blazer and gray turtleneck sweater. It was warm outside, but he knew he'd be in an air-conditioned room all day, and it would be chilly.

"They're including me in some of their briefings. It helps us get a better perspective on what's happening over there. We can't broadcast what I hear, but it's useful information, and the President wants advice on how I think he should translate it to the media. I think I can help him on that." It was exactly what she'd suspected the night before. Jack was becoming the President's spin doctor.

"Telling the American people the truth might be an interesting way to go on it. It would certainly be new and different," she said, looking at her husband. Sometimes she didn't like his willingness to massage the truth, in order to put the "right" spin on things. He had a way of doing that which unnerved her. Maddy was much more of a black and white person. It was either true, in her point of view, or it wasn't. But Jack saw a rainbow of opportunities and subtler shadings. To him, the truth had a million hues and meanings.

"There are different versions of the truth, Mad. We just want to find the one that people will be most comfortable with."

"That's bullshit and you know it. This isn't PR, it's about the truth."

"I guess that's why I'm going to be there today and you're not. What are you doing today, by the way?" He glossed right over what he had just said to her, and the implications of it.

"I don't know. Hang around here, I guess. Relax. Maybe I'll do some shopping." She would have liked to go shopping with a friend, but she hadn't done that in years. She never had time to cultivate friends anymore, Jack monopolized all her spare time and kept her too busy, and the rest of the time she was working. And the only people they saw socially were somehow related to business, like having the McCutchinses to Virginia for the weekend.

"Why don't you take the plane and go to New York for the day? You can shop there. You'd like that." She nodded as she thought about the suggestion.

"That might be fun. There's an exhibit at the Whitney I'd like to see too. Maybe I can squeeze it in. You really don't mind if I take the plane?" It was a fantasy life, and she never forgot that. He provided luxuries and opportunities for her that she would never have dreamed possible while she lived in Knoxville. It reminded her of what he had said to her the night before, that she'd have no career at all if it weren't for him. It was painful to hear him say it, but she couldn't deny it. Everything good that had ever happened to her, she was sure, was because of Jack.

He called their pilot before he left, told him to expect Madeleine there by ten o'clock, and to get clearance for a flight to La Guardia with a return that evening to Washington. "Have fun," he said with a smile as he left, and she thanked him. It made her realize again that there were small sacrifices she made for him, but in exchange, he gave her so much. It was hard to justify ever being annoyed at him.

She arrived at the airport at ten-fifteen, with her hair neatly pulled back, in a white linen pantsuit. Their pilot was waiting for her and half an hour later, they took off and headed for New York. They landed at La Guardia at eleven-thirty, and at noon, she was in the city. She went to Bergdorf Goodman and Saks, and then walked up Madison Avenue, stopping at her favorite shops. She skipped lunch and arrived at the Whitney Museum at three-thirty. It was a golden life, and she loved it. Jack took her to Los Angeles too, New Orleans, San Francisco, Miami, and now and then to Las Vegas for the weekend. She knew she was spoiled, but she was grateful to him for it. She never lost sight of the many benefits of her life with Jack, or the career he had given her. And she knew that what he said was true, that it was all because she was Mrs. Jack Hunter. She utterly believed what he said, that without him, she'd be nothing. Believing that gave her an odd kind of humility, which others found both ingenuous and appealing. She took nothing for granted and had no sense of her own importance, only his. He had even convinced her that the awards she'd won had been his doing.

She was back at La Guardia at five o'clock, they were cleared to leave at six, and she let herself into their house on R Street at seven-thirty. It had been a perfect day, and she'd had fun. She had bought a couple of pantsuits, some bathing suits, and a great new hat, and she was in good spirits as she walked in with her trophies, and saw Jack sitting on the couch with a glass of wine, watching the seven-thirty broadcast. It was full of news of Iraq again, and Jack seemed intent on what he was hearing.

"Hi sweetheart," she said comfortably, the animosity of the past week seemed to have dispelled between them the night before, and she was in better spirits. She was happy to see Jack, and he turned to her with a smile at the first break in the broadcast.

"How was your day, Mad?" he asked, pouring himself another glass of wine.

"Fun. I did a lot of shopping, and I went to the Whitney. How was yours?" It was a thrill for him to play spin doctor to the President, and she knew it.

"Terrific. I think we've got a handle on things." He looked pleased and as though he felt very important, which he was. No one who knew him was ever unaware of it, and certainly not Maddy.

"Anything you can tell me about, or is it all top secret?"

"Pretty much." She would know it from what they gave her to report on the news. What she would never know, nor would anyone else, was the reality, or the original, undoctored version. "What are we doing for dinner?" he asked as he turned off the set.

"I can whip something up if you want," she said, setting down her packages. She still looked impeccable and beautiful after her long day of shopping. "Or I can order something in."

"Why don't we go out? I've been locked up all day with a bunch of guys. It might be nice to see some real people." He picked up the phone and made reservations for them at nine o'clock at Citronelle, which was the most fashionable restaurant in Washington at the moment. "Go put on something pretty."

"Yes, sir." She smiled at him, and disappeared upstairs to their bedroom with all the things she'd bought in New York, and she returned an hour later, bathed, combed, perfumed, in a simple black cocktail dress and high-heeled sandals, with her diamond studs and a pearl necklace. Jack bought her pretty things from time to time, and she looked wonderful in them. The diamond studs and her eight-carat engagement ring were her prize possessions. Not bad for a kid from a trailer park in Chattanooga, she often admitted to him, and he called her "poor white trash" when he wanted to really tease her. She didn't love it, but it was true. She couldn't deny it to him, although she had come so far and grown so far beyond it. It was obvious that he thought calling her that was funny, although hearing the words always made her wince at the image he conjured.

"You clean up pretty good," he said by way of a compliment and she smiled at him. She loved going out with him, being his, and letting the whole world see it. The thrill of being married to him had never dimmed for her, even now that she was a star in her own right.

More people knew her than him now, or it was fairly
even. He was the tycoon behind the scenes, the man
the President consulted for media advice, but she was
the woman other women and girls wanted to be,
and the face that many men dreamed of. She was the
presence in their living room, the voice they trusted,
the woman who told them the truth about tough things,
as best she could, as she had about Janet McCutchins
and countless other women like her. Maddy had a lot of
integrity, and it showed. And it came in a hell of an attractive package. As Greg said about her constantly, she
was "gorgeous." She looked it now, as they left for the
restaurant for dinner.

Jack drove her himself, which was rare for him, and
they chatted about New York on the way. It was obvious
that he could say nothing about his meetings. And once
at Citronelle, they were taken by the headwaiter to a
highly visible table. Heads turned, and people commented on who they were and how beautiful she was.
The women looked at Jack too, he was a handsome
man, with a sexy smile, eyes that took everything in, and
a great deal of presence about him. Everything about
them exuded success and power, and in Washington
that was important. Dozens of people stopped at their
table to chat with them, mostly politicians, and one of
the President's advisers. And every few minutes someone would come hesitantly up to them and ask Maddy
for her autograph, and she would scribble it for them
with a warm smile, and chat with them for a few minutes.

"Don't you get sick of that, Mad?" Jack asked as he
poured her another glass of wine. The waiter had left it

chilling in a bucket next to their table. It was Château Cheval Blanc 1959, Jack was an expert on fine wines, and this was a great one.

"Not really. I think it's sweet that they know who I am, and they care enough to ask." She was always gracious about it, and people came away from meeting her feeling as though they'd made a new friend, and liking her even better in person than on TV. Approaching Jack was a little more daunting, he was a lot less friendly.

It was nearly midnight when they left the restaurant, and on Sunday, they flew down to Virginia for the day. Jack hated missing a minute he could spend there. He rode for a while, and they had lunch outside. It was a hot day, and he commented that it was going to be a great summer.

"Are we going anywhere?" Maddy asked on the way back. She knew he hated to make plans, and he liked deciding at the last minute and just springing it on her. He would arrange for a stand-in for her on the news, and then he'd whisk her away. But she liked it better when she had a little advance notice. Sometimes he only told her the day before or that morning. And she could never say that she needed more time. They didn't have kids, and he was her boss, so if he decided she was leaving with him, there was no one to say that she couldn't. She was always free to go with him.

"I haven't decided about the summer yet," he said vaguely. He never asked her where she wanted to go, but he always picked places she loved in the end. Life was full of surprises with Jack. And who was she to complain? Without him, she would never be able to go to these places. "I guess we'll go to Europe." She knew it was all the warning she'd get, and maybe all she needed.

"Let me know when to pack," she teased, as though she had nothing to do, and could drop everything at a moment's notice. But sometimes that was exactly what he expected of her.

"I will," he acknowledged, and then took some papers out of his briefcase, which was the signal that he had nothing more to say to her for the moment.

She read a book the rest of the way home, it was one that the First Lady had recommended to her, a work about crimes of violence against women, and it was full of depressing but interesting statistics.

"What's that?" he asked, pointing at the book as they landed at National.

"Phyllis gave it to me. It's about crimes of violence against women."

"Like what? Cutting up their credit cards?" he said with a smile, and there was a pained look in Maddy's eyes as he said it. She hated it when he belittled issues that were important to her. "Don't get yourself too wound up over this commission, Mad. It's a great image-maker for you, which is why I suggested it, but let's not get crazy with it. You don't need to become the leading champion for battered women."

"I like what they're doing, and where they're going with it. It's something I really care about, and you know that." She spoke to him quietly but emotionally as they taxied down the runway after they landed.

"I just know how you are. You can get awfully overboard about things. This is about image, Mad, not about becoming Joan of Arc. Keep your perspective. A lot of what they say about abused women is just plain crap."

"Like what?" she said, feeling a cold chill run down her spine, as she wondered what he was really saying to her.

"All that garbage about date rape and sexual harassment is just that, and probably more than half the women who are either kicked around by their husbands or allegedly murdered by them deserved it." He said it with the utmost conviction as she stared at him.

"Are you serious? I can't believe you mean that. What about me? Do you think I deserved what Bobby Joe did to me? Is that what you think?"

"He was a small-time punk, and a drunk, and God only knows what you may have said to provoke him. A lot of people fight, Mad, some take a few pokes at each other, some get hurt, but that doesn't necessarily warrant a crusade, and it's not a national emergency. Believe me, if you asked her privately, I'm sure Phyllis is doing it for the same reasons I wanted you to. It looks good." Maddy felt sick as she listened.

"I can't believe what I'm hearing," she said in a whisper. "Her mother was abused by her father for all her married life, and Phyllis grew up with that. So did I. So do a lot of people, Jack. And in some cases, beatings aren't enough, they have to kill the women just to prove how tough they are, and how worthless the women are. What does that sound like to you, just your ordinary fight? When was the last time you kicked a woman down the stairs, or hit her with a chair, or took a hot iron to her, or put bleach in her eyes, or burned her with lit cigarettes? Do you have any idea what these people go through?"

"You're getting wound up, Mad. Those are the exception, not the rule. Sure, there are a few nutcases out there, but they kill other guys too. No one ever said the world isn't full of crazy people."

"The difference is that some of these women live with their assailants, or even eventual murderers, for ten or twenty or fifty years and let them continue to abuse them, and possibly kill them."

"Then it's the women who're sick, isn't it? They can always put a stop to it by walking out, but they don't. Hell, maybe they like it." She had never felt as frustrated in her life as she did listening to him, but he was not only the voice of ignorance, but the voice of most people in the world. And she wondered if she could get through to him. She felt helpless.

"They're too scared to walk out most of the time. Most of the men who threaten to kill their wives eventually do. The statistics are devastating, and these women instinctively know that. They're too scared to move out, or to run away. They have kids, they have nowhere to go, a lot of them don't have jobs, some or most of them have no money. Their life is a dead end, and there's a guy telling them that if they make a move, he'll kill them or their kids, or both. What would you do in a case like that? Call your attorney?"

"No, I'd get my ass out of Dodge, just like you did."

And then she tried a new concept on him. "That kind of abuse is a habit. It's familiar. It becomes normal to you. You grow up with it, you see it all the time, they tell you you're rotten and bad and you deserve it, and you believe it. It's mesmerizing, it makes you feel paralyzed.

You're isolated and alone and scared and you have nowhere to go, maybe you even want to die because that seems like the only way out." There were tears in her eyes as she said it. "Why do you think I let Bobby Joe kick me around? Because I loved it? I thought I had no other choice, and I believed I deserved it. My parents told me I was bad, Bobby Joe told me it was all my fault, I didn't know anything else until I met you, Jack." He had never laid a hand to her, and in her mind not beating her was all it took to be a good husband.

"Just keep that in mind the next time you give me a bad time, Mad. I've never laid a hand on you, and I never would. You're a lucky woman, Mrs. Hunter." He smiled at her and stood up, they were at the terminal, and he had lost interest in the topic that was so important to her.

"Maybe that's why I feel I owe it to the others, the ones who aren't as lucky, to help them," she said, wondering why she felt so uncomfortable about what he had just said to her. But he was obviously tired of the subject, and neither of them mentioned it again as they left the plane and went back to their house in Georgetown.

They spent a quiet night, she made pasta, and they both read, and they made love when they went to bed, and Maddy wasn't sure why, but she knew that her heart wasn't in it. She felt distant and strange, and depressed, and as she lay in bed afterward she thought of the things he had said about abused women. All she knew was that something about what he'd said, or the way he'd said it to her, had hurt her. And when she fell asleep that night, she dreamed about Bobby Joe and she woke up in the middle of the night, screaming. She could almost see him in front of her, his eyes filled with hate, his fists were pummeling her, and in the dream, Jack had been standing there, shaking his head and watching her, and she knew it was all her fault as she walked away, and Bobby Joe came at her again and hit her.

Chapter 6

THINGS WERE BUSY AT THE OFFICE the next day. There were reams of things to read about the fighting in Iraq, and the U.S. casualties that had occurred over the weekend. Five more Marines had been killed, and a plane had been shot down, taking two young pilots with it. No matter what Jack did to help the President put a positive spin on it, there was no way to change the facts, or the depressing truth that people on both sides were going to die there.

She was at work until eight o'clock that night, when she came off the air. They were going to a black tie dinner at the home of the Ambassador of Brazil, and she had brought an evening dress with her so she could change at the office. But just as she was getting dressed, the intercom in her dressing room rang, and it was her husband.

"I'll be ready in five minutes."

"You have to go without me. I've got a meeting that just got called." But this time she knew why. She was sure that the President was concerned with public reaction to the deaths in Iraq since the fighting had begun there.

"Your meeting is at the White House, I assume."

"Something like that."

"Will you come later?" She was used to going to parties alone, but she liked it better when Jack was with her.

"I doubt it. We've got some things to work out. I'll see you at home later. If I finish early, I'll come to the dinner, but I already called to tell them I won't make it. Sorry, Maddy."

"That's okay. This isn't looking good in Iraq, is it?"

"It'll be fine. It's something we're just going to have to live with." And if he did his job right, he was going to convince the public of that, but Maddy wasn't sold on it, and Greg hadn't been either when they talked about it. But they made no editorial comments on the news. Their opinions were not a part of their broadcasts. "I'll see you later."

She finished dressing after that, she was wearing a pale pink gown that looked exquisite with her creamy coloring and dark hair, and she was wearing pale pink topaz earrings that sparkled as she put a pink satin stole over her evening gown, and left her office. Jack had left the car for her, and had taken a company car and driver to the White House.

The Embassy was on Massachusetts Avenue, and it looked as though about a hundred people were there. They were speaking Spanish and Portuguese and French, and there was wonderful samba music in the background. The Brazilian Ambassador and his wife entertained with a lot of elegance and flair, and everyone in Washington loved them. And as she looked around, Maddy was pleased to see Bill Alexander.

"Hello, Maddy," he said with a warm smile, as he came to stand beside her. "How are you?"

"Fine. How was your weekend?" she asked him. He felt like a friend now, after all they knew about each other.

"It was uneventful. I went up to Vermont to see my kids. My son has a house there. That was an interesting meeting the other day, wasn't it? It's amazing to realize how many of us are touched by domestic violence, or violent crimes, in one way or another. The amazing thing is that we all think everyone else has such a normal life, and it's just not true, is it?" His eyes were a deep blue, almost the same color as hers, but darker, his full head of white hair was neatly combed, and he looked handsome in his dinner jacket. He was about six feet four, and Maddy looked doll-like beside him.

"I learned that a long time ago." Even the First Lady hadn't been exempt from violence in her childhood. "I used to feel so guilty because of my youth, and I still do sometimes, but at least I understand that it happens to other people too. But somehow, you always feel like it's your fault."

"I guess the trick is understanding that it's not. At least not in your case. When I came back to Washington, at first I felt as though everyone who looked at me was either saying or thinking that I killed Margaret." She looked surprised by what he'd said, and looked up at him gently as she asked the next question.

"Why would you think that?"

"Because I think I did. I realize only too well now that what I did was very foolish."

"It might have come out the same way anyway, it probably would have. Terrorists don't play fair, Bill. You know that."

"It's a little hard to absorb when the price to pay is someone you love. I don't know if I'll ever really understand it, or accept it." He was so open and so honest with her, and she liked him even better for it. And everything about him suggested that he was a gentle person.

"I don't think violence can be understood," Maddy said softly. "What I dealt with was a whole lot simpler, and I don't think I ever really understood it either. Why would anyone want to do that to a person? And why did I let him?"

"No options, no choices, no exits, no one to help you, nowhere to turn. Does any of that sound right?" he asked thoughtfully, and she nodded. He seemed to have a perfect grasp on the situation. Far more so than her husband, or a lot of people.

"I think you've got it just right," she smiled at him. "What do you think about Iraq?" she asked, changing the subject.

"That it's a damn shame we had to go back in there. It's a no-win situation, and I think the public is going to be asking hard questions. Particularly if we start losing boys at the rate we did this weekend." She agreed with him completely, in spite of Jack's certainty that he could put a spin on it that would make people buy it and continue to support the President's action. Jack was a lot more optimistic about it than she was. "I hated to see us do it," Bill went on. "I think people are afraid the gain isn't enough to warrant the losses." She wanted to tell him that he could thank Jack for that, but she didn't.

Maddy was glad to hear Bill agree with her and they chatted for a little while, and he asked her what her plans were for the summer.

"I'm not sure yet. I have a story to finish. But my husband hates making plans. He just tells me when to pack my suitcase, usually the day we're leaving."

"Well, that must keep life interesting," Bill said with a smile, wondering how she did that. Most people needed more warning. He couldn't help wondering too how her kids felt about it. "Do you have children?"

She hesitated for a fraction of an instant before she answered. "No, I don't actually." But it didn't really surprise him. She was young and had a demanding career, and she still had lots of time ahead of her to have children. And it was hardly party conversation to tell him that she couldn't, that it had been a condition of Jack marrying her to have her tubes tied.

"At your age, you have lots of time to think about children." And knowing what he did, he couldn't help wondering if her traumatic childhood had made her postpone having children. In her case, he would certainly have understood that.

"What are you doing this summer, Bill?" she asked, changing the subject.

"Normally, we go up to Martha's Vineyard. But I thought that might be difficult for me now. I gave my house to my daughter for the summer. She has three kids, and they love it there, and if I want to go up, I can always stay in the guest room." He seemed like a nice man, and it was obvious that he was close to his children.

They continued talking for a while, and a very interesting French couple joined them. They were diplomats and fairly young, and a few minutes later the Ambassador from Argentina stopped to say hello to Bill and they chatted easily in Spanish. Bill was completely fluent. Maddy was surprised a few minutes later to discover that Bill was her dinner partner, and she apologized for monopolizing so much of his time beforehand.

"I didn't realize we'd be sitting together."

"I'd like to tell you I engineered it," he laughed, "but I don't have that much pull. I guess I'm just lucky."

"So am I," she said comfortably as he tucked her hand into his arm and walked her into dinner.

It was a lovely evening. She sat next to the senior Democratic Senator from Nebraska, on her other side, whom she had never met, and whom she had always admired. And Bill kept her entertained with stories about his years teaching at Princeton and Harvard. He had obviously enjoyed it, and his brief career as a diplomat had been both interesting and rewarding, until its tragic ending.

"And what do you think you'll do now?" Maddy asked him over dessert. She knew he was writing a book, and he said he was almost finished.

"To be honest with you, Maddy, I'm not sure. I was thinking about teaching again, but I've done that. It's been interesting writing the book. But after this, I'm just not sure what direction I should go in. I've had several offers from academic institutions, one of them of course being Harvard. I'm actually tempted to go out west for a while, maybe teach at Stanford, or spend a year in Europe. Margaret and I always loved Florence. Or maybe Siena. I've also been offered the opportunity to teach for a year at Oxford, on American foreign policy, but I'm not sure I want to do that, and the winters are a little rough. Colombia spoiled me, at least as far as the weather."

"You have a lot of choices," she said admiringly, but she could see why everyone wanted him. He was intelligent and warm and open to new ideas and unfamiliar concepts. "What about Madrid, since you speak such perfect Spanish?"

"There's an option I hadn't even thought of. Maybe I should learn to bullfight." They both laughed at the unlikely image, and Maddy was almost sorry when they got up from dinner. He had been a wonderful dinner partner, and at the end of the evening, he offered to drive her home, but she told him she had a car and driver with her.

"I'll look forward to seeing you at the next meeting of the commission. It's such an intriguing, eclectic group, isn't it? I don't feel as though I have much to offer. I'm not very knowledgeable on the subject, at least not in the areas of abuse, or domestic violence. I'm afraid my brush with violence is a little unusual, but I'm flattered that Phyllis asked me."

"She knows what she's doing. I think we'll make a good team once we focus on our direction. I'm hoping that we get some media attention. People need to have their eyes opened on the issues concerning abuse and women."

"You'll make an excellent spokesperson for us," he said as she smiled at him again, they chatted for a few minutes, and then she went home, and found Jack reading in bed, looking relaxed and peaceful.

"You missed a good party," she said, taking off her earrings, and stepping out of her shoes as she stopped to kiss him.

"By the time we finished, I figured you'd be through with dinner. Anyone interesting there?"

"Lots of people. And I ran into Bill Alexander. He's a nice person."

"I've always thought he was pretty boring." Jack dismissed him and closed his book with an appreciative glance at his wife, even without her earrings and shoes, she looked particularly smashing. "You look great, Mad." He looked as though he meant it, and she leaned down to kiss him again.

"Thank you."

"Come to bed." He had a familiar gleam in his eye that she recognized instantly, and a few minutes later when she joined him, he was more than willing to prove it to her. There were some benefits to not having kids. They never had to pay attention to anyone else, all they had to concentrate on, when they weren't working, was each other.

And after they made love, Maddy lay in his arms and snuggled next to him, feeling comfortable and sated.

"How did things go at the White House?" she asked sleepily with a yawn.

"Pretty well. I think we made some sensible decisions. Or the President did. I just tell him what I think, and he puts it in the hopper with what everyone else says, and figures out what he wants to do about it. But he's a smart guy, and he does the right thing most of the time. It's a tough spot to be in."

"Worst job in the world, if you ask me. You couldn't pay me all the money on the planet to do it."

"You'd be great at it," he teased, "everyone in the White House would be well dressed, they would be beautiful, the White House would look wonderful, and everyone would be polite and compassionate and thoughtful about what they said, and all your Cabinet members would be bleeding hearts. A perfect world, Mad." But in spite of the seeming compliment, to her it somehow felt like a put-down, and she didn't answer. As she drifted off to sleep, she forgot about it, and the next thing she knew it was morning, and they both had to get to work early.

They were both in the office by eight o'clock, and she and Greg sat down and did some work together on a special he was working on about American dancers. She had promised to help him with it, and she was still in his office at noon, when they both became aware of a lot of scurrying and running around in the hallway.

"Now what?" Greg asked as he looked up, wondering what had happened.

"Shit. Maybe things are heating up in Iraq. Jack was with the President last night. They must be cooking up something." They both walked into the hallway to see what people were saying. Maddy was first to collar one of the associate producers. "Anything major?"

"A flight to Paris just blew to smithereens twenty minutes out of Kennedy. They claim you could hear the explosion all over Long Island. No survivors." It was the abbreviated version of what had happened, but as Greg and Maddy checked the news desk, they learned what little more there was. No one had claimed responsibility for the explosion, but Maddy was sure there was more to the story, even if they did not yet know the details.

"We got an anonymous call from someone who sounds like they knew what they were talking about," the producer said to them. "They say the airline knew before they boarded the flight that there had been a threat. They might even have known as early as noon yesterday, and they didn't stop it." Greg and Maddy looked at each other. That was insane. No one could have let something like that happen. It was a U.S. owned airline.

"Who's your source?" Greg asked with a frown.

"We don't know. But they knew their stuff. They gave us a lot of fairly traceable details. All we know is that the FAA got some kind of warning yesterday, and it sounds like they didn't do anything about it."

"Who's tracking that for you?" Greg asked with interest.

"You are, if you want to. Someone's got a list of people to call. The caller gave us some pretty specific names and directions." Greg raised an eyebrow as he looked at Maddy.

"Count me in too," she said, and they both headed for the assistant producer who supposedly had the list, as she commented on it. "I don't believe that. They don't board planes if there are bomb threats on them."

"Maybe they do, and we just don't know it," Greg muttered.

They got the list of names to call, and two hours later, they sat on opposite sides of Maddy's desk, staring at each other in disbelief. The story was consistent with everyone they talked to. There had been a warning, but not a specific one. The FAA had been told that an outbound flight out of Kennedy was going to have a bomb on it sometime in the next three days. That was all they were told, and all they knew, and an executive decision had been made at the highest level to tighten security but not to stop their outbound flights unless they found evidence of a bomb or had further information. But there had been no further warning.

"That's pretty vague," Maddy admitted in their defense. "Maybe they just thought it was an idle threat." But they had also suspected that the threat emanated from one of two terrorist groups, both of which had committed similar atrocities before, so they had reason to believe it.

"There's more to this than meets the eye," Greg said suspiciously, "I smell a rat somewhere. Who the hell can we call for a source deeper inside the FAA?" They had exhausted all their resources, and as they sat thinking about it, Maddy had an idea, and got up from her chair with a look of purpose.

"What've you got?"

"Maybe nothing. I'll be back in five minutes." She didn't say anything to Greg, but she went upstairs in the private elevator to see her husband. He had been at the White House the night before, and with a threat of that magnitude, he might have heard something, and she wanted to ask him.

He was in a meeting when she got there, and she asked his secretary to go in and ask him if he'd come out for a minute, it was important. He followed her out of the conference room with a worried look a minute later.

"Are you okay?"

"I'm fine. I'm working on the plane that went down. We got a tip that there was a warning about the bomb in a general way, but the flight went out anyway. They all did. I guess no one knew which flight the bomb might be on." She explained to him quickly, but he didn't seem too upset or particularly startled.

"It happens that way sometimes, Mad. There's not a hell of a lot anyone could have done. The warning sounds pretty vague, and could have been unfounded."

"We can tell the truth about it now, at least if there's a story here. Did you hear anything last night?" She was looking at him intently. Something in his eyes told her it was not an unfamiliar story to him.

"Not really," he said vaguely.

"That's not a real answer, Jack, this is important. If they were warned, they should have stopped the flights. Who made the decision?"

"I'm not telling you I know anything about it. But if they were warned, in a general way, what do you think they could have done? Stop *all* outbound flights out of Kennedy for three days? Christ, they might as well have shut down all U.S. aviation. They couldn't do that."

"How did you know it was all 'outbound' flights, and that the threat covered a three-day span? You knew, didn't you?" And then she suddenly wondered if that was why he had been called to the White House on such short notice, to advise them of what to say to the American public, if anything, or maybe even what to do, or not do about it. And how to cover their asses if a plane did go down at some point. But even if the decision hadn't been his, which it couldn't have been, he might well have been an important voice in the ultimate decision about whether or not to warn the public.

"Maddy, you can't shut down *all* outbound flights out of Kennedy for three days. Do you know what that means? At that rate, you'd have to shut down all incoming too, in case the blast hit them. This country would have gone haywire, and our economy with it."

"I don't believe this," she said, suddenly in a white

fury. "You and God knows who else decided to just go ahead with business as usual and not warn anyone, because our *economy* would be affected? And you'd disrupt flight schedules? Tell me this didn't happen the way I think it did. Tell me four hundred and twelve people didn't die to spare our aviation industry a disruption. Is that what you're telling me? It was a *business* decision? Who the hell decided that one?"

"Our President, you fool. What do you think? That I make decisions like that? It was a major issue, but the threat just wasn't specific enough. They couldn't do a goddamn thing about it, except check every plane with a fine-tooth comb before it went out. And if you quote me, Mad, I'll fucking kill you."

"I don't give a damn what you do. This is about people and lives and babies and children, and innocent people who got on an airplane with a bomb on it because no one had the balls to shut down Kennedy for three days. But goddammit, Jack, they should have!"

"You don't know what you're talking about. You don't shut down a major international airport for three days for a bomb threat, not and stay in business."

"They shut it down for snow, for chrissake, and the economy stays afloat. Why not for a bomb threat?"

"Because they'd have looked like fools and everyone would have panicked."

"Oh, okay, I guess four hundred lives is a small price to pay in order to avoid a panic. My God, I can't believe what I'm hearing. I can't believe you knew and you didn't do a *fucking* thing about it."

"What did you expect me to do? Go to JFK and hand out leaflets?"

"No, you asshole, you own the network. You could

have blown the whistle on this, anonymously if you wanted to, and forced them to shut down the airport."

"And the door to the White House would have been slammed in my face forever. You think they wouldn't have known who leaked something like that? Don't be ridiculous, and *don't*," he said, grabbing her arm and yanking her hard with it, "*ever* call me an asshole. I knew what I was doing."

"You and the boys you were playing with last night killed four hundred and twelve people at noon today," she almost spat the words at him and her voice was shaking. She couldn't believe he had been a party to it. "Why don't you just buy a gun, and start shooting people? It's cleaner, and a lot more honest. Do you know what this means? It means that business is more important than people. It means that every time some woman gets on an airplane with her kids, she doesn't know if someone has been warned that there's a bomb on it, but for the sake of big business, she and her kids are a walking sacrifice, because no one thinks they're important enough to warrant a 'disruption.'"

"They're not, in the larger scale of things. You're naive. You don't understand. Sometimes people have to be sacrificed for larger interests." She felt as though she was going to throw up as she listened. "And I'll tell you something, if you breathe a word of this, I will personally drag you back to Knoxville and leave you on Bobby Joe's doorstep. If you say a goddamn word, you're going to have to answer to the President of the United States and I hope they throw your ass in jail for treason. This was a security issue, and it was handled by people who knew what they were doing and have the highest possible clearance. This is not some little whining, psychotic housewife we're talking about, or some fat slobbering Senator. If you open up this can of worms, you're going to have the President on your neck, and the FBI, and the FAA, and every major agency in this country, and I'm going to watch you go down in flames with it. You are *not* touching this one. You don't know a goddamn thing about it, and they'll turn on you so fast, and bury you in about five minutes. You'll never win this one."

She knew there was some truth to what he said, everyone would lie about it, and it would be the biggest cover-up since Watergate, and more than likely the public would never believe her. She was one small voice in a sea of much bigger ones who would not only out-shout her, they would see to it that she was discredited forever. They might even kill her. The thought of it was frightening, but the thought of letting the public down and not telling them the truth made her feel like a traitor. They had a right to know that the people on Flight 263 had been sacrificed to economic concerns. And to the people who had made that decision, they meant nothing. "Did you hear what I just said to you?" Jack asked her with a terrifying look in his eyes. He was beginning to scare her. He would be the first one to take her down, before even the others could, if she jeopardized his network.

"I heard you," she said numbly. "And I hate you for it."

"I don't give a damn what you think or feel about this. I only care about what you do, and it goddamn better be the right thing this time, or you're finished. With me, and the network. Is that clear, Mad?" She looked at him for a long moment and then turned on her heel and walked swiftly down the stairs, back to her own floor.

She didn't even wait for the elevator, and when she got back to her office, she was pale and shaking.

"What happened? Did he know anything?" Greg asked. He had figured out instantly where she'd gone, and he'd never seen her look the way she did when she returned to her office. She was deathly pale and she looked sick, but for a moment she said nothing.

"No, he didn't" was all she said, and she took three aspirin with half a cup of coffee. And not surprisingly, ten minutes later the head producer came in and looked sternly at both of them before issuing a warning.

"I have to clear your copy before you go on the air tonight, both of you. Anything that deviates from what's approved, we cut you off and go to commercial. You got that?"

"Got it," Greg said quietly, and he knew where it came from, just as Maddy did. Greg didn't know what had been said upstairs, but he knew it couldn't have been pretty. Just looking at Maddy's face told its own story. He waited until the producer left and then looked across at Maddy, his eyes full of questions. "I take it he knew," Greg said softly. "You don't have to tell me if you don't want to." She looked long and hard at Greg and nodded.

"I can't prove that. And we can't say it. Everyone involved will deny it."

"I think we better not touch this one, Mad. This is one very large hot potato. Too big for us, I think. If they knew, you can be damn sure, everyone involved covered their asses. This one had to be run by the big boys." It impressed him to realize that Jack Hunter was now considered one of them. He had heard for a while that Jack had become the President's spin doctor. He was obviously playing in the big leagues.

"He said he'd kick me off the show if I touch it." She looked less impressed than Greg had thought she'd be as she said it. "I don't care about that, I hate lying to the public."

"Sometimes we have to," Greg said carefully, "even though I don't like it either. But the big guys would hang us out to dry on this one."

"Jack said I'll wind up in jail, or something pleasant like that."

"Isn't he getting a little cranky?" Greg said with a wry smile, and Maddy laughed in spite of herself, and then remembered the way he had grabbed her arm and shaken her. She had never seen him as enraged, or as frightened. But this was a big one.

They wrote their copy for the show that afternoon, and it was checked carefully by the producer. And half an hour later, it was returned to them with further edits. The piece on the air disaster was about as bland as it could be, and the powers that be upstairs wanted them to rely mostly on video footage to convey the story.

"Be careful, Mad," Greg whispered to her, as they sat at their desks in the studio, waiting to go on the air, after the countdown had started. And she only nodded. He knew what a crusader she was, and what a purist. It would have been just like her to take a kamikaze dive into the danger zone, by exposing the truth after all, but this time he was pretty sure she wouldn't do it.

She read off the piece about the crash of Flight 263, and her voice nearly broke once. She sounded somber and respectful as she spoke of the people on board, and the number of children. And the footage they showed underlined the tragedy even further. They had just shown the last shots, of some video footage someone on Long Island happened to get of the explosion, and Maddy was about to close when Greg saw her fold her hands on the desk, and look away from the TelePrompTer, and all he could feel as he watched her was terror. He mouthed the words "Maddy, don't . . ." because he could see on the monitor he was off camera, but she didn't see him. She was looking straight into the camera she was facing, right into the faces and hearts and homes of the American public.

"There are a lot of rumors flying around about the crash today," she began cautiously, "some of them very disturbing." Greg could see the producer stand up behind the set, with a look of panic. But they didn't cut away to commercial. "There have been rumors that the FAA was warned in advance, that 'some' mysterious, unknown flight outbound from Kennedy might be carrying a bomb, 'sometime' this week. But there is no evidence to support that rumor. We know nothing more right now than that four hundred and twelve lives were lost, and we can only assume that if the FAA was warned, they would have shared that information with the public." She was coming close to the line, but she didn't cross it, as Greg held his breath and watched her, as she continued. "All of us here at WBT would like to extend our condolences to the friends and families and loved ones of those who died on Flight 263. It is a tragedy beyond measure. Goodnight. I'm Maddy Hunter." And with that, they cut to commercial, and Greg looked pale as Maddy sat grim-faced and took her mike off.

"Shit, you terrified me. I thought you were going to blow it. You damn near did, didn't you?" She had raised a question, but not provided the damning answer to it. And she could have.

"I said what I could," which wasn't much, they both knew. And as she stood up, off camera now, she saw the producer in the doorway, talking to her husband. Jack walked straight toward her purposefully, and stopped when he reached her.

"You skated pretty close to the line on that one, didn't you, Maddy? We were ready to cut you off at any second." He didn't look pleased, but he no longer looked angry. She hadn't betrayed him, and she could have. Or she could have tried at least, although they wouldn't have let her get far.

"I know you were," she said coldly, her eyes looked like bright blue stones as they met his. Something terrible had happened between them that afternoon, and she would never forget it. "Are you satisfied?" she asked in a tone as icy as the look she gave him.

"You saved your own ass, not mine," he said so no one else could hear them. The producer had already walked away, and Greg had gone back to his office. "You were the one on the line here."

"The public got cheated."

"They would have been pissed out of their minds, if every flight in and out of Kennedy had been canceled for three days."

"Well, I'm glad we didn't piss them off, aren't you? I bet the people on Flight 263 were real glad too. It's a lot better to kill people than to make them angry," she said grimly.

"Don't push your luck, Maddy," he said ominously,

and she could see that he meant it. She said nothing, and walked right by him to her office. Greg was just leaving when she got there.

"Are you okay?" he whispered, not sure how close Jack was; he had stayed in the studio to talk to the producer.

"Not really," she said honestly. "I don't know what I am. Heartsick mostly. I sold out, Greg," she said, fighting back tears. She hated herself for it.

"You had no choice. Get past it. This was too big for you to tackle. How is he?" he asked, referring to her husband. "Pissed? He shouldn't be. You gift-wrapped it for him, and you sure got the FAA off the hook, and everyone else with it."

"I think I scared him," she said, smiling through her tears.

"Never mind him, you scared the shit out of me. I thought I was going to have to put my jacket over your face to shut you up, before someone killed you. They might have, you know. They would have said you had a psychotic break, that you've been unstable for months, under psychiatric care, schizoid, they'd have done everything they had to. I'm glad you didn't do anything really stupid." She was about to say something just as Jack walked into her office.

"Get your things, we're leaving." He didn't even bother to acknowledge Greg. Jack was satisfied with Greg's ratings, but he had never liked him, and never bothered to pretend he did. But he spoke to Maddy now like a servant, just someone to be ordered around and carry out his orders. She picked up her handbag and walked out of the office without saying a word. She wasn't sure how, but she knew that after today things would be different between them. They each felt betrayed by the other.

Jack followed her to the elevator, and they rode downstairs in silence, and it was only once they were in the car that he spoke to her again. "You came damn near close to ending your career today. I hope you know that."

"You and your friends killed four hundred and twelve people. I can't even imagine how that must feel. Compared to that, my career doesn't mean much."

"I'm glad you think so. You were playing with fire out there. You were told to only read your approved copy."

"I thought the death of more than four hundred people merited some small comment. I didn't say anything you could object to."

They sat in silence again until they got home, and then he looked at her with contempt, as though to remind her that she was unimportant. "Pack your bags, Mad. We're leaving tomorrow."

"For where?" she said without interest.

"Europe." As usual, he offered no details, and hadn't asked her.

"I'm not going," she said firmly, determined this time to fight him.

"I didn't ask you. I told you. You're off the air for two weeks, I want you to cool off and remember what the ground rules are before you go back on the show again. Elizabeth Watts is covering for you. She can do it permanently, if you'd prefer it." He wasn't pulling any punches. Elizabeth Watts was the anchorwoman whose place Maddy had taken when she got there. She still covered for Maddy during vacations. It was in her contract, although she was still bitter about having been unseated by Maddy.

"I don't really care at this point, Jack," Maddy said coolly, "if you want to fire me, go ahead." Her words were brave, although she felt a tremor of terror as she watched him. In some ways, although he had never been physically violent with her, he had always scared her. The power he exuded from every pore was not only directed at others, but at her as well.

"If I fire you, you'll be washing dishes somewhere. You'd better think of that before you shoot your mouth off. And yes, you are going with me. We're going to the South of France, Paris, and London. And if you don't pack your things, I will. I want you out of the country. You're not giving comments, interviews, or editorials of any kind. You are now officially on vacation."

"Was that the President's idea, or yours?"

"Mine. I run the show here. You work for me. You're married to me. I own you," he said with a force that took her breath away as she listened to him.

"You don't own me, Jack. I may work for you, and I'm married to you, but you don't own me." She said it softly, and firmly, but she looked frightened. Ever since her childhood, she had hated confrontation and conflict.

"Am I packing or are you?" he asked, without further comment.

She hesitated for a long moment, and then walked through their bedroom to her dressing room, and took out a suitcase. There were tears in her eyes when she did it, and she was crying openly as she tossed bathing suits and shorts and T-shirts and shoes into the suitcase. All she could think as she did it was that things never changed much. Bobby Joe may have pushed her down the stairs, but Jack had done a good job of it today, without ever touching her, or barely. What was it about men like them that made them think they owned you? Was it the men she chose, or did she ask for it? It hadn't quite come clear to her, as she folded four linen dresses and put three pairs of high heels into the suitcase. Twenty minutes later, she was finished and went to take a shower. Jack was in his bathroom packing.

"What time are we leaving tomorrow?" she asked when she saw him again in their bedroom.

"We leave here at seven o'clock in the morning. We're flying to Paris." It was all she knew about the trip, but she really didn't care now. He had made his point, and she had bought into it. For all her brave words, she had proved to both of them that he owned her.

"I guess there's one advantage to having your own plane," she said as she climbed into bed with him.

"What's that?" he asked, thinking she was making idle conversation.

"At least we know there won't be a bomb on it. That's a definite plus," she said, and turned her back to him as she got into bed beside him. He didn't answer her as he turned off the light, and for once, he didn't touch her.

Chapter 7

THEY ARRIVED IN PARIS AT TEN P.M. local time, and there was a car waiting for them. It was a beautiful warm night as they drove to the Ritz, and got there at eleven o'clock. The Place Vendôme was brightly lit, and the doorman recognized them immediately. But in spite of the beauty of the scene, it was anything but romantic to Maddy. For the first time in years, she felt like a prisoner. Jack had crossed over the line. And she looked blank and felt numb as she walked into the lobby behind him.

She usually loved going to Paris with him, but not this time. There was nothing but ice and pain between them, and for the first time in years she felt the sick feeling of being abused, and she knew that although he hadn't battered her, he might as well have. It was a side of him she had never before confronted, and she wondered now how often and in how many ways this had happened. She had never allowed herself to think of it before, but now the feelings were no different than they had been in Knoxville with Bobby Joe. The setting was just fancier, but she realized now that she was still the same person. She was just as trapped as she had been then. Jack's words of the night before still echoed in her ears as they brought the bags in, "I own you." And she had agreed by coming with him.

The suite at the Ritz was as beautiful as it always was. They had a view of the Place Vendôme, a living room and bedroom and two baths. The entire suite was done in pale yellow satin. And the hotel had filled three vases with long-stemmed yellow roses. She would have loved it if she hadn't felt so heartsick over Jack.

"Is there any particular reason why we're here?" Maddy asked him lifelessly as he poured himself a glass of champagne, and offered her one. "Is it just to keep me off the air, or is there some better reason?"

"I thought we needed a vacation," he said simply, and all the fury of the day before seemed to have vanished as she took the glass of Cristal from him. She didn't even want it, but she needed something to numb her. "I know how much you like Paris and I thought it would be fun for us."

"After everything you've said to me in the past two days, how can you say that?" The prospect of anything being "fun" with him was absurd.

"Because that was business, and this isn't," he said calmly. "You walked right into something that was a matter of national security and you had no business being there. Maddy, I was trying to protect you."

"That's bullshit," she said, sipping the champagne. She was not yet ready to forgive him for his threats, his words, or his saying that he owned her. But she didn't want to argue with him either. She was exhausted and depressed.

"Why don't we just put that behind us, and enjoy Paris? We both needed a vacation." She felt as though she needed a lobotomy, or maybe a new husband. She had never felt as betrayed by him in all the years they'd been married. And she couldn't help wondering how, or if, they would recover. "I love you, Mad," he said, moving closer to her, as he ran his fingers sensually up the arm that he had used the day before to shake her. She still remembered the feeling, and knew she always would.

"I don't know what to say to you," she said honestly, "I'm angry and hurt, and maybe even a little bit scared of you. I feel sick over everything that happened." She was always scrupulously honest with him, far more so than he was with her.

"That's why we're here, Mad. So we can forget our jobs, our work, our problems, our differences of opinion. We came here," he said, snuggling up to her, and putting his glass down on the Louis XV table, "to be lovers." But she didn't feel like being lovers. She just wanted to hide and lick her wounds, and be alone for a while until she understood what she was feeling. But he wouldn't let her do that. He was kissing her, and he started unzipping her dress, and before she could stop him, he had her bra off.

"Jack, don't . . . I need some time . . . I can't . . ."

"Yes, you can," he said, covering her lips with his own, and nearly swallowing her, and then his mouth moved to her breasts, and her dress seemed to disappear along with her underwear, and he laid her on the floor and was kissing her and caressing her, and his tongue was so powerful and so effective that she wanted to muster all her strength to resist him, but found she couldn't. And much to her chagrin, after a moment more, she knew she didn't want to stop him. He took her there, on the floor, as they rose and fell in each other's arms, and their climax was so swift and so powerful that she didn't expect it. She was his again, and she lay breathless for a time, clinging to him, and wondering how it had happened, and why.

"Well, that's one way to start a vacation," she said, feeling foolish. Their lovemaking had been entirely sensual, and so powerful it was like a tidal wave of feeling that had run through her, but there had been nothing loving about it. If anything, it had only proven yet again that he owned her. But she felt powerless to fight it. "I don't know how that happened," she said, looking at him, as he lay naked on the floor beside her.

"I could show you, if you like. Maybe some more champagne would help." He propped himself up on his elbow as he lay there, and smiled at her. She wasn't sure if she hated him now or not, but one thing was certain about Jack, he was fatally handsome, and she had never been able to resist him. He gave her no choice.

She looked at him sadly, and propped herself up to look at him as he handed her another glass of champagne. She didn't really want it, but she took it, and sipped it. "I hated you yesterday. That was the first time I ever felt that way about you," she confessed, and he looked nonplussed.

"I know you did. That's a dangerous game to play. I hope you learned a lesson." It was a thinly veiled warning, which she heard.

"What lesson was I supposed to learn?"

"Not to put your nose where it doesn't belong. Just stick to what you know, Mad. All you have to do is read the news. It's not your job to pass judgment on it."

"Is that how it works?" She was feeling a little drunk, and for once she didn't mind.

"That's how it's supposed to. Your job is to look beautiful and read your stuff off the TelePrompTer. Let someone else worry about how it gets there, and what it says."

"That sounds pretty simple," she giggled as she said it, but a sob caught in her throat. She felt somehow as though she had not only been demoted, but diminished as a person, and she had been.

"It is simple, Maddy. And it's simple between us. I love you. You're my wife. It's not good for us to fight, or for you to challenge me like that. I want you to promise me you won't do that anymore."

"I can't do that, Jack," she said honestly. She didn't want to lie to him, no matter how much she hated conflict. "Yesterday was a matter of professional ethics and morality. I have a responsibility to the people who watch me."

"You have a responsibility to me," he said in silken tones, and for an instant, she felt frightened again, but she wasn't sure why. There was nothing threatening about him now, in fact he was caressing her again, in ways that were infinitely distracting. "I told you what I want . . . I want you to promise me you're going to be a good girl." His tongue was traveling across the most sensual places of her body, in between saying things to her that confused her.

"I am a good girl, aren't I?" She giggled uncontrollably as she said it.

"No, you're not, Mad . . . you were a bad girl yesterday, a very bad girl, and if you do it again, I'll have to punish you for it . . . maybe I'll have to punish you now," he said, teasing her, but he didn't sound ominous, just seductive, "I don't want to punish you, Mad . . . I want to please you," and he was, almost too much so. But she didn't have the energy to stop him, she was too tired and too confused, and the champagne was making her feel fuzzy. For once, she didn't mind being drunk. It helped.

"You do please me," she said in a husky voice, momentarily forgetting how angry she had been at him. But that was then, and this was now, and this was Paris. It was hard to remember how furious she'd been at him, how betrayed she felt, and how frightened. And as she tried to remember it, she found she couldn't as he started making love to her again, and her whole body felt as though it were on fire.

"Are you going to be a good girl now?" he asked, taunting her, torturing her with pleasure. "Do you promise?"

"I promise," she said breathlessly.

"Promise again, Mad. . . ." He was a master at what he was doing, it had taken long years of practice. "Promise me again. . . ."

"I promise . . . I promise . . . I promise . . . I'll be good, I swear." All she wanted now was to please him, and from the distance, she knew she hated herself for it. She had sold out to him again, given herself to him again, but he was too powerful a force to resist.

"Who owns you, Mad . . . who loves you? . . . I own you . . . I love you . . . Say it, Maddy. . . ."

"I love you . . . you own me. . . ." He was turning her inside out and outside in, and as she said the words, he began making love to her so hard that he hurt her. She gave a small squeak of pain, and tried to move away from him, and he held her pinned down to the floor with all his might, and continued pounding into her as she murmured in pain, but he wouldn't stop, he only pounded harder. She tried to say something to him, and he crushed his mouth down on hers, as he pounded her into the floor as hard as he could, and then he came with a great shuddering, and as he did, he reached down and bit her nipple. It was bleeding when he finally stopped, and she was too dazed to even cry. She wasn't sure what had happened. Was he angry, or did he love her? Was he punishing her, or did he want her so badly that he didn't even know he hurt her? She was no longer sure if what she felt for him was love or desire or hatred.

"Did I hurt you?" he asked, looking innocent and concerned. "Oh my God, Mad, you're bleeding, I'm so sorry. . . ." There was a trickle of blood from her left breast where he had bitten her nipple, and she felt as though her insides had been pummeled, and they had been. Maybe he had meant what he said, and he had punished her, and yet his eyes were full of love as he took a wet cloth from around the champagne and put it on her nipple. "I'm sorry, baby. I wanted you so much, I went crazy."

"It's okay," she said, still feeling confused, and more than a little dizzy. He helped her up, and they left their clothes on the floor and walked into the bedroom. All she wanted to do was go to bed. She didn't even have the energy to take a shower. And she knew that if she had let herself, she might have fainted.

Jack put her to bed ever so gently, and she smiled up at him as the room went around them in gentle circles.

"I love you, Maddy." He was looking down at her,

and she tried to concentrate on seeing him, but the room was spinning too swiftly.

"I love you too, Jack," she said, slurring her words, and a moment later she was asleep, as he stood over her and looked at her. He turned off the light and walked back into the living room, and poured himself a glass of whiskey. He drank it neat as he looked out at the Place Vendôme, and he seemed pleased with himself. The lesson had been delivered. She had learned.

Chapter 8

JACK TOOK MADDY TO TAILLEVENT, Tour d'Argent, Chez Laurent, and Lucas Carton for dinner. They dined out elegantly every night, and had lunch on the Left Bank in little bistros. They shopped and went to antique shops and art galleries. And he bought her an emerald bracelet at Cartier. It was like a second honeymoon, and she was apologetic about getting drunk the first night. She still had very odd memories of it, some of them very sexy, and others tinged with an aura of something ominous and scary and sad. She drank very little after that. She didn't need to. With Jack showering her with attention and gifts, she was drunk on romance. He did everything he could to seduce her. And by the time they left for the South of France, she was completely under his spell again. He was a master at the game.

They stayed at the Hôtel du Cap in Cap d'Antibes, and had a fabulous suite overlooking the ocean. They had a private cabana, where they spent their days, and it was just secluded enough for him to make love to her, which he did repeatedly. He was more loving and more amorous than ever. And at times, Maddy felt as though her head were spinning. It was as though everything she had felt before, the anger, the outrage, the betrayal, had been some kind of a delusion, and this was the only reality she knew. They were there for five days, and she hated to leave at the end of it, and go to London. They had chartered a boat and gone to Saint-Tropez, shopped in Cannes, and had dinner in Juan les Pins and when they got back to the Hôtel du Cap at night, he took her dancing. It was peaceful and happy and romantic. And he had never made love to her as often. She could hardly sit down by the time they got to London.

London was more businesslike, but he still made an effort to be with her. He took her shopping, and for dinner at Harry's Bar. They went dancing at Annabel's, and he bought her a small emerald band at Graff's to go with the bracelet he'd bought her in Paris.

"Why are you spoiling me like this?" she asked, laughing, as they walked out of Graff's onto New Bond Street.

"Because I love you, and you're my star anchor." He beamed at her.

"Aha! Are these bribes instead of a raise?" She was in good spirits, and yet beneath it all, she was confused. He was so loving, and yet before the trip he had been so cruel.

"That must be it. I was sent here by the controller to seduce you," he said, looking mock stern and she laughed at the answer. She wanted to love him, and wanted him to love her.

"You must want something, Jack," she teased. And he did. He wanted her body day and night. She was beginning to feel like a sex machine, and once or twice, while they made love, he had reminded her that he "owned" her. She didn't like the term, but it seemed to turn him on to say it to her, so she didn't say anything to him. If it meant that much to him, she could let him say it, although now and then, she couldn't help wondering if he believed it. He didn't own her. They loved each other. And he was her husband. "I'm beginning to feel like Lady Chatterley," she said, laughing at him, when he peeled her clothes off again the moment they got back to their hotel room. "What kind of vitamins are you taking? Maybe you're taking too many."

"There's no such thing as too much sex, Mad. It's good for us. I love making love to you when we're on vacation." But he didn't do badly when they were at home either. He seemed to have an insatiable appetite for Maddy. And most of the time, she liked it, except when he got too rough with her, or carried away, as he had in Paris.

But he did it again on their last night at Claridge's. They had been dancing at Annabel's, and the moment they got back to their suite and closed the door, he slammed her against the wall, pulled down her pants, and nearly raped her. She tried to make him wait, or go into the bedroom with her, but he shoved her against the wall and wouldn't stop, and then he dragged her into the bathroom and took her on the marble floor, while she begged him to stop. He was hurting her again, but he was so excited he didn't hear her. And afterward, he apologized, and lifted her gently into a tub of warm water.

"I don't know what you do to me, Mad. It's all your fault," he said, as he rubbed her back, and a moment later, slipped into the water with her. She looked at him suspiciously, worried that he would want her again, but this time when he began caressing her, he took her ever so gently. Life with him was a constant merry-go-round of pleasure and pain, terror and passion, infinite gentleness coupled with just a hint of something terrifyingly brutal and cruel. It would have been hard to explain to anyone, and would have embarrassed her to do so. He made her do things sometimes that afterward made her feel awkward. But he assured her that there was nothing wrong with it, they were married and he loved her, and when he hurt her, he always told her that she drove him so insane, it was her fault. It was flattering, but nonetheless, at times, very painful. And she felt continually confused.

When they flew home at last, their two weeks seemed more like a month's vacation. She felt closer to him than she had in a long time, and they had done some fun things. For two weeks, he had turned his full attention on her. He hadn't left her side for a minute, he had spoiled her in every possible way, and made love to her so many times that she could no longer keep track of what they had done, or how often they'd done it.

The night they got back to the house in Georgetown, Maddy felt as though she'd been on a honeymoon with him, and Jack kissed her as he followed her into the hallway. He carried their bags upstairs, along with the suitcase she'd bought to accommodate the new things she'd bought in London and Paris. She listened to their messages on the machine, while Jack went downstairs to get the mail, and Maddy was surprised to hear four messages from her co-anchor, Greg Morris. He sounded serious on the machine, and she glanced at her watch, but it was too late to call him back.

There was nothing interesting in the mail, and after a snack, they both showered and went to bed, and got up early the next morning.

They chatted on the way to work, and Maddy left Jack in the lobby, and went upstairs to her office. She was anxious to see Greg and tell him about the trip, and she was surprised when she didn't see him in his office. She went on to her own, and read all her messages and mail, and as usual, there was a stack of fan mail. At ten o'clock, when she still hadn't seen Greg, she got worried. She went out to her secretary and asked her if Greg was sick, and Debbie looked at her, and was obviously feeling awkward.

"I . . . uh . . . he . . . I guess no one told you," she said finally.

"Told me what?" Maddy said with a look of panic. "Did something happen to him?" Maybe he had an accident, and no one had wanted to upset her while she was away.

"He left," she said bluntly.

"For where?" Maddy didn't understand what she was saying.

"He doesn't work here anymore, Mrs. Hunter. I thought someone would have told you. Your new co-anchor starts on Monday. I think you're on alone. Greg left the day after you went on vacation."

"He *what*?" She couldn't believe what she was hearing. "Did he have an argument with someone and walk off the set?"

"I don't know the details," she lied, but she didn't want to be the one to tell her. And the words weren't out of her mouth before Maddy was flying down the hall to the producer's office.

"What in hell happened to Greg?" she asked, as the producer looked up at her. Rafe Thompson was a tall, tired-looking man who looked as though he had the weight of the world on his shoulders, and at times he did.

"He's gone" was all he answered.

"I know that much. Where? And when? And why? I want answers to those questions," she asked, as her eyes blazed.

"There was a change in format on the show. He didn't fit in. I think he's going to be doing sports on NBC now. I don't know the details."

"Bullshit. That's what Debbie told me. Who does know the details?" But she already knew the answer to her question, and she went up to Jack's office without waiting another minute. She walked right into his office without being announced, and looked at him from across his desk. He had just put down the phone and his desk was covered with papers, the price to pay for a two-week vacation. "Did you fire Greg?" she asked without preamble, and he looked at her for a long moment.

"We made an executive decision," he said calmly.

"What does that mean, and why didn't you tell me when we were in Europe?" She felt as though she'd been tricked.

"I didn't want to upset you, Mad. I thought you deserved a real vacation."

"I had a right to know that you fired my co-anchor." It explained the four messages on her machine the night before, and the tone of Greg's voice. She realized now that he had sounded upset, and it was no wonder. "Why did you fire him? He's terrific. And so were his ratings."

"We didn't think so," Jack said smoothly. "He's not as good as you are, sweetheart. We needed someone stronger as a balance to you."

"What do you mean 'stronger'?" She didn't understand what he was saying, and she was upset about the decision and the way it had been handled.

"He's too soft, too effeminate, you run right over him, and you're a lot more professional than he is. I'm sorry. You need someone with a little more personality and a lot more experience."

"So who did you hire?" she asked, looking worried. She was still upset about Greg, she had loved working with him, and he was her closest friend.

"Brad Newbury. I don't know if you remember him. He used to do news from the Middle East on CNN. He's terrific. I think you're going to love working with him," Jack said firmly.

"Brad Newbury?" Maddy looked stunned. "He can't even make a war zone sound exciting. Whose idea was that?"

"It was a collective decision. He's a pro, and a seasoned reporter. We think he's the perfect counterpoint to you." Maddy hated his style, and had never liked him. And the few times they'd met he'd been arrogant and condescending to her.

"He's dry and he's dull, and he has no appeal on the air," she said, looking frantic. "For God's sake, he's going to put everyone to sleep. He even made the trouble in the Middle East sound boring."

"He's a very skilled reporter."

"And so is Greg. Our ratings had never been higher."

"*Your* ratings had never been higher, Mad. His were starting to slip. I didn't want to worry you, but he would have taken you down with him."

"I just don't understand it," she said, "and I don't know why you didn't tell me."

"Because I didn't want to upset you. This is business, Maddy. Show business. We have to keep our eye on the ball here." But she was still depressed about it when she got back to her office and called Greg.

"I can't believe this, Greg. No one told me. I thought you were sick or something when you didn't come in by ten o'clock. What the hell happened after I left? Did you piss someone off?"

"Not that I know of," he said, still sounding devastated. He had loved working with her, and they both knew their show was a hit. But he understood more about it than she did. "The morning after you left, Tom Helmsley," who was the executive producer of the show, "called me in and told me they were letting me go, firing me, to be exact. He said we had gotten too informal, too close, and we were beginning to remind senior management of Abbott and Costello."

"Now where the hell did that come from? When was the last time we made a joke on the show?"

"Not lately, but I think the key word is *close* here. I think someone feels we were too personal, too close. Hell, Maddy, you're my best friend. I think someone in your life doesn't like that." He didn't want to spell it out for her, but he might as well have.

"You mean Jack? Greg, that's crazy." She couldn't believe that. That was no reason to fire him, and Jack would never have jeopardized the ratings of the show for personal reasons. But Brad Newbury was certainly an odd choice. She wondered if Greg meant that Jack was jealous of him, but she didn't think so.

"It may sound crazy to you, Mad. But it's called isolation. Have you ever thought of that? How many friends do you have? How often does he let you see anyone? He had no choice with me, we work together. But he took care of that, didn't he? Think about it."

"Why would he want to isolate me?" She sounded confused, and Greg wondered how much he should say to her. He had noticed it for a long time, but obviously she hadn't, and he assumed that she was in denial about it.

"He wants to isolate you, Mad, because he wants to control you. He runs your life, makes all your decisions for you, he never consults you about the show. He doesn't even tell you till the night before you leave for Europe. He treats you like a paper doll, for chrissake, and when he doesn't like what you do, he tells you that you came from poor white trash, and tells you you'd be back in a trailer park without him. How often has he told you that without him, you'd be nothing? Do you know what kind of bullshit that is? Without *you,* he'd have the lowest-rated news show on any network. If you ever left WBT, you'd be snapped up by any major network you wanted. Now what does all that sound like to you, Mad? A loving husband, or something much more familiar?" She had never let herself string it all together before, but listening to him, she was suddenly terrified. What if he did want to isolate her? And suddenly she remembered all the times he had said to her recently that he "owned" her. It made her shudder to think about it.

"It sounds like abusive behavior, doesn't it?" she said barely audibly.

"Now there's a news flash for you. So what else is new?" Greg answered. "Are you telling me this has never had a ring of familiarity to you? The only thing he doesn't do is kick the shit out of you on Saturday nights, but he doesn't need to do that, he controls you in every other way, and when you misbehave and he doesn't like what you do, he yanks you off to Europe and gets you off the air for two weeks and fires me. I'd say you're married to a control freak." He didn't want to say "abuser," but it meant the same thing to him.

"Maybe, Greg," she said, torn between defending Jack and sympathizing with her co-anchor. He hadn't painted a pretty picture for her, and she didn't disagree with him. She just didn't know what to do.

"I'm sorry, Mad," he said quietly. She meant a lot to him, and for a long time, he had hated the things Jack did to her. And what broke his heart was that Maddy seemed not to notice. But Greg did. And Greg was sure that all of that was part of why they'd fired him. It was too dangerous to have him close to Maddy. "What he's doing to you is abusive."

"It sounds like it," she admitted sadly. "But I'm not sure. Maybe we're overreacting, Greg. He doesn't beat me." She knew better than that, she just didn't want to see it, or hear it. But it was hard to avoid.

"Do you think he respects you?"

"I think he loves me" was her instant answer, particularly after their recent trip to Europe. "I think he wants what's best for me, even if he's not always right in the way he does it." Greg disagreed with her, and all he wanted her to do was think, and take a closer look at the life she led with Jack.

"I think even abusive men love the women they abuse. Do you think Bobby Joe loved you?"

"No, I don't." She couldn't believe Greg was comparing Jack to him. It was a terrifying thought, and she didn't want to hear it. It was one thing to think Jack was abusive, another to listen to Greg say as much to her. It made the terror of abuse far too real to her again.

"Well, maybe Bobby Joe didn't love you. But think about some of the things Jack does to you. He moves you around like a thing, an object he's bought and paid for. How loving is it for him to tell you that without him, you'd be nothing? And he wants you to believe that." Worse yet, she did, and Greg knew that. "Maddy, he wants you to think he owns you." As he said the words, she felt a chill run down her spine. Those had been Jack's words to her in Europe.

"What makes you say that?"

"Because he's not abusing me, and he doesn't own me. Maddy, I want you to do something for me." She thought he was going to ask her to talk to Jack about getting his job back and she was willing to do it, although she didn't think Jack would listen to her.

"I'll do whatever you want," she promised.

"I'm going to hold you to that. I want you to go to a group for abused women."

"That's silly. I don't need one." She was surprised by the suggestion.

"I want you to decide that after you've been there. I don't think you have any idea what's happening to you, or who's doing it to you. I want you to promise me you'll do it. I'll find one for you." It was exactly what she had tried to do for Janet McCutchins, but she had been covered with bruises, and Maddy wasn't. "I think it'll open your eyes, Mad. I'll even go with you."

"Okay . . . maybe . . . if you find one. What if someone recognizes me?"

"You can say you came to lend me support. Maddy, my sister went through this. She attempted suicide twice before she figured out what was happening to her. I went with her too. It was like a replay of *Gaslight,* and she had four kids with him."

"What happened to her?"

"She divorced him, and she's married to someone terrific now, but it took three years of therapy to get her there. She thought that just because he didn't beat the shit out of her like my dad did to our mom, that he was a hero. Not all forms of abuse leave bruises." She knew that, but part of her still wanted to believe that what Jack did was different. She didn't want to feel like a victim, or that Jack was an abuser.

"I think you're crazy, but I love you. What are you going to do now, Greg?" She was worried about him, and she was trying not to think about what he'd said about Jack. It was just too threatening to her. She had already started trying to convince herself that Jack wasn't really abusive. Greg was upset and confused, she told herself.

"I'll be doing sports on NBC. They made me a great offer and I start in two weeks. Do you know who they have for you yet?"

"Brad Newbury," she said, sounding depressed about it. She was going to miss Greg more than she could tell him. And maybe it would be worth going to an abuse group with him, just so she could see him. She was sure that Jack wasn't going to let her socialize with him. He'd find a way to cut Greg out of her life completely, "for her own good," and make it impossible for her to see him. She knew that much about her husband.

"The guy from CNN?" Greg said in disbelief when she mentioned Brad's name. "You've got to be kidding. He's awful."

"I think our ratings are going to go straight down the tubes without you."

"No, they won't. They've got you. It'll be okay, kid. Just think about what I said. That's all I want you to do. Think about it." Doing the news with Brad was the least of her problems.

"I will," she said, but without much conviction. And for the rest of the morning, every time she thought about Greg she felt anxious. The things he had said to her had touched a nerve somewhere, and she was doing everything she could to deny them. When Jack said he "owned" her, all he meant was that he loved her with a passion. But now that she thought about it, even their lovemaking had an odd quality to it, especially lately. He had hurt her more than once, and in Paris pretty badly. It had taken a week for her nipple to heal, and when he made love to her on the marble floor at Claridge's, he had hurt her back and she could still feel it. But that hadn't been intentional, he was just insatiable and highly sexed, and he thought her desirable. And he didn't like making plans. How abusive was it to take her to Paris, to stay at the Ritz, even without much notice? And he had bought her a bracelet at Cartier and a ring at Graff's. Greg was crazy, and probably just upset that he'd been fired, which was understandable. And the craziest thing of all was comparing Jack to Bobby Joe. They had absolutely nothing in common, and Jack had saved her from him. But the one thing she couldn't figure out was why she felt sick every time she thought about the things Greg had said to her. He had made her incredibly nervous. But just thinking about abuse did that to her.

She was still haunted by Greg's words when she went to the First Lady's commission on Monday, and sat next to Bill Alexander. He had a tan, and said he'd visited his son again in Vermont since they last met, and his daughter in Martha's Vineyard, over the weekend.

"How's the book coming?" she whispered, as the meeting began.

"Slowly, but well," he smiled at her, admiring her, as everyone did. She was wearing a blue cotton man's shirt, and white linen slacks, and she looked summery and pretty.

The First Lady had invited a guest speaker to come and speak to them about abuse. Her name was Eugenia Flowers. She was a psychiatrist who specialized in victims of abuse, and a supporter of numerous women's causes. Maddy had heard of her, but never met her. Dr. Flowers went around the room, talking to each of them from where she sat. She was personable and warm and looked like a grandmother, but her eyes were sharp, and she seemed to know exactly what to say to everyone. She asked questions of each of them about what they thought abusive behavior was, and most of them said pretty much the same thing, that it meant hitting or beating or battering the victim.

"Well, that's true," she agreed amiably, "those are the

obvious ones." And then she listed several others, some of them so perverted and obscure that it made each of them wince to think about them. "But what about other forms? What do you think those might be? Abusers wear many hats and many faces. What about controlling someone, their every act and every move, every thought? Destroying their confidence in themselves, isolating them, frightening them? Maybe just driving too fast in a dangerous situation until you terrify them? Or threatening them? Disrespecting them? Making someone believe that white is black and black is white, until you confuse them completely, or taking money from them, or telling them they'd be nothing without you, that you 'own' them? Taking their free will away from them, or forcing them to make reproductive choices they don't want, either having babies one after the other, or constant abortions, or maybe even not allowing them to have children at all? Do any of those sound like abuse to you? Well, they are, classic forms in fact, and they're just as painful, just as dangerous, just as lethal, as the kind that leave bruises." Maddy felt as though she couldn't breathe as she listened. She went deathly pale, and Bill Alexander noticed, but said nothing to her.

"There are many kinds of violence against women," the speaker went on, "some of them obvious, all of them dangerous, some of them more insidious than others. The most insidious are the subtle ones, because the victims not only believe them, but blame themselves for them. If the abuser is clever enough, he can use all of them, and convince his or her victim that it was all their fault. An abuse victim can be driven to suicide, drug abuse, crippling depression, or even murder.

Abuse of any kind, at any time, is potentially fatal to the victim. But the subtler forms are the hardest to stop, because it's harder to see them. And worst of all, the victim is so convinced most of the time that it's her fault, that she goes back for more, and helps the abuser do it, because she feels she owes it to him, and she feels so guilty and so bad and so worthless that she knows he's right and she deserves it. She believes that she would be nothing without him." Maddy felt faint as she listened, the woman was describing her marriage to Jack in every detail. He had never laid a hand on her, except the one time he had grabbed her arm, but he had done everything the woman had described, and Maddy wanted to run out of the room screaming. Instead she felt paralyzed in her chair.

The woman went on for half an hour, and then the First Lady opened up the meeting to questions. Most of them were about what could be done to protect these women not only from the abusers but from themselves, and how to stop it.

"Well, first, they have to recognize it. They have to be willing to. But like abused children, most of these women protect their abusers, by denying, and blaming themselves. It's too painful most of the time to admit what's happening to them, and to tell the world about it. What they feel is shame, because they believe everything they've been told by the abuser. So first, you have to help them to see it, then you have to help them remove themselves from the abusive situation, and that's not always easy. They have lives, they have kids, they have homes. You're asking them to pull up stakes and run away from a danger they can't see and aren't even sure is a real danger. The problem is that it's just as real and just as dangerous as a gun pointed at them, but most of them don't know it. Some do, but most of the time, they're just as scared as the others. And I'm talking about smart, educated, sometimes even professional women, who you may think should know better. But no one is exempt from being a victim of abuse. It can happen to anyone, and it does, in the best jobs, the best schools, with high incomes or low. Sometimes it happens to beautiful, smart women that you can't believe would fall for it. Sometimes they're the easiest targets. Women who are more streetwise are less apt to buy the bullshit. They're the ones who get the shit kicked out of them. The others are tortured more subtly. Abuse doesn't know color, it doesn't know race, it doesn't know neighborhoods, or socio-economic rules. It touches everyone. It can happen to any of us, particularly if we have a background that predisposes us to it.

"For instance, a woman who has seen domestic violence at home as a child, say with a physically abusive father, may think that a man who never beats her physically is a great guy, but he may be ten times more abusive than her father, much subtler and far more dangerous. He can control her, isolate her, threaten her, terrorize her, insult her, belittle her, demean her, disrespect her, withhold affection or money from her. Abandon her, or threaten to take away her children, but she won't have a mark on her, and he tells her she's one lucky woman and what is worse, she believes it. And you'll never be able to put him in jail, because when you nail the bastard for what he did to her, he'll tell you that she's crazy, stupid, dishonest, psychotic, and lying to you about him. And worse yet, she probably believes it. Those women have to be pulled slowly out of relation-

ships, and gotten off the ledge to safety. But they'll fight
you all the way, defend him to the death, and their eyes
open very slowly." Maddy felt as though she were going
to cry before the meeting ever ended, and it was all she
could do to remain outwardly calm until it was time to
leave, and her knees were shaking when she finally
stood up. Bill Alexander looked down at her, and wondered if she was suffering from the heat. He had seen
her go pale half an hour before, and she was nearly
green by the time it was over.

"Would you like a glass of water?" he asked kindly.
"It was an interesting meeting, wasn't it? Though I'm
not sure what we're supposed to do to help women in
that kind of situation, except maybe educate and support them." Maddy sat down again then and nodded at
him. The room was beginning to spin as she listened to
him, and fortunately, no one else had noticed that she
was feeling ill, as he went to get her a glass of water.

She was still sitting there, waiting for him, when the
guest speaker came over to talk to her.

"I'm a great admirer of yours, Ms. Hunter," she said
smiling down at Maddy, who was unable to get up, and
smiled wanly at her. "I watch your broadcast every
night. It's the only way I know what's going on in the
world. I particularly liked your editorial on Janet
McCutchins."

"Thank you," Maddy said through dry lips, just as Bill
appeared with a paper cup full of water, and he couldn't
help wondering if she was pregnant. The speaker
watched her take a sip, and her eyes seemed kind and
warm as she watched Maddy intently. Maddy stood up
when she finished it, and she didn't want to admit to
anyone how wobbly her legs were. She was beginning

to wonder how she was going to walk outside to get a taxi, and Bill seemed to sense her distress.

"Do you need a ride anywhere?" he asked chivalrously, and without thinking, Maddy nodded.

"I have to go back to the office." She wasn't even sure if she could go on the air, and for a moment she wondered if it was something she'd eaten. But she knew better than that now. It was someone she'd married.

"I'd like to get together with you sometime," Dr. Flowers said, as Maddy said good-bye to her and the First Lady. She handed Maddy a card, and Maddy thanked her and left, but she tucked the card into her shirt pocket. Coupled with what Greg had said, she felt as though she'd had a double dose of it, and she wasn't sure if it was reality or a nightmare. But whatever it was, it had hit her like a freight train. And she looked it as she rode down in the elevator with Bill. He had parked his car outside, and she followed him to it in silence.

He opened the door for her, and she got in, and a moment later, he slid behind the wheel and looked at her with concern. She looked awful. "Are you all right? I thought you were going to faint in there." She nodded, and said nothing for a moment. She was thinking about lying to him, and telling him she had the flu, but suddenly she just couldn't. She felt totally lost, and utterly alone, as though everything she had trusted and believed in and wanted to believe had been torn from her, and she felt like an orphan. She had never felt as terrified or as vulnerable as she did at that moment. Tears began to slide down her cheeks, as he gently reached out and touched her shoulder. And without meaning to, she began to sob, but there was nothing she could do to stop.

"It's very upsetting listening to these things," he said gently, and then instinctively he put his arms around her and held her. He didn't know what else to do, but it was what people had done for him when he was distraught about his wife, and what he would have done for his children in the same situation. There was nothing sensual or inappropriate about what he did. He just held her while she cried, until her sobs finally abated, and she looked up at him. What he saw in her eyes was raw terror. "I'm here, Maddy. Nothing bad is going to happen to you. You're all right now." But she shook her head then and began to cry again. Nothing was all right, it hadn't been in years, and maybe it never would be. She suddenly realized how endangered she had been, how demeaned, and how isolated from anyone who might have seen it, or could have helped her. Systematically, Jack had eliminated all her friends, even Greg, and she was his solitary, unprotected prey. Suddenly everything he had done and said to her over the years, and even recently, took on a new and intensely ominous meaning. "What can I do to help you?" Bill asked her, as she clung to him and cried, as she had never been able to, to any man in her life, starting with her father.

"My husband does every single thing that woman talked about today. Someone said exactly the same thing to me a few days ago and I never saw it. But when she started talking about it, I knew . . . he has completely isolated and abused me for the last seven years, and I thought he was a hero because he didn't beat me." She sat back against the seat and stared at Bill in shock and disbelief, and he looked desperately worried about her.

"Are you sure?"

"Completely." He had even abused her sexually, she realized now. He wasn't rough by accident, or because he was so passionate about her. It was yet another way of demeaning and controlling her. It was a seemingly acceptable way to hurt her, and he had done it for years. It was incredible to her now that she had never understood it. "I can't begin to tell you the things he's done to me. I don't think she left out a single one of them." Her lip trembled as she looked at Bill. "What am I going to do now? He says I'd be nothing without him. He calls me poor white trash sometimes, and says I'll wind up back in a trailer park without him." It was exactly what Eugenia Flowers had just described to them and Bill looked at her in complete amazement.

"Is he joking? You're the biggest name in news in the entire country. You could get a job anywhere. The only way you'll ever see a trailer park again is if you buy one." She laughed at the remark, and sat staring out the window for a long moment. She felt as though her house had just burned down and she had no idea where to live. She couldn't even imagine going home to Jack, or facing him, now that she had a clearer picture of what he had done to her. But it was still hard for her to believe. She silently told herself that maybe he hadn't meant to, maybe she was wrong.

"I don't know what to do," she said quietly. "Or what to say to him. I just want to ask him why he acts the way he does."

"Maybe he doesn't know anything different," Bill said fairly, "but that's no excuse for abusing you. What can I do to help?" He wanted to, but he was as much at a loss as she was.

"I have to think about what I'm going to do," she said thoughtfully, as he turned the key in the ignition, and then turned to look at her again.

"Would you like to stop for a cup of coffee?" It was all he could think of to calm her.

"I'd like that." He had been a real friend to her, and she was grateful for it. She could sense his warmth and sincerity, and she felt safe sitting next to him. She had felt peaceful and safe when he put his arms around her. She knew instinctively that this was a man who would never hurt her. And when she thought about Jack, she knew the difference. There was always an edge to him, an angle, he always said things that put her down, and made her feel as though she were less than he was, and he was doing her a huge favor. Bill Alexander acted as though he was grateful to have the opportunity to help her, and she sensed correctly that she could be honest with him.

They stopped at a small café, and she still looked pale when they sat down at a corner table. Bill ordered tea, and she ordered a cappuccino.

"I'm sorry," she said apologetically, "I didn't mean to involve you in my personal dramas. I don't know what happened to me. What she said overwhelmed me."

"Maybe it was just meant to be. Destiny that she would be there. Maddy, what are you going to do now? You can't go on living with a man who's abusive to you. You heard what she said, it's like having a gun to your head. You may not see it clearly yet, but you're in grave danger."

"I think I'm beginning to understand that. But I can't just leave."

"Why not?" To him, it seemed simple. She needed to

get out, so Jack couldn't hurt her any further. That much was clear to him, if not to Maddy.

"I owe him everything I am, and have. He made me what I am. I work for him. Besides, where would I go? What would I do? If I leave him, I have to quit my job too. I wouldn't know where to go, or what to do. Besides," she said, as tears filled her eyes again, "he loves me."

"I'm not as certain of that as you are," Bill said firmly. "It's not love to treat someone the way Dr. Flowers described to us. Do you really think he loves you?"

"I don't know," she said, overwhelmed by conflicting emotions of terror and remorse. She felt guilty for what she was thinking and saying about him. What if she was wrong? If in Jack's case, it was different?

"I think you're afraid, and you're in denial again. What about you, Maddy, do you love him?"

"I thought I did. My last husband broke both my arms and my leg at various times. He tortured me, and pushed me down the stairs. He put a lit cigarette out on my back once." She still had the scar although you could barely see it. "And Jack saved me from him. He drove me to Washington in a limousine and gave me a job, a life. He married me. How can I walk out on him?"

"Because he's not a good guy, from what you've said. It's just subtler and less obvious to you than what your first husband did, but you heard Dr. Flowers, it's just as lethal. And he wasn't doing you a favor when he married you. You're the best thing that ever happened to him, and a prize asset in his business. He's not a philanthropist, he's a businessman, and he knows exactly what he's doing." You heard the doctor. He is controlling you."

"And if I leave?"

"He might replace you on the show with someone else, and go on to torture someone else. You can't cure him, Maddy. You have to save yourself. If he wants to change himself, he can get treatment. But first, you have to get out, before he finds some other way to hurt you, or you get too demoralized to leave. You've seen it now. You know what's happening. You have to save yourself, and not think of anyone else. You're risking your life and your well-being. You may not have bruises this time. But if he's doing everything you say, you can't afford to waste a minute. Get away from him."

"He'll kill me if I leave him." The last time she had said that had been nine years before, but she suddenly knew that it was just as true this time. Jack had a lot invested in her, and he was not going to take kindly to her quitting or disappearing.

"You have to go somewhere safe. Do you have family?" She shook her head. Her parents had died years ago, and she had lost contact with her relatives in Chattanooga. She could stay with Greg, but it was probably the first place Jack would look, and then he'd blame Greg for her leaving, and she didn't want to endanger him. And she had no other real friends. Jack had seen to that. And it seemed ridiculous for someone as well known as she was to stay in a safe house. But maybe she'd have to do that. "What about staying with my daughter and her family at the Vineyard? She's about your age, and there's room for you there. And she has lovely children." Just hearing that made her think about what Jack had done, and Bobby Joe before him. She had had six abortions while she was married to Bobby Joe, the first two because he said he wasn't ready to have kids, and the others because she didn't want his children, or to bring a child into the life she led with him. And Jack had insisted that she have her tubes tied when they got married. Between the two of them they had seen to it that she would never have children. They had both convinced her that it was the best thing for her, and she'd believed them. She not only felt devastated suddenly, but incredibly stupid for listening to them. They had both deprived her of the chance to have kids.

"I don't know what to think, Bill, or where to go. I need some time to think about this."

"Maybe you can't afford it," he said, thinking about everything Dr. Flowers had said. If she was right, Maddy needed to make a move very quickly. There was no point waiting any longer. "I don't think you should spend a lot of time making this decision. If he gets help, if things change, if you work it out, you can always go back later."

"What if he won't let me?"

"Then it means he hasn't changed, and you don't want him." It was exactly what he would have said to his daughter, and he wanted to do whatever he could to protect and help her, and she was grateful for it. "I want you to give this some thought, and take action quickly. He may also realize that things have changed, and you're more aware. If he senses that, he may feel endangered, and make things worse for you. That's not a good situation for you to be in." None of it was, and she knew that, and as she glanced at her watch, she realized that she had to be in makeup in ten minutes, and she told Bill regretfully that she had to go back to work.

They walked outside a few minutes after that, and got back in his car and he drove her to the office. But before he left her there, he turned to her with a worried expression. "I'm going to be worried sick about you, until you do something about this. Promise me you're not going to try and ignore it. You've had your awakening, now you have to do something constructive about it."

"I promise," she said, smiling at him, but she had no idea what to do yet.

"I'll call you tomorrow," he said firmly, "and I want to hear some progress. Or I'm going to kidnap you myself and take you to my daughter."

"That sounds pretty good at the moment. How can I thank you?" she said, feeling grateful to him again. He had been like a father to her, and she felt as though they were friends. She trusted him totally, and never thought for a moment that he might divulge what she had confided to him. But he reassured her on that score himself before she left him.

"The only way you can thank me, Maddy, is to do something about it. I'm counting on you to do that. And I'm here if you need me." He jotted his number down on a piece of paper for her, and she tucked it into her handbag, thanked him again, kissed him on the cheek, and ran hurriedly into the building. It was going to be her first day on the air with Brad Newbury, and she had to change, have her hair done, and get makeup. And as she disappeared, Bill sat watching her, awed by everything she had told him. It was hard to imagine that a woman like her could be cowed by anyone, or willing to believe that she would be friendless, jobless, and back in a trailer park if she ever left her husband. It was about as far from the truth as you could get, but only Maddy didn't know that. She proved everything Eugenia Flowers had said about psychological abuse, and it amazed him. And as he drove away, Maddy was on her way to makeup.

She met Brad Newbury there, and stared at him as they combed his hair and did his makeup. He looked incredibly pompous to her, and she still couldn't believe that Jack had hired him to work with her. But he made an effort to be pleasant to her as they chatted and he watched her get her hair done. He had told her he was pleased to be working with her, but he acted as though he were doing her a favor. And she said politely that she was looking forward to it. But it only made her miss Greg more, and she found herself thinking about him, and then Bill Alexander when she went back to her office to put her dress on. She had no idea what she was going to do about Jack now. But she had no time to think about it. She was going on the air in less than three minutes. And she made it to her desk just in time. She just had time to catch her breath before they started the countdown.

As soon as they went on the air, she introduced Brad, and they were off and running. He had a dry, technical style, and as they worked together, she had to acknowledge that he was intelligent and knowledgeable, but his style was so different from hers that they seemed totally out of sync and in particular contrast to each other. She was warm and personable and down to earth, while he was aloof and distant. There was none of the harmony and ease she'd shared with Greg and she couldn't help wondering what the ratings were going to tell them.

They hung around and chatted for a while until they went on the air again, and it went a little smoother this time, but not enough to impress anyone. The broadcast felt flat to her, and the producer was frowning when she left the set. She'd gotten a message that Jack had late meetings that night, and he was leaving the car for her. But in the end, she decided to walk a few blocks, and then take a cab. It was a warm night and it was still light outside, but she had the funny feeling someone was watching her, and she decided she was paranoid. It had been such an upsetting day, her imagination was running wild. And maybe about Jack too. She was beginning to question the conclusion she'd come to, and she felt disloyal to him having said what she had to Bill. Maybe Jack wasn't any of the things she had accused him of, there were a myriad of explanations for his behavior.

But when she got out of the cab, she saw two policemen standing near her house, and an unmarked car across the street, and she wondered what had happened. On her way into the house, she stopped and asked them.

"Just keeping an eye on the neighborhood," they smiled, and she went in. But two hours later, she saw that they were still there, and she mentioned it to Jack when he came in at midnight.

"I saw them too. Apparently one of the neighbors is having some kind of security problem. They said they'd be there for a while, and not to worry about it. Maybe the Supreme Court judge down the street is having a death threat. Anyway, it makes the neighborhood that much safer for the rest of us." But then he scolded her for not taking the driver and using a cab. He told her he wanted her to use their car and driver whenever she went out.

"It's no big deal. I wanted to walk," she said, but she suddenly felt awkward with him. If he was everything she thought, she didn't even know what to say to him. And she felt guilty again. He was so sweet about the car.

"How did it go tonight with Brad?" he asked when he came to bed. And suddenly she almost shuddered, wondering if he was going to make love to her. All she knew was that she didn't want to.

"Pretty flat, I thought," she answered about her new co-anchor. "He's all right, but not very exciting to watch. I looked at the tape of the five o'clock, and there's no life in the show."

"Then put some in it," he said bluntly, putting the responsibility on her shoulders. And she found herself staring at him as though he were a complete stranger. She didn't even know what to say to him, or what was true now. Was he abusive to her, or did he just like to have control of things, and manage her life because he cared about her? What exactly had he done that was so bad? Give her a fabulous career, or a lovely house, or a car and driver to get to work, beautiful clothes, terrific jewelry, trips to Europe, and a jet plane she could use to shop in New York anytime she wanted? Was she crazy or why had she imagined that he was so abusive? She was just telling herself that she had imagined all of it, and it had been disloyal of her to even think about it, when he turned out the light and turned slowly to her with an odd expression. He was smiling at her, and he reached out a hand and gently touched her breast, and then before she could stop him, he had grabbed her so hard, it made her gasp, and she begged him to stop.

"Why?" he said, sounding cruel, and then he laughed at her. "Why, baby? Tell me why? Don't you love me?"

"I love you, but you're hurting me. . . ." There were tears in her eyes as she said it, and he pulled away her nightgown and revealed the rest of her, and then he dove between her legs and made her moan with excitement. It was the same game he had played with her before, of alternating pain and pleasure. "I don't want to make love tonight," she tried to say, but he didn't listen, he grabbed a handful of her hair and sharply pulled her head back, kissed her neck so sensually that her entire body tingled, and then entered her with such force that she thought he would rip right through her. He rode her so hard that it made her cry out, and as she clawed at him to make him stop, he turned gentle again, and she lay in his arms and cried in despair as he came and shuddered violently inside her.

"I love you, baby," he whispered into her neck, as she wondered what that word meant to him, or how she would ever escape him. There was something violent and terrifying about their loving. It was a subtle way of terrifying her that she had known before and never recognized, but now that she knew what it was, what she sensed most in his love for her was danger. "I love you," he said again, sounding sleepy this time.

"I love you too," she whispered back, as tears slid from her eyes, and the worst part of it was that she did.

Chapter 9

THERE WERE TWO POLICEMEN STILL outside their house when Jack and Maddy left for work the next day, and security seemed tighter than usual when they got to the office. They were asking everyone for passes, and she had to go through the metal detector three times before they were satisfied that the alarm that went off was due to her bracelet and nothing else.

"What's going on?" she asked Jack.

"Just routine, I guess. Someone must have complained that we were getting sloppy." She didn't think about it after that, and she went upstairs to meet with Brad. They had agreed to spend some time together and work on their presentation. Their styles were so different that Maddy had asked for some rehearsals so they could get more comfortable with each other. There was more to the news than just reading it off a TelePrompTer, contrary to what Jack said.

She called Greg after that, to tell him about meeting Dr. Flowers, but he was out. And she decided to go out and get a sandwich. It was a glorious afternoon and there was a breeze that softened the heat that was so typical of Washington summers. And again, when she went out, she had the feeling she was being followed. But when she turned around and looked, she saw nothing suspicious. All she saw were two men, strolling behind her, laughing and talking. And as soon as she got back to her office, Bill called her.

He wanted to know how she was, and if she had made any decisions.

"I don't know," she confessed, "maybe I'm wrong. Maybe he's just difficult. I know this sounds crazy. But I love him and I know he loves me."

"You're the best judge of that," Bill said quietly, "but after listening to Dr. Flowers yesterday, I can't help wondering if you're back in denial. Maybe you should call her, and see what she thinks."

"She gave me her card, and I was thinking about it."

"Call her."

"I will. I promise." She thanked him again for the day before, and promised to call him the next day just to reassure him. He was a nice man, and she was grateful for his friendship and concern.

For the rest of the afternoon, she worked on her current stories in progress and the five o'clock went a little more smoothly with Brad, but not much. And she was irritated at how awkward he was. What he said was intelligent, but the way he delivered it made him sound like a novice. He had never before been a co-anchor, and in spite of his intelligence, he had absolutely no charm or charisma or style.

She was still annoyed about it when she left work. Jack was going to the White House for a meeting. He told her to take the car, and lock the doors when she got home, which seemed silly to her. She never left them open. And with policemen stationed near their house, they were safer than ever. It was such a nice night that she had the driver stop before their house, and she walked the last few blocks through Georgetown. It was dusk by then, and she felt happier and more relaxed than she had the day before. She was thinking about Jack when she got to the last corner, and from nowhere a hand reached out, and before she could move away, someone grabbed her, and pulled her into the bushes. She had never been held with such force, and she couldn't see his face, as he grabbed her from behind and pinned her arms back. She started to scream, but he put a hand over her mouth, and she fought like a tigress, and then kicked him hard in the shins with one foot, while trying to maintain her balance with the other. And she continued to struggle with him, feeling panic rise in her, and then as she wrestled with him, they both lost their balance and fell, and in an instant he was on top of her and grabbing at her skirt, trying to push it up with one hand, as he tried to yank her pants down with the other. But he needed both hands to accomplish what he wanted, which left her mouth free again and she screamed as loud as she could, and suddenly she heard running all around her, and just as he pulled her pants down and started to unzip his own, someone yanked him off her. He almost flew through the air with the force of it, and Maddy lay on the ground for an instant, gasping. And suddenly there were policemen everywhere and lights flashing, someone helped her to her feet, as she pulled her clothes up and she caught her breath. Her hair was disheveled and the back of her skirt was filthy, but she was unharmed, and shaking, as one of the policemen held her.

"Are you all right, Mrs. Hunter?"

"I'm fine, I think." They were putting her assailant in the back of a van, and she was shaking all over as she watched them. "What happened?"

"We got him. I was sure we would. It was just a matter of time before he showed his hand. He's a sick bastard, but he'll go back to prison for this. We couldn't do anything until he grabbed you."

"Have you been watching him?" She looked startled, she had assumed he was a random attacker.

"Ever since he started sending you letters."

"Letters? What letters?"

"One a day for about the last week, I think. Your husband met with the lieutenant." She nodded, not wanting to look as stupid as she felt, and wondering why Jack had said nothing about it to her. The least he could have done was warn her. And suddenly she remembered the things he'd said, about wanting her to take the car, and lock the doors when she got home. But he hadn't told her why, so she had felt perfectly safe walking the last few blocks home, right into the arms of a stalker.

She was still feeling shaken when Jack got home that night, and he already knew what had happened. The police had called him at the White House to tell him the stalker had been caught.

"Are you all right?" he asked, looking worried. He had even left the meeting a little early, at the President's urging. The President was concerned by the call from the police, and relieved that Maddy hadn't been seriously injured.

"Why didn't you tell me?" Maddy looked pale as she asked her husband.

"I didn't want to scare you," he said simply.

"Don't you think I had a right to know? I walked home tonight, and that's how he got me."

"I told you to take the car," he said, looking both irritated and worried.

"I didn't know I was being stalked, for chrissake. Jack, I'm not a child. You should have told me."

"I didn't see any point. The police were watching you, here, and they tightened security at work." It explained the feeling she'd had for the past two days, of being followed. She had been.

"I don't want you making all my decisions for me."

"Why not?" he asked. "You couldn't make them yourself, if I let you. You need to be protected."

"I appreciate that," she said, trying to sound grateful, but feeling stifled, "but I'm a grown woman, I have a right to make decisions and choices. I need friends. And even if you don't like the decisions I might make, I have a right to make them."

"Not if they're the wrong ones. Why should you be burdened with that? I've been making all your decisions for the last nine years. What's changed?"

"Maybe I grew up. It doesn't mean I don't love you."

"I love you too, which is why I protect you from being foolish." He absolutely wouldn't concede that she had a right to at least some independence. She was trying to reason with him, to prove what she feared wasn't true, but he was unwilling to relinquish even one iota of control to her, even about her own life. "You're a pretty girl, Mad, but that's all you are, sweetheart. Let me do your thinking for you. All you have to do is read the news, and look pretty."

"I'm not a moron, Jack." She sounded angry as she said it, and she was still shaken by what had happened earlier that evening. "I can do more than just comb my hair and read the news. For chrissake, how dumb do you think I am?"

"That's a loaded question," he smiled derisively at her as he said it, and for the first time in her life, she wanted to slap him.

"That's insulting!"

"It's the truth. As I recall, Mad, you never went to college. In fact, I'm not even sure if you finished high school." It was the ultimate put-down, insinuating that she was too stupid and uneducated to think. He said it to humiliate her, but this time he only made her angry. He had said as much before to her, and she had never fought back when he said it.

"It didn't stop you from hiring me, did it? Or from getting you the best ratings in the business."

"I told you. People respond to pretty faces. Now, shall we go to bed?"

"What does that mean? That you're horny, and feeling 'passionate' again? I've already been mauled once this evening."

"Watch it, Maddy." He took a step closer to her, and she could see fury in his eyes. She was shaking, but she didn't step back from him. She was tired of being abused by him, under whatever title he gave it. But passion no longer convinced her. "You're out of line," he hissed into her face.

"So are you when you hurt me."

"I don't hurt you. You want it, and you love it."

"I love you, but I don't like the way you treat me."

"Who've you been talking to? That little black punk you used to work with? Did you know he used to be a bisexual, or does that come as a surprise to you?" He was trying to demean Greg and to shock her, but instead she was outraged.

"Yes, I did know, as a matter of fact. And it's none of my business, or yours either. Is that why you fired him? If it is, I hope he slaps you with a discrimination suit, because you deserve it."

"I fired him because he was a rotten influence on you. There were rumors about you two. I spared you the embarrassment of discussing them with you, and kicked his ass out, where it belongs."

"That's a disgusting thing to say. You know I've never cheated on you."

"So you say. But just in case, I thought I'd remove the temptation."

"Is that why you hired that pompous mummy who can't even read the news? He's using a TelePrompTer the size of a billboard. And he's going to flush your ratings right down the toilet."

"If they go, baby, you go with them, so you'd better hope he puts some jazz into his delivery pretty quickly. You'd better carry him just like you did your little black boyfriend. Because if the ratings hit the skids, you might just be out of a job, and then you can come home and scrub floors, because there's nothing else you know how to do, is there?" He was saying disgusting things to her, and all his pretense of loving her was falling by the wayside. Just listening to him made her want to hit him.

"Why are you doing this, Jack?" There were tears in her eyes as she asked him, but he seemed not to care, as he walked up to her, grabbed a handful of hair, and yanked it, to get her attention.

"I'm doing it, you little crybaby, because you need to remember who's in charge here. You seem to have forgotten. I don't want to hear any of your threats anymore, or your demands. I'll tell you what I want to, when I want to, if I want to. And if I don't tell you a goddamn thing, it's none of your fucking business. All you have to do is your job, read the news, once in a while do a special report, and get into bed at night and not whine at me about how much I hurt you. You don't even know what it's like to be hurt, and you better pray you never find out. You're lucky I bother to fuck you at all."

"You're disgusting," she said, feeling sick as she listened. He had no respect for her whatsoever, and certainly no love for her. She wanted to tell him she was leaving, but she was afraid to. And the police were gone now that they had caught her stalker. She was afraid of Jack suddenly, and she knew he could see it.

"I'm tired of listening to you, Mad. Now get in bed, and stay there. And I'll let you know what I want to do about it." She stood trembling in front of him for a long moment, and thought about refusing to get into bed with him, but she thought it would be worse if she did that. What had once been a somewhat roughshod style of making love to her had been becoming increasingly violent, ever since she had defied him over the story about Janet McCutchins. He was punishing her.

She went upstairs and got into bed without a word, and prayed that he wouldn't make love to her. And by some miracle, when he finally came to bed, he turned over without speaking to her, and didn't. Maddy was overwhelmed with relief.

Chapter 10

MADDY DIDN'T GO TO WORK with Jack the next day. He had to leave early, and she said she had some calls to make before she left for work, and he didn't ask any questions. No mention was made of the night before, he didn't apologize to her, and she didn't say anything about it. But as soon as he left, Maddy dialed Eugenia Flowers's office and made an appointment. The psychiatrist agreed to see her the next day, and she wondered how she would get through one more night with Jack. It was clear to her now that she had to do something before he really hurt her. It no longer seemed enough for him to demean her and call her poor white trash, he was beginning to openly abuse her, and she was starting to think that all he felt for her was hatred and contempt.

And as soon as she got to the station, Bill called her.

"How's it going?"

"Not so great," she said honestly. "Things seem to be getting a little rougher."

"They're going to get worse if you don't get out of there, Maddy. You heard what Dr. Flowers said."

"I'm seeing her tomorrow." And then she told him about the stalker. She knew the story was coming out in the paper that afternoon, and she had to identify the suspect in a lineup.

"Oh my God, Maddy, he could have killed you."

"He tried to rape me. Apparently, Jack knew all about it, but he never told me. He doesn't think I'm bright enough to make decisions, since I never went to college."

"You're one of the brightest women I know, Maddy, what are you doing?"

"I don't know. I'm scared," she admitted to him. "I'm afraid of what will happen if I go."

"I'm afraid of what will happen if you don't. He could kill you."

"He won't do that. What if I never get another job? What if I wind up back in Knoxville?" She sounded panicked. It was all racing through her head.

"That's not going to happen. You'll get a better job. Knoxville is over for you, Maddy. You have to see that."

"What if he's right? What if I'm too dumb to get hired by anyone else? He's right, I never did go to college." He had made her feel like a fraud.

"So what, for Heaven's sake?" It frustrated him, listening to her. She made it impossible to help her. "You're beautiful and young and talented. You've got top ratings on the show. Maddy, even if he were right, and you had to scrub floors, which will never happen, you would still be better off out of there. He treats you like dirt, and he might hurt you."

"He never has before," but that wasn't entirely true

either. He didn't hurt her as badly as Bobby Joe, but she had a scar where Jack had bitten her nipple in Paris. His form of violence was just subtler and more perverse than her previous husband's, but just as damaging to her psyche.

"I think Dr. Flowers is going to tell you the same thing I have." They chatted for a few more minutes and he asked her to lunch, but she had to see the lineup at lunchtime.

And when Greg called her late that afternoon, he said the same things to her Bill had. "You're playing with fire, Mad. The son of a bitch is crazy in his own way, and one of these days he's going to get you. Don't wait for that to happen. Get your ass out of there pronto." But for some reason she was paralyzed with doubt, and couldn't bring herself to do it. What if he got really angry at her? And what if he did love her? After all he'd done for her, she couldn't bring herself to desert him. It was a classic portrait of abuser and abused, as Dr. Flowers told her on the phone, but she also understood that Maddy was immobilized by fear. Dr. Flowers didn't push her the way Bill and Greg had. She knew that Maddy had to wait until she was ready. And Maddy felt relieved after she talked to her. She had been thinking of their conversation, and the meeting time they had set, when she went out to lunch. And Maddy was distracted on the way back from lunch. And as she walked into the building, she never saw the young woman watching her from across the street. She was pretty and young, wearing a black miniskirt and high heels, and she never took her eyes off Maddy.

She was there again the next day, when Maddy went out to lunch with Bill. She met him downstairs, and they went to 701 on Pennsylvania Avenue for lunch, and they made no secret of it. They had nothing to hide. They were serving on the First Lady's commission together, and Maddy knew that even Jack couldn't object.

They had a very nice lunch, and talked about a variety of subjects. And she told him about her conversation with Dr. Flowers, and how understanding she was.

"I hope she helps you," Bill said, looking worried. From what he could see, she was in a very dangerous situation, and he was frightened for her.

"So do I. Something has changed between Jack and me," she explained to Bill, as though she were trying to explain it to herself, and still couldn't. But there was a viciousness now to her exchanges with Jack that had never been there before. Dr. Flowers had told her that it was because he sensed that she was moving away from him, and he was going to do everything he could to terrorize her back into his control. The more independent, and the healthier she got, the less he would like it. Dr. Flowers had warned her to be careful. Even nonviolent abusers could change their tactics at any moment, and Maddy had felt that from Jack from time to time.

She and Bill talked about it for a long time, and he told her he was going to the Vineyard the following week, but he hated to leave her. "I'll give you my number there before I go. And if something happens, I can always come back." It was as though he felt responsible for her now, particularly so since he now knew she had virtually no friends to support her, except for Greg, who had gone to New York for his new job.

"I'll be fine," she said unconvincingly, but she didn't want to be a burden on him with her problems.

"I wish I could believe that." He was going to stay for two weeks, and he was hoping to finish his book while he was there. He was also looking forward to sailing with his children. He was an avid sailor. "I still wish you'd come up sometime. I think you'd enjoy it. The Vineyard is lovely."

"I'd love it. We're supposed to go to our farm in Virginia for a few days, but Jack is so involved with the President these days, we never go anywhere, except for our trip to Europe." As he listened to her, Bill marveled at how a man who owned a television network, and was close to the President, could be an abuser, and how a woman who was literally a star in her own right, successful, highly paid, beautiful, and intelligent, could let him. It was truly a scourge that had no respect for class or money or power or education, just as Dr. Flowers had said.

"I hope that by the time I get back, you've made a move and you are out of there. I'm going to worry about you until you do that," he said, and then looked seriously at her. She was so lovely, and so decent, and had so much warmth and charm and integrity, he couldn't understand how anyone could do this to her. He enjoyed her company, and had come to count on talking to her every day. Their friendship was rapidly becoming a strong bond between them.

"If your daughter comes to see you in Washington, I'd love to meet her," Maddy said warmly.

"I think you'd like her," he said, smiling. It was odd for him to realize that Maddy and his daughter were the same age, but his feelings for Maddy were slowly evolving into something different. He saw her as more of a woman than a child, and in many ways, she was far more worldly and sophisticated than his daughter. Maddy had been exposed to many more things, and some of them not so pleasant. But she seemed more of a friend and companion to him than a contemporary of his daughter's.

It was three o'clock when they left the restaurant, and when Maddy went back to work, there was a pretty girl with long dark hair and a miniskirt standing in the lobby. She looked right at Maddy, and Maddy had the odd feeling that there was something familiar about her, but she couldn't place her. The girl looked straight at her, and then turned away, as though she wanted to see Maddy, but didn't want to be recognized by her. And then as soon as Maddy went upstairs, she asked the guard what floor Miss Hunter's office was on, but instead of telling her, he directed her to Jack's office. Those were the standard instructions. Any inquiries for Mrs. Hunter went directly to her husband, and were screened by him, although Maddy didn't know that. No one had ever told her. And it didn't shock anyone who asked for her. It was, after all, a reasonable screening process.

The girl in the miniskirt rode up in the elevator, and a secretary asked if she could help her.

"I'd like to see Mrs. Hunter," she said clearly. She looked as though she was in her early twenties.

"Is this personal or business?" the woman asked, jotting down a note. The girl's name was Elizabeth Turner.

"Personal," she said, hesitating for only an instant before she answered.

"Mrs. Hunter isn't seeing anyone today, she's very busy. Perhaps you'd like to explain the nature of your business to me, or leave a note, and I'll see that she gets it." The girl nodded and looked faintly disappointed. But she took the piece of paper the secretary handed to her, and wrote a quick note, which she handed back to the woman at the desk a few minutes later. The secretary flipped it open, glanced at it, and then back at the girl, and stood up, looking somewhat nervous. "Will you wait a moment, please, Miss . . . er . . . Turner." The girl only nodded as the secretary disappeared, and handed the note to Jack less than a minute later. He looked at it and at the secretary with a look of fury.

"Where is she? What the hell is she doing here?"

"She's at the reception desk, Mr. Hunter."

"Bring her in here." His mind was racing as he tried to decide what to do, and all he could hope was that Maddy hadn't seen her. But she wouldn't recognize her anyway, so maybe it made no difference.

The girl was ushered in a moment later, and Jack stood looking at her. The look in his eyes was cold and hard, but the smile he wore when he greeted her spoke volumes. Maddy knew absolutely nothing about the girl.

Chapter 11

MADDY SLIPPED AWAY QUIETLY when she went for her meeting with Dr. Flowers. The only one who knew she was seeing her was Bill Alexander. And the doctor looked as grandmotherly and calm when Maddy walked in as she had the first day they'd met at the White House.

"How are you, my dear?" she said warmly. Maddy had explained her situation with Jack quickly and succinctly when she'd called before, but she hadn't had time to go into all the details.

"I learned a lot from you the other day," Maddy said as soon as she sat down in one of the doctor's comfortable leather chairs. She had a cozy office that looked like she had bought everything in it at a garage sale. Nothing matched, chairs were worn, and all of the paintings looked like they'd been done by her children. But it was tidy, and warm, and Maddy felt suprisingly at home. "I am the product of an abusive home, my father beat my mother every weekend when he got drunk.

And I married a man, at seventeen, who did the same thing to me," she said in answer to Dr. Flowers's questions about her past.

"I'm sorry to hear that, my dear." Dr. Flowers looked compassionate and concerned, but the grandmotherly tone was in sharp contrast to her eyes, which seemed to understand and see everything. "I know how painful that can be, not just physically, but the kind of scars it can leave. How long were you married?"

"Nine years. I didn't leave until he had broken my leg and both arms, and I'd had six abortions."

"I'm assuming you divorced him." The all-knowing eyes looked hard at Maddy.

Maddy nodded, looking thoughtful. Just talking about it brought back agonizing memories. She could see Bobby Joe in her mind's eye, just as he had looked the day she left him. "I ran away. We lived in Knoxville. Jack Hunter rescued me. He bought the television station where I worked, and offered me a job here. He came to pick me up in Knoxville with a limo. And as soon as I got here, I divorced my husband. Jack and I got married two years later, a year after my divorce was final."

Dr. Flowers was interested in more than words, and she heard a great deal more than people told her. She had had a practice of abused women for forty years, and she knew all the signs, sometimes before her patients even recognized them. There was a long silence as she watched Maddy's eyes.

"Tell me about your current husband," Dr. Flowers said quietly.

"Jack and I have been married for seven years, and he's been good to me. Very good to me. He established my career, and we live lavishly. We have a house, a plane, I have a great job, thanks to him, a farm in Virginia, that's actually his. . . ." Her voice trailed off as Dr. Flowers watched her. She already knew the answers to the unspoken questions.

"Do you have children?"

"He has two sons by a former marriage, and he didn't want any more when we got married. We talked about it pretty thoroughly, and he decided . . . *we* decided that I should have my tubes tied."

"Are you pleased with that decision, or do you regret it?"

It was an honest question, and it deserved an honest answer. "Sometimes. When I see babies . . . I wish I had one." Her eyes filled suddenly with tears as she said it. "But Jack was right, I guess. We really don't have time for children."

"Time has nothing to do with it," Dr. Flowers said quietly. "It's a matter of desire, and need. Do you feel as though you *need* a baby, Maddy?"

"Sometimes I do. But it's too late now. I had the tubes cut as well as tied, to be sure. They can't reverse it." Maddy's voice sounded sad.

"You could adopt, if your husband is willing. Would he be?"

"I don't know," Maddy said in a choked voice. Their problems were so much more complicated than that. She had only explained it briefly to Dr. Flowers on the phone.

"About adopting a baby?" Dr. Flowers looked surprised by what Maddy had just told her. She didn't expect that.

"No, about my husband. And what you said the other day. It came on the heels of a conversation I'd just had with a co-worker. I . . . he thought . . . I think . . ." Tears rolled down her cheeks as she finally said it. "My husband is abusive to me. He doesn't beat me like my first husband did. He has never laid a hand on me, not literally. He shook me recently, and he's . . . sexually . . . pretty rough on me sometimes, but I don't think he does it on purpose, he's just very passionate. . . ." And then she stopped, and looked Dr. Flowers in the eye. She had to tell her. "I used to think he was rough, but he isn't . . . he's cruel, and abusive, and he hurts me. Intentionally, I think. He controls me. Constantly. He makes all my decisions for me. He calls me poor white trash, reminds me that I'm uneducated, and tells me that if he fired me, I'd go right down the tubes and no one would ever hire me. He never lets me forget that he saved me. He doesn't let me have friends, he isolates me. He makes me feel like dirt. He lies to me, and belittles me, and makes me feel rotten about myself. He humiliates me, and lately he frightens me. He's getting rougher in bed, and he threatens me. I never let myself look at it before, but he does just about everything you talked about the other day." The tears continued to roll down her cheeks as she said it.

"And you let him," Eugenia Flowers said quietly. "Because you think he's right and you deserve it. You think the ugly secret you carry around with you is that you're every bit as bad as he says, and if you don't do exactly what he says, everyone will know it." Maddy nodded as she listened. It was a relief to hear the words, because it was exactly what she did think. "And now that you're aware of it, Maddy, what are you going to do about it? Do you want to stay with him?" It was an honest question, and she wasn't afraid to tell the truth, no matter how crazy it sounded.

"Sometimes. I love him. And I think he loves me. I keep thinking that if he understood what he's doing to me, he wouldn't do it. Maybe if I loved him more, or could help him understand how hurtful it is, he would stop doing it. I don't think he really wants to hurt me."

"That's possible. But unlikely," she said, looking right at Maddy. But she wasn't passing judgment on her. She was opening doors and windows for her. What she wanted to give her more than anything was perspective. "What if he wanted to hurt you, if you knew it was intentional? Would you still want to stay with him?"

"I don't know . . . maybe. I'm scared to leave him. What if he's right? What if I can't find a job, and no one ever wants me?" Dr. Flowers silently marveled that this exquisite creature could think that no one would ever love or employ her. But no one ever had loved her, not her first husband or her parents, or even Jack Hunter. Of that, Dr. Flowers was certain. Not through any fault of Maddy's. But she had chosen men who had wanted nothing more than to hurt her.

But she had yet to see it, and Dr. Flowers knew that. "I thought it was all so simple. I thought when I left Bobby Joe that I'd never let myself be abused again. I swore that no one would ever hit me. And Jack doesn't. Not with his hands at least."

"But it's not that simple, is it? There are other forms of abuse that are even more destructive, like the kind of abuse he practices on you, where he hits at your soul and your self-esteem. If you let him, Maddy, he'll destroy you. That's what he wants to do, what you've let him do for seven years. And you can continue letting him do that, if you want to. You don't have to leave him. No one is going to make you."

"The only two friends I have are telling me that I have to go, or he will destroy me."

"He might. He almost certainly will, one way or another. He doesn't even have to do it himself. Eventually, you'll do it for him." It was a terrifying prospect. "Or you'll just wither away inside. What your friends are saying to you isn't inconceivable. Do you love him enough to risk that?"

"I don't think so . . . I don't want to . . . but I'm scared to leave him, and . . ." she gulped on a sob as she said it, "I'd miss him. We've had such a good life. I love being with him."

"How does he make you feel when you're with him?"

"Important. Well . . . no . . . that's not true. He makes me feel stupid, and lucky to be with him."

"Are you stupid?"

"No," Maddy laughed, "only about the men I fall in love with."

"Is there anyone else at the moment?"

"No, not really . . . well, not in a romantic sense. Bill Alexander is a good friend. . . . I told him all about it the day you came to the commission."

"And what does he think?"

"That I should pack my bags as soon as I can and get out before Jack does something terrible to me."

"He already has, Maddy. And what about Bill? Are you in love with him?"

"I don't think so. We're just good friends."

"Does your husband know that?" Dr. Flowers looked concerned.

"No . . . he doesn't." Maddy looked frightened as she answered. And the doctor looked at her for a long moment.

"You have a long road to go, Maddy, until you reach safety. And even when you get there, you'll want to go back sometimes. You'll miss him, and the way he makes you feel, not the bad times, but the good ones. Abusive men are very clever, there's a tremendous potency to that particular kind of poison. It makes women want more, because the good times are so sweet. But the bad times are pretty awful. It's a little bit like giving up drugs, or smoking, or any other kind of addiction. Abuse, as terrible as it is, is addictive."

"I believe that. I'm so used to him, I can't imagine living without him. And then there are other times when I just want to run away and go somewhere where he can't touch me."

"What you need to do, and I know it sounds hard, is get so strong that he can't touch you wherever you are, because you won't let him. It has to come from you, because no one else can really protect you. Friends can hide you from him, and keep him away, and if you want it badly enough, you'll sneak off and go back to him, for the drug he gives you. But it's a dangerous one, as dangerous, or perhaps even more, than any other. Do you think you're strong enough to give it up?"

Maddy nodded thoughtfully. This was what she wanted. She knew that. All she needed now was courage. "If you help me." There were tears in Maddy's eyes.

"I'll do that. It may take us some time, be patient with yourself. And when you're ready, you'll leave him. You'll know when, when you've had enough and are strong enough to do it. And in the meantime, you have to do everything you can to keep yourself safe, and not risk letting him abuse you more than he has already. He'll sense this, you know. Abusers are like jungle animals, they have highly honed perceptions and defenses. What we have to do is sharpen yours now. But if he senses his prey getting away from him, he'll try to pen you in, by making you feel frightened, and crazy and hopeless. He'll convince you that there's no way out, that you'd be nothing without him. And a part of you will want to believe him. But the rest of you knows better. Cling to that as much as you can. That's what's going to save you, the part that doesn't want to be abused anymore, or taken advantage of, or damaged or belittled. Listen to that voice, and try not to listen to the other." Not for an instant had she doubted that Jack was abusive. From everything she'd heard that day, she was certain of it, and she could see in Maddy's eyes how badly she'd been wounded by it. But she wasn't beyond repair, or salvation, she had a lot going for her, and Dr. Flowers knew she'd find the way out sooner or later, when she was ready, and not before. She had to find the way out herself, or it would have no meaning for her.

"How long do you think it'll take us to do this?" Maddy asked with a look of concern. Bill Alexander had wanted her to leave Jack the day she told him about it. But she couldn't do that yet.

"That's a hard thing to measure or predict. You'll know when you're ready, it could take days or months or years. It depends how frightened you are of him, and how much of you is willing to believe him. He's going to make you a lot of promises, and threaten you, he's going to try everything he can to keep you, like a drug dealer offering you your drug of choice. That drug at the moment, for you, is abusive behavior. And when you try to give it up, it's going to scare him, and make him more abusive."

"That sounds awful," Maddy said with a look of embarrassment about her addiction to abuse, but she knew there was some truth in it. It sounded right to her, and hit a familiar chord.

"Don't be ashamed of it. Many of us have been there. The brave ones admit it. It's difficult for other people to believe that you would love a man who would do that to you. But it goes back a long way, a long time, to what people told you about yourself in your childhood. If they told you you were worthless and wrong and terrible and unlovable, it's a powerful message for the dark side. What we have to do now is fill you with light, and convince you that you're a wonderful person. And I can tell you one thing, not only are you going to find another job in the first five minutes you're free, there are going to be men, good men with healthy attitudes, flocking at your feet as soon as they know the door is open. But it doesn't matter until you believe it." Maddy laughed at the vision she conjured. It was certainly an appealing picture, and very comforting to hear. She felt better already. She felt utterly confident in Dr. Flowers's ability to get her out of the mess she was in. And she was grateful that she was willing to help her. Maddy knew just how busy the doctor was.

"I'd like you to come back and talk to me in a few days, about how you're feeling. About yourself, about him. And I'm going to give you a special number where you can call me, night and day. If anything happens that scares you, Maddy, or if you believe yourself in danger, or even if you're just upset, call me. I carry my cell phone everywhere, you can always reach me." She was a one-woman wife-abuse hotline. And Maddy was relieved to know that, and grateful for her help.

"I want you to know, Maddy, that you're not alone.

There are a lot of people out there who want to help you, and you can do this, if you want to."

"I want to." She said it in barely more than a whisper, and she said it with less certainty than her supporters might have liked. But as always with Maddy, it was honest. "That's why I came here. I just don't know how to do it. I don't know how to get free of him. Part of me believes I'll never make it without him."

"That's what he wants you to believe. Then you'll need him, and he can do anything he wants to you. People in healthy relationships don't make decisions for each other, don't conceal information, don't tell each other they're worthless or that they're poor white trash and will wind up back in the gutter if the other one leaves. That's abuse, Maddy. He doesn't need to throw bleach in your face, or hit you with a hot iron to prove that. He doesn't have to. He does enough damage with his mouth and his mind, he doesn't need to use his hands to hurt you. What he does is very effective." Maddy nodded in silence.

Half an hour later she left and went back to her office. And as she walked into the building, she didn't see the girl with the long black hair standing near the entrance again, watching her. And she was still there at eight o'clock that night, across the street this time, when Maddy got into the car to go home. She seemed to be waiting for something. But Maddy never saw her. And when Jack came out a little while later and hailed a cab, the girl scurried away, concealing her face from him so he wouldn't see her. They had already said everything they had to say, and she knew she'd get nowhere with him.

Chapter 12

THE NEXT DAY, WHILE MADDY WAS working on some research on a story about the Senate Ethics Committee with Brad, the phone rang, and someone listened for a long time and said nothing when Maddy answered. For a moment, she was frightened. She wondered if it was another stalker, or a crank call of some kind, but then they hung up, and when she went back to work again, Maddy forgot about it.

The same thing happened that night at home, and this time she told Jack, and he shrugged it off, and told her it was probably just a wrong number. He teased her about being afraid of her own shadow, just because one nutcase had stalked her. Given her high visibility on the air, it wasn't surprising that she'd had a stalker as far as he was concerned. Most celebrities had them. "It goes with the territory, Mad," he said calmly. "You read the news. You should know that." Things had calmed down again between them, but she was still annoyed that he hadn't warned her about the stalker. He said that she had better things to think about, and security issues involving talent on the air were his problem. But she continued to believe he should have told her.

She was talking to the First Lady's private secretary on the phone Monday, about changing the date of the next commission meeting. The First Lady had to join the President for a state dinner at Buckingham Palace. And she was trying to mesh schedules with Maddy and the other eleven people on the commission, and Maddy was frowning distractedly as she went over dates, when a young woman walked into her office. She had long straight black hair, and she was wearing jeans and a white T-shirt. She looked neat and clean, but inexpensively dressed, and very nervous, as Maddy glanced up and wondered what she wanted and who she was. She had never seen her before, and thought she'd been sent by another department at the network, or maybe she just wanted an autograph. Maddy noticed that she didn't have a badge, and was carrying a bag of doughnuts. And suddenly, she wondered if that was how the girl had gotten into the building.

"No thanks." Maddy smiled at her and waved her out, but the girl didn't move, she just stared at her, and for an instant, Maddy panicked. What if this was yet another stalker? Maybe she had a gun, or a knife, or was mentally ill. She realized now that anything was possible, and she thought about hitting the panic button under her desk, but didn't. "What is it?" She put her hand over the phone and asked her.

"I need to talk to you," the girl said, and Maddy eyed her with suspicion. There was something about her that made Maddy extremely nervous.

"Would you mind waiting outside?" Maddy asked

firmly, and the girl reluctantly left her office, carrying the bag of doughnuts.

Maddy gave Phyllis Armstrong's secretary three possible dates and the secretary promised to get back to her, and as soon as she'd hung up, Maddy picked up her intercom and spoke to a receptionist at a desk in the hallway.

"There's someone waiting for me outside. I don't know what she wants. Would you talk to her and find out, and then call me?" Maybe she was a celebrity hound or an autograph seeker, or wanted a job. But Maddy was annoyed that she had walked in on her with such ease. Given what had happened recently, it was unnerving.

The intercom rang a few minutes later, and Maddy picked it up quickly. "She says she needs to speak to you. It's a personal matter."

"Like what? She wants to kill me? She has to tell you what it is, or I'm not seeing her." But as she said the words, she looked up, and the girl was standing in her office doorway with a look of determination. "Look, this isn't how we do things here. I don't know what you want, but you have to talk to someone before you can talk to me." She said it firmly and calmly, with her fingers resting lightly on the panic button, and her heart pounding. "What do you want from me?"

"I just want to talk to you for a few minutes," she said, and Maddy realized the girl was about to cry, and the doughnuts had vanished.

"I don't know if I can help you," Maddy said hesitantly, and then suddenly wondered if this had to do with her being on the commission about violence against women, or one of her stories. Maybe this girl knew she'd be sympathetic. "What's this about?" Maddy asked, mellowing a little.

"It's about you," she said in a trembling voice, and when Maddy looked at her more closely she saw that the girl's hands were shaking.

"What about me?" Maddy asked cautiously. What had this girl come to tell her? But as she looked at her, she had a very odd feeling.

"I think you're my mother," she said in a whisper, so no one else could hear them if they were walking by, and Maddy looked as though she'd slapped her as she recoiled in her chair.

"Your *what*? What are you talking about?" Maddy's face had gone white, and now her hands were shaking, as they continued to rest on the panic button. She had an instant concern that this girl was some kind of nutcase. "I don't have any children."

"Did you ever?" The girl's lips were trembling and her eyes were already beginning to fill with disappointment. For her, this had been a three-year search for her mother, and she sensed that she was about to hit a dead end again. She had already had several. "Did you ever have a baby? My name is Elizabeth Turner, I'm nineteen years old, my birthday is May fifteenth, and I was born in Gatlinburg, Tennessee, in the Smoky Mountains. I think my mother was from Chattanooga. I've talked to everyone I can, and all I know is that she was fifteen when I was born. I think her name was Madeleine Beaumont, but I'm not sure of that. And one person I talked to said I look a lot like her." Maddy was staring at her in disbelief, as her hand moved slowly off the panic button and onto her desk.

"What makes you think I'm that person?" Her tone gave away nothing.

"I don't know, I know you're from Tennessee. I read that in an interview one time, and your name is Maddy, and . . . I don't know . . . I sort of think I look like you a little bit, and . . . I know this sounds crazy." There were tears running down her cheeks now from the sheer stress of approaching her, and the fear of yet another disappointment. "Maybe I just wanted you to be the right person. I've watched you a lot on TV, and I really like you." There was a long, deafening silence in the room, while Maddy weighed the situation, and tried to figure out what to do about it. Her eyes never left the girl's, and as she looked at her, she slowly felt walls dissolving within her, surrounding places she hadn't touched in years, and thought she would never allow herself to feel again. She didn't want this to be happening, but it was, and there was nothing she could do now to change it. She could end it easily. She could tell her that she wasn't the same Madeleine Beaumont, that Tennessee was full of them, even though Beaumont was her maiden name. She could say she had never been to Gatlinburg, and that she was sorry, and wish her luck. She could say everything she needed to, to get rid of her, and never see her again, but as she looked at her, she knew she couldn't do that to this girl.

Without a word, she got up and closed the door to her office, and then stood looking at the girl, who claimed to be the baby she had given up at fifteen, and thought she'd never see again. The baby she had cried for and mourned for years, and whom she no longer allowed herself to think of. The child she had never told Jack about. All he knew about were the abortions.

"How do I know that's who you are?" Maddy asked in a voice that was rough with grief and fear and the remembered pain of giving up her baby. She had never seen her after the delivery, and only held her once. But this girl could have been anyone, the child of a nurse who'd been there, a neighbor's child who wanted to blackmail her and make some money. There were damn few people who knew, and Maddy had been grateful that none of them had ever surfaced. She had worried about it for years.

"I have my birth certificate," the girl said awkwardly, pulling a folded piece of paper from her purse. It was dog-eared and folded into a tiny wad, as she handed it to Maddy. And she handed her a tiny baby picture with it, as Maddy stared at it in silent agony. It was the same one they had given her, taken at the hospital, red-faced and brand new, wrapped in a pink blanket. Maddy had kept it in her wallet for years, and finally threw it away, for fear that Jack would find it. Bobby Joe knew, but he had never cared much about it. Lots of girls they knew got pregnant and gave up babies for adoption. Some girls had them a lot younger than she had. But in the years since, it had become her darkest secret.

"This could be any baby," Maddy said coldly, "or you could have gotten this picture from someone else, from the hospital even. It doesn't prove anything."

"We could have blood tests, if you thought maybe I could be your daughter," the girl said sensibly, and Maddy's heart went out to her. She had done a brave thing, and Maddy wasn't making it easy for her. But what this girl was volunteering to do was destroy her life, and make her face something that she had finally put away, and didn't dare touch now. And how could she tell Jack?

"Why don't you sit down for a minute," Maddy said,

sitting down slowly in the chair next to her, and staring at her. She wanted to reach out and touch her. The girl's father had been a high school senior in Maddy's school, they didn't even know each other well, but she liked him, and she went out with him a couple of times, during one of the spells when she and Bobby Joe broke up. He was killed in a car accident three weeks after the baby was born and she'd already given her up. She never told Bobby Joe who the father was, and he didn't care much, although he'd beaten her up over it once or twice, but it was just another excuse to abuse her, once they were married. "How did you come here, Elizabeth?" She said her name carefully, as though even saying that much would commit her to a fate she was not yet prepared to face. "Where do you live?"

"In Memphis. I came here by bus. I've been working since I was twelve to save up enough money to do this. I always wanted to find my real mother. I tried to find my father too, but I couldn't find out anything about him." She still didn't know what Maddy's answer to her was, and she looked extremely nervous.

"Your father died," Maddy said quietly, "three weeks after you were born. He was a nice boy, and you look a little like him." But she looked a great deal more like her mother, their coloring and features were the same, even Maddy could see it. It would have been hard to deny her, even if she wanted to. And Maddy couldn't help wondering how the story was going to look in the tabloids.

"How do you know about him?" Elizabeth looked confused as she stared at her, not sure what it meant now. She was a bright girl, but she was overwhelmed by the impact of what she was doing, as was Maddy, and neither of them was thinking clearly.

Maddy looked at her for a long time, her most secret wish having just come true, and not sure yet if that wish would become a nightmare, if she would be betrayed, or if this girl would turn out to be an impostor, but it seemed unlikely. Maddy opened her mouth to speak, and a sob came before the words, as she reached out and put her arms around the girl in the chair next to hers. It was a long time before she could say the words she had thought would never be hers, in an entire lifetime. "I'm your mother." Elizabeth gave a sharp gasp, and her hand flew to her mouth as her eyes filled with tears and she looked up at Maddy, and then pulled her closer. And they just sat there for a long time, holding each other and crying.

"Oh my God . . . oh my God . . . I didn't really think it was you . . . I just wanted to ask you . . . oh my God. . . ." They sat there for a long time, rocking back and forth and holding each other, and then they held hands, and just looked at each other. Elizabeth was smiling through her tears, and Maddy was still too shaken to know what she thought. The only thing she knew was that beyond the miracle of time and circumstance, they had found each other. And Maddy had no idea what to do about it. This was just the beginning after so many years.

"Where are your adoptive parents?" Maddy asked finally. All she had been allowed to know was that they lived in Tennessee, had no other children, and were gainfully employed. She knew nothing else about them. In those days, all the records were sealed, and the information given to either side was so minimal you could never find each other. It was done for that purpose. And over the years, as things changed legally, regarding old sealed adoptions, Maddy had never wanted to make any effort to find her. She figured it was too late, and it was something she had to let go of, rather than cling to. But now here she was.

"I never knew them," Elizabeth explained, still wiping the tears from her eyes, as she clung to her mother's hand. "They died when I was a year old, in a train wreck, and I was state-raised till I was five, in an orphanage in Knoxville." It turned Maddy's stomach to realize that she was living in Knoxville at the same time and was married to Bobby Joe, and could have taken her back if she had to. But she had no way of knowing where the child was. "I grew up in foster homes after that. Some of them were okay, some of them were pretty awful. I moved around the state a lot, I never stayed in any of them more than six months, I didn't really want to. I always felt like an outsider, and some of them were mean to me, so I was happy to move on to the next one."

"And no one ever adopted you again?" Maddy looked horrified as Elizabeth shook her head.

"I guess that's why I wanted to find you. I almost got adopted once or twice, but my foster parents always decided it was too expensive. They had kids of their own, and they couldn't afford another one. I stay in touch with some of them, particularly the last ones. They have five kids, and they were nice to me. They were all boys, and I almost married my oldest brother, but I figured it'd be too weird, so I didn't. I'm living on my own in Memphis now, I'm going to City College and working as a waitress. When I finish school, I'm going to move to Nashville, and try to get a job singing in a nightclub." She had the same spirit of survival as her mother.

"Can you sing?" Maddy asked with surprise,

suddenly wanting to know everything about her. Her heart ached as she thought of her in orphanages and foster homes, and never having real parents. But remarkably, she seemed to have survived it, from what Maddy could see superficially at least. She was a lovely-looking girl, and as she glanced at her, she realized that they had both crossed their legs at the same time, in exactly the same way.

"I like to sing. I guess I have a pretty good voice. That's what people tell me."

"Then you can't be my daughter," Maddy laughed, with tears in her eyes again. She was overwhelmed with emotion as they continued to hold hands, sitting in Maddy's office. And miraculously, for once, no one had interrupted them. It was a rare, quiet morning. "What else do you like to do?"

"I like horses. I can ride anything on four legs. But I hate cows. One of the families that fostered me had a dairy farm. I swore I'd never marry a farmer." They both laughed at that. "I like kids. I write to all my foster brothers and sisters, except for a few of them. Most of them were good people. I like Washington." She smiled at Maddy then. "I like you on TV . . . I like clothes . . . I like boys . . . I like the beach. . . ."

"I love you," Maddy blurted out, although she didn't even know her. "I loved you then too. I just couldn't take care of you, I was fifteen and my parents wouldn't let me keep you. I cried over it for years. I always wondered where you were and if you were okay, and if people were being good to you. I told myself you'd been adopted by wonderful people who loved you." It broke her heart to think that that hadn't been true, and the child had grown up between foster homes and state institutions.

"Do you have kids?" Elizabeth wanted to know. It was a reasonable question. And Maddy shook her head with a look of sorrow. But she did now. She had a daughter. And this time, she wasn't going to lose her. She had already made that decision.

"No, I don't. I never had children, and I can't now." Elizabeth didn't ask her why, she was respectful of the fact that they didn't know each other. And given the patchwork quilt that her past had been, Maddy was impressed by how polite she was, and well behaved, and how educated she sounded. "Do you like to read?" Maddy asked, curious about her.

"I love it," Elizabeth confirmed, another trait she had inherited from her mother, along with her perseverance and courage and dogged pursuit of her objectives. She had never given up on finding her mother. It was all she'd ever wanted.

"How old are you now?" Elizabeth asked her, just to be sure she'd originally guessed Maddy's age right. Elizabeth wasn't sure if Maddy had been fifteen or sixteen when she gave up her baby.

"I'm thirty-four." They were more like sisters, and looked it, than mother and daughter. "And I'm married to the man who owns this network. His name is Jack Hunter." It was pretty basic information, but after she said it, Elizabeth stunned her.

"I know. I met him last week, in his office."

"You what? How did you do that?" It seemed impossible to Maddy.

"I tried to ask for you in the lobby, and they wouldn't let me see you. They sent me right up to his office. I talked to his secretary, and I'd written you a note, it just said that I wanted to ask you if you were my mother.

She took it to him, and then she brought me in to see him," she said innocently, as though it were a perfectly logical sequence of events, and it was in some ways. Except that Jack hadn't said a word about it to Maddy.

"And then what happened?" Maddy asked, with her heart pounding again, just as it had when Elizabeth said Maddy was her mother. "What did he say to you?"

"He told me that he knew for a fact that I was wrong, that you'd never had any children. I think he thought I was a fake, or trying to blackmail you or something. He told me to go away and never come back again. I showed him my birth certificate and the picture, and I was afraid he would take them away from me, but he didn't. He just told me that wasn't your maiden name, but I knew it was, so I thought he might be lying to protect you. And then I wondered if maybe he didn't know, and you never told him."

"I never did," Maddy said honestly. "I was afraid to. He's been very good to me. He got me out of Knoxville nine years ago, and paid for my divorce. He made me who I am today, and I didn't know how he'd feel if I told him, so I didn't." But he knew now, and he hadn't said a word to her. She wondered if it was because he thought it was a hoax and didn't want to worry her, or if he was saving it for ammunition. Given what she'd come to believe of him recently, she thought the latter more likely, and couldn't help wondering when he was going to tell her. He was probably saving it for just the right moment, when it would do the most damage. And then she felt instantly guilty for what she was thinking. "Well, he knows now," Maddy said with a sigh, looking at the girl. And then she looked at the girl squarely. "What are we going to do now, about all this?"

"Nothing, I guess," Elizabeth said practically. "I don't want anything from you. I just wanted to find you, and meet you. I'm going back to Memphis tomorrow. They gave me a week off from work, but I have to go back now."

"That's it?" Maddy looked surprised that she wanted so little from her. "I'd like to see you again, Elizabeth, and get to know you. Maybe I could come to Memphis."

"I'd like that. You could stay with me, but I don't think you'd like it." She smiled shyly. "I rent a room in a boarding house, and it's pretty small and smelly. I spend all my money on school . . . and on finding you. I guess I won't have to do that now."

"Maybe we could stay in a hotel together." The girl's eyes lit up at that, and Maddy was touched. She seemed to have no expectations whatsoever.

"I'm not going to tell anyone about this," Elizabeth said shyly, "just my landlady and my boss, and one of my foster moms, if that's okay with you. But I won't tell anyone if you don't want me to. I don't want to cause you any trouble." She herself was unaware of the implications of a public exposé for Maddy.

"That's nice of you to say, Elizabeth, but I don't know what I'm going to do about it myself. I have to think about that and talk it over with my husband."

"I don't think he's going to like it." Maddy didn't think so either. "He didn't look real happy to see me. I guess it was kind of a big surprise."

"Yes, I would say that," Maddy smiled at her. It was certainly a shock, even to her, but she was pleased now. It was suddenly exciting having a daughter. It was the end to a mystery for her, a healing of an old wound she had resigned herself to for years, but it had always been there. And now this was a blessing like no other. "He'll get used to it. We all will." Maddy invited her to lunch then, and Elizabeth looked thrilled and told her mother to call her "Lizzie." They went to a coffee shop around the corner, and Maddy cautiously put an arm around her shoulders as they walked along, and over a club sandwich and a hamburger, Lizzie told her everything she could think of about her life, her friends, her fears, her joys, and then she asked Maddy a million questions. This was the meeting she had always dreamed of, and the one Maddy had never dared to.

It was three o'clock when they got back, and Maddy had given her all her phone numbers and fax numbers, and gotten hers, and she promised to call her often to see how she was doing. And as soon as she got things squared away with Jack, she wanted to have her to Virginia for the weekend. And when she told her she'd send the plane for her, Lizzie's eyes grew big as saucers.

"You guys have your own plane?"

"Jack does."

"Wow! My mom is a TV star, and my dad has a jet plane! Holy Moses!"

"He's not exactly your father," Maddy corrected gently, nor would he want to be, Maddy easily suspected. He didn't enjoy interacting with his own sons, let alone take on Maddy's illegitimate daughter. "But he's a nice man," and as she said it, she knew she was lying to her. But it was too complicated to explain how unhappy she was, and that she was in therapy to try to get up the courage to leave him. She just hoped that Elizabeth had never been abused, as she had been. But there had been no tales of that over lunch, and in spite of never having had a real home, she seemed remarkably well adjusted. And as much as it depressed her to think so, Maddy wondered if Lizzie had done better in the end where she was, than if she'd been watching Bobby Joe shove her mother down the stairs, or listening to Jack abuse her. But she couldn't let herself off the hook as easily as that, and she felt guilty for what she had never done for her daughter. Just thinking the word now gave her a tremor. A daughter. She had a daughter.

Maddy kissed Elizabeth good-bye when she left, and they hugged for a long moment, and then she looked down at the girl's face with a smile and spoke softly to her. "Thank you for finding me, Lizzie. I don't deserve you yet, but I'm so happy to know you."

"Thank you, Mom," Lizzie whispered and they both wiped away tears as Maddy watched her go. It was a moment in her life that she knew neither of them would ever forget, and for the rest of the day she was in a daze, and she was still distracted when Bill Alexander called her.

"What's new with you today?" he asked comfortably, and Maddy laughed at the question.

"You wouldn't believe me if I told you."

"That sounds pretty mysterious. Anything important happen?" He wondered if she was going to tell him she had left her husband, but he had begun to realize she wasn't there yet.

"I'll tell you when I see you again. It's kind of a long story."

"I can't wait to hear it. How's it going with your co-anchor?"

"Slowly. He's a nice guy, but it's like dancing with a rhinoceros for the moment. We're not exactly graceful together." She was waiting for their ratings to take a dive, they had already gotten hundreds of letters, complaining about the disappearance of Greg Morris. And she wondered what Jack would do when he saw them.

"You'll adjust to each other eventually, it's probably a little bit like marriage."

"Maybe." She sounded unconvinced. Brad Newbury was smart, but they were not an exciting duo, and it was inevitable that their viewers would notice.

"How about lunch tomorrow?" he asked casually. He was still concerned about her, and wanted to be sure that she was all right, after everything she had told him. Besides, he liked her.

"I'd love it," Maddy answered without hesitating.

"You can tell me your long story then. I can hardly wait to hear it." They agreed on a place, and Maddy was smiling to herself when she hung up, and a little while later she went in to hair and makeup.

The broadcasts went well, and she met Jack in the lobby afterward. He was talking on his cell phone, and the conversation continued into the car and halfway home, and when he finally hung up, she didn't say anything to him.

"You're looking serious tonight," he said, looking unconcerned. He had absolutely no idea that she had met Lizzie, and she didn't say a word to him about it, until they were in their house, and he was rummaging for something to eat in the kitchen. They had agreed not to go out to dinner, and neither of them was very hungry. "Anything special happen today?" he asked casually. With Maddy, silence was often an indicator of something important she wasn't saying. She looked at him, and nodded. She had been groping for the right words for a while, and then finally decided to come right out and say it.

"Why didn't you tell me that you'd had a visit from my daughter?" Her eyes never left his as she asked the question, and she saw something cold and hard come into his, a burning ember that was rapidly being kindled by anger.

"Why didn't you tell me you had a daughter?" he asked just as bluntly. "I wonder how many other secrets you've kept from me, Mad. That's a pretty big one." He sat down at the kitchen counter with a bottle of wine, and poured himself a glass, but he didn't offer one to Maddy.

"I should have told you about it, but I didn't want anyone to know. It happened ten years before I met you, and I just wanted to put it behind me." As always, she was honest with him. Her only sin with him so far was one of omission, not commission.

"Funny how things bounce back at you sometimes, isn't it? Here you thought you had gotten rid of her, and she pops right back up like a bad penny." It hurt her to hear him say that, and she resented it. Lizzie was a great girl, and Maddy already felt protective of her.

"You don't need to call her that, Jack. She's a good kid. It's not her fault I had her when I was fifteen and gave her up. She seems like a decent person."

"How the hell do you know?" he said, spitting fire at her, and she could already feel the blaze as he watched her. "She could be talking to the *Enquirer* tonight. You may be seeing her face on TV tomorrow, talking about her famous mom who abandoned her. Lots of people do that. You don't even know if she's for real, for God's sake. She could be a fraud. She could be a lot of things, and she probably is, just like her mother." It was the ultimate put-down, that she was "as bad as her mother."

Maddy caught the implication clearly, and thought instantly of Dr. Flowers. This was the kind of abuse they
had talked about, subterranean, vicious, demeaning.

"She looks just like me, Jack. It would be hard to
deny her," Maddy said calmly, not addressing any of the
slurs he'd made on her, but trying to address facts and
nothing further.

"Every hick in Tennessee looks like you, for chris-
sake. You think black hair and blue eyes is so unusual?
They all look like you, Maddy. You're not special."
Maddy ignored yet another ugly comment.

"What I want to know from you is why you didn't tell
me that you saw her. What were you saving it for?" The
moment when it would hurt her most, she guessed, when
it would knock the wind right out of her, and shock her.

"I was trying to protect you from what I assumed was
a blackmailer. I was going to check her out before I told
you." It sounded reasonable, and chivalrous, but she
knew him better.

"That was nice of you. I appreciate it. But I would
have liked to know about it, as soon as you saw her."

"I'll remember that the next time one of your bastard
kids shows up. By the way, how many of them are
there?" She didn't dignify what he said with an answer.

"It was nice seeing her," Maddy said quietly, "she's a
sweet girl." She looked sad and wistful as she said it.

"What did she want from you? Money?"

"She just wanted to meet me. She's spent three years
looking for me. I've spent a lifetime thinking about her."

"How touching. She'll come back to haunt you again,
I can promise you that. And it's not going to be a pretty
story," he said cynically, pouring himself another glass
of wine, and staring at her in fury.

"It could be. It's very human. These things happen to people."

"Not nice people, Mad," he said, relishing the words, and the wounds he was inflicting on her. "That doesn't happen to nice women. They don't go around having babies at fifteen, and then dropping them on the church steps like so much garbage." It cut her to the quick as she listened.

"That's not how it happened. I don't suppose you'd care to hear the whole story?" She owed him that much at least, he was her husband, and she felt guilty for never having told him.

"No, I wouldn't," he cut her off, "I just want to know what we're going to do about it when the story breaks and you look like a slut on national TV. I have a show to worry about, and a network."

"I think people will understand it." She was trying to maintain her dignity, outwardly at least, but inside, he had hit his mark. She felt an ache in her soul at the portrait he was painting of her. "She's not an ax murderer, for chrissake, and neither am I."

"No, just a whore. Poor white trash. I wasn't far off the mark, was I?"

"How can you say things like that to me?" she asked, facing him, with a look of pain in her eyes, but it didn't touch him. He wanted to hurt her. "Don't you know how much that hurts me?"

"It should hurt. You can't be proud of yourself, and if you are, you're crazy. And maybe you're that too, Mad. You lied to me, you abandoned her. Did Bobby Joe know about it?"

"Yes, he did," she said fairly, but at that time, it had been much more recent.

"Maybe that's why he kicked the shit out of you. That explains it. You left that part out when you whined about him. I'm not so sure now that I blame him."

"That's bullshit!" Maddy blazed back at him. "I don't care what I did. I didn't deserve the way he treated me, and I don't deserve it now. What you're doing isn't fair, and you know it."

"Lying to me about her wasn't either. How do you think I feel? You're a whore, Mad, a cheap slut. You must have been out fucking around when you were twelve, for chrissake. It makes me wonder who you are now. I feel like I don't even know you."

"That's not fair," and he had completely dodged the issue of not having told her. "I was fifteen, and I was wrong, but it was a terrible thing to have happen to me. Nothing in my life has ever been so sad or so painful. Even being kicked around by Bobby Joe wasn't as bad. When I left her, it ripped my heart out."

"Tell her that, don't tell me. Maybe you can write her a check for it. But don't try using any of my money. I'll be watching."

"I've never used your money for anything," she shouted at him, "I use my own, for everything I do," she said proudly.

"Like hell you do. Who do you think pays your salary? That's my money too," he said smugly.

"I earn it."

"The hell you do. You're the most overpaid anchor in the business."

"No," Maddy shot at him, "Brad is, and he's going to fuck your show right out the window. I can hardly wait to see it happen."

"And when it does, sister, you'll go with it. In fact,

the way you've been behaving these days, and treating me, I'd say your days are numbered. I'm not going to put up with your bullshit for a lot longer. Why the fuck should I? I can throw your ass out of here anytime I want to. I'm not going to sit here forever while you lie to me, steal from me, victimize me. My God, woman, I can't believe the abuse I take from you." Just listening to him stunned her. He was the abuser and he was pretending to be the victim. But Dr. Flowers had warned her of that technique and it was very effective. In spite of what she knew and felt, he actually made her feel guilty and defensive. "And just to make things clear, don't try bringing your little brat around here. She's probably a whore, just like her mother."

"She's my daughter!" Maddy shouted at him in total frustration. "I have a right to see her if I want to, and I live here."

"Only for as long as I say you do, and don't you forget that." And with that, he got up and walked out of the room, and Maddy stood there gasping. She waited until she could hear him moving around upstairs, and then quietly closed the kitchen door and called Dr. Flowers. She told her everything that had happened, about Lizzie finding her, and Jack not telling her she'd been looking for her, and his utter fury at having been lied to.

"And how do you feel, Maddy? Right now. Honestly. Think about it."

"I feel guilty. I should have told him. And I never should have left her."

"Do you believe all the things he says you are?"

"Some of them."

"Why? If he came to you with your story could you forgive him?"

"Yes," she said instantly, "I think I'd understand it."

"Then what does it say about him that he can't do that for you?"

"That he's a shit," Maddy said, looking around her kitchen, and listening to Dr. Flowers.

"That's one way to put it. But you're not. That's the point here. You're a good person who had a very sad thing happen to her, that's one of the worst things that can happen to a woman, having to give up a baby. Can you forgive yourself for it?"

"Maybe. In time."

"And what about the things Jack is saying to you? Do you think you deserve them?"

"No."

"Think what that says about him. Listen to what he's saying about you, Maddy. None of it's true, but all of it is aimed to hurt you, and it does, and I don't blame you for it." She heard footsteps in the hall then, and told Dr. Flowers she had to go, but at least the doctor had given her some perspective. And an instant later, the door flew open and Jack strode into the room with a look of suspicion.

"Who were you talking to? Your boyfriend?"

"I don't have a boyfriend, Jack, and you know it," she said meekly.

"Who was it then?"

"A friend."

"You don't have friends. No one likes you. Was it that little black faggot you love so much?" Maddy winced at what Jack was saying, but she didn't answer. "You'd damn well better not tell anyone about this. I don't want you wrecking my show. You say a word about this to anyone, and I'll kill you. Do you understand me?"

"I understand you," she said with her eyes filled with

tears. He had said so many hurtful things in the past hour, she didn't know which had hurt most. They all did.

She waited for him to leave the room, and then dialed the hotel where Lizzie was staying. She knew she'd be there till the morning.

They rang her room, and a second later, Lizzie answered. She'd been lying on her bed, thinking about Maddy. She'd watched her on the news that night and couldn't stop smiling.

"Maddy . . . I mean Mom . . . I mean . . ."

"Mom is fine." Maddy smiled at the now familiar voice, and realized that Lizzie sounded just like her. "I just called to tell you I love you."

"I love you too, Mom. God, that sounds good, doesn't it?"

There were tears running down Maddy's cheeks as she answered. "It sure does, sweetheart. I'll call you in Memphis. Have a safe trip back." She didn't want anything to happen to her now that they had found each other, and when she put the phone down again, she was smiling. No matter what Jack said to her, or did to her because of it, he couldn't take that away from her now. After all these years, and so many losses, she was a mother.

Chapter 13

BILL AND MADDY MET AT the Bombay Club for lunch, and she was wearing a white linen Chanel pantsuit when she walked in, with her sunglasses on her head and a straw handbag over her shoulder. She looked like an ad for the joys of summer, and he looked happy to see her. He looked handsome and tan, and his white hair was in sharp contrast to his blue eyes and sun-tanned face, as he stood up and watched Maddy walk toward him. She looked a lot happier than she had the last time he saw her and he was pleased to see it.

He ordered white wine for both of them, and they chatted for a few minutes before looking at the menu. Several well-known politicians were there, and a Supreme Court judge Bill knew from their days at Harvard.

"You seem pretty chipper today," he smiled at her, "are things a little quieter on the home front?"

"I wouldn't say that, but Dr. Flowers has been a big help, and something wonderful happened to me."

Every time he met her, for one reason or another, he was afraid she was going to tell him she was pregnant. He didn't know why it bothered him so much, but now that he knew more about Jack, he particularly didn't want her to get trapped in that marriage. And a baby would certainly do that.

"You said something about it yesterday. Am I allowed to ask, or is it top secret?"

She laughed at the way he said it. "I think your security clearance is adequate for this, Ambassador. Besides, I trust you, but yes, it is a secret."

"You're not having a baby, Maddy, are you?" He said it in an undervoice, looking worried, and she smiled like the Mona Lisa, as he felt a tremor of worry run through him.

"It's funny you should say that." Her answer instantly convinced him. "What made you ask that?"

"I don't know. Just a feeling. The last time I saw you at the commission you nearly fainted. And it was just something you said yesterday that concerned me. I'm not sure that would be good news for you at this point. It would certainly lock you into your marriage with an abusive husband. Is that it then?" He looked disappointed but resigned as he asked her, and was surprised when she shook her head.

"No, I'm not pregnant. As a matter of fact, I'm unable to have children." It was funny talking about things like that with him, but she felt incredibly comfortable with him. As she had with Greg when they met, but for different reasons, she felt completely at ease with Bill. And now that he knew about her situation with Jack, she trusted him implicitly with her secrets, and she knew instinctively that he wouldn't betray her.

"I'm sorry to hear that, Maddy," he said at her admission to him, "I know that must be a great sorrow to you."

"It is, or it was at least. But I don't have a right to complain. It happened by choice. I had my tubes tied, at Jack's request, when we got married. He didn't want more children." Bill wanted to say that it was selfish of him, but he refrained from comment. "But something amazing happened yesterday," she beamed at him over her glass of wine and it was hard for him to ignore how beautiful she was. She was like a ray of sunshine to him. For months he had been depressed over his wife's death, and he was still struggling with it. But every time he saw Maddy, he felt happy, and he cherished their friendship. He was flattered by the trust she put in him, and her openness in talking about things he suspected she talked to no one else about. And he wasn't mistaken.

"I can't stand the suspense," he said as he waited. "What happened?"

"Well, I don't know if I should start at the beginning or the end." She seemed to hesitate, and he laughed in anticipation. He could tell that it was something that had pleased her greatly.

"Start at the middle if you want, but just tell me!"

"All right, all right . . . maybe at the beginning. I'll try to do this quickly. When I was fifteen, I was already involved with Bobby Joe, whom I eventually married after graduation. He dumped me a couple of times, and one night I went to a party with another boy," she hesitated then and frowned. Jack was right. Any way she told it, she sounded like a whore, and it was easy to figure out what Bill would think of her. She didn't want to make excuses to him, but as she looked at him, she was worried.

"What is it?"

"You're not going to think much of me when I tell you." And it mattered to her. More than she had realized when she began her story, and she wondered if she should never have started.

"Let me be the judge of that. I think our friendship will survive it," he said calmly.

"Your respect for me may not." But she was willing to take the chance. She thought a lot of him and was willing to expose herself to him, in order to share this with him. "Anyway, I went out with someone else. And I shouldn't have, but I slept with him. He was very smooth, and handsome, and a nice kid. I wasn't in love with him, but I was lonely and confused, and flattered by his attention."

"You don't have to defend it, Maddy," he said softly, "it's okay. People do that. I'm a big boy, I can take it." She smiled gratefully at him. It was a far cry from being called a slut and a whore, and poor white trash, by her husband.

"Thank you. That was confession number one. Confession number two is that I got pregnant. I was fifteen, and my father almost killed me for it. I didn't even figure it out till I was four months pregnant. I was young and pretty stupid, and it was too late to do anything about it. I was poor. I probably would have had to have it anyway, even if I'd figured it out sooner."

"You had the baby?" He sounded startled, but not judgmental. There was a distinct difference, and she was acutely aware of it as she nodded.

"I had the baby. Although until yesterday, almost

nobody knew that. I went to another town for five months, and I went to school there, and I had it. A little girl," in spite of herself, tears filled her eyes as she said it. "I only saw her once, and they gave me a picture of her when I left the hospital. That's all I ever had of her, and eventually I even threw that away because I was afraid Jack would find it. I never told him. I put her up for adoption, and I went home, as though nothing had happened. Bobby Joe knew, but he didn't care, and we started going out again."

"Was the baby's father involved at all?"

"No, I told him I was pregnant, but he didn't want any part of it. His parents owned a hardware store, and they thought we were trash, and I guess we were. They convinced him it was probably someone else's. I don't think he believed them, but he was too scared to go against them, and I hardly knew him. I called him when the baby was born, and he never returned my call. And three weeks later, he was killed in a head-on collision. I don't think he ever knew about the baby. I never knew who adopted her," she went on a little breathlessly. Telling him was harder and more emotional than she had expected, and he took her hand in his own under the table, to give her courage. He still had no idea what was coming. He just thought it was something she felt she had to tell him. "In those days, adoption records were sealed, and there would have been no hope of finding out, so I never tried. I married Bobby Joe after I graduated, and eight years later, I left. We got divorced, and I married Jack. And I know it was wrong of me, but I never told him. I just couldn't. I was afraid he wouldn't love me if I told him," she choked on her tears again, and the waiter waiting to take their order kept a discreet distance. "I never told him," she repeated. "It was a piece of my past I never touched myself. I just couldn't bear to think about it." There were tears in Bill's eyes as he listened. "And yesterday," she said, smiling through her tears, as they ran down her cheeks and she squeezed his hand, "she walked into my office."

"Who?" He was afraid to say, although he could almost guess, but it seemed too extraordinary to be possible. Things like that only happened in books and movies.

"My daughter. Her name is Lizzie," Maddy said proudly. "It took her three years to find me. The people who adopted her died within a year, and she wound up in a state orphanage in Knoxville, where I was living, and I never knew it. I thought she was happy then. I wish I'd known," she said wistfully, but at least they had found each other now. That was all that mattered at this point. "She's been in foster homes for all these years, and she's nineteen years old now. She lives in Memphis. She goes to school and she works as a waitress, and she's just beautiful. Wait till you meet her!" Maddy said proudly. "We spent five hours together yesterday, and she went back to Memphis today, but I'm going to bring her back soon. I didn't say anything to her, but I'd like her to live here, if she wants to. I called her last night," Maddy said, holding tightly to his hand, as her voice cracked completely, "she called me . . . Mom. . . ." He squeezed her hand harder as she said it. It was an amazing story, and touched his heart.

"How on earth did she find you?" He was in awe of Maddy's honesty, and the outcome of the story. It was the proverbial happy ending.

"I'm not sure. She just kept looking. I think she went

back to Gatlinburg, the town where she was born, to
see if anyone remembered anything. She had my age on
her birth certificate, and she went to the local schools,
until she found a teacher who remembered. They told
her my name was Madeleine Beaumont, and I guess
they remembered. The amazing thing is that no one
made the connection between that person and Maddy
Hunter. But it's been nearly twenty years, and I guess
there's not much similarity between the two. But she
figured it out from watching me on the news. I've never
talked publicly about my past much. There's not a lot to
be proud of." In fact, with Jack's help, she was profoundly ashamed of it.

"Yes, there is a lot to be proud of," Bill said quietly,
and signaled to the waiter to leave them alone for a few
more minutes.

"Thank you, Bill. Anyway, I guess she followed me
back to Chattanooga, and somehow she figured out what
nobody else has. She says she watches me on the news,
and she read somewhere that my maiden name was
Beaumont. She's a voracious reader," Maddy said
proudly and Bill smiled as he listened. She was suddenly
a mother. Nineteen years late, but better late than never.
And her daughter had appeared at just the right moment. "She came to the network, and tried to see me,"
and at that piece of the story, Maddy's face clouded, "and
they sent her to see Jack instead. He has some crazy sys-
tem that directs people to him, if they ask for me. He
claims it's a screening process for my own protection, but
I realize now that it has to do with controlling me and the
people I do and don't see. He lied to her," she said in disbelief, "he told her my maiden name wasn't Beaumont,
and that I wasn't from Chattanooga. And I don't know if

she didn't believe him, or she's just as stubborn as I am, but she got into the building somehow yesterday, pretending she was delivering doughnuts, and she walked into my office. At first, I thought she was going to attack me. She had this odd look on her face and she was very nervous. And then she told me. And that's it. And now I have a daughter." She beamed at him. It was too good to believe, too wonderful to resist, as she smiled at him, and he wiped tears away from his own eyes.

"That's quite a story," and then he wondered something. "What did Jack say to all this? I assume you told him."

"I did, and when I asked him why he didn't tell me, he said he thought she was a hoax and figured she was trying to blackmail me. But he had a lot more to say about my concealing it from him. He's livid about it, and I guess he's right. It was wrong of me, and I know that. I was scared, if that's an excuse. And maybe I was right too, because now he's calling me a slut and a whore, and threatening to fire me. He wants no part of it. But I'm not going to let her go now that I've found her."

"Of course not. What's she like? As beautiful as her mother?"

"A lot more so. Bill, she's gorgeous, and so sweet and loving. She's never had a real home, or a mother. There's so much I want to do for her." Bill only hoped that she was as decent a person as Maddy thought. But whether she was or not, he understood that Maddy wanted her in her life now. "Jack says he won't let her in the house. And he's worried about the scandal, and the impact on my image if it gets out."

"Are you?"

"Not at all," she said honestly. "I made a mistake. It happens to people. I think people would understand that."

"From an image standpoint, I think it's more positive than negative, if you care. But I think there are far more important issues here. It's a very touching story," he said quietly.

"It's the happiest thing that has ever happened to me. I don't deserve to be this lucky."

"Oh yes, you do," he said emphatically. "Did you tell Dr. Flowers about it?"

"Last night. She was very excited for me."

"I'm not surprised to hear that, Maddy. So am I. It's a beautiful gift, and you deserve it. It would have been a tragedy for you to be childless all your life, and the girl deserves a mother."

"She's as happy as I am."

"I'm not surprised by Jack's reaction, by the way. He's a real son of a bitch to you at every opportunity. The things he said to you are unforgivable, Maddy. He's just trying to bully you and make you feel guilty." It was his stock in trade, and they both knew that.

They ordered lunch then, and settled in to talk some more. The afternoon flew by, and it was two-thirty before they knew it.

"What are you going to do about all this?" he asked with a lot of concern. She had some decisions to make, only some of which involved her newfound daughter. She still had an abusive husband to contend with, and he wasn't about to disappear by magic.

"I don't know yet. I think I'll go down to Memphis in a few weeks, to see her. I'd like her to transfer to school here."

"I might be able to help you with that. Let me know when you're ready."

"Thank you, Bill. I still have to deal with Jack. He's terrified of a scandal in the tabloids."

"So what? Do you really care about that?" Bill asked reasonably, and she shook her head as she thought about it.

"I guess I only care about Jack's reaction to it. He'll torture me over it." They both knew that was true, and Bill was worried about the effect on Maddy.

"I wish I weren't leaving for the Vineyard tomorrow," he said, looking worried. "I could stay here, if you want me to, but I'm not sure what I could do to make him behave. I still think the only solution is for you to leave him."

"I know. But Dr. Flowers and I agree that I'm not ready. I owe him so much, Bill."

"Does Dr. Flowers agree with that too?" He looked disapproving and Maddy smiled sheepishly.

"No, she doesn't. But she understands that I can't leave yet."

"Don't wait too long, Maddy. One of these days, he might hurt you. He may not be satisfied with just abusing you emotionally, and up the ante."

"Dr. Flowers thinks he's going to get worse as I get more independent."

"Then why stay? It just doesn't make sense to risk what he might do to you. Maddy, you have to move quickly." The extraordinary thing was that she was beautiful, employed, intelligent, she was the woman that every other woman in the country envied and wanted to be. As far as they knew, she was the spirit of independence, and she had the resources to get out of a bad situation. But abuse was more complicated than that, as she knew only too well, and Bill was learning. It was a tar pit full of guilt and terror, which had her too paralyzed to escape, even though everyone else thought she could do it. She felt as though she were moving in slow motion, but no matter how hard she tried, she could move no faster. And she felt as though she owed Jack her life. What Bill feared, watching her from the sidelines, was that Jack would eventually hurt her physically as well as emotionally, particularly if he could no longer control her. But even she saw what was happening. She was just too frightened still to do anything about it. It had taken her eight years to flee Bobby Joe, and Bill could only hope that this time she wouldn't wait much longer.

"Will you call me at the Vineyard, Maddy? I'm going to be worried sick about you." It was true, she had been much on his mind lately, far more than he understood or had expected. He was still grieving for his wife, and somewhat obsessed with her, as he finished the book he'd written about her. And yet lately, he was constantly distracted, and sometimes cheered, by thoughts of Maddy. "I'll call you at the office." He was afraid to call her at home, and add jealousy to the weapons Jack used to torment her.

"I'll call you. I promise. I'll be fine here. I have a lot to do, and we're probably going to Virginia for a few days. I'd love to have Lizzie there, but I don't think Jack would allow it."

"I just wish you were out of there," he said grimly. He had no personal stake in it, no romantic involvement with her. But as one human being watching another being tortured, he felt helpless and angry, and desperate to do something to help her. At times, it reminded him of the endless months when his wife was being held hostage. He was constantly waiting for news of her, and frustrated by the fact that he could do nothing to free her. It was what had driven him finally to do whatever he could on his own. And in his naïveté, he had killed her, or at least felt responsible for it. In some ways, this was a painfully similar situation. "I want you to be very careful," he admonished her, when he left her at her car, outside the restaurant. "Don't do anything to put yourself in jeopardy. This may not be the right time to confront him. You don't have to prove anything, Maddy. You don't have to win his consent. All you have to do is get out when you're ready. He's not going to free you, you have to free yourself, and run like hell till you reach the border." In some ways, it was like fleeing a Communist country.

"I know that. I left my wedding ring on the kitchen table, and ran like hell, the day I left Bobby Joe. It took him months to figure out where I was, and by then Jack had taken over. I had more security than the Pope for my first few months at the network."

"You may have to do that again for a while." He stood looking at her long and hard, as they both stood next to her car. "I don't want him to hurt you." Or worse, kill her if he snapped somehow, but Bill didn't say that to her. But Bill thought he was capable of it. He was a man without ethics or soul. In Bill's opinion, he was a sociopath, a man without a conscience. "Take care of yourself," and then he smiled at her, thinking of her daughter, "Mom. I like thinking of you as a mother. It suits you."

"So do I. It feels great." She beamed at him.

"Enjoy it. You deserve it." He gave her a warm hug then, and he was still standing on the sidewalk walking as she drove off, and two hours later, a huge bouquet of flowers came to her office. The flowers were all in pale shades of pink, with pink balloons and a pink teddy bear, and the card read, "Congratulations on your new daughter. Love, Bill." She put the card in a drawer and smiled as she looked at the flowers. It was a sweet thing to do, and she was touched. She called to thank him, but he was still out, and she left a message on his machine, thanking him, and telling him how much she loved it.

She was still smiling about the flowers and her lunch with Bill, when Jack walked into her office an hour later.

"What the fuck is that?" he said, furious at the pink balloons and the bear. It was easy to figure out the implication of it.

"It's just a joke. It's no big deal."

"The hell it isn't. Who sent it?" He looked for a card, but couldn't find one, while she frantically tried to figure out who to say they had come from.

"They're from my therapist," she said benignly, and then realized instantly that wasn't the right answer either. She'd seen one years ago, and Jack had made her stop going. He had been very threatened by him, and told her the therapist was incompetent. In the end, it was easier to stop seeing him. It was part of Jack's master plan, she realized now, to isolate her.

"When did you start that again?"

"Actually, she's just a friend. I met her at the Commission on Violence Against Women."

"Spare me. What is she? Some kind of dyke women's libber?"

"She's about eighty years old, and has grandchildren. She's a very interesting woman."

"I'll bet. She must be senile. Anyway, if you shoot your mouth off to enough people, Mad, you'll be reading about yourself in the tabloids soon. And I hope you enjoy it when it happens, because you'll be out of a job when it does. So if I were you, I'd keep my mouth shut. And tell that little bitch from Memphis to keep hers shut too, or I'll sue her ass for slander."

"It wouldn't be slander if she claims to be my daughter," Maddy said, sounding calmer than she felt, "it's true. And she has a right to say it. But she promised me she won't. And don't call her a little bitch, Jack. She's my daughter." She said it clearly and politely and he turned to look at her with a malevolent expression.

"Don't tell me what to do, Maddy. Remember me? I own you."

She was about to respond to him when her secretary walked into the room, and she decided not to. But that was the key here. Jack believed he owned her. And for the past nine years, she had let him think that, because she also believed it. But no longer. She just didn't have the guts to act on it yet, but at least her mind was clearing. And a few minutes later, he left and went back upstairs to his office.

And almost as soon as he did, the phone rang. It was Bill. He had gotten her message, and was pleased.

"I love the flowers!" she said, beaming again, and only slightly shaken by her husband's visit. She was glad she had thought to take the card off, or she'd have been in a far worse situation. "That was such a nice thing to do. Thank you, Bill. And for lunch too."

"I already miss you," he said, sounding young and a

little awkward. He hadn't sent flowers to anyone but his wife in years, but he had wanted to acknowledge the return of Maddy's daughter. He knew how much it meant to her, and he was deeply moved by what she'd told him, and her confidence in him. He would never betray her. All he wanted was to help her. They were friends now. "I'm going to miss you while I'm gone," he said. It was a funny thing for him to say, and they both noticed it. But she realized she was going to miss him too. She was coming to rely on him, or at least on knowing that he was nearby, although they didn't see each other often. But they had begun talking daily. At least they could still do that while he was at the Vineyard, except on weekends, when he couldn't call her, with good reason. It was too dangerous for her. "I'll be back in two weeks, Maddy. Try to be careful till then."

"I will. I promise. And have fun with your children."

"I can't wait to meet Lizzie." It was as though a whole piece of her had been returned, that she had almost forgotten was missing. She had never realized what a big part of her had been taken from her, and now that it was back, she knew it with her heart and soul.

"You'll meet her soon, Bill. Take care," she said gently, and a minute later, they hung up, and she sat staring out the window, thinking of Bill and the flowers he had sent her. He was a nice man, and a good friend, and she was so glad she had met him. It was funny how life worked sometimes, the things it took away, and the gifts it gave one. She had lost so much in her life, and then found other people, other places, other things, but she felt at one with her past now. All that remained was to ensure the safety of her future. She only hoped that fate would be kind to her again.

And in his house on Dunbarton Street, Bill was also staring out the window. But his prayers for Maddy were more specific. He was praying for her safety. Every fiber of his being told him that she was in danger. Far more than she knew.

Chapter 14

For the two weeks while Bill was away, things were fairly peaceful for Maddy. She and Jack took a week off and went to Virginia, and he was always in better spirits there. He enjoyed his horses and his farm, and he flew back to Washington several times for meetings with the President, on a variety of issues. And whenever he was away, or out riding somewhere, Maddy would call Bill at the Vineyard. Before that, he had continued to call her daily at the office.

"Is he behaving himself?" Bill asked her with a worried tone.

"Everything's fine," she reassured him. She wasn't having a good time, but she wasn't in danger either. Jack always backed down after periods when he'd been particularly horrible to her. It was as though he wanted to prove it was all her imagination. As Dr. Flowers had pointed out, it was a classic scheme of *Gaslight*, so that she would not only seem, but feel, crazy, if she complained about how he behaved with her. And he was doing just that in Virginia. He pretended to not be upset about her daughter, though he did tell her he thought Maddy shouldn't go to Memphis. She might be recognized, and it was too hot there anyway. And he wanted her close to him. He had been unusually amorous to her there, but gentler again, and more civilized, so that her claims that he had hurt her in Paris sounded silly. But she didn't argue with him about anything now, and Dr. Flowers warned her, when they talked, that that in itself might make him suspicious. But she was being honest with Bill when she said she felt safe there. "How's the book?" she asked him. He reported on it to her daily.

"Finished," he said proudly, on their last weekend away. They were both anxious to get back to Washington. And the commission was meeting on Monday. "I can't believe it."

"I can't wait to read it."

"It's not exactly happy reading."

"I don't expect it to be, but I'm sure it's wonderful." She knew she had no right to be, but she was proud of him.

"I'll get you a clean copy as soon as it's retyped. I'm anxious for you to read it." And then there was an odd silence. He wasn't sure how to say it to her, but he had been thinking a lot about her, and worrying about her constantly. "I'm anxious to see you too, Maddy. I've been worried sick about you."

"Don't be. I'm fine. And I'm going to see Lizzie next weekend. She's coming to Washington to see me. I can't wait to introduce you to her. I've told her all about you."

"I can't imagine what you'd say about me," he sounded embarrassed. "I must seem like a prehistoric monument to her, and I'm not very exciting."

"You are to me. You're my best friend, Bill." She was closer to him than she had been to anyone in years, except Greg, who had a new girlfriend in New York, and still called when he could get through to her. But they had both figured out that when Jack took his calls, she never got the messages. And when he answered and she was there, he never put the calls through to her. She and Bill were more careful about the timing and circumstances of their phone calls.

"You're very special to me too," Bill answered her, not knowing what to say. He was confused about his feelings for her, part daughter, part friend, part woman, in alternating combinations, and she felt the same way about him. Sometimes he seemed like a brother to her, and at other times, she was startled by her feelings for him. But neither of them had ever attempted to define it to the other. "Let's have lunch before the commission on Monday. Can you do that?"

"I'd love to."

And she was even more confused by how nice Jack was to her over their last weekend in Virginia. He brought her flowers from the garden, and breakfast in bed, and went for walks with her, and told her how important she was to him. And when he made love to her now, he was kinder and gentler to her than he had ever been. It was as though the abuses of the past were a figment of her imagination. And she felt guilty again for the things she had said about him to Bill and Greg and Dr. Flowers, and she wanted to correct the bad impression she had left with them about her very loving husband. She was beginning to wonder if it was all her fault. Maybe she just brought out the worst in him. When he wanted to be, and when she was nice to him, he was such an incredibly sweet person.

She tried explaining it to Dr. Flowers the morning they got back, and Dr. Flowers sounded harsh to her when she issued a warning.

"Be careful, Maddy. Look at what you're doing. You're falling into his trap again. He knows what you were thinking, and he's making sure to prove you wrong, and to make you feel it's your fault." She made it sound so Machiavellian that Maddy felt sorry for Jack as she listened. She had truly maligned him, and now Dr. Flowers believed her. But she didn't say anything about it to Bill when they had lunch, for fear he would say the same thing Dr. Flowers had. Instead, they talked about his book. He had already sold it to a publisher several months before, through an agent.

"What are your plans for the fall?" he asked her carefully, wanting to hear that she was leaving her husband. But she never mentioned it at lunch, and she looked happier and more relaxed than he had seen her since he'd known her. Something seemed to be going well, but he was just as worried about her. And like Dr. Flowers, he was afraid that Jack was going to lure her back into his trap, and keep her there forever, alternately abusing and confusing her until she could stand it no longer. But she said nothing about leaving to him.

"I want to try and get the show back on track. Our ratings have taken a sudden dive. I thought it was because of Brad, but Jack thinks I'm in a slump too, and my delivery isn't what it should be. He said my stories have been really boring. I want to research some specials to do this fall, and see if we can't put some zip back into it." As usual, Jack was blaming her for something that wasn't her fault, Bill suspected, but she was more than willing to believe him. It wasn't that she was stupid. It was that she was mesmerized, and he was infinitely convincing. But unless one knew the pattern, it was difficult for people outside the inner circle to see it. And Maddy was too close to see.

Bill was tempted to call Dr. Flowers about it, after he and Maddy had lunch, but he knew that as ethical as she was, now that Maddy was her patient, Dr. Flowers wouldn't discuss her with him, and he understood that. He just had to sit and watch what was happening to her, and step in when he saw an opportunity to help her, but for the moment there was none. And once again he was reminded of Margaret, and his long months of waiting, to rescue her and bring her back to safety. What pained him most to remember was the outcome. And this time he didn't want to make the same mistake, and frighten the enemy by moving in. More than anyone, he knew that Jack was a formidable opponent, a terrorist of the utmost skill. And Bill wanted more than anything to save her. He just hoped he could do it this time.

The commission was moving ahead well, and they were talking about having more frequent meetings. The First Lady had brought six more people in, and they were devising a campaign for the fall, of ads against domestic violence and crimes against women. There were six different ads being worked on, and subgroups that were being formed. He and Maddy were on a subcommittee on rape, and the things they were learning were appalling. There was another subcommittee concentrating on murders, but neither he nor Maddy had wanted to be on it.

And the weekend after they both got back, Lizzie came to town again, and Maddy put her up at the Four Seasons. She invited Bill to have tea with them, and he was impressed when he met her. She was as beautiful as Maddy had said, and every bit as bright as her mother. And given the few advantages she'd had, she sounded surprisingly educated. She had been diligent about going to school, enjoyed her courses at the city college in Memphis, and she was obviously a voracious reader.

"I'd like to get her into Georgetown next term, if I can," Maddy said to him, as they sat having tea in the lobby. And Lizzie said she was excited about it.

"I've got some connections that might be helpful there," Bill volunteered. "What do you want to study?"

"Foreign policy, and communications," Lizzie said without hesitation.

"I'd love to get her an internship at the network, but that's not possible," Maddy said regretfully. She hadn't even told Jack Lizzie was there, and Maddy wasn't going to tell him about it. He was being so much nicer to her that she didn't want to upset him. He was talking about taking her back to Europe in October, but she hadn't told Bill yet. "If Lizzie comes to school here, we're going to get her a little apartment in Georgetown."

"Make sure it's safe," Bill said, looking worried. They had both been horrified by the statistics on rape they'd learned that week at the commission.

"Don't worry, I will," Maddy nodded, thinking of the same thing. "She should probably have a roommate." And when Lizzie went to powder her nose, Bill told Maddy how lovely he thought her.

"She's a terrific girl, you must be very proud of her," he said smiling at Maddy.

"I am, though I have no right to be." Maddy was taking her to the theater that night. She had told Jack she was going to a women's dinner related to the commission, and he wasn't pleased, but since it involved the First Lady, he understood.

And when Lizzie came back to the table, they talked about school some more, and her plans to move to Washington, to be closer to her mother. It was like a fairy tale come true, for both of them. But Bill felt with utter certainty that they both deserved it.

It was five o'clock when he finally left them, and a few minutes later, Maddy left Lizzie at the hotel, and went home to see Jack and change for the theater. She and Lizzie were going to a new production of *The King and I,* and Maddy was excited about taking Lizzie to her first musical play. There were a lot of treats in store for them, and Maddy could hardly wait to get started.

When she got home, Jack was relaxing and watching the weekend broadcast. The weekend anchors had been doing better in the ratings than she and Brad were, but he still refused to listen to Maddy that it was Brad's fault. He just wasn't up to being on screen as an anchor. Jack's plot to get rid of Greg had backfired badly. But he was continuing to blame it on Maddy, and insisted it was her fault. And although the producer agreed with her, he was too afraid to tell Jack that. No one liked to cross him.

Jack had made plans to have dinner with friends, although he didn't like going out without her on the weekend, and she left him as he was getting dressed. And he kissed her lovingly before she went out, and she was pleased that he was being so nice to her. It was so much easier this way. And she couldn't help wondering if the bad times were behind them.

She picked Lizzie up at the hotel in a cab, and they

went straight to the theater, and Lizzie was like a little girl as she watched the play, and applauded frantically when it was over.

"It's the best thing I've ever seen, Mom!" she said emphatically, as they left the theater, just as Maddy noticed a man with a camera out of the corner of her eye, watching them. There was a brief flash, and then he disappeared. It was no big deal, Maddy thought, he was probably just a tourist who had recognized her, and wanted her photograph, and she forgot about it. She was too busy talking to Lizzie to care about much else. They'd had a wonderful evening.

Lizzie got into the cab with her, and Maddy dropped her off at the hotel, and after giving her a hug, promised to meet her the next morning for breakfast. Once again she would have to hide Lizzie from Jack. She hated lying to him, but was going to tell him she was going to church, because he never went with her. And after that, Lizzie was flying back to Memphis, and Maddy was going to spend the day with her husband. It had been perfectly orchestrated, and she was thrilled with the evening they'd spent, and pleased with herself as she walked into the house in Georgetown a few minutes later.

Jack was in the living room, watching the late news when she walked in, and she smiled broadly at him, still riding the crest of the wave of joy she'd shared with Lizzie all evening at *The King and I*.

"Did you have fun?" he asked innocently, as she came to sit next to him, and Maddy nodded with a smile.

"It was interesting," she lied to him, and she hated doing it, but she knew she couldn't tell him she'd been

with Lizzie. He had flatly forbidden Maddy to see her
again.

"Who was there?"

"Phyllis, of course, and most of the women on the
commission. They're a good group," she said, aching to
change the subject.

"Phyllis was there? My, that's clever of her. I was just
watching her on the news, at a temple in Kyoto. They
arrived there this morning." Maddy stared at him for an
instant, not sure what to say to him. "Now, why don't
you tell me who you were really with. Was it a guy? Are
you fucking around?" He grabbed her throat with one
hand, and held it there, gently squeezing, while she
tried not to panic and looked him squarely in the eye.

"I wouldn't do that to you," she said, as she felt her
airway slowly closing.

"Then where were you? Try telling me the truth this
time."

"I was with Lizzie," she whispered.

"Who the fuck is that?"

"My daughter."

"Oh, for God's sake," he said, shoving her away from
him, as she fell backward on the couch, feeling a rush of
air in her lungs with considerable relief. "Why the hell
did you bring that slut here?"

"She's not a slut," Maddy said quietly. "And I wanted
to see her."

"You're going to get yourself smeared all over the
tabloids. I told you to stay away from her."

"We need each other," she said simply, as he stared at
her in fury. It infuriated him when she didn't obey his
orders.

"I told you, for your own good, you can't afford it. If

you think your ratings are lousy now, wait till you see what happens when someone leaks that story. And more than likely, she will."

"All she wants is to see me. She doesn't want publicity," Maddy said quietly, sorry that she had lied to him and that he was so angry about it. But his rigidity about her seeing Lizzie didn't give Maddy many options.

"That's what you think. How can you be so stupid? Wait till she starts hitting you up for money, if she hasn't already. Or has she?" He narrowed his eyes as he looked at her. "You know, you're getting to be more trouble than you're worth. If it isn't one goddamn thing, it's another. Where is she now?"

"At a hotel. The Four Seasons."

"Lucky for her. And you're telling me she's not interested in the money?"

"I'm telling you that she wants a mother," Maddy tried to soothe him, but he looked furious as he strode across the room, and then stood looking at her, with irritation and contempt.

"You're always doing something to screw me over, aren't you, Mad? If it's not an editorial about that nutcase Paul McCutchins was married to, it's fucking up your ratings, and now this . . . you're going to get sucked right down the tubes with this. Watch if I'm not right on this one, Mad. And when that happens, believe me, you'll be damn sorry." But he didn't say another word about it, he just stomped upstairs, and slammed the door to his bathroom, as Maddy sat in the living room for a little bit, trying to figure out how to explain to him how much it meant to her, and how sorry she was that she had upset him. It was all her fault, she knew, because she had lied to him about having had a baby.

Maybe if she had told him from the first, he wouldn't have been so upset by it. But all she could do was apologize, and try to be discreet about it now. The one thing she knew was that she was not going to give up her daughter, now that they had found each other at last.

She went upstairs quietly, after she turned off the lights, and by the time she'd changed into her nightgown, he was in bed, with his eyes closed and the lights off. But she was sure he wasn't sleeping, and when she got into bed with him, he spoke to her without opening his eyes. "I hate it when you lie to me. I feel as though I can't trust you anymore. You're always doing something to hurt me."

"I'm so sorry, Jack," she said, touching his face with her hand, and forgetting totally that he had nearly strangled her half an hour before when he accused her of cheating on him. "I don't mean to upset you. But I really want to see her."

"I told you, I don't want you to. Can't you get that into your head? I never wanted kids in the first place, and neither did you," he said, opening his eyes and looking at her. "And I sure didn't want to get stuck with some nineteen-year-old little whore from Memphis."

"Please don't say things like that about her," Maddy begged him, but what she really wanted was for him to forgive her, for lying to him, betraying him, and having her illegitimate child appear seven years after they were married, when she'd never even told him about her in the first place. She realized it was a lot to ask him to swallow. But she couldn't help wishing that his reaction were more like Bill's. He had really liked Lizzie when they met.

"I want you to stop seeing her," Jack said, looking at her with conviction. "You owe me that much, Mad. You never told me she existed, now I want her to disappear again from both our lives. You don't need her, you don't even know her."

"I can't do that. I can't have kids. And I never should have given her up in the first place."

"Even if it costs you our marriage?" It was a hell of a threat.

"Is that what you're saying to me, that it will?" she asked, looking horrified. He was threatening her, and forcing her to make a choice that would break her heart. But at the moment, she didn't want to leave him either. He had been so nice to her for the past few weeks that she'd been beginning to think that things were working out between them. And now this had happened. She wished she hadn't lied to him so she could take Lizzie to the theater.

She was desperate to see her daughter and didn't know what to do about it without upsetting her husband.

"It's a possibility," Jack said, in answer to her question about her seeing Lizzie being a threat to their marriage. "This was never part of the deal. In fact, it very emphatically wasn't. You entered this marriage on a fraudulent basis, you told me you'd never had kids. You lied to me. I could have our marriage annulled for that."

"After seven years?" She looked shocked.

"If I can prove you defrauded me, and lied to me, which you did and I can, then there is no marriage. You'd better think of that before you drag her into our lives any further. Give it some serious thought, Mad. I mean it." And with that, he turned over and closed his eyes, and five minutes later, he was snoring, as Maddy stared at him. She didn't know what to do or say. She didn't want to give Lizzie up again. She couldn't do that to her, or herself. But she didn't want to lose Jack either. He had given her so much, and the abuses she had accused him of were beginning to seem like figments of her imagination, and Lizzie wasn't. Maddy felt as though it was she who had behaved badly toward him, and now he was the victim, just as he had said to her. She lay in bed for hours that night, thinking about it, and feeling guilty toward him.

But in the morning, she still had no answers. She explained to him that she was going to say good-bye to Lizzie at the hotel, and have breakfast with her, and then she'd be back and they could spend the day together.

"You'd better tell her you're not going to see her again, Mad. You're playing with fire here. With me, and with the press. It's a high price to pay for some kid you don't even know, and will never miss if you kiss her off now."

"I told you, Jack," she said honestly. She didn't want to lie to him again. It was one more sin to add to her many others, as he saw it. "I can't do that."

"You have to."

"I won't do that to her."

"You'd rather do it to me, wouldn't you? That says a lot to me, about what you think about this marriage." He looked pained as he said it. The consummate victim.

"You're not being reasonable about this," she tried to explain it to him, but he brushed her away with a look of outrage.

"*Reasonable?* Are you kidding me? Are you nuts? What drugs are you on? How reasonable does it seem to you to spring your bastard kid on me after never telling me you had one?"

"That was wrong of me, I agree. But I'm not asking you to see her, Jack. I want to."

"Then you're even crazier than I think you are. How about a family portrait on the cover of *People?* Would that be enough for you? Because that's what's going to happen sooner or later. And then you can kiss your ass good-bye with the public."

"Maybe not," she said quietly, "maybe they'd be more understanding about it than you are."

"Shit. For chrissake, will you come to your senses?"

They argued about it for half an hour. And Jack had to leave to play golf with two of the President's advisers, but not before he warned Maddy not to see Lizzie ever again. But Maddy left to meet Lizzie for breakfast and they had a nice time, and Lizzie noticed that she looked upset, but Maddy denied it. She didn't want to upset her, and she didn't tell her that she wouldn't see her again. Instead she promised to have her back soon for another weekend, and told her she'd let her know what she found out about Georgetown. They kissed and hugged when she left, and Maddy gave her money for the cab to the airport, but although she'd offered it, Lizzie wouldn't take more than that. She was very conscientious about not taking anything from her mother beyond the plane ticket, and the hotel, and cab fare. Maddy had offered to open a bank account for her, and Lizzie had categorically refused it. She didn't want to take advantage of her mother. But Maddy knew that Jack would never have believed that.

Maddy was back by noon, and Jack was still out. And she called Bill and told him everything that had happened.

"It was all my fault," she said miserably, "I shouldn't have lied to him."

But Bill disagreed with her. "He's being a bastard about this, and pretending to be the victim. He isn't, Maddy. You are. Why can't you see that?" He was more frustrated about it than ever. They talked for nearly an hour, and at the end of it, Maddy sounded even more depressed. It was as though she couldn't understand what Bill was saying to her. He wondered if she'd ever swim free of the chains that bound her. She seemed to be going backward lately instead of forward.

And that night when Jack came home, he said not a word about Lizzie. Maddy wasn't sure if it was a good sign or not, or if he was just saving himself for another ultimatum. But she did everything she could to please him. She made a nice dinner for him, and spoke pleasantly. They made love that night, and he was sweeter to her than ever, which made her feel even more guilty for making him so unhappy.

And the next day when they went to work, just as Jack had predicted, the whole thing blew up in their faces. The picture the man at the theater had taken of Lizzie and Maddy was on the front of every tabloid, in several variations. And someone had either talked or guessed at the truth. The banner headlines read "Maddy Hunter and Her Long Lost Daughter." It told as much as they knew, that Maddy had had a baby at fifteen and given it up for adoption. There were several interviews with Bobby Joe, and a teacher at her old school. The tabloids had really done their home-work.

Jack was in her office and in her face with samples of every tabloid. "Pretty, isn't it? I hope you're proud of this. And what the fuck are we supposed to do? We've been selling you as the Virgin Mary for the last nine years, and now you look like what you are, Mad. A fucking whore, for chrissake. Shit, why the hell didn't you listen to me?" The photograph of her and Lizzie made them look like twins, they looked so much alike. And Jack was raging around her office like a bull with a dagger in his side. But there was no denying what had happened.

Maddy called Lizzie in Memphis to warn her, and when Jack finally left and went back to his own office, she called Dr. Flowers and then Bill, and they both said almost the same thing. It wasn't her fault, and it wasn't as bad as she thought. The public loved her. She was a good person, and she'd made a youthful mistake, and knowing about it would only make them love her more and sympathize with her. The picture of her and Lizzie was actually very sweet, they had their arms around each other.

But Jack had done everything he could, and very suc-cessfully, to make her feel terrified and guilty. And even Lizzie had cried when she called her.

"I'm so sorry, Mom. I didn't want to make trouble for you. Is Jack really mad?" She was worried about Maddy. She hadn't liked Jack when she met him, and she thought he was pretty scary. There was something sinis-ter about him.

"He's not happy, but he'll get over it." It was a gentle understatement.

"Is he going to fire you?"

"I don't think so. Besides, I don't think the union will let him. It would be discriminatory," unless Jack could get her on the morals clause in her contract. But whether or not he could, he was furious with her, and she was in agony over the pain she had caused him. "We just have to ride it out. But promise me, you won't talk to any reporters."

"I swear. I never did, and I wouldn't. I wouldn't do anything to hurt you. I love you." She was sobbing at the other end, and Maddy did what she could to reassure her.

"I love you too, sweetheart. And I believe you. They'll get bored with it eventually. Try not to worry about it too much."

But the tabloid TV shows began stalking her by noon, and the network was going crazy. Every magazine in the country had called, wanting an interview about it.

"Maybe we should give them what they want," the head of PR suggested finally. "How bad could it be? So she had a baby at fifteen. It's happened before. She didn't kill it, for chrissake, and it's kind of a sweet story now, if we work it right. What do you think, Jack?" He looked hopeful as he glanced at his employer.

"I think I want to kick her ass from here to Cleveland. That's what I think," Jack said in instant response to the question. He had never been as furious at her, or had as much reason to be. "She's a fool for even admitting to that little bitch that she was her mother. Mother. What the hell does that mean in a case like this? She fucked some high school jock and got knocked up and dumped the kid the minute she was born. And now she goes around looking saintly and talking about her daughter. Shit, a cat has more relationship with its litter than Maddy does with this dumb bitch from Memphis. The girl's just riding on Maddy's coattails, and she doesn't see it."

"There may be a little more to it than that," the head of PR said delicately. He was startled by the vehemence of Jack's reaction to the situation. He'd been under a lot of pressure lately. The ratings for Maddy's show had been slipping daily, which may have been part of why he was so angry at her. But they all knew that that wasn't her fault, and they had said as much to Jack, but he didn't want to hear that either.

He was still steaming when they went home that night, and he tried to extract a promise from Maddy that she wouldn't see Lizzie again, but she wouldn't agree to it. And by midnight, he was so angry, he slammed out of the house and didn't come back until the next morning. She had no idea where he went, but when she looked, she could see TV cameras outside, and she didn't dare go after him. All she could do now was what she'd told Lizzie to do. Sit tight. Lizzie was staying at a friend's so they didn't find her at the boarding house, and her boss had given her the rest of the week off from the restaurant, because he was so impressed that she really was Maddy Hunter's daughter.

The only one who wasn't impressed was Jack. He was anything but impressed. He put her on a two-week suspension from the show for the disruption she was causing all of them, and he told her to clean up her act, give up her kid, and not to come back to work until she did that. She was in total disgrace with him, and he told her, with veins throbbing in his head, that if she ever lied to him again, about *anything*, he was going to kill her. And all she felt, as she listened to him, was guilty. Whatever happened, it was always her fault.

Chapter 15

AS SEPTEMBER ROLLED ON, the tabloids began to lose interest in Maddy and her daughter. Reporters turned up at the restaurant in Memphis once or twice, but Lizzie's boss hid her in the back room until they left, and eventually they stopped coming. It was a little harder for Maddy, who was more exposed, and had more trouble avoiding the press than Lizzie. At Jack's insistence, she made no comments to anyone, and other than the one picture of them at *The King and I*, there wasn't much to go on. Maddy neither denied nor confirmed that Lizzie was her daughter, although she would have liked to tell them that she was very proud of her, and she was thrilled that Lizzie had found her. But for Jack's sake, she didn't.

She and Lizzie had agreed that she shouldn't come to Washington for a while, but Maddy was still pursuing a place for her at Georgetown University, and Bill was doing whatever he could to help her. Lizzie was an easy sell. She had good grades, and terrific recommendations from her teachers in Memphis.

The First Lady's commission met again, and Bill was happy to see Maddy there. But he thought she seemed stressed, and tired, and worried. The tabloid attack had taken a toll on her, and she said that Jack was still giving her a hard time about it. He was giving her a bad time about her ratings too, and claiming now that it was because of the scandal over her illegitimate daughter. But Bill knew most of it from his daily calls to her. What he didn't know, and wasn't sure of now, was if she would ever leave her husband. She had stopped talking about it, and seemed to be blaming herself for most of their problems.

Bill was so upset about the situation she was in that he took Dr. Flowers aside at one of their commission meetings, and said something to her about it. She didn't divulge any secrets to him, and all she could do was reassure him.

"Most women put up with abuse for years," she said sensibly, intrigued by both his interest and his reaction. He seemed almost frantic with worry about Maddy. "And this is the subtlest, most insidious kind. Men like Jack are good at it. He makes her feel responsible for what he does, and portrays himself as the victim. And the thing you have to remember, Bill, is that she lets him."

"What can we do to help her?" He wanted to, desperately, but he had no idea how to do it.

"Be there for her. Listen. Wait. Tell her honestly what you think and see. But if she wants to feel guilty about Jack, she will. She'll probably work her way through it eventually. You're doing everything you can for the moment." She didn't say it to him, but she knew from Maddy that he called her daily, and she valued his friendship. Dr. Flowers couldn't help wondering what else was there, but Maddy was staunch in her insistence that they were no more than friends, and that neither of them had romantic motives. Dr. Flowers was not quite as certain. But whatever it was, she liked Bill, and had a great deal of respect for both him and Maddy.

"I'm just worried that one of these days, his subtleties are going to give way to something more obvious. I'm still afraid he's going to hurt her."

"He's hurting her now," she said clearly. "But men like him don't usually get violent. I can't promise you he won't, but I think he's smarter than that. Although the closer he gets to losing his prey, the worse it's going to get for her. He's not going to let her go kindly."

They chatted for a little while longer after Maddy had left that day, and Bill wasn't encouraged when he drove home. He had only once before in his life felt that helpless. And he couldn't help wondering if his own fears that Maddy would get hurt were based on his own experience when his wife had been kidnapped and then murdered. Until then, he had never truly believed that anything as terrible as that could happen.

And the following week, he gave Maddy the clean manuscript of his book to read. She was halfway through it on the weekend, with tears streaming down her face, when Jack saw it.

"What the hell are you reading to make you cry like that?" he asked with curiosity. They were in Virginia over a rainy weekend, and she'd been lying on the couch all afternoon, crying and reading. Bill's description of what it was like when his wife was kidnapped by terrorists tore her heart out.

"It's Bill Alexander's book. It's very well written."

"Oh, for chrissake, why would you want to read crap like that? The guy is such a loser, it's hard to believe he could write anything worth reading." Jack had total disregard for him, and it was obvious he didn't like him. He would have liked him even less, hated him in fact, if he had suspected how much support he gave Maddy. And she wondered if Jack sensed it.

"It's very moving."

Jack didn't mention it again, but when she went to look for the manuscript that night, she couldn't find it, and she finally asked Jack if he'd seen it.

"Yeah, I thought I'd spare you another night of tears over it. I put it where it belongs. In the garbage."

"You threw it out?" She was shocked that he'd done it.

"You've got better things to do with your time. If you did a little more research, the ratings for your show would be better."

"You know how much research I do," she said defensively. She'd currently been working on a scandal brewing at the CIA, and another story about Customs violations. "And you also know my research is not the problem."

"Maybe you're getting old, kid. You know, the public doesn't like women over thirty." He said anything he could to undermine her.

"You had no right to throw that book out. I wasn't finished. And I promised to return the manuscript to him." She was upset, and Jack looked totally indifferent to it. It was just another form of disrespect for her, and for Bill Alexander. Fortunately, it had been a copy and not the original.

"Don't waste your time, Mad." He went upstairs to

their bedroom then, and when she came to bed, he made love to her. And she had noticed lately that he was getting rough with her again, as though to punish her for her many transgressions. He wasn't so brutal with her that she could complain, and when she said something to him, he told her that she had imagined he was rough with her. He tried to convince her that he had been gentle with her, but she knew better.

And the following week, when they were back in Washington, Brad startled everyone by solving the show's biggest problem. He talked to Maddy before he went to see Jack, but he told her he had realized that being an anchor was no easy task, even with as competent a co-anchor as Maddy.

"I always thought I was good at the on-air stuff, but it's a lot different hanging out of a tree or off a tank, for a two-minute sound bite." He smiled at her ruefully, "I don't think I have the knack for this. And to be honest with you, I haven't enjoyed it." He had already taken a job with another network, to be their correspondent in Asia. He was going to be based in Singapore, and he could hardly wait to leave. And although Maddy had begun to like him better, she was relieved that he was going. She couldn't help wondering what Jack's reaction would be.

As it turned out, he made almost no comment about it whatsoever. A memo went out the next day, saying that Brad was leaving and that he had agreed to finish out the week. They had a provisional contract for the first six months, because Brad himself hadn't been sure he would like it. Maddy could tell by looking at Jack that he wasn't pleased, but he admitted nothing to her. All he said was that it put an even greater burden on her now, until they found someone else to co-anchor with her.

"I hope your ratings don't shoot right down the tubes," he said, sounding worried. But his fears rapidly proved to be unfounded. Rather than going down, they skyrocketed as soon as Brad left the show the following week, and the producer even suggested to Jack that they let her continue solo. But he insisted that she wasn't strong enough to carry the show alone, and he wanted someone to anchor with her. It was yet another way of putting her down. But in the meantime, their ratings were back at an all-time high, and Maddy was happy about it, even if Jack didn't acknowledge it.

But in spite of the ratings, which were an enormous relief to her, she still sounded down to Bill whenever he called her. She had been beating herself up over the show for a long time. She missed working with Greg. And she said she missed Lizzie. She wasn't sure what the problem was, but she admitted to him that she was in lousy spirits. They improved markedly when Bill called her to tell her he had gotten Lizzie into Georgetown. She had the grades and the skills, and she had sent in a wonderful application. But it was one of the most popular schools in the country, and there had been some question for a while as to whether they could find a place for her. He had called several of his contacts, and based on Bill, and the recommendations Lizzie had gotten from her teachers, they had decided to accept her. And Maddy was thrilled for her. She told Bill she was going to get her a little apartment in Georgetown, and she and Lizzie could see each other whenever they wanted. Maddy was ecstatic, and deeply grateful to him.

"Wait till I tell her!"

"Tell her I had nothing to do with it," Bill said with humility. "She really earned this herself. All I did was open a few doors, but it would never have happened if she didn't deserve it."

"You're a saint, Bill," Maddy smiled again. She had been mortified when she had to tell him that Jack had thrown his manuscript out, but it didn't surprise him. He had sent her another copy, and she read it in spare moments at the office. She had just finished it the day before, and they talked about it for some time. She thought it was going to have tremendous impact. It was not only intelligent, but honest and warm, and overwhelmingly human.

And that weekend, she told Lizzie in person about Georgetown. Jack went to Las Vegas for the weekend, with a group of men, and Maddy took a flight to Memphis. They went out to dinner and had a good time, and made plans. Maddy promised to find her an apartment in December, before Lizzie started the term at Georgetown after Christmas. Lizzie couldn't believe her good fortune.

"Don't get me anything too expensive," she said with a worried frown. "If I'm going to school full-time, I can only work nights and weekends."

"And when do you think you're going to do your homework?" Maddy asked, sounding like a mom, and loving every minute of it. "You can't work if you're going to get good grades, Lizzie. Think about it." But there wasn't much to think about from Lizzie's perspective. She had already put herself through a year and a half of college, by working every minute.

"Did they offer me a scholarship?" She still looked worried.

"No, but I am. Don't be silly, Lizzie. Times have changed. You have a mom now." And one who made a healthy living on one of the highest-rated news shows in the country. She had every intention of putting Lizzie through college, and paying for her apartment and expenses. And she explained that to her in no uncertain terms. "I don't expect you to support yourself. You deserve a break. You've had enough hard times." She felt she had a lot to make up to her for, and all she wanted now was to do that. She couldn't undo the past, but she could at least ensure her future.

"I can't let you do that. I'll pay you back one day," Lizzie said solemnly.

"You can support me in my old age," Maddy laughed, "like a devoted daughter." The truth was that they were already devoted to each other, and once again, they shared a terrific weekend with each other. They had discovered rapidly that they shared a lot of the same views, had much the same taste in clothes and the things they liked. The only thing they differed on, vehemently, was music. Lizzie was addicted to punk rock and country western, both of which Maddy hated. "I just hope you outgrow it," Maddy teased her, and Lizzie swore she wouldn't.

"The stuff you listen to is so corny, yuk!" Lizzie teased her back.

They went on long walks together, and spent a quiet morning together on Sunday after they went to church. And then Maddy flew back to Washington, and got home before Jack got in from Vegas. He had said he'd be in around midnight. And she hadn't told him where she was going, and she didn't intend to tell him when he returned. Lizzie was still a time bomb between them.

She was unpacking her small bag when the phone

rang on Sunday night, and she was surprised to hear Bill's voice when she answered. He never called her at home, usually only in the office, in case Jack answered.

"Is this a bad time?" he asked, sounding nervous.

"No, it's fine. I just came back from seeing Lizzie. She's ecstatic about Georgetown."

"I'm glad to hear it. I've been thinking about you all day. I'm glad you're all right. I don't know why, but I was worried about you." But that wasn't unusual for him either. Ever since she'd walked into his life, she was all he could think of. She was in such a tough situation. She felt she owed Jack so much that she believed she had to take whatever he dished out to her, and so far Bill hadn't been able to convince her of anything different, even though she had begun to realize that Jack was abusive. It was intensely frustrating for Bill. And he worried constantly about her. He had even mentioned her to his children, who were intrigued that he knew her. "Is your husband around?" he asked cautiously. He suspected he wasn't if she was talking about Lizzie.

"No. He went to Las Vegas for the weekend. They were going to have dinner there and see one last show, and come home pretty late. He said midnight, but I bet he won't be home till three or four in the morning."

"What about dinner then?" he was quick to ask her, relieved to find her alone. "I was just about to make myself some pasta and a salad. Can I interest you in something simple? Or we could go out if you prefer." He had never invited her to dinner before, although they had had lunch several times, and she always enjoyed spending time with him. He had become her mentor and her confidant, and in some ways, her guardian angel. And with Greg gone, he had become her best friend.

"Actually, I'd love to have dinner with you," she smiled at the invitation. And they both thought his place was a good idea. There was no point starting rumors, and given the level of interest in her the tabloids had, they could have. And neither of them wanted that kind of problem. "Do you want me to bring anything? Wine? Dessert? Napkins?" She sounded happy that she was going to see him.

"Just bring you. And don't expect too much. My cooking is pretty plain. I've really only learned in the past year."

"Don't worry about it. I'll help you."

She arrived at his house half an hour later, with a bottle of red wine in one hand, and wearing a white sweater and blue jeans. And with her hair hanging straight down her back, she looked more like Lizzie than ever. And Bill commented on it.

"She's such a cute kid," Maddy said proudly, as though they'd shared an entire lifetime together.

Maddy was very impressed by how proficient Bill actually was in the kitchen. He was wearing a starched blue shirt and jeans, and he had rolled up his sleeves, and made an excellent salad. He heated the French bread he had bought for her, and his fettuccine Alfredo was delicious. And the red wine she'd brought was perfect with it. And as they sat in his comfortable kitchen, looking out at the garden he loved, they talked about many things. His diplomatic posts, his academic career, his book, and her show, and eventually his children. They were completely at ease with each other, as friends should be. He found he could talk to her about anything, even his concerns about his daughter's marriage. He thought she worked too hard, had had too many kids in too short a time, and he was worried that his son-in-law was too critical of her. They sounded like a nice family, and Maddy would have envied him more than she did, if she didn't have Lizzie.

"I never realized how important children were, until I couldn't have them. I was stupid to let Jack talk me into that, but it was so important to him, and he'd done so much for me, I felt like I owed him that too. All my life, people have told me what to do about having kids or not having them, or giving them up, or seeing to it that I couldn't have them." It seemed incredible now talking about it with him, but the bitterness and anguish had gone out of it for her to some degree, now that she had found Lizzie. "Imagine if I never had, think of how sad my life would have been, never to have children."

"It's hard to imagine. My children are what make my life worth living," he admitted. "Sometimes I think I was more involved with them than Margaret. She was a lot more casual about it. I was always more worried about them, and a little overprotective." But Maddy could understand that better now. She was constantly worrying about Lizzie, that something might happen to her, and the greatest gift in her life would suddenly vanish. As though it was too sweet a gift to deserve, and she would be punished by having Lizzie disappear.

"I'll always feel guilty for giving her up. It's a miracle she came out of it as well as she did. In some ways, she's a lot healthier than I am," Maddy said with admiration, as he put a cup of chocolate mousse in front of her, and she tasted it. Like everything else he had served, it was delicious.

"She didn't have the hard hits you did, Maddy. It's amazing you're as whole as you are. Although I'm sure she had some tough times too, in foster homes and orphanages. That can't have been easy for her either. Thank God you have each other." And then he asked her an odd question. "Now that you have her, and you see what it's like, would you ever want more kids?"

"I'd love it, but I don't think there's much chance that will happen," she smiled wistfully at him, "I didn't give any others away, and I can't have any . . . the only way I'd have kids would be if I adopted, and Jack won't let me." It saddened him to hear that Jack was still so much a part of the equation. She was saying nothing about leaving him these days. She hadn't made her peace with the situation she was in, but she hadn't gotten up enough courage to leave either. And she still felt she owed him so much, particularly after the grief she'd caused him over Lizzie, and her deception.

"What if there were no Jack? Would you adopt?" It was a pointless question, but he was curious about it. She obviously liked kids, and took so much pleasure in her newfound relationship with her daughter. She was a surprisingly good mother, although she was a novice at it.

"Probably," she said, looking surprised herself. "I've never thought about it. Mostly because I never thought I'd leave Jack. And even now, I don't know if I'll ever have the guts to do it."

"Do you want to? Leave Jack, I mean." Sometimes he thought she did, and sometimes he didn't. It was an area of her life that was full of guilt, confusion, and conflict. But in his eyes at least, it was certainly not a marriage. All she was was a victim.

"I would like to leave all the agony and the fear, and the guilt that I feel when I'm with him . . . maybe what

I'd really like is to have him without all that, and I don't think it's possible. But when I think of leaving him, I think of leaving the man I thought he would be, and has been from time to time, and used to be. And when I think of staying, I think of staying with the bastard he can be, and is much too often. It's hard to reconcile those two things. I'm never quite sure who he is, or who I am, or who I'd be leaving." It was as sensibly as she could put it, but it explained it a little better to him.

"Maybe we all do that a little, though to a lesser degree." In a way, she was frozen in indecision because both sides weighed equally with her, whereas in his mind, the abuse Jack perpetrated on her should have tipped the balance. But he hadn't had the abusive childhood she had, which had predisposed her to letting Jack do whatever he wanted to her, no matter how abusive. It had taken her nearly nine years, seven of them married to him, to realize that he and Bobby Joe actually had a lot in common. What Jack did to her was just more subtle.

"Even in my case," Bill went on, "I forget some of the things Margaret did that used to annoy me. When I look back now, and remember the years we shared, it all looks so perfect. But we had our differences, as most people do, and a couple of tough times. When I accepted our first diplomatic post, and wanted to leave Cambridge, she threatened to leave me. She didn't want to go anywhere, and she thought I was crazy. As it turned out," he looked sadly at Maddy, "she was right. I should never have done it. She'd be alive today if I hadn't."

"You can't say that," Maddy said softly, reaching across the table to touch his hand gently. "What happens is destiny. She could have died in a plane crash, been hit by a car, killed in the street, gotten cancer . . . you couldn't know what would happen. And you must have thought you were doing the right thing."

"I did. And I never thought Colombia would be as dangerous as it was, or that we'd be so much at risk there. If I had understood that, I'd never have taken the job."

"I know that," Maddy said, with her hand still on his, and he took it in his own and held it. It was so comforting to be with her. "I'm sure she knew it too. It's like saying you should never take a plane because they crash sometimes. You have to lead your life as best you can, and take reasonable risks. Most of the time, it's worth it. You can't beat yourself up over it. That's not fair. You deserve better than that," she said simply.

"So do you," he said with her hand in his, as he looked at her across the table. "I wish you believed that."

"I'm trying to learn," she said softly, "I've had a lot of years of people telling me I didn't. It's hard not to hear that."

"I wish I could take all that away from you. You deserve a much better life than you've had, Maddy. I wish I could protect you, and help you."

"You do. More than you know. I'd be lost without you." She told him everything now, all her hopes, all her fears, all her problems. There was nothing he didn't know about her life, far more than Jack did. And she was grateful to Bill for being there for her.

He poured them each a cup of coffee then, and they strolled outside to sit in his garden. The air was cool, but it was still pleasant, as they sat on a bench, and he put an arm around her. It had been a perfect evening, after a lovely weekend.

"We'll have to do this again sometime," he said quietly, "if you can." It had been lucky for him that Jack was in Vegas.

"I don't think Jack would understand it," she said honestly. She wasn't even sure she did. She knew Jack would be angry if he knew about the dinner with Bill Alexander. But she had already decided not to tell him. There seemed to be a lot she wasn't telling him these days.

"I'm here for you, Maddy, if you need me. I hope you know that," he said, turning to look at her in the light from his living room, and the moonlight.

"I know that, Bill, thank you." Their eyes held for a long minute, and then he pulled her closer to him, and they sat there together for a long time, saying nothing, just silent, and at peace, comfortable with each other, as good friends should be.

Chapter 16

OCTOBER SEEMED MORE HECTIC than usual to everyone. The social season was in full swing. The world of
politics seemed more fraught with tension than usual.
The trouble in Iraq was still claiming lives, and people
were unhappy about it. And Jack threw her a curve and
hired another co-anchor for her. He was better than
Brad, but he was extremely difficult, and jealous and
hostile to Maddy. His name was Elliott Noble. He had
co-anchored before, and although he was cold as ice, he
was good, and at least this time their ratings didn't suf-
fer. They even improved slightly. But he was miserable
to work with, unlike Greg, or even Brad eventually.

A week after Elliott started, Jack announced that he
was taking Maddy to Europe. He had three days of meetings in London, and he wanted Maddy to go with him.
She didn't think she should leave the show so soon after
Elliott had started, and she was worried that people
might think he had come to replace her. But Jack insisted
that no one would believe that and he was adamant about

her going. She agreed to, but at the last minute, she caught a bad cold, and had an ear infection, and couldn't fly with him. So he went without her, and he was annoyed about it. He decided to stay a week as a result, and visit friends in Hampshire over the weekend. And she was just as glad, it gave her a chance to see Lizzie, and even look at some apartments with her. They had fun doing it, but didn't find anything they liked. They had plenty of time. They didn't need a place for her till December. And Bill took them both out to dinner.

And on the way home, Maddy stopped to pick up a few things at the market for breakfast, and she was startled when she saw Jack's name on the front page of the tabloids. "Is Maddy Hunter's Hubby Still Mad About Her Baby?" was the line that caught her eye, and just below it "Sweet Revenge: Looks Like He Has a New Baby of His Own." And with it, there was a picture of him with another woman. It was hard to know if they had doctored it, or if it was the genuine article. But there was a photograph of him leaving Annabel's, hand in hand with a very pretty, very young blond woman. And his expression was startled. Maddy's was even more so as she stared at it, and then put it on the counter with her other things. She read it carefully when they went home, and she admitted to Lizzie that she was upset about it.

"You know how those things are. He was probably in a big group or something, or maybe she's just a friend, or someone else's wife or date. They're pretty disgusting, and most of it is just lies anyway. No one ever believes them," Lizzie said, comforting her mother, which was entirely possible, but Maddy felt as though she had been slapped as she stared at Jack and the woman standing next to him in the picture.

He hadn't called her in two days by then, and she decided to call him at the number he'd left her. It was Claridge's, and they reminded her that he was gone for the weekend, and she didn't have that number. She didn't say anything about it after that, but thoughts of it festered all through the weekend, and when he came home on Monday, she was seething.

"You're in a great mood," he said jovially, when he came home on Monday night. "What's the matter, Mad? Does your ear still hurt?" He was in terrific spirits, and without saying a word, she took out the tabloid she had saved to show him. He glanced at it for a minute, without looking concerned, and then shrugged his shoulders as he grinned at her. "So? What's the big deal? I was in a group and we walked out together. That's not a crime, as far as I know." He didn't seem to feel at all guilty, and made no attempt to apologize for it, which was either gutsy of him, or reassuring, and Maddy was not sure which as she looked at him.

"Were you out dancing with her?" Maddy never took her eyes from his.

"Sure. I danced with a lot of people that night. I didn't fuck her, if that's what you're asking." He came right to the point, and he was starting to look annoyed at her for doubting him. "Is that what you were accusing me of, Mad?" He made it sound as though she were the one at fault, and not his fidelity that was in question.

"I was worried. She's pretty cute, and the story made it sound like you were out with her."

"The stories on you make you look like a two-bit whore, but I don't believe them, do I?" She reeled from what he said like a punch in the stomach.

"That's not a nice thing to say, Jack," she said softly.

"It's true, isn't it? Nobody has showed up with my illegitimate brats, have they? If they did, then you'd have
a right to bitch. But as I see it, you don't have much to
say now. And given the lies you've told me, and the
things you've concealed from me, who would blame me
if I cheated on you?" As usual, it was entirely her fault,
and she deserved it. And even thinking about it, she
knew he was partially right. She still hadn't told him she
was moving Lizzie to Washington, or that she saw Bill
from time to time, and talked to him daily. Jack had
successfully managed to turn it around and make her
feel guilty, rather than addressing the issue of whether
or not he'd been unfaithful.

"I'm sorry. It just looked . . ." She sounded flustered,
and felt awful for what she'd thought about him.

"Don't be so quick to point fingers, Mad. What's happening at work?" As he always did, he completely dismissed what she'd said. The only time he hung on to a
subject was when it suited his purposes, and this didn't.
He had used it to bludgeon her, and as usual, she stood
corrected.

In fact, because of what she'd said to him, and what
she had thought when she saw the picture of him, he
accused her several times of flirting with her new co-
anchor on the air. Elliott was young, single, and good-
looking, and Jack started telling her that there were
rumors about them, which severely upset her. She
talked to Bill about it and he pointed out to her that
Jack was just trying to divert her attention, but she still
thought he believed it and felt terrible about it.

And what he said about Elliott was nothing compared

to what he said about Bill, when someone told him that they had seen them at the Bombay Club, having lunch together.

"Is that why you pulled that crap on me about Annabel's? What was that? Some kind of red herring? Are you fucking that old fart, Mad? If you are, I feel sorry for you. Maybe that's all you can get now."

"That's disgusting!" She flew at him in a rage, incensed at the accusation and the way he talked about Bill. There was nothing old or dull about Bill. He was interesting and fun and good and decent, and extremely good-looking. And the funny thing was that although he was twenty-six years older than she was, it never even occurred to her when they were together.

And things only got worse when he questioned one of the receptionists behind her back, and she said something inane about Bill's calls. He tricked her into admitting that Bill called Maddy almost every day. Jack was in her office, accusing and threatening her, five minutes later.

"You little whore! What the hell is going on with you two? When did that start? On your goddamn bleeding heart commission about women? Don't forget that that son of a bitch got his wife killed. Maybe he'll do you the same favor if you're not careful."

"How can you say that?" Tears filled her eyes instantly at the brutality of his words. She didn't know how to defend herself, and there was no way she could prove that she wasn't sleeping with Bill Alexander. "We're just friends. I have never cheated on you, Jack." The look in her eyes implored him to believe her. Instead of hating him for what he had said to her, she was devastated by it.

"Tell that to someone who believes you. I know better, remember? I'm the guy you lied to about your baby."

"That was different." She was sobbing as she sat at her desk, as he pounded her with his words.

"No, it isn't. I don't believe a word you tell me anymore, and why should I? I have every reason not to trust you. Your so-called 'daughter' is proof of that, if you need a reminder."

"We're just friends, Jack," she was talking about Bill again, and he refused to listen. He slammed out of her office so hard he almost broke the glass door as he left, and Maddy sat shaking at her desk. She was still in tears when Bill called half an hour later, and she explained what had happened to him.

"I don't think you should call me anymore. He thinks we're having an affair." And they certainly couldn't go to lunch now. She felt as though she were cutting off her life support, but she had no choice, as she saw it. "I'll call you. It's simpler," she said sadly.

"He has no right to talk to you that way." Bill was outraged, and she had cleaned it up considerably for him. If he had actually heard what Jack said, he would have been beside himself. "I'm so sorry, Maddy."

"It's all right. It's my own fault. I made him mad when I accused him of going out with someone in London."

"You saw a picture of him, for God's sake. That was hardly an unreasonable assumption." He was convinced Jack had lied to her about it, but he didn't say so. And then, sounding depressed over all of it, he asked her a pointed question. "How much of this are you going to take, Maddy? The man treats you like dirt under his feet. Can't you see that?"

"I see it . . . but he's right too. I lied to him about Lizzie. I provoke him. I even lie to him about you. I wouldn't want him talking to some woman every day either."

"Do you want us to stop talking?" Bill asked, sounding panicked. But she was quick to reassure him.

"No, I don't. But I understand how Jack feels."

"I don't think you have the remotest idea how he feels, or even *if* he feels," Bill disagreed with her. "I think he's so manipulative and so evil that he knows just how to play you and make you feel guilty. He's the one who should be apologizing to you, and feeling guilty!" He sounded desperately upset as they continued to hash it out, and finally agreed that she would call him every day, and they would put a halt to their lunches for a while, or maybe have lunch from time to time quietly at his place. It seemed sneaky to her too, but it seemed better not to be seen in public, and neither of them wanted to stop seeing each other. She needed at least one friend, and other than Lizzie, he was all she had.

The atmosphere remained tense at home for several days, and then, as luck would have it, she and Jack went to a party at the home of a Congressman Jack knew, and Bill was there. They had gone to college together, and he had forgotten to tell Maddy that he was going.

Jack reacted instantly the moment Bill walked into the room, and he leaned over and squeezed Maddy's arm so hard it was white when he let her go again. But the message to her was clear.

"If you so much as speak to him, I'm going to drag you out of here so fast you won't know what hit you." He whispered the words close to her ear.

"I understand," she whispered back. She avoided Bill's eyes, to get the message to him that she couldn't talk to him, and whenever he moved near, she went to stand next to Jack, to reassure him. She looked nervous and pale, and felt awkward for the entire evening, and when Jack went to the bathroom at one point, she looked at Bill imploringly, and he drifted past her with a worried look. He had instantly seen the tension on her face.

"I can't talk to you . . . he's furious . . ."

"Are you okay?" He was sick about her. He had seen what was happening, and had made a point of not saying anything to her.

"I'm fine," she said, and turned away, but Jack came back just as Bill was walking away from her, and he sensed instantly what had happened. Jack walked purposefully across the room to her and spoke between clenched teeth in a tone that terrified her.

"We're leaving. Get your coat."

She thanked the hostess graciously, and they left a few minutes later. They were the first to leave, but dinner was over and it didn't cause any comment. Jack had explained that they both had early meetings the next day. Only Bill looked upset after they left, and he knew he couldn't call to find out how she was. Jack was already lashing out at her verbally in the car as they drove away, and she was tempted to jump out of the car and run away. He was in a frenzy over Bill.

"What kind of fool do you think I am, for chrissake? I told you not to talk to him . . . I saw the look in your eyes when you looked at him . . . why didn't you just pull up your skirt, rip your pants off, and wave them at him?"

"Jack, please . . . we're friends, that's all. I told you. He's mourning his wife. I'm married to you. We're on the same commission. That's all there is to it." She spoke as quietly as she could, trying not to provoke him any further, but it was hopeless. He was in a total rage.

"Bullshit, you little bitch! You know goddamn well what you're doing with him, and so do I. And so does all of fucking Washington, probably. What kind of fool does that make me? I'm not blind, Maddy, for chrissake. Jesus, the shit I take from you. I just can't believe it." She said not another word as they drove home, and Jack slammed every door in the house but he never touched her. She lay cowering in their bed all night, terrified of what he would do to her, but he did nothing. And he was as cold as ice the next day when she poured his coffee.

And he issued only one warning. "If you ever speak to him again, I'm going to throw your ass out on the street where you belong. Do you understand?" She nodded silently, fighting back tears, and terrified at the prospect. "I'm not going to put up with that bullshit. You humiliated me last night. You never took your eyes off him, and you looked like a bitch in heat while you did it." She wanted to argue with him and defend herself, but she didn't dare. She just nodded, and drove with him in silence to the office. The only sensible thing to do after that was to call Bill and tell him she couldn't see or talk to him anymore. And she knew she should. But he was the lifeline she was holding on to, the thin thread between her and the abyss she was so terrified to fall into. And she didn't know what it was, or why, but she knew she had a special bond to him, and no matter how much Jack threatened her, she couldn't give up her contact with Bill, whatever the cost, or the risk. She knew that what she was doing was dangerous, but no matter how sternly she told herself that, what she knew most of all was that she couldn't stop now.

Chapter 17

*M*ADDY WAS STILL IN DISGRACE with Jack, and calling Bill very cautiously every day from her office, when she heard a shout one afternoon from the newsroom. She was talking to Bill at the time, and she listened for a second to the noise outside, and then told him something must have happened.

"I'll call you back," she said, and hung up, and hurried outside her office to see what the fuss was. Everyone was crowding around a monitor, and at first she couldn't see what they were watching. But within seconds, someone moved aside, and she could hear and see the bulletin that had interrupted all broadcasts on every network. President Armstrong had been shot, and was being rushed by helicopter to Bethesda Naval Hospital in critical condition.

"Oh my God . . . oh my God . . ." Maddy whispered . . . all she could think of as she watched was the First Lady.

"Get your coat!" the producer shouted at her. "We

have a helicopter for you at National." A cameraman was already standing by, and someone handed her her handbag and her coat, and she ran into the elevator without stopping to talk to anyone. The same bulletin had announced that the First Lady was with him. And as soon as Maddy got in the car that was waiting to take her to National, she called the office back on her cell phone. The producer had been standing by, waiting to hear from her.

"How did it happen?" she asked quickly.

"They don't know yet. Some guy just came out of a crowd at him and shot him. One of the Secret Service guys took a hit, but no one's dead yet." *Yet.* That was the key word here.

"Is he going to make it?" She had her eyes closed as she listened.

"We don't know that yet either. It doesn't look good. There's blood all over the place on what they're showing now. They just showed it all in slow motion. He was shaking hands as he left some perfectly innocuous group, and a guy who looks like *Father Knows Best* just let him have it. They got him. He's in custody now, but they haven't released his name yet."

"Shit."

"Stay in touch. Get everything you can. Doctors, nurses, Secret Service. The First Lady, if they let you see her." He knew they were friends, and no relationships were sacred in this business. She knew they expected her to fully exploit every possible opportunity, no matter how tasteless. "We've got a crew going out to meet you by car, if you need a break. But I want you on this one."

"I know. I know."

"And stay off your phone, in case we have to call you."

"I'll be in touch." She turned the radio on in the car, but it was all the same thing for the next five minutes, and hesitating for only a fraction of an instant, she called Bill, to let him know where she was going. "I can't stay on long," she explained rapidly. "I have to keep the line clear. Have you heard?"

"I just heard it on the radio. My God, I can't believe it." It was like Kennedy all over again, except it was worse. This wasn't just politics or history. She knew them.

"I'm on my way to Bethesda now. I'll call you."

"Be careful." There was no need for her to be. She was in no danger. But he said it anyway, and after they hung up, he stared out the window into his garden, thinking about her.

For the next five hours, Maddy's life was completely crazy. There was an area roped off for the press at the hospital, and coffee stations for them outside. The press secretary came to talk to them every half hour. And they were all trying to corner every possible member of hospital personnel they could. But for the moment, there was no news, and no story.

The President had been in surgery since noon, and at seven o'clock, he hadn't come out yet. The bullet had pierced his lung, and damaged his kidney and spleen. There was a lot of reconstructive work to do. Miraculously, it hadn't touched his heart, but he had had massive internal bleeding. And no one had seen the First Lady. She was waiting for him in the recovery room, watching the surgery on closed circuit TV. And there was nothing more to say, until he got out of surgery and they evaluated how he was doing. The doctors estimated that he would be there until midnight. And so would Maddy.

There were over a hundred photographers in the lobby, on couches, on chairs, sitting on their camera bags, some sprawled on the floor in corners. There were a sea of Styrofoam cups all around, bags of fast food, and a cluster of reporters stood outside, smoking. It looked like a war zone.

Maddy and the cameraman she'd been assigned had stationed themselves in a corner of the room, and they were talking quietly to a group of reporters they knew, from other networks and major newspapers.

She had done a piece for the five o'clock news, standing outside the hospital, and at seven they shot her in an area they'd been assigned inside the lobby. Elliott Noble was back at the station doing a solo, and communicating with her regularly. She did another piece for the eleven o'clock news, but there wasn't much to say, except what they'd been told. The doctors attending the President were guardedly hopeful.

It was nearly midnight when Jack called her on her cell phone. "Can't you get anything more interesting than that, Mad? Christ, we're all running the same boring stuff. Have you tried to see the First Lady?"

"She's waiting outside the OR for him, Jack. No one but the Secret Service and the hospital staff has been in to see her."

"Then put a white gown on, for chrissake." He was always pushing her to get more and do better.

"I don't think anyone knows anything more than we do. It's in God's hands at this point." There was no way to know yet if he'd survive it. Jim Armstrong wasn't a young man, and amazingly he'd been shot once before. But that time the bullet had only grazed him.

"I assume you're going to stay there tonight," Jack said pointedly. It was more a directive than a question, but she'd been planning to do that.

"I want to be here if anything happens. They're calling a press conference when he gets out of surgery. They promised us one of the surgeons."

"Call me if anything big breaks. I'm going home now." He was still at the office, most of the staff was still there. It had been an endless day and it looked like it was going to be a long night. But the days ahead would be worse, if the President didn't recover. Maddy only hoped for the First Lady's sake that he'd make it. There was nothing any of them could do now but pray. It was in the hands of the gods and the surgeons.

After Jack called, Maddy sat around drinking more coffee for a while. She'd had gallons, and had barely eaten all day. But she felt too heartsick over what had happened to be hungry.

A little while later, she called Bill, and wondered if he was asleep as she let the phone ring. He answered finally, and she was relieved that he didn't sound sleepy.

"Are you sleeping?" she asked hesitantly. He recognized her voice instantly and was pleased she'd called him. He'd seen all her broadcasts from the hospital, and was keeping his TV on, in case she came back on.

"Sorry, I was in the shower. I was hoping you'd call me. How's it going?"

"There's nothing much going on," she said, sounding tired, but happy to talk to him. "We're just sitting around waiting. He should be out of surgery soon. I keep thinking about Phyllis." Maddy knew how much she loved her husband. They all knew it. She made no secret of it. They'd been married for nearly fifty years, and Maddy couldn't bear the thought of it ending this way for them.

"I don't suppose you've been able to see her?" Bill inquired, but he hadn't seen the First Lady on any broadcast, on any channel.

"She's upstairs somewhere. I wish I could, not for us, but just to let her know that we're thinking of her," Maddy answered.

"I'm sure she knows that. God, you wonder how things like this happen. With all the security, it still does from time to time. I saw the original tape in slow motion. The guy just stepped right up and plugged him. How's the injured Secret Service guy doing?"

"They operated on him this afternoon, and they say he's in serious, but stable condition. He was lucky."

"I hope Jim will be too," Bill said solemnly. "How are you? You must be exhausted."

"I'm getting there. We've been standing around here all afternoon, waiting for something to happen." It reminded them both of Dallas and John Kennedy. It was before she was born, but she had seen all the footage on it, and he'd been in grad school.

"Do you want me to bring you some food?" he asked, sounding concerned about her, and she smiled at the suggestion.

"There must be two thousand doughnuts here, and all the fast food in Washington. But thanks for the offer." She noticed a cluster of doctors moving toward a microphone, and told him she had to go.

"Call me if anything happens. Don't worry about waking me. I'm here if you need me." Unlike Jack, who only complained that their broadcast was too boring.

One of the doctors was wearing a surgical cap and paper slippers over his shoes, and green surgical scrubs, and Maddy correctly guessed he had just come from surgery, as he stepped up to the podium they'd set up in the lobby. And instantly, all the news crews were crowded around him.

"We don't have anything dramatic to tell you," he said, looking serious, as cameras all over the room began focusing on him, "but we have every reason to be optimistic. The President is a strong, healthy man, and from our perspective, the surgery was successful. We've done everything we can right now, and we'll keep you posted with bulletins through the night, as he progresses. He's under heavy sedation right now, but he was regaining consciousness when I left him. And Mrs. Armstrong asked me to thank all of you. She said she's very sorry," he said with a tired smile, "that you all have to sleep here. She wishes you didn't have to. That's all for now," he said, and left the podium without further comment. They had been told earlier that there would be no questions. He had told them all the doctors knew themselves. The rest was in God's hands.

Her cell phone rang almost as soon as the doctor left them. It was Jack. "Get an interview with him."

"I can't, Jack. They already told us he won't do it. The man's been in surgery for twelve hours, and they're telling us everything they know."

"Like hell they are. They're feeding you press kit crap. For all we know he's brain dead."

"What do you suggest I do? Crawl into Armstrong's room through the heat vent?" She was tired, and annoyed that he was being so unreasonable and so demanding. They were all in the same boat. They had to wait for whatever announcements were made, and harassing the surgeons wasn't going to get them more information.

"Don't be cute, Mad," Jack said, sounding annoyed. "Do you want to put your viewers to sleep, or are you working for some other network?"

"You know what's happening here. We're all getting the same stuff," she said, sounding exasperated.

"That's my point. Get something different." He hung up on her without saying good-bye, and a reporter from a rival network smiled at her and shrugged in sympathy.

"I'm getting the same crap from the head of our newsroom. If they're so smart, why don't they come down here and do it."

"I'll have to remember to suggest that," Maddy smiled back at him, and settled into a chair with her coat over her, until the next press announcement.

A team of doctors came back to them at three in the morning, and those who were asleep woke up to hear what they had to tell them. It was more of the same. The President was still holding his own. He had regained consciousness, was still in critical condition, and his wife was with him.

It was a long night, and in spite of another release at five, no one gave them any significant news until seven in the morning. Maddy was awake and drinking coffee by then. She had slept about three hours in disjointed little bits and pieces, and she was feeling stiff from sleeping curled up in a chair all night. It was like spending a night at the airport during the snowstorm.

But at least at seven, the news was a little better. They admitted that he was uncomfortable and in considerable pain, but he had smiled at his wife, and sent his thanks to the nation. And his team of surgeons was extremely pleased with him. And they actually dared to say that they had every reason to believe he was going to make it, barring complications.

And half an hour later, the White House released the identity of the man who had shot him. He was now being referred to as "the suspect," although half the country had seen reruns of the tape that showed how he had shot the President. The CIA believed that it was not part of a plot to assassinate the President. The suspect's son had been killed in the action in Iraq that summer, and he felt that the President was to blame for it. He was a man with no previous criminal record, no history of violence, or mental instability, but he had lost his only child in a war he didn't understand and didn't care about, and had been depressed ever since. He was in custody, and being watched carefully. The rest of his family was shocked. His wife was apparently hysterical. He had been, until that moment, a respected member of the community, and a reasonably successful accountant. And it saddened Maddy to think about it.

She sent a note to Phyllis Armstrong through one of the press secretaries, just to let her know that she was there, and praying for her. And she was stunned when a note came back from her a few hours later. She had just jotted the words, "Thank you, Maddy. He's doing better, thank God. Love, Phyllis." But Maddy was enormously touched that she had taken the time to write it.

Maddy went on the air again at noon, with the latest report, that the President was resting comfortably, and although still listed in critical condition, they were hoping that he would soon be out of danger.

"If you don't give me something interesting soon,"

Jack said when he called her after the broadcast, "I'm going to send Elliott over to do it."

"If he can get anything different than the rest of us can, then send him," she said, sounding exhausted. For once, she was too tired to be affected by Jack's threats and accusations.

"You're boring me to tears," he accused her.

"I'm stuck with what they're feeding us, Jack. No one else is getting anything better." But it didn't stop Jack from calling every few hours and complaining to her. And when Bill called her at one o'clock, she was relieved to hear him.

"When was the last time you ate?" he asked with genuine worry.

"I can't remember," she smiled. "I'm so tired, I'm not hungry."

He didn't offer to come by. He just showed up twenty minutes later, with a club sandwich and some fruit, and a couple of soft drinks. He looked like the Red Cross arriving, as he showed up, and picked his way through the sea of reporters in the lobby till he found her, and forced her to sit in a chair and eat while he watched her.

"I can't believe you did this," she grinned broadly at him. "I didn't even realize it, I was starving. Thank you, Bill."

"It makes me feel useful." He was amazed by how many people were there, reporters, cameramen, sound crews, producers, all milling around the hospital lobby. They were spilling out into the street, where the news vans were parked helter skelter. It looked like a disaster area, and it was. And he was pleased that she ate all of her sandwich. "How long are you going to have to stay here?"

"Until he's out of the woods, or we drop, whichever comes first. Jack is threatening to send Elliott to replace me, because my broadcasts are so boring. But there's not much I can do about it." And as she said the words, the press secretary stepped up to the podium again, and everyone rushed to their feet and pressed forward, and Maddy had to go with them.

This time they told them that it was going to be a long, slow haul, of painstaking progress, and the press secretary suggested that some of them might want to go home, and get spelled off by their colleagues. The President was making a good recovery. There were no complications, and they had every reason to believe that he would continue to improve.

"Can we see him?" someone shouted.

"Not for several days," the press secretary answered.

"What about Mrs. Armstrong? Can we talk to her?"

"Not yet. She hasn't left her husband's side for a minute. And she's going to stay here until he recovers. She's sleeping right now, and so is he. Maybe you should get some sleep too," the press secretary said with the first smile they'd seen in twenty-four hours. And then he left, and promised to come back to them in a few hours, as Maddy turned off her microphone and looked up at Bill. She was so tired she could hardly see straight.

"What are you going to do now?" he asked her.

"I'd give my right arm to go home for a shower, but Jack would probably kill me for leaving."

"Can't he send someone to replace you?" It seemed inhuman to just stay there.

"He could, but I don't think he will. Not yet anyway. Jack wants me here. But I'm not doing anything anyone else couldn't do. You heard what they give us. It's pretty much packaged. They're telling us what they want us to know, but if they're telling the truth, it sounds like he's doing okay."

"Don't you believe them?" Bill was surprised by her skepticism, but it was her business to be that way, and ferret out any inconsistencies in their story. She was good at that, which was why Jack wanted her to stay there.

"I do," she said sensibly, "But the truth is, he could be dead for all we know." It was an awful thing to say, but it was possible certainly. "I don't think they'd lie about it unless they had to for national security. In this case, I think they're being pretty honest. At least I hope so."

"So do I," Bill said with fervor.

He stayed with her for another half hour, and then he left. And at three, Jack finally let her off the hook, and told her to go home and change, and come back to the studio for the five o'clock broadcast. She barely had time to do it, and she knew she wouldn't have time for a nap. He had already told her to come back to the hospital after the seven-thirty broadcast. And after she went home and changed into a dark blue pantsuit, she knew she could sleep in on the gurneys for the press at the hospital, she was almost reeling by the time she got to hair and makeup. Elliott Noble was there too, and he looked at her with admiration.

"I don't know how you do it, Maddy. If I'd been at that hospital for the last twenty-seven hours, they'd be carrying me out on a stretcher. You've done a great job there." Though not according to her husband. But she was touched by the compliment, and knew she'd earned it.

"I'm just used to it, I guess. I've been doing this for a long time." It made them feel more like colleagues, and she liked him a little better. At least for once he'd been decent to her.

"How do you think the President really is?" Elliott asked her in an undertone.

"I think they're probably telling us the truth on this one," she answered. And somehow, with his help, she got through the five o'clock broadcast and the seven-thirty, and she was back at the hospital at eight-fifteen, just as Jack told her to do. He had stopped in to see her between the two shows, looking fresh and rested, and gave her a whole new set of orders, criticisms, and directions. He didn't even ask if she was tired. He didn't care if she was. This was a crisis and she had to deliver. But she never failed him. And although he didn't acknowledge it, everyone else did. She was one of a few veterans of the first night when she got back to the hospital. Most of the other networks had replaced their people with fresh teams, and she had a new cameraman and a new soundman. And miraculously someone felt sorry for her and brought her a gurney in the lobby, so she could get some sleep between press releases. And when she told Bill about it on the phone, he urged her to use it.

"You'll get sick if you don't get some sleep," he said sensibly. "Have you had dinner?"

"I ate between broadcasts, in my office."

"Something nourishing, I hope." She grinned at what he said. He had a lot to learn about her business.

"Health food actually. Pizza and doughnuts. Standard fare for reporters. I'd have withdrawal if I didn't eat that. I only eat real food at dinner parties."

"Do you want me to bring you something?" he offered, sounding hopeful, but she was too tired to see him.

"I think I'm going to hit my gurney and try to sleep for a couple of hours. But thanks anyway. I'll call you in the morning, unless something major happens here." But nothing did. It was a peaceful night, and she went home to shower and change in the morning.

As it turned out, she was at the hospital for five days, and on the last day, she finally saw Phyllis for a few minutes, though not in an interview. The First Lady had sent for her, and they chatted in the hallway outside the President's room, standing among the Secret Service. The President was being guarded closely. Although his assailant was in custody, they weren't taking any chances. And Maddy could imagine they felt very guilty that they hadn't stopped the bullet.

"How are you holding up?" Maddy asked the First Lady with obvious concern. She looked a hundred years old, and was wearing a hospital gown over a pair of slacks and a sweater. But she smiled at Maddy's question.

"Better than you probably. They're taking wonderful care of us. Poor Jim is feeling pretty rotten, but he's much better. This is a little rough at our age."

"I'm so sorry it happened," Maddy said sympathetically. "I've been worried about you all week. Everyone is taking care of him, but I wasn't sure how you were faring."

"It's quite a shock, to say the least. But we're muddling through. I hope you can all go home soon."

"I'm going home tonight actually." The press secretary had announced that the President was no longer in critical condition. And everyone in the lobby cheered at the news. Most of them had been there for days, and they were so relieved some of them cried when they heard it. By then, only Maddy had been there since the beginning. And they all admired her for it.

When she got home that night, Jack was there, watching rival stations. He glanced up at her, and never got up off the couch to greet her. He wasn't even grateful for what she'd given him for the past five days. Her life, her soul, her spirit. And he didn't tell her that their ratings were the highest of any network, but she had heard it from the producer. She had even managed to do a story on the dozens of people who had to be moved to other hospitals, to clear an entire floor for the President, his nursing staff, and the Secret Service. And everyone had been cheerful and pleasant about being moved. They were happy to do what they could for him, and they'd been told that their hospital stays elsewhere would be paid for by the White House. None of them were critically ill. They were all convalescing, so it had been all right to move them.

"You look like shit, Mad" was all Jack said to her, and it was true. She looked exhausted, but she had still managed to look presentable on the air when she had to. But her face was drawn and pale, and there were deep circles under her eyes.

"Why are you so mad at me all the time?" She looked puzzled. Admittedly she had done some things to upset him in the past few months. Everything from her editorials, to her relationship with Lizzie, to her talks with Bill. But her real crime was that she was less in his control now, and he hated her for it. Dr. Flowers had warned her about that. She had said that he wouldn't take kindly to it, and she'd been right. It was very threatening to him. But as the thought that he hated her crossed Maddy's mind, she was suddenly reminded of what Janet McCutchins had said to her four months before, that her husband hated her, and Maddy had refused to believe it. But she believed it of Jack now. He certainly acted like it.

"I have reason to be mad at you," he said coldly. "You've betrayed me every way you could in the last few months, Mad. You're just lucky I haven't fired you yet." The *yet* was supposed to terrify her, and make her feel that he would at any moment. And he might. But what she really felt was anxious. It was so hard standing up to him, and taking the consequences for it. But lately, she felt she had to. Finding Lizzie, and knowing Bill, had somehow changed her. She felt as though she had found herself, as well as her daughter. And it was obvious that Jack didn't like it. That night when they went to bed, he didn't even talk to her, and he was icy with her the next morning.

Jack was harder than ever on her these days, and he alternated constant criticism with the cold shoulder. He had very little pleasant to say to her, and she didn't care as much. She got her comfort from Bill whenever they talked. And one night when Jack was out, she went to Bill's house again for dinner. He made steak for her this time, because he thought she was still working too hard and needed some real nourishment. But the best nourishment he gave her was the nurturing he lavished on her, and the obvious affection he showered on her.

They talked about the President for a while. He had been in the hospital for two weeks by then, and he was going home in a few days. Maddy and a few others of the elite group had been allowed to interview him briefly, and he looked thinner and very worn. But he was in excellent spirits, and he thanked everyone for their devotion and their kindness. And she had interviewed Phyllis too, who was equally gracious.

It had been an extraordinary two weeks, and Maddy was pleased with the coverage they'd given their viewers, even if Jack wasn't. She had even won the respect of her co-anchor, Elliott Noble. He thought she was an extraordinary reporter, and so did everyone else at the network.

Bill looked at her with a smile full of tenderness and admiration as they sat in his kitchen after dinner. "So what are you going to do now to keep yourself amused?" It wasn't every day the President got shot, and after that, everything else she covered would seem anticlimactic.

"I'll think of something. I have to find Lizzie an apartment." It was the beginning of November. "I still have another month to do that."

"Maybe I can look at some with you." He was less busy than he had been, now that his book was finished. And he was talking about teaching again. He'd had offers from both Yale and Harvard. Maddy was pleased for him, but she knew she'd be sad if he left Washington. He was her only friend there. "It won't be till next September," he reassured her. "I thought I'd try my hand at another book after the first of the year. Maybe fiction this time." She was excited for him, but at the same time, she had a sense that she wasn't dealing with her own life. She was increasingly aware of how abusive Jack was, but all she was doing was treading water. But Bill didn't press her about it. Dr. Flowers had said she would do something about it when she was ready, and it might take her years to confront him. Bill had almost resigned himself to it, although he worried about her. But at least her two weeks of covering the President at the hospital had kept her away from Jack, and too busy to deal with him, although he'd been eternally shouting at her on the cell phone. Bill could always hear it in her voice when he called her. Everything was always her fault. It was pure *Gaslight*.

"What are you doing for Thanksgiving?" Bill asked her as they finished dinner.

"Nothing much. We usually go to Virginia, and spend it quietly. Neither of us has family. Sometimes we go to our neighbors'. What about you, Bill?"

"We go to Vermont every year." But she knew it would be hard for him this year. It was going to be his first Thanksgiving at home without his wife, and he was dreading it, she knew, from their conversations.

"I wish I could invite Lizzie, but I can't. She's going to have Thanksgiving dinner with her favorite foster parents. She seems okay with it." But nonetheless, Maddy was disappointed not to be with her for their first Thanksgiving, but they had no choice.

"What about you? Will you be okay?" he asked, sounding worried.

"I think so." But she wasn't as sure now. She had talked to Dr. Flowers about it, who was begging her to go to a group for battered women. And Maddy had promised her she would. It was starting right after Thanksgiving.

Maddy saw Bill the day before they left, and they were both in somber moods. He because of his wife, and she because she had to go away with Jack, and their relationship was so tense. It seemed to be electrified by undercurrents. And Jack was watching her like a hawk. He didn't trust her anymore. He hadn't caught her with Bill again, and Bill didn't call her anymore, except on her cell phone. He waited for her to call him most of the time. The last thing he wanted was to cause her more trouble.

On the day before Thanksgiving, she met him at his house. He made tea for her, and she brought him a box of cookies, and they sat in his cozy kitchen and chatted. The weather had turned cold, and he told her it had already snowed in Vermont, and he and his children and grandchildren were planning to go skiing.

She stayed with him for as long as she could, and then finally, she told him she had to get back to the office.

"Take care of yourself, Maddy," he said gently, with eyes full of feelings for her that couldn't be expressed. They both knew it would have been wrong to do so. Neither of them had ever done anything they'd regret, out of respect for each other. Whatever it was they felt went unexplained and unsaid. It was only with Dr. Flowers that she questioned what she felt for him. They had an odd relationship, and yet she knew they both counted on it. They were like two survivors from sinking ships that had met in troubled waters. She clung to him now before she left, and he held her as a father would a child, with strong arms and a loving heart, and he made no demands of her.

"I'm going to miss you," he said simply. They knew they couldn't talk to each other over the weekend. Jack would have been suspicious if Bill called on her cell phone. And she didn't dare call him.

"I'll call you if he goes out riding or something. Try not to be too sad," she said, concerned about him. She knew how hard it was going to be to celebrate the holiday without Margaret. But he wasn't thinking of his wife now, only Maddy.

"I'm sure it'll be hard, but it'll be good to see the children." And then, without thinking, he kissed the top of her head, and held her for one last minute. When they left each other that afternoon, they were both sad, at what they had once had and lost, and could no longer have. And Maddy was silently grateful as she drove away, that at least they had each other. All she could do was thank God for him.

Chapter 18

THE TIME MADDY SPENT IN VIRGINIA with Jack over the holiday was difficult and fraught with tension. He was in a bad mood most of the time, and he locked himself in the study frequently for clandestine phone calls. And this time, she knew it couldn't be the President, because he was still convalescing, and the Vice President was running the country for the moment. And Jack had never been close to him. His ties were to Jim Armstrong and no one else.

And once, when she picked up the phone to call Bill, thinking Jack was out, she accidently heard him talking to a woman. She hung up immediately, without listening to what they were saying. But it made her wonder. He had been so quick to explain the photograph of the woman he'd been with at Annabel's in London, but he had been very removed from her in the past month, and they rarely made love anymore. It was a relief in some ways, but it also puzzled her. For all their married life, his sexual appetite had been insatiable and voracious.

And he seemed disinterested in her now, except when he complained to her, or accused her of something he claimed she had done.

She managed to call Lizzie on Thanksgiving Day, and Bill the following night, when Jack went to talk to one of the neighbors about their horses. Bill said the holiday had been rough, but the skiing was great, so that was something. He had made turkey with the kids. And Maddy and Jack had eaten theirs alone in stony silence, but when she tried to talk to him about the tension between them, he brushed her off, and told her it was her imagination, which she knew it wasn't. She had never been as unhappy, except when Bobby Joe was abusing her. In some ways, this felt no different, it was just subtler. But it was hurtful and confusing and sad.

She was relieved when they finally got on the plane to go home, and Jack commented on it with a tone of suspicion. "Any particular reason you're so happy to go home?"

"No, I'm just anxious to get back to work," she said, fobbing him off. She didn't want to get in a fight with him, and he seemed to be itching to start one.

"Is there someone waiting for you in Washington, Mad?" he asked nastily, and Maddy just looked at him in despair.

"There's no one, Jack. I hope you know that."

"I'm not sure what I know about you. But I could find out if I wanted," he said, and she didn't answer. Discretion seemed the better part of valor. Silence the only choice.

And the next day after work, she went to the abuse group she had promised Dr. Flowers she'd attend. She really didn't want to go. It sounded depressing to her, and she had told Jack she had a meeting to attend for the First Lady's commission. She wasn't sure he believed her, but he didn't challenge her for once, and he had plans of his own. He said he was meeting people for business after work.

But Maddy felt depressed again when she walked into the address where the abuse group was held. It was a ramshackle house, in a bad neighborhood, and she felt sure it would be full of dreary, whining women. She just wasn't in the mood to go. But she was surprised when she saw the women arrive, in jeans, and business suits, some young, some old, some pretty, and others plain and unattractive. It was a motley assortment, but most of them seemed to be intelligent and interesting, and some were very lively. And as the group leader came in and sat down, her eyes were warm as she looked at Maddy.

"We only use first names here," she explained. "And if we recognize each other, we don't discuss it. We don't greet each other if we meet on the street. We don't tell anyone who we saw, and what we heard. What we say here never leaves this room. It's important that we feel safe here." Maddy nodded, and believed her.

They sat down on threadbare chairs, and introduced themselves by their first names, and many of them seemed to know each other from previous visits to the group. There were twenty women usually, sometimes more, sometimes less, the leader explained. They met twice a week, and however often Maddy wanted to come was fine. It was an open enrollment. There was a coffeepot in the corner, and someone had brought cookies.

And one by one, they began to speak, and talk about

what they were doing, what was happening in their lives, what they worried about, or were pleased about, or what they were afraid of. Some were in terrifying situations, some had left husbands who had mistreated them, some were straight, some were gay, and some had children, but the common bond they all shared was that they had been tormented by abusers. Most of them seemed to have had abusive families as children, but some of them didn't. Some of them had had seemingly perfect lives, until they met the men and women who abused them. And as Maddy listened to them, she felt herself relax as she hadn't in years. What she was hearing was so familiar, so real, so much of what she knew that it was like taking off a suit of armor, and breathing fresh air. She felt as though she had come home, and these women were her sisters. And almost everything they described sounded like the relationship she had lived, not only with Bobby Joe, but with Jack in recent years. As she listened to them, it was like hearing her own voice, and her own story, and she knew with utter conviction that Jack had abused her since the day he met her. All the power, all the charm, all the threats, all the control, all the gifts, all the insults, all the humiliation and the pain, it was something they had all experienced. And he was such a classic portrait of an abuser that it embarrassed her that she hadn't understood it sooner. But even when Dr. Flowers had described it at the commission several months before, it hadn't been as clear to her as it was now. And suddenly she no longer felt shame over it, or embarrassment. She felt relief, and the only thing she had done wrong was accept all the blame he had heaped on her, and allowed herself to feel guilty for it.

She told them about her life with him, and the things he did and said to her, the words he used, the tone, the accusations, and his reaction to Lizzie, and they all nodded and sympathized, and pointed out to her that she had a choice. It was her responsibility what she did about it.

"I'm so scared," she whispered, as tears ran down her face, "what will happen to me if I leave him? . . . What if I can't make it without him?" But no one ridiculed her for the words, or told her she was stupid for what she was feeling. They had all been scared too, and some of them had good reason to be. One of the women's husbands was in prison for trying to kill her, and she was terrified of what would happen when he came out in a year or so. Many of them had been physically abused, as she had been by Bobby Joe. Some of them had walked out on whole lives, and nice homes, and two of them had even abandoned their children, but they had felt they had to save themselves before their husbands killed them. They knew it wasn't admirable, but they had fled, in whatever way they could. And others were still struggling to get out, and weren't even sure they could, like Maddy. But the one thing she knew after talking to them was that every hour, every day, every minute she stayed, she was in danger. Suddenly, she understood what Bill and Dr. Flowers and even Greg had been saying to her. Until then, she couldn't really hear it. But now, at last, she could.

"What do you think you're going to do now, Maddy?" one of the women asked her.

"I don't know," she said honestly, "I'm so scared, I'm afraid he'll see what's inside my head, or hear what I'm thinking."

"The only thing he's gonna hear clearly is you slamming the door in his face and running like hell. He won't hear nothing till you do that," a woman with no teeth and scraggly hair said. But in spite of the way she looked and the rough things she said, Maddy liked her. These women, she knew now, were what was going to save her. She had to save herself, she also knew, but she needed their help. And for whatever reason, she could hear them.

She felt like a new person as she left them, but they also warned her that it wouldn't happen by magic. No matter how good she felt from the common experience they shared, and the validation they gave her, she still had to do the work, and it wasn't going to be easy. She also knew that.

"Giving up abuse is like giving up drugs," one of the women told her bluntly. "It's the hardest thing you'll ever do, because it's familiar to you. You're used to it. You don't even know it's happening anymore. It's the only way you know or think someone loves you." Maddy had heard this before, but she still hated hearing it. She now realized it was true. She just didn't know what she was going to do about it, except come here.

"Don't expect too much of yourself at first," one of the others said to her, "but don't hang around for 'one last time,' one last round, one last shot at it . . . it may be your last one. Even the guys who don't lay a hand on you get crazy sometimes. He's a bad person, Maddy, a lot worse than you think, and he could kill you. He probably wants to, but doesn't have the balls. Get your ass out of there before he finds them. He doesn't love you. He doesn't care about you, not in any way you want . . . his love for you is hurting you. That's what he wants, and that's what he's gonna do. He ain't never gonna change. He'll just get worse. And the better you get, the worse he'll be. You're in a lot of danger."

She thanked them all when she left, and she drove home thoughtfully, mulling over everything they'd said. She didn't doubt any of it. She knew it was true. And she also knew that for some crazy reason, she wanted Jack to stop hurting her and to love her. She wanted to show him how, part of her even wanted to explain it all to him, so he could stop doing the things that hurt her. But she also knew now that he never would. He would just go on hurting her more and more. And even if she thought she loved him, she had to leave him. It was a matter of survival.

She called Bill from the car before she got home, and told him what it had been like. And he sounded relieved for her. He just prayed that they would give her the strength she needed, and she'd act on it.

And it was as though Jack sensed it when she got home. He looked at her strangely and asked her where she'd been, and she told him again it was a meeting relating to the commission. She even took a chance and told him it was a group for battered women they had wanted to check out, and it was very interesting, but just hearing about it made him angry.

"What a bunch of sick fucks that must have been. I can't believe they expect you to meet with people like that." She opened her mouth and started to defend them, and then she closed it. She knew now that even doing that, and tipping her hand to that extent, could put her in danger with him. And she was no longer willing to risk it. She had learned that much. "What are you looking so smug about?" he accused her, and she looked

as noncommittal and nonthreatening as she could, and
refused to let him make her feel anxious. She was prac-
ticing what they had taught her that night at the meeting.

"It was actually pretty boring," she said wisely, "but I
promised Phyllis I'd do it." He eyed her cautiously and
nodded. He seemed satisfied with her answer. For
once, it had been the right response.

And that night, for the first time in a while, he made
love to her, and he was rough with her again, as though
to remind her of his power. And no matter what she'd
heard, he was still in control and always would be. But
as she had before, she said nothing to him. She went to
her bathroom and showered afterward, but no amount
of water or soap seemed to wash the horror of him off
her. She went back to bed without a sound, and was relieved when she heard him snoring.

She got up early the next day, and she was in the
kitchen when he came downstairs, and everything
seemed the same as always between them. But she felt
like a prisoner now, chipping away at the walls, silently
digging a tunnel to safety, no matter how long it took.

"What's with you?" he snapped at her as she handed
him his coffee. "You've been acting strange." She
prayed he couldn't read her mind. She was almost sure
he could, but she wouldn't let herself believe it. But just
hearing him, she knew she was already becoming different, and that in itself put her at risk.

"I think I'm getting the flu or something."

"Take vitamin C. I don't want to have to get a stand-
in for you if you're sick. It's so goddamn much trouble."
He didn't even have to find the stand-in himself, but at
least he had bought her story about not feeling well.

But just listening to his tone, she was aware of how constantly rude to her he was these days.

"I'll be okay. I can go on anyway." He nodded, and picked up the paper, and Maddy stared blindly at *The Wall Street Journal*. All she could do now was pray that he didn't figure out what she was thinking. But with any luck at all, he wouldn't. She had to make a plan, she knew, and escape before he destroyed her. Because one thing she knew now for sure was that the hatred she had suspected he felt for her was real, and far worse than she had feared.

Chapter 19

DECEMBER WAS BUSY AS USUAL. Parties, meetings, plans for the holidays. Every embassy seemed to be giving a cocktail party, a dinner, or a dance, whenever possible including their national traditions. It was part of the fun of living in Washington, and Maddy had always enjoyed it. In the early days of their marriage, she had loved going to parties with Jack, but in the past months, as things became more and more strained in their relationship, she hated going out with him. He was always jealous of her, watched her with other men, and afterward accused her of some misdeed or inappropriate behavior. It was stressful going anywhere with him, and she was not looking forward to Christmas this year.

What she really wanted this year was to include Lizzie in her holidays, but with Jack forbidding her to have anything to do with the girl, Maddy knew that there was no way she could. Either she had to confront him and make a battle of it, or she had to give up the idea completely. There was no compromise with Jack. It was his way or no way. She was stunned to realize that she had never noticed that before, nor how he belittled her ideas and needs, and made her feel either foolish or guilty for them. It was something that, for years, she had readily accepted. She wasn't even sure now how the change had come, but in the past months, as she came to understand how truly disrespectful of her he was, she had a constant need to fight her increasing sense of oppression. But however much at odds she was with him, she knew in her heart of hearts that she still loved him. And that in itself was terrifying, because it left her vulnerable to him.

She couldn't wait, she knew now, for that love to stop. Love had nothing to do with it. Even loving and needing him in some ways, she knew that she had to walk away. Every day she stayed with him was dangerous for her. And she had to constantly remind herself of it. She was also aware that if she had tried to explain it to anyone, no one would have understood, except those who had gone through the same process. To anyone else, the conflicting emotions and guilt she had would seem utterly crazy. Even Bill, with all his concern for her, didn't really understand it. The only thing that helped him at all was the fact that he was learning a great deal on the commission about the subtle and not-so-subtle forms of violence against women. And it was hard, in the true sense of the word, to call what Jack did "violence," but it was the epitome of abusive behavior. Outwardly, he paid her well, had rescued her, provided her with security, a lovely home, a country house, a jet plane she could use anytime, beautiful clothes, gifts of jewelry and furs, vacations in the South of France. How could anyone in their right mind call him abusive? But Maddy and the people who saw the relationship under a finer microscope knew only too well what evil lurked there. All the cells of the disease were present, carefully concealed beneath the trappings. But hour by hour, day by day, minute by minute, Maddy could feel his poison devour her. She lived in constant fear.

And there were even times these days, when she felt that Bill was annoyed with her. She knew what he wanted from her, although she wasn't sure why, but he wanted her to get out and find her way to safety. And watching her stumble and fall, advance and retreat, see clearly and then let herself be consumed by guilt until it paralyzed and blinded her, was frustrating for him. They still spoke on the phone every day, and were cautious about how often they had lunch together. There was always the risk that someone would see her going to his house, and make an assumption that would be not only inaccurate but disastrous for her. They were always circumspect even when they were alone. The last thing Bill wanted to do was burden her with more problems. She had enough, he felt, without his adding to them.

The President was back in the Oval Office by then. He was working half days, and tiring easily, he said, but when Maddy saw him at a small tea they gave, she thought he was looking better and much stronger. Phyllis looked as though she'd been through the wars, but she beamed every time she looked at her husband. Maddy envied her that. She couldn't even imagine what it would feel like. She was so used to the tensions in her own relationship that it was hard to imagine living without them. She had come to take that kind of stress and pain for granted. And more than ever lately.

Jack was harsher with her than he'd ever been, quicker to jump down her throat over anything she said, and constantly accusatory about her behavior. It was as though, night and day, at work or at home, he was waiting to pounce on her, like a mountain lion poised to attack his prey, and she knew just how lethal he could be. The things he said were devastating. The way he said them even more so. And yet, there were still times when she found herself thinking how charming he was, how intelligent and how handsome. What she wanted to learn most of all was how to hate him, not just to fear him. She had far greater insight now, thanks to her abused women's group, into what motivated her, and what she was doing. And she knew now that in some subtle, unseen way, she was addicted to him.

She was talking about it to Bill one day, in mid-December. The network Christmas party was the next day, and she wasn't looking forward to it. Jack's latest battle call that she was flirting with Elliott on the air had escalated to his accusing her several times of sleeping with him. She was sure he knew that wasn't true, but he said it to upset her anyway. And he had even made a comment about it to their producer, which made her wonder now if Elliott's days on the show with her were numbered. She had thought about warning him, but when she said as much to Greg on the phone when he called, he told her not to. It would only make more trouble for her, which was probably exactly what Jack wanted.

"He's just trying to make you feel like hell, Mad," Greg said practically. He was happy in New York, and talking about marrying his new girlfriend, but she had suggested he give it more time. She didn't think much of marriage these days, or at least thought he should be cautious.

And as she sat in Bill's kitchen on a Thursday afternoon, she felt infinitely tired and disillusioned. She wasn't looking forward to Christmas this year, and she was trying to figure out how to get to Memphis to see Lizzie, or have her come to Washington, without Jack knowing. She had finally found a small apartment for her the previous weekend. It was cheerful and bright, and Maddy was in the process of having it repainted. She had made the deposit with a cashier's check, and she was confident that she could pay the rent, without Jack ever finding out about it.

"I hate lying to him," Maddy said quietly over lunch with Bill. He had bought some caviar for them, and they were enjoying one of their rare, comfortable moments together. "But it's the only way I can do what I want and need. He's so unreasonable about Lizzie, and forbade me to see her." What wasn't he unreasonable about, Bill thought, but for once he didn't say anything to her. He was less talkative than usual, and she wondered if something was bothering him. She knew the holidays were hard for him. And Margaret's birthday was that week, which was painful too. "Are you okay?" she asked, as she handed him a piece of toast with caviar, squeezed some lemon on it, and he took it from her.

"I don't know. This time of year always makes me nostalgic. Particularly this year. It's hard not to look back sometimes, instead of forward." But Maddy thought he'd been better lately. He still talked about his wife a great deal, but he seemed to be torturing himself less over what had happened. He and Maddy had talked about it often, and she kept urging him to forgive himself, but it was easier said than done. She had the impression that when he wrote the book, he had worked his way through it. But the sorrow of her loss still weighed on him.

"The holidays are tough," Maddy conceded. "At least

you'll be with your kids." They were going to Vermont again, and she and Jack were going to Virginia, which she knew would be a lot less fun than what he was doing. Bill and his children were planning an old-fashioned Christmas. Jack hated holidays, and other than a few expensive gifts for her, made as little fuss about them as possible. He had been disappointed each year on Christmas as a child, and as an adult, refused to pay homage to it.

Bill surprised her by what he said next. "I wish I could spend Christmas with you, Maddy." He smiled sadly at her as he said it. It was an impossible dream, but a sweet thought. "My children would love to have you with us."

"So would Lizzie," she said, sounding resigned. She had already picked out wonderful Christmas gifts for her, and she had bought a few small things for Bill. She kept finding silly little gifts that reminded her of him, CDs, a warm scarf that looked just like him, and a set of old books that she hoped he would love. Nothing important and expensive, but all very personal, as tokens of the friendship they both cherished. She was saving them for the day before he left for Vermont, and was hoping to have lunch with him one last time before they both left town and went their separate ways until after New Year.

She smiled up at him then, as they ate the last of the caviar. He had bought pâté, and cheese and French bread, and a bottle of red wine. It was a very elegant picnic he had provided for her, a safe haven from the tensions of the world she lived in. "Sometimes I wonder why you put up with me. All I do is moan and whine about Jack, and I know that to you, it must look like I'm not doing anything about it. It must be hard to sit by and watch sometimes. How do you stand me?"

"That's an easy one to answer," he smiled back at her. And took her breath away by what he said next, without pretense or hesitation. "I love you." There was an instant's pause as she absorbed it, and realized what he meant. He meant it in the same way she would have said it to Lizzie, as protector and friend, not as a woman would say to a man, or vice versa. At least that was how she understood it.

"I love you too, Bill," she said softly. "You're my best friend in the world." What they shared had even surpassed what she'd shared with Greg, who seemed to have moved on to his own life. "You're like my family, almost like a big brother."

But having said it, he was not going to back down. He stood very close to her, and put a hand on her shoulder. "That's not how I meant it, Maddy," he said clearly. "I mean it in a deeper sense, as a man. I love you," he repeated, and she stared at him, not sure how to answer. He understood that too, and tried to put her at ease. But he was glad he had finally said it to her. It had been a long time coming. Six months of great intimacy, in all the ways that mattered. He was part of her daily life now, and only wished he could be more so. "You don't have to answer if you don't want to. I don't expect anything from you. I think I've been waiting for the last six months for you to change your life, and do something about Jack. But I understand how hard that is for you. I'm not even sure you ever will. I think I accept that. But I don't want to wait until you do, or if you do, to tell you that I love you. Life is short, and love is very special." She was bowled over by what he was saying to her.

"You're very special too," she said softly and leaned toward him to kiss him on the cheek, but he turned slightly, and she wasn't sure how it happened, if she had done it, or he, but the next thing she knew she was kissing him, and he her, profoundly from their hearts and with considerable passion. And when they stopped, she looked at him with amazement. "How did that happen?"

"I think it was a long time coming," he said, putting his arms around her, and worrying that he might have upset her. "Are you okay?" He looked down at her, and she nodded and leaned her head against him. He was considerably taller than she was, and she felt safe and happy in his arms, in a way she knew she had never known before. This was something completely different, and in its newness, it was both wonderful and scary.

"I think I am," she said, looking up at him and trying to sort out her feelings. And then he kissed her again, and she did nothing to resist. On the contrary, she realized now that it was all she wanted. But it made what Jack had said about her true. She had never cheated on him, never looked at another man before, and she realized now that she was in love with Bill, and she had no idea what to do about it.

They sat down at the kitchen table, holding hands, and looked at each other. It was suddenly a whole new world between them. He had thrown open a door that they had both been standing near, and Maddy had never realized how grandiose the vista would be once he did it. "This is quite a Christmas gift," she said with a shy smile, and he smiled broadly.

"Yes, it is, Maddy, isn't it? But I don't want you to feel pressured. I didn't plan this. I didn't expect it any more than you did. And I don't want you to feel guilty about it." He knew her well now. There were times when just breathing made her feel guilty, and this was a lot more than breathing. This was living.

"How am I supposed to feel? I'm married, Bill. I'm doing everything he accuses me of, and none of it was ever true before. Now it is . . . or it could be . . ."

"That depends how we handle it, and I suggest we move *very* slowly." Although he knew now that he would have liked to move a great deal more quickly. But out of respect for her, he knew he couldn't. "I want to make you happy, not screw up your life." But it certainly complicated it. And it forced her to look at her relationship with Jack in a way she had been avoiding. She had been catapulted into an entirely different situation with their first kiss.

"What am I going to do?" she asked Bill, but she was asking herself the same question. She was married to a man who treated her abominably. But in spite of that, she had a sense of loyalty to him, or at least that was what she called it.

"You're going to do what's right for you. I'm a big boy. I can deal with it. But whatever you decide about me, or about us, you still have to do something about Jack. You can't hide from that forever, Maddy." He was hoping that his love, and her knowing it now, would give her the strength she needed to escape him. In a sense, although she didn't want to think about it that way, he was her passport to freedom. But she was determined not to use him. She sensed that, if she wanted it to be, he could be her future. Bill Alexander was not a man to take lightly.

They chatted over lunch after that, eating cheese and drinking wine, and he made her laugh a little bit about their situation. He told her that, although he didn't recognize it at first, he had fallen in love with her right from the beginning.

"I think I did too," she admitted to him, "but I was afraid to face it. It seemed like the wrong thing to do, because of Jack." And it still was, but it was stronger than she now, or either of them. "Jack will never forgive me for this, you know," she said unhappily. "He'll never believe this hasn't been going on all along. He'll tell everyone in the world that I've been cheating on him."

"He might have done that anyway, if you leave him." And Bill prayed now more than ever that she would, for both their sakes. He felt as though an exquisite butterfly had landed on his hand, and he was afraid to touch or catch it. He just wanted to admire it and love it. "I think he's going to say some pretty ugly things, when you get free of him, regardless of me. He's not going to thank you for it, Maddy." It was the first time he had said "when" instead of "if," and they both heard it. "The truth is, he needs you, more than you need him. You needed him to fulfill your fantasies about safety and marriage. But he needs you to feed his sickness, to satisfy his bloodlust, if you will. An abuser *needs* a victim." She didn't answer him as she thought about it, and then silently she nodded.

It was after three o'clock when she left him, reluctantly. She wanted to stay with him, and they kissed for a long time before she left. There was a new dimension to their relationship now, a door that had been opened and could not be closed again, nor did either of them want to.

"Take care of yourself," he whispered to her. "Be careful."

"I will." And then she smiled at him as he held her. "I

love you . . . and thank you for the caviar . . . and the kisses. . . ."

"Anytime," he smiled back at her, and he stood in the doorway and waved, as she drove away. They both had a lot to think about. Particularly Maddy.

She was instantly nervous when her secretary told her Jack had called her twice in the last hour. She sat down at her desk, took a breath, and called his intercom number, terrified suddenly that someone might have seen her leaving Bill's house. And her hands were shaking when he answered.

"Where the hell have you been?"

"Christmas shopping," she said quickly. The lie had come to her so easily that she was startled at her own willingness to deceive him. But she certainly couldn't tell him where she had been, or what she'd been doing. Although she'd thought about it on the way back, wondering if the right thing to do was to tell him the truth, that she was desperately unhappy with him, and in love with someone else. But she knew that it would be an invitation to him to abuse her. Unless she could leave immediately. And she knew she wasn't ready. In this case, honesty was not necessarily the right answer or at least not yet.

"I was calling you to tell you that I have to meet with President Armstrong tonight." Hearing that surprised her. The President didn't seem well enough to her yet to be having evening meetings, but she didn't question him about it. It was easier not to. And she decided instantly that her suspicions about him were probably based on her own bad behavior. She hated to think about it that way. But she knew that whatever her feelings for him, what was happening with Bill was not the right thing for a married woman to be doing, however damaged and flawed the marriage happened to be.

"That's okay," she said in answer to his plans. "I need to pick some things up on my way home." She wanted to buy some wrapping paper, and a few little gifts for her secretary and researcher, to give them at the Christmas party, more like stocking stuffers. She had already bought them both Cartier watches. "Do you need anything?" she asked, trying to be nice to him, to make up for her transgressions.

"What are you in such a good mood about?" he asked suspiciously, and she put it down to Christmas. He told her not to wait up for him, that it could be a long meeting, which made her even more doubtful about what he was doing. But she said nothing to him.

She did both her broadcasts that night feeling as though she were walking on air, and she called Bill twice, both before and after.

"You make me very happy." And very scared, she wanted to add, but didn't. They didn't talk about what they were going to do, but savored the sweetness of it. She told him she was going to a nearby mall after work, to buy some things. And he told her he'd call her when she got home, since Jack was going to be out. And he didn't believe her husband was meeting with the President either. Phyllis had told them both, at the commission a few days before, that Jim was exhausted by late afternoon, and asleep by seven every night.

"Maybe Jack is sleeping with him," Maddy teased, in unexpectedly good spirits.

"That would be a new twist." Bill laughed at the suggestion, and they promised to talk later.

Maddy left work in one of the network cars, since Jack had their usual car and driver. She was happier being alone just now anyway. It gave her time to think and dream about Bill. She parked at the mall, and went into a large drugstore to buy ribbon, tape, and wrapping paper, so she could wrap her presents.

The store was full to the rafters with Christmas shoppers, women with crying kids, men looking confused at what they were supposed to buy, and the usual shoppers who filled the mall during the nights before the holidays. Not surprisingly, it was busier than ever. And the toy store next door had a Santa Claus who had people lined up all the way into the parking lot to see him. It put Maddy in a good mood just seeing all of it. It felt like the spirit of Christmas, and suddenly, thanks to Bill, she was beginning to enjoy it.

She had a dozen rolls of red wrapping paper in her arms, and a cart full of perfume and tape and chocolate Santa Clauses and small Christmas ornaments, when she heard a strange sound from somewhere above her. It was so loud that it startled her at first, and she saw others stop and look, not able to understand it either. It was a loud *boom!* and then a sound like a waterfall, like a wall of rushing water. She couldn't hear anyone. The music stopped, and suddenly there were screams as the entire mall went dark, and before she had time to panic or even open her mouth, she saw the entire ceiling cave in just beyond her. And as it did, Maddy's entire world suddenly vanished into blackness, and everything around her disappeared.

Chapter 20

WHEN MADDY WOKE UP, SHE felt as though there were an entire building lying on her chest. She opened her eyes and was aware that they hurt and were filled with dirt, but she couldn't see anything, and there was a strange smell of dust and fire all around her. She was aware that she was warm, and every part of her body felt very heavy. And then she realized that something had fallen on her. She tried to move, and at first, she thought she couldn't. She could move her feet, but there was something holding her legs down, and her entire upper body was pinned down, but little by little, as she struggled to get free, she found she could move the various weights that had fallen on her. She didn't realize it, but it took her more than an hour to free herself until she could sit in a little ball in the small space she was confined to. And what she noticed as she worked on it, at first, was that all around her was silence. And then, after a while, she began hearing moans and screams, and people calling to each other in the distance. And as she sat up, she was sure she could hear a baby crying somewhere. She had no idea what had happened or exactly where she was.

And in the parking lot, far from where she lay, cars had been blown up. The front of several buildings had been blown away. There were fire trucks everywhere, and people were running and shouting. People bleeding from everywhere were running into the parking lot, and injured children were being put on gurneys and rushed into ambulances. It looked almost like a movie set, and the people who were talking to the police and firemen in a daze said that the whole building had collapsed in a single instant. In fact, four of the stores in the mall had been destroyed, and there was a huge crater outside the drugstore where Maddy was. The crater stood now like a yawning hole where only instants before a truck had been. There had been an explosion of such magnitude that windows in buildings as much as five blocks away had shattered. And as the news crews arrived, the Santa Claus from the toy store was carried out with a tarp over him. He had been killed instantly, along with more than half of the children who had been waiting to see him. It was a tragedy of such huge proportions that no one could quite absorb it.

And deep inside the store where Maddy sat curled in a little ball, she was trying to figure out how to get out from under the rubble that held her prisoner. She tried clawing at it, pushing it away, bracing herself against it, but at first nothing moved, and with a sense of total panic she was having trouble breathing. And then, in the darkness, she heard a voice very near her.

"Help . . . help . . . can anyone hear me?" The voice

sounded weak, but it was comforting to know that someone was close by, as Maddy listened.

"I can. Where are you?" There was so much dust that Maddy could hardly take a breath. But she turned in the direction of the voice, as she listened carefully in the darkness.

"I don't know. I can't see," the voice answered. They were all enveloped in total blackness.

"Do you know what happened?"

"I think the building fell on us . . . I hit my head . . . I think it's bleeding. . . ." It was a woman's voice, and Maddy thought she could hear the baby again. But she couldn't hear much else. An occasional voice . . . a scream . . . she was listening for sirens, hoping for help, but she couldn't hear them. There was too much concrete blocking them to allow any of them to hear the chaos outside or the rescue vehicles that were shrieking toward them from all over the city. Calls had even gone out to Virginia and Maryland. No one knew anything yet except that there had been a huge explosion and a lot of people injured and killed.

"Is that your baby?" Maddy asked, as she heard it crying again.

"Yes . . ." the voice said weakly. "He's two months old. His name is Andy." The girl sounded as though she were crying. And Maddy would have been too, except she was still too much in shock to feel her own emotions.

"Is he hurt?"

"I don't know . . . I can't see him." She sobbed then, and Maddy closed her eyes for a minute, trying to think straight. Something terrible must have happened to bring the whole building down on them, but she couldn't figure out what yet.

"Can you move?" Maddy inquired. Talking to the girl was helping her keep her own sanity, as she tried to push various places again, and what felt like a boulder behind her moved a little, though barely more than a few inches. It was in the opposite direction from where the voice was coming.

"I can't move at all," the voice answered, "there's something on my legs and my arms . . . and I can't reach my baby."

"They're going to send us help, you know." And as Maddy said it, they were both aware of the sound of muffled voices in the distance, but there was no way to know if they were rescuers or victims. And then, as Maddy tried to think of what to do, she remembered that her cell phone was in her handbag. If she could find it, she could call for help, or maybe they would find her more easily. It was a crazy idea, but it gave her something to do, as she groped the area immediately around her and found nothing except dirt and rocks and jagged pieces of broken concrete. But she had a better sense of the small area surrounding her, as she did it. And she tried again to move the walls of her makeshift cell, and at one end, she was able to move some boards about a foot from her and enlarge her airspace. "I'm trying to get to you," she told the girl encouragingly, and for a long moment, there was silence; and it scared her. "Are you okay? . . . Can you hear me?" There was a long pause, and then the voice again.

"I think I was sleeping."

"Don't sleep. Try to stay awake," Maddy said firmly, still trying to think, but nothing would come. She was still in shock herself, and she was aware, as she moved, of a blinding headache. "Talk to me . . . what's your name?"

"Anne."

"Hi, Anne. My name is Maddy. How old are you?"

"Sixteen."

"I'm thirty-four. I'm a reporter . . . on TV. . . ." But there was no answer again. "Wake up, Anne . . . how's Andy doing?"

"I don't know." He was whimpering so Maddy knew he was alive, but the girl sounded weaker. God only knew how badly injured she was, or when anyone would find them.

And as Maddy continued to struggle within her cave, outside fire trucks continued to arrive from every district. Two of the stores were in flames, four had collapsed, and dismembered bodies were being removed from the areas closest to the center of the explosion, some of them far beyond recognition. There were hands and feet and arms and heads everywhere. Everyone ambulatory was being removed, and ambulances were taking away those who couldn't move under their own steam. They were trying to clear the area for rescue workers and volunteers. The Center for Disaster Control and National Emergencies had been called and they were organizing teams as bulldozers began to arrive. But the balance of the remaining structures was too delicate to use them, and there were too many victims to jeopardize by using machinery that might ultimately create a bigger problem.

There were scores of news crews on the scene, and broadcasts all over the country had been interrupted to bring viewers the news that the biggest disaster in the nation's history, since the bombing in Oklahoma City in '95, had occurred in Washington. There were already over a hundred known casualties and no way to assess how many more there would be, and a screaming child with her arm blown off had already been filmed by every camera crew on the scene as she was rushed away by rescue workers. Her identity was unknown and no one had claimed her yet. But there were dozens of others like her. Hurt, dazed, injured, maimed, dead, and dying, being brought out of the wreckage.

Bill had been watching television peacefully in his den, when the first bulletin flashed across the screen, and he sat up with a look of horror. Maddy had told him she was going there after work, and he instantly ran to the phone and called her. There was no answer. He called her cell phone next and a recording told him the subscriber he had called was out of range, and as he continued to watch the news, he felt a wave of rising panic. He almost called the network to find out if they knew where she was, but he didn't dare. There was always the possibility that she was on the scene, covering it herself, but he decided to wait to see if she called him. He knew she would if she had time, and if she wasn't trapped somewhere beneath the rubble. All he could do now was pray she wasn't. And all he could think of was the moment when he had first realized that Margaret had been kidnapped by masked men carrying machine guns.

Jack was aware of the situation too. His cell phone rang within instants of the blast, and he looked at the woman he was with, with dismay. This was not the evening he had planned. He had set it up so carefully, as he always did, and he was irritated by the interruption.

"Find Maddy and tell her to get her ass over there. She should be home by now," he directed, and then hung up. They already had two crews on the scene, and a third one was on its way, the producer had said. And the pretty blonde he was with at the Ritz Carlton asked him what had happened.

"Some asshole blew up a shopping mall," he said, and flipped on the TV. And they both sat and stared at what they saw. It was a scene of total destruction and utter chaos. "Jesus," he whistled through his teeth. Neither of them had realized the magnitude of the disaster until they saw it. They sat there silently for a while, and then he picked up his cell phone and called the network. "Did you find her?" he barked into the phone. It was a hell of a story, but even to a practiced eye like his, there were moments of what they were shooting that brought tears to his eyes. And next to him the girl he had only met the week before was crying softly. A fireman had just carried away a dead baby and its mother.

"We're trying, Jack," the frazzled producer said. "She's not home yet, and her cell phone is off."

"Goddammit, I told her never to do that. Keep trying. She'll turn up." And then as he snapped his phone shut, a strange thought wandered across his mind, but he rejected it instantly. She had said she was going to buy wrapping paper and some things, but she usually hated malls and shopped in Georgetown. There was no reason on earth why she would be there.

"Can you hear me, Anne?" Maddy's voice penetrated through the concrete again, but it took her longer to rouse the other voice this time.

"Yes . . . I can . . ." and as she answered, they heard another voice. A man's this time, and he sounded surprisingly close to Maddy.

"Who is that?" the voice asked. He sounded strong and loud, and he said he had dislodged some rocks and a beam and crawled a long way to get to them, but he had no idea which way he was going, or where he was.

"My name is Maddy," she answered firmly, "and there's a girl here called Anne . . . she's not with me, but I can hear her. I think she's hurt and she has a baby."

"How about you? Are you okay?" She had a headache, but it wasn't worth reporting to him.

"I'm fine. Can you move any of this stuff around me?"

"Keep talking, and I'll try." She hoped he was big and strong. Strong enough to move mountains if he had to.

"What's your name?"

"Mike. And don't worry, lady. I bench-press five hundred pounds. I'll get you out of there in no time." But she could hear him struggling as he continued to talk to her, and Anne dropped out of the conversation again, as Maddy called out to her, but the baby was crying louder than ever.

"Talk to your baby, Anne. If he hears you, he might not be so scared."

"I'm too tired," Anne said weakly, as Maddy continued to talk to Mike, and he sounded a few inches closer.

"Do you know what happened?" Maddy asked him.

"Damned if I know. I was buying shaving cream and the goddamn roof fell on top of me. I was going to bring my kids. I'm glad I didn't. Was anyone with you?"

"No, I was alone," Maddy answered, while she tried clawing at the rocks and dirt again, but all she did was break her nails and hurt her fingers. Nothing was moving.

"I'm going to try and dig in the other direction," he finally said, as Maddy felt a wave of panic wash over her. The thought of the friendly voice leaving her aroused a sense of abandonment in her like no other she had ever known. But they had to get help, and if one of them could get to it, the others would be saved too.

"Okay," she said. "Good luck. When you get out," she made a point of saying "when" and not "if," "I'm a reporter, tell my network I'm here. I have a feeling they're out there somewhere."

"I'll come back for you," he said clearly. And a few minutes later, his voice disappeared again, and no others came. She was left alone in the darkness with her solitude, Anne, and her crying baby. And she kept wishing for her cell phone, not that it would have made much difference. She couldn't even have told them where they were, only where they had started. But for all she knew, they had been thrown a long way. There was nothing to identify where they were trapped now.

And as Bill continued to watch the news, he felt a rising sense of panic. He had called her a dozen times, and only got her answering machine. And her cell phone was still off. Finally in desperation, he called the network.

"Who is this?" the producer asked irritably, surprised the caller had even gotten through.

"I'm a friend of hers, and I was just concerned. Is she covering the story?"

There was a pause and then the producer decided to answer him honestly. "We can't find her either. Her cell phone's off, and she's not home. She could have gone to the scene independently, but no one's seen her. But there are a hell of a lot of people there. She'll turn up eventually. She always does," Rafe Thompson, the producer, reassured him.

"It's not like her to disappear," Bill pointed out to the producer in a worried tone, and Rafe couldn't help wondering how the man on the phone knew that, but he was obviously worried. A lot more than Jack was. All Jack had done was yell at them to goddamn fucking find her. And the producer had a fairly good idea of what Jack had been doing when he found him. A giggling female voice had been laughing in the background when Jack answered the first time.

"I don't know what to tell you. She'll probably call in pretty soon. She might be at a movie or something." But Bill knew she wasn't, and the fact that she hadn't called him to tell him she was okay was making him panic. He wandered around his living room for another ten minutes after that, keeping an eye on the TV, and finally he couldn't stand it. He picked up his coat and his car keys, and hurried outside. He didn't even know if he could get near the scene, but he had to try. He didn't know why, but he knew he had to be there. Maybe he could find her.

It was after ten o'clock as Bill sped the entire way, an hour and a half after the blast that had destroyed two city blocks, killed a hundred and three at last count, and injured dozens of others. And this was just the beginning.

When he got there, it took him twenty minutes to pick his way past the emergency vehicles and debris, and there were so many volunteers on hand to help that no one asked him for passes, badges, or ID, they just let him through, and he stood outside the toy store with tears in his eyes, praying he would find her in the crowd outside.

And within minutes, someone handed him a hard hat, and asked him to help carry debris from inside. He followed them in, and it was so terrifying just being there that all he could hope was that Maddy was anywhere but there, and had just forgotten to turn on her cell phone.

And inside her cave, Maddy was thinking of him, as she braced her full weight against a piece of concrete, and was stunned when she moved it. She tried again, and it moved another few inches, and every time it did, Anne's ever-weakening voice seemed to grow closer.

"I think I'm getting somewhere," she said to Anne, "keep talking to me. I need to know where you are. I don't want to make things worse . . . can you feel anything? Is there dirt falling on you anywhere?" She wasn't sure if she was near her head or her feet, but the last thing she wanted to do was drop a piece of concrete on her or her baby. But it was almost as much work moving the concrete as it was to keep Anne talking.

Maddy was even talking to herself now as she pushed and shoved and clawed, and she gave a shove so mighty that she nearly hurt herself, and much to her amazement, as she did, a huge chunk of concrete gave way, and she was able to move it aside, and create a hole big enough to accommodate her upper body, and she started to crawl through it. And as soon as she did, she knew she had found Anne. Her voice was so close to her, and the first thing she touched was Andy. He was lying near his mother's hand, just out of reach, and squirming freely. Maddy couldn't see him, but she could feel him and she pulled him to her. And he howled in terror as she did. She had no idea if he was hurt or not, but she set him down again, and crawled through the hole toward Anne. But for a moment, the girl said nothing, and then Maddy touched her. She wasn't even sure if she was still breathing.

"Anne . . . Anne . . ." She gently touched her face, and as she let her hands rove over her cautiously, she thought she knew what had happened. There was a huge beam across the girl's upper body, crushing her, and Maddy could feel from the dampness of her clothes that she was bleeding. And another beam lay across her legs. She was completely pinned down, and although Maddy tried frantically, she could do nothing to free her. The beams were heavier than the concrete, and what she didn't know was that there was more concrete pinning the beams down. "Anne! . . . Anne! . . ." She kept saying her name, as the baby whimpered next to them, and then finally the girl stirred and spoke to Maddy.

"Where are you?" She didn't understand what had happened.

"I'm here. I'm with you. Andy's fine, I think." Relative to his mother at least.

"Did they find us?" Anne was starting to drift off again, and Maddy was afraid to shake her, given the damage she realized Anne had sustained when the beams fell on her.

"Not yet. But they're going to. I promise. Hang on." Maddy picked up the baby then, and held him close to her as she crouched next to Anne, and then trying to keep the girl from giving up, she put his face next to Anne's, as they must have done when he was born, and Anne began to cry softly.

"I'm going to die, aren't I?" There was no honest answer to that question, and they both knew it. She was
no longer sixteen. She had grown to full maturity in a
matter of instants, and she might as well have been a
hundred just then.

"I don't think so," Maddy lied. "You can't. You have
to stick around for Andy."

"He doesn't have a daddy," she volunteered. "He
gave him up when he was born. He didn't want him."

"My baby didn't have a daddy either," Maddy said,
trying to reassure her. At least she was talking, which
was something. Lizzie hadn't had a mommy either,
Maddy thought with fresh guilt, but she didn't say anything to Anne.

"Do you live with your mom and dad?" Maddy
asked, still trying to keep her talking, as she cradled the
baby close to her, and noticed that he had stopped crying. She put a finger under his nose, and was relieved to
find he was still breathing. He was asleep.

"I ran away when I was fourteen. I'm from
Oklahoma. I called my mom and dad when he was
born, and they don't want either of us. They got nine
other kids, and my mom said all I am is trouble. . . .
Andy and I are on welfare." It was a tragedy, but nothing so dire as what was happening to them now. Maddy
couldn't help wondering if either of them would survive
it, or she would. She wondered now if they would be
found long after they had died, part of a larger, still
more hideous story. But she was determined not to let
that happen, for their sakes. This baby had a right to
live, and so did the child who was his mother. Saving
them was her only goal.

"When he grows up, you can tell him about this. He'll think you were wonderful and brave, and you are . . . I'm very proud of you," she said, choking back tears, thinking of Lizzie. They had found each other after nineteen years, and now Lizzie might lose her again. But she couldn't let herself think of it. She had to keep her head clear, and she noticed as she talked to Anne that she was feeling dizzy. She wondered when they would run out of air. If they would be gasping, or just drift off to sleep, snuffed out like candles. She started humming to herself, and crooning softly to Anne and the baby, but Anne had stopped talking again, and nothing Maddy did seemed to wake her. When Maddy touched her, she moaned, so she knew Anne was still alive, but she seemed to be fading fast.

And outside the toy store, Bill had finally found her crew from the network. He identified himself and found he was talking to the producer he had talked to earlier on the phone. He was on the scene now, directing camera crews and reporters.

"I think she's in there," Bill said grimly. "She told me she was going to buy wrapping paper, and she was going to come here to buy it."

"I was having a weird feeling about that," Rafe Thompson admitted to him, "and I figured I was crazy. Not that it makes any difference. They're doing their best to pull people out." He was wondering how Bill knew her, and then he said they were on the First Lady's commission together. Rafe thought he seemed like a nice guy. He had spent hours helping them rescue people. His coat was torn, his face was filthy by then, and his hands were bleeding. And everyone was looking stressed and exhausted. It was after midnight, and

Maddy hadn't turned up yet. Rafe had talked to Jack several times, who was still screaming at them from the Ritz Carlton. He had been less than sympathetic about Maddy's disappearance, and said she was probably "fucking around somewhere" and he was going to kill her when he found her. Rafe and Bill were far more concerned that the people who had set the bomb had already done that. And so far, no one had taken responsibility for it.

They didn't even mention on the air that Maddy might be trapped in the bombed-out mall. They had no way of knowing if she was, and there was no point reporting it till they knew something. But by four in the morning, the rescue workers were beginning to make serious progress. It had been almost eight hours of tireless work, and it was nearly five when a man called Mike was rescued. He seemed to be bleeding from everywhere, but he had dug around in the debris endlessly, and created tunnels and caves by moving concrete and beams, and had rescued four people with his efforts. And as he came out, he explained to the men who rescued him that there had been two more women he'd found but couldn't get to. Their names were Maddy and Anne, and one of them had a baby. And he did the best he could to give the rescuers a sense of direction, as he was put in an ambulance and taken away. Rafe heard about it moments later and came to tell Bill, while the workers went back inside to follow Mike's vague directions.

"She's in there," Rafe came to tell Bill grimly.

"Oh my God . . . did they find her?" He was afraid to ask if she was dead or alive, and Rafe didn't look reassuring.

"Not yet. One of the men they just brought out said there were two women he couldn't reach . . . one of them is Maddy. She told him she was a reporter on TV and what network she works for." It was the worst of their fears confirmed, and all they could do was wait. It was another two hours of watching bodies pulled out, survivors carried away with missing limbs, and watching dead children brought back to be identified by sobbing parents. By seven, Bill just stood there and cried. It was impossible to believe she was still alive. It had been nearly eleven hours. And he wondered if he should try to call Lizzie, but he had nothing to tell her. By then, the whole country knew of the tragedy. It was the work of madmen.

Bill and Rafe were sitting on some of the sound equipment when a fresh team went in, and a Red Cross worker offered them both Styrofoam cups of coffee. Rafe took one gratefully but Bill just couldn't.

Rafe had asked Bill no further questions about his relationship to Maddy, but as the night wore on, it was obvious that he cared a lot about her, and Rafe felt sorry for him.

"Hang in there. They'll find her eventually." The question that still pounded through both their minds was if she'd be alive when they did.

And as they waited for the rescue teams, Maddy was crouched in a ball, clutching the baby, but Anne hadn't spoken to her in hours. She didn't know if she was sleeping or dead, but none of her efforts to make her talk to her had been fruitful in a long time. Maddy had no idea what time it was, or how long they had been there, and then finally, when the baby stirred and started to cry again, his mother heard him.

"Tell him I love him . . . ," Anne whispered, and startled Maddy. The voice next to her sounded ghostly.

"You have to stick around and tell him that yourself," Maddy said, trying to sound optimistic. But she wasn't anymore. She was short of air, and drifting in and out of consciousness herself as she held the baby.

"I want you to take care of him for me," Anne said, and then grew quiet again. And then after a while, "I love you, Maddy. Thank you for being here with me. I would have been really scared without you." Maddy was scared herself, even with Anne and the baby, but tears rolled down her cheeks as she leaned over and kissed the injured girl on the cheek, thinking of Lizzie.

"I love you too, Annie. . . . I love you a lot . . . now you have to get well. We'll be out of here soon. And I want you to meet my daughter." Anne nodded, as though she believed her, and then smiled in the darkness, and Maddy could sense it if not see it.

"My mom used to call me Annie. She still loved me then," Anne said sadly.

"I'll bet she still loves you now. And she's going to love Andy when she sees him."

"I don't want her to have him," she said, sounding stronger and very determined. "I want you to take care of my baby. Promise you'll love him." Maddy had to gulp back sobs as she answered, and she knew that neither of them could afford the air or the energy it would cost them. And just as she was about to say something to her, she heard voices in the distance, strong ones, loud ones, and as she listened, she realized they were calling her name.

"Can you hear us, Maddy? Maddy? . . . Maddy Hunter . . . and Anne . . . can you hear us? . . ." She wanted to scream with excitement as she listened and called to them as loudly as she could.

"We hear you! WE HEAR YOU!!! We're here . . ." The voices came closer as she spoke rapidly to Annie. "They're coming to get us now, Annie . . . hang on . . . we'll be out of here in a few minutes." But in spite of the noise Maddy made, Annie had drifted off to sleep again, and because of it, the baby started crying loudly. He was tired and hungry and frightened. But so was Maddy.

The voices continued to approach until they sounded only inches away, and she identified herself to them. She described the cave they were in, as best she could, and Annie's circumstances, without terrifying her completely, and she said she was okay and holding the baby.

"Is the baby hurt?" another voice asked, wanting to know what kind of rescue team they needed.

"I don't know. I don't think so. And I'm not either," except for a ferocious bump on the head and a whopping headache. The baby's mother was another story.

But even once they knew where they were, it took them another hour and a half to free them. They had to move the dirt away inch by inch, and the concrete just as slowly. They were afraid that the whole structure would collapse on them if they moved too quickly, and Maddy gave a scream of relief and pain when they shone a powerful beam into her eyes through a hole the size of a saucer. She couldn't stop herself from sobbing and she told Annie what was happening, but she didn't answer.

The hole grew bigger as Maddy watched and they talked to her, and five minutes later, she passed Andy through it, and she saw how filthy he was when they

shone the flashlight on him. There was dried blood on
his face from a small cut on his cheek, but other than
that, his eyes were wide and he looked beautiful to
Maddy. She kissed him as she handed him through and
a pair of powerful male hands took him and vanished.
But there were four others left to work on freeing her
and Annie, and in another half hour they had made a
space big enough for Maddy to crawl through, and she
turned before she left and touched Annie's hand. The
girl was silent and sleeping, which was merciful. It was
going to be ugly work to free her, and Maddy slid past
the men at the entrance to the hole they'd made, and
two of them moved in to work on Annie, as one of the
men led Maddy back through the crawl space they'd
made, and she crawled on her hands and knees back to
the entrance. From there, powerful hands lifted her up
and she was carried over concrete and debris and steel
pilings that were twisted everywhere like an evil forest,
and before she knew it, she was in bright daylight.

It was ten o'clock in the morning, almost fourteen
hours after the mall had collapsed and she had been
trapped there. She tried to ask someone if the baby was
okay, but there was so much chaos around her that no
one seemed to hear her. Others were still being pulled
out, and there were bodies under tarps, crying people
waiting for news of their families, rescue workers shouting to each other, and suddenly in the midst of it all, she
saw him standing there, waiting for her. It was Bill, and
he was almost as filthy as she was, from his efforts to
help the others. But as he saw her, he was wracked by
sobs, and grabbed her from the man who was holding
her. All he could do was cling to her and cry, as she did.
There were no words to tell her what he had felt, how

vast his fears had been, how terrible her terrors. It
would take years to explain it to each other, and all they
had now was the single instant of love and relief of this
unforgettable moment.

"Thank God," he whispered as she clung to him, and
he handed her gingerly to a team of paramedics. But
she appeared miraculously undamaged, and then forgetting Bill for an instant, but still holding tightly to his
hand, she turned to one of the rescue workers.

"Where's Annie? Is she okay?"

"They're working on it," he said, looking grim. He
had seen too much that night, as they all had. But each
survivor was a victory. Each one saved a gift they had all
prayed for.

"Tell her I love her," Maddy said fervently, and then
turned back to Bill, her eyes filled with everything they
felt for each other. And for one terrible instant, she
wondered if this was her punishment for falling in love
with him, if she had no right to this. But she pushed the
thought away as though it had been a boulder trying to
crush her, and she wouldn't let it, as she hadn't let the
walls of their tiny cave crush Annie or the baby. She was
Bill's now. She had a right to be. She had lived for this.
For him. And for Lizzie. And with that, they put her in
an ambulance, and without hesitating, Bill climbed in
with her. And as he looked out the window at the back
of the ambulance as they drove away, Bill saw Rafe,
watching them, and crying. He was happy for both of
them.

Chapter 21

WHEN MADDY GOT TO THE HOSPITAL, they put her in the trauma unit where the others were who had been rescued from the mall, and she asked instantly about the baby. She was told he was doing fine. And the doctors were amazed to find she had no broken bones, no internal injuries. She had a concussion, a few scrapes, and minor bruises. Bill couldn't believe how lucky she'd been, and as he sat with her, he told her what he knew of what had happened. All anyone knew so far was that a group of militants had exploded the bomb. In a message to the President only an hour before, they had said it was their statement against the government. They sounded like lunatics. And they had killed more than three hundred people, almost half of them children. The sheer horror of it made Maddy shudder.

She told Bill what she'd seen as the ceiling collapsed, and what it had been like being trapped with Annie and the baby. And all she hoped now was that they would both survive it. She was worried about Annie, but not

nearly as worried as Bill had been about Maddy. It had
been just as bad as what he had gone through with
Margaret, and Maddy told him sympathetically that no
one should have to go through that twice in a lifetime.

They talked for a few more minutes then, and the
doctors wanted to do some more tests on her, just to be
thorough in their evaluation, and she and Bill agreed
that he should leave, in case Jack came to see her. Bill
didn't want to cause her any trouble at this point.

"I'll come back in a few hours," he said, as he leaned
over and kissed her. "Take it easy."

"You too. Get some sleep." She kissed him again, and
could hardly bring herself to relinquish his fingers. As
soon as he left, the doctors took her away and com-
pleted their examination. And when she was brought
back to her room, Rafe came in with a news crew. Jack
had sent them. Rafe didn't tell Maddy what a bastard he
thought Jack was for not coming to see her himself, and
he didn't ask her about Bill. He didn't need to. Whatever else might have been happening between them,
it was obvious to the producer of her show that the
guy really loved her, and just as obvious to him now that
Maddy loved him.

She told them what she could about what had happened, from her perspective, and told them, on camera,
how brave Annie had been. "She's sixteen years old,"
Maddy said, impressed and proud, and then she saw an
odd look in Rafe's eyes, and when they turned the camera off, she asked him a question.

"She's okay, isn't she, Rafe? Did you hear something?"

He hesitated, wanting to lie to her, but he couldn't
bring himself to do it. She'd find out anyway, and it

didn't seem fair not to tell her. "The baby is going to be okay, Mad. But they couldn't get his mom out."

"What do you mean, they couldn't get her out?" She was almost shrieking as she said it. She had kept her alive for fourteen hours and now they were telling her they couldn't free her? That was impossible. She refused to believe it.

"They'd have had to use dynamite. She was in a coma when they took you out, Maddy. They gave her life support, but she died half an hour later. Her lungs were crushed, and she had bled so much internally the rescue docs said they could never have saved her." Maddy made a sound like an animal as she heard him. It was a keening, groaning sound, as though the girl had been her own child. She couldn't bear to think of it. And what was going to happen to her baby? Rafe said he didn't know anything about that, and they left her to rest shortly after. But not before he told her, choking on sobs himself, how glad he was that she had made it.

Everyone was. Lizzie cried hopelessly when Maddy called her in Memphis to tell her she was all right. Lizzie had stayed up all night to watch the news coverage and when she didn't see Maddy on camera with the news crews, she called her at home, but no one answered. She had sensed somehow that Maddy was trapped there.

And Phyllis Armstrong called her and told her how relieved she and Jim were, and what a tragedy it was, particularly the deaths of all those children. They both cried, thinking of it, and after she hung up, Maddy asked a nurse about the baby. Andy was still at the hospital, being observed, as he would be for the next few days. The child protection authorities hadn't picked him up yet. And after the nurse left the room, Maddy got up quietly and went to the nursery to see him. He barely looked like more than a newborn, and Maddy asked a nurse if she could hold him. They had bathed him and combed his hair. He was blond and had big blue eyes, and they had wrapped him in a blue blanket. He looked immaculate and Maddy could see how pretty Annie must have been as she looked at her baby. And as she held him, all she could think of was Annie, asking her to take care of her baby. And soon he would be left to the same fate her own had been, going from orphanages to foster homes into the hands of strangers, with no real parents to love or claim him. It made Maddy's heart ache as she held him.

And as she did, he looked at her intently and she wondered if he recognized her voice as she crooned to him. He seemed to lose interest after a while, and drifted off to sleep in her arms. And Maddy cried as she thought of Annie. It had been an odd turn of fate that had left them together in the rubble. She set the baby down gently in the hospital bassinette and went back to her own room, still crying over Annie.

Maddy was stiff and achy, and incredibly tired, but she didn't have any serious injuries and she realized how incredibly lucky she had been. She was staring out the window and thinking how odd it was that life spared some, and took others, with no seeming rhyme or reason. It was hard to guess why she had been one of the lucky ones, and Annie wasn't. She had had so much more life left to live than Maddy. And as she thought about the mysteries of life, Jack walked into the room with a solemn expression.

"I guess I don't need to ask where you've been all

night for once." The "for once" was unnecessary, but typical of him. "How are you doing, Maddy?" He looked and felt awkward. He had never really believed she was in the wreckage in the first place. It sounded like hysteria to him, and he was surprised to learn she had been, but relieved to know she had survived. "That must have been pretty rough," he said, as he leaned over and kissed her, and a nurse brought a huge vase of flowers into the room, from the Armstrongs.

"Yeah, it was pretty scary," she said thoughtfully. He was the master of understatement, and dismissal. But this was a tough one to belittle. Being trapped in a bombed building for fourteen hours definitely qualified as a major trauma, however Jack called it. She thought about telling him about Annie and the baby, and how much it had touched her, but she decided not to. He wouldn't have understood.

"Everyone was worried about you. I figured you were out somewhere. I just didn't think you were in there. Why would you be?"

"I went to buy wrapping paper," she said simply, eyeing him. He had retreated to the other side of the room, as though he needed to keep his distance, and so did she now, for her own safety.

"You hate malls," he said, as though that would change it all now, and she smiled at him.

"I guess now I know why. They're fucking dangerous," she said and they both laughed. But the tension was high between them. She hadn't sorted it all out yet after the night before, but she had even thought about it while she was trapped in the debris, trying to keep Annie going. It occurred to her that if she ever survived what she'd just been through, she would have faced the

greatest terror in her life. She didn't need to face any
more than that, or impose it on herself, or risk herself
again. She would have faced the greatest enemy, looked
death in the eye. She didn't need to punish herself anymore, and she had promised herself she wasn't going to.
And seeing him there, sitting awkwardly across the
room from her, she knew she couldn't. He couldn't
even have enough love in his heart to walk across the
room and hold her in his arms and tell her he loved her.
He couldn't. He probably loved her as much as he
could, she realized, but that didn't say much. And as
though sensing something strange happening between
them, he stood up and walked over to her, and handed
her a gift-wrapped box. She took it without a word, and
opened it, and there was a narrow diamond bracelet inside. It was very pretty, and she thanked him. What she
didn't know was that he had bought two of them at the
Ritz Carlton when he checked out that morning. One
for her, for what she'd gone through at the mall, and the
other for the girl he'd spent the night with. But even
without knowing that, Maddy handed it back to him
with a serious expression.

"I can't accept it. I'm sorry, Jack," she said, and his
eyes narrowed as he watched her. He could sense the
prey slipping slowly away from him, and for an instant
she thought he was going to grab her, but he didn't.

"Why not?"

"I'm leaving you." She stunned herself with her
words, but not as much as she stunned Jack. He looked
as though she had hit him.

"What the fuck is that all about?" As usual, he covered up his own sins and weaknesses by being nasty to
her.

"I can't do this anymore."

"Do what?" he asked, pacing the room, unwilling to simply accept it and leave her. He looked like a tiger stalking his prey, but he didn't frighten her as he once had. And she knew she was safe here. There were people all around them, just beyond her doorway. "What is it that you can't do? Live a life of luxury? Go to Europe twice a year? Travel on a private jet? Get jewelry whenever I'm dumb enough to buy it for you? What a tough life to put up with, for a slut from Knoxville." He was at it again.

"That's the trouble, Jack," she said, sounding tired, and leaning back against her pillow as she watched him. "I'm not a slut from Knoxville. I never was. Even back then when I was poor and unhappy."

"Bullshit. I don't recall that you were ever from the right side of the tracks, or even knew what they looked like. Hell, you were a whore when you were a kid. Look at Lizzie."

"Yeah, look at her. She's a great kid, and a decent person in spite of some pretty rotten breaks, thanks to me. I owe her something now. And I owe myself something."

"You owe me everything. And I hope you realize you'll be out of a job if you leave me." His eyes glittered like steel.

"Possibly. I'll let my lawyers handle that, Jack. I have a contract with the network. You can't just throw me out without notice or compensation." She had gotten braver and smarter while fighting for her life in the rubble. She wondered how he could think that the things he was saying to her would convince her to stay with him. But once they might have, out of pure intimidation. That was the sad part.

"Don't threaten me. You won't get a dime out of me with that bullshit. And don't forget the prenup you signed. You walk out of my house empty-handed. It's all mine, even your fucking pantyhose. You walk out on me, Maddy, and all you've got is the hospital gown you're wearing."

"What do you want from me?" she asked sadly. "Why do you want me to stay? You hate me."

"I have every right to hate you. You lie to me. You've cheated on me. I know you have a boyfriend who calls you every day. How fucking dumb do you think I am?" Not dumb. Mean. But she didn't say it to him. She was brave, not foolish.

"He's not a boyfriend. We've just been friends till now. I have never cheated on you. And the only thing I've ever lied to you about is Lizzie."

"I'd say that's a big one. But I'm willing to forgive you. I'm the victim here, not you. I'm the one who's gotten screwed over in this deal, and I'm still willing to put up with you. You don't know how lucky you are. Just wait till you're starving and back in some shit hole in Memphis, or Knoxville, or wherever the hell you wind up with your bastard kid. You'll be begging me to come back," he said, slowly approaching the bed as she wondered what he would do next. There was a look in his eyes she'd never seen before, and she was instantly reminded of everything she'd been told in her abuse group. When he would sense his prey leaving him, he would do everything he could to stop her. Whatever he had to. "You're not leaving me, Mad," he said, standing over her, as she trembled. "You haven't got the balls for that. You're too smart for that. You're not going to throw a golden life and your whole career out the window, are you?" He was wheedling and terrifying, and there was an implied threat just in the way he looked at her. "Maybe you got hit on the head last night. Maybe that's what happened to you. Maybe I ought to knock some sense into you to get you thinking straight again. How about it, Maddy?" But as he said it to her, she felt everything rise up in her, and she knew that if he laid a hand on her, she'd kill him. She was not going to let him do this again, drag her back and torture her and humiliate her and convince her she was dirt and deserved all the misery and accusations he heaped on her. And the look in her eyes would have terrified him if he'd understood it.

"If you lay a hand on me, here or anywhere else, I swear I'll kill you. I've taken all the shit from you I'm ever going to. You cleaned the floor with me, but it's all over, Jack. I'm not coming back. Find someone else to dump on, and abuse, and torture."

"Oh listen to the big girl threatening her daddy. Poor baby. Do I scare you, Mad?" he asked, laughing at her, but she was out of bed now and facing him. The time had come. The game was over.

"No, you don't scare me, you son of a bitch. You make me sick. Get out of my room, Jack. Or I'll call for security and have you thrown out."

He stood looking at her for a long moment, and then came and stood so close to her she could have counted the hairs in his eyebrows if she'd cared to. "I hope you die, you fucking bitch. And you will. Soon, I hope. You deserve to." She couldn't tell if it was a direct threat or not, and it scared her, but not enough to make her change her mind. And as she watched him spin on his heel and walk out of the room, there was an insane instant of wanting to stop him and beg him to forgive her. But she knew she couldn't. That was the sick part of her, begging her to go back, feeling guilty, wanting him to love her at any price, no matter how much pain she had to take from him in order to get it. But that part of her was no longer in control anymore, and she watched him go silently, without making a move. And when he was gone, she was engulfed by sobs of pain and loss and guilt. However much she hated him, and however evil he was, like a malignancy on her soul, no matter how deep she gouged to cut him out, she knew she would never forget him, and he would never forgive her.

Chapter 22

THE DAY AFTER THEY RESCUED HER, Maddy went back to the nursery to see Andy again, and they told her the social worker had come to see him that morning. They were taking him the next day and placing him in a foster home, until they could arrange for long-term placement. And she went back to her room with a heavy heart. She knew she would never see him again, just as once she had known it about Lizzie. But God had given her a second chance with her, and now she wondered if Andy and his mother had come into her life for a reason.

She thought about it all afternoon, and later talked to Bill when he came to see her. He knew about her visit from Jack the day before, and he was both relieved and worried. He didn't want him coming back to hurt her. Now that Jack knew that she was leaving him, there was no telling what he would do, and he urged Maddy to be careful. She was going to pick up her things at the house when she left the hospital, and she agreed to take someone with her to do it. She was going to hire a security guard from the network. And Bill had promised to buy her some clothes to leave the hospital, but she wasn't worried about Jack. She felt surprisingly free. And although it pained her to have said what she had to him, she was amazed that she didn't feel guilty. She knew that she would again, at some point. She'd been warned about that. But she knew she had done the right thing. Jack was a cancer that would have killed her if she let him.

But she was haunted about Annie's baby. "I know this sounds crazy," she finally admitted to Bill, "but I promised her I'd take care of him. I guess I should at least let the social worker know that I'd like to know where they place him." Bill thought that was a good idea, and they talked more about the disaster in the mall. One of the perpetrators of it had been apprehended. He was a twenty-year-old boy with a history of mental disorders, and a prison record. And he had apparently done it with two partners, who hadn't been found yet. There were memorial services everywhere for the victims, and it made it even worse that it was almost Christmas. And Bill had already told her he was thinking of not going to Vermont, and staying in the city to be with her.

"Don't worry about me. I'll be fine," she promised. She felt surprisingly well, aside from a few aches and pains, and she had already decided to move into Lizzie's apartment with her. She was arriving in a week, and they were going to spend Christmas together. And she didn't mind sharing a bedroom with Lizzie, at least for the time being.

"You can stay with me if you like," he said hopefully, and she smiled at him as he kissed her. He had been extraordinary to her since the disaster at the mall, and long before that.

"Thank you for the offer, but I'm not sure you're ready for a roommate."

"That wasn't exactly what I had in mind," he said, blushing a little. She loved his gentleness and the kindness he constantly showed her. They had a lot to look forward to now, and to discover about each other. But she didn't want to rush it either. She needed to recover from a lifetime of abuse, nine years of Jack, and Bill was still wending his way through the grief process over Margaret. But there was certainly room in their lives now for each other. What she wasn't sure of was where Andy fit in, and yet she knew she wanted to make a place for him, even if only for an occasional visit, to honor a promise made to his mother. Maddy was not going to forget that.

And she said as much that night to Lizzie on the phone when they talked. Lizzie had been so panicked about the explosion at the mall, that she was calling her mother several times daily.

"Why don't you adopt him?" she said with a nineteen-year-old's simplicity, and Maddy told her that was ridiculous. She didn't have a husband now, might have lost her job, she didn't even have her own apartment. But after she hung up, the idea rolled around in her head like a marble in a shoebox. And at three o'clock in the morning, still awake, Maddy wandered into the nursery, sat in a rocking chair, and held him. He was sleeping peacefully in her arms when a nurse came in and told her she should be in bed. But she couldn't. She felt as though a force greater than she was pushing her toward him, and she could no longer resist it.

She was waiting nervously in the hall when the social worker came for him in the morning, and Maddy asked if she could speak to her for a minute. She explained the situation to her, and the woman looked interested but startled.

"I'm sure it was a very emotional moment for you, Mrs. Hunter. Your lives were all in danger. No one would expect you to honor a promise like that. That's a major decision."

"I know it is," Maddy explained. "It isn't just that. . . . I don't know what it is . . . I think I've fallen in love with him," she said about the blue-eyed baby Annie had asked her to take care of.

"The fact that you'd be single isn't a handicap. Although it could be a burden for you," the social worker said to her. Maddy hadn't mentioned that she might be out of a job, but she had enough money put away in her own name to be secure for quite some time. She had been cautious with what she'd made over the years, and had a healthy nest egg for her and Lizzie, and even a baby. "Are you telling me you want to adopt him?"

"I think so," Maddy said, feeling a wave of love wash over her for him. It felt like the right thing to do, for her, if no one else. She had no idea how Bill felt. But she couldn't give up her dreams for him now either. She had to do what was right for her. And if it worked out for both of them, it would be a blessing for everyone, not just her and the baby. But she at least wanted to ask him how he felt about it. "How long do I have to decide?"

"A while. We're placing him in a temporary foster home. They're a family who have helped us out before, but they're not interested in adoption. They do this out of the goodness of their hearts, for religious reasons. But a baby like this will be in high demand. He's healthy, white, eight weeks old. He's what everyone wants to adopt. And there aren't many like him these days."

"Let me think about it. Would I have any kind of priority?"

"As long as there's no family to object, and we're researching that now, he could be yours very quickly, Mrs. Hunter." Maddy nodded, and a few minutes later, the social worker left her room, after giving Maddy her card. And when Maddy went back to the nursery later on, she felt her heart ache, knowing he wouldn't be there. She was still down about it when Bill came to see her a little later. He had bought her a pair of gray slacks, a blue sweater, a pair of loafers and some underwear, and a new coat, and some toiletries and makeup and a nightgown.

She complimented him on how well he'd done, and everything fit perfectly. She was leaving the hospital the next day, and had agreed to stay with him, until she could set up Lizzie's apartment. She thought she could do it in a week. She wanted to pick up her things at Jack's, and she had to get back to work. She had a lot to do, and she sat talking to Bill about all of it, and then brought up the baby. She told him she was thinking of adopting him, and he looked startled when she said it.

"You are? Are you sure that's what you want to do, Maddy?"

"Not entirely. That's why I'm talking about it to you. I'm not sure if it's the craziest idea I've ever had, or the best thing I've ever done . . . or what I was meant to do. I just don't know," she said, looking troubled.

"The best thing you've ever done was leave Jack Hunter," he said firmly. "This could be the next best thing, after Lizzie." He smiled at her. "I must say, you threw me a curve on that one, Maddy." It underlined to him how much older than she he was. He had loved his children when they were young, and he loved his grandchildren now, but taking on a baby at his age was more than he had bargained for, although he was crazy about her daughter. "I'm not sure what to say." He was being honest about it.

"Neither am I. I'm not sure if I'm asking you or telling you, or if either is relevant. We don't have any idea yet where things are going with us, or if it will work out, no matter how much we love each other." She was being honest about that, and he admired her for it. And what she said was true. He was in love with her, but whether or not it would prove to be a relationship for life, or one that even worked short-term, neither of them could judge yet. This was just the beginning for them. They hadn't even been to bed yet, although the prospect of it was certainly appealing. But a baby was a major commitment. They had no argument about that. "All my life," she struggled to explain to him, "people have been telling me what to do in that area, as well as every other. My parents made me give Lizzie up. Bobby Joe made me have abortions early on, and then I had them because I didn't want his kids. Jack forbade me to have kids, so I had my tubes tied. And then he forbade me to see Lizzie. And now this baby comes along, and I want to be sure that I do what I need to do, what's right for me, not just for you. Because if I give him up, in order to have you, maybe I'll always feel that I gave up something I shouldn't have. On the other hand, I don't want to lose you over a baby who isn't mine anyway. Do you see what I mean?" she asked, looking confused, and he smiled and sat down next to her on the bed, and put an arm around her and pulled her close to him.

"Yes, I see what you mean. Although it sounds a little complicated when you say it. But I don't want to take something away from you that's right for you either. You'd wind up hating me for it, or feeling cheated someday. Particularly since you've never had a baby since Lizzie, and you're not able to, and you missed nineteen years of her life. I've had all that. I don't have a right to deprive you of it." It was what Jack should have said to her seven years before when he married her, but hadn't. But they hadn't been honest with each other, and this was extraordinarily different. Bill had absolutely nothing in common with Jack Hunter. And the woman she was now bore no relation to the woman she had been when she married Jack. It was a whole new world.

"On the other hand," Bill went on, wanting to be scrupulously honest with her, so he didn't mislead her, "I don't know if I'm willing to turn the clock back that many years, or even if I'd want to. I'm a lot older than you, Maddy. You should be having babies at your age. I should be having grandchildren. This kind of makes me face that. It's something for both of us to think about. I don't think it's even fair for a baby to have a father my age." She was sad to hear him say it, and she didn't agree with him, but she didn't want to sell fatherhood to him either.

"There's nothing wrong with having a father your age," she said, believing what she said. "You'd be wonderful with a baby. Or a child. Or anyone." It was kind of a crazy conversation anyway, since they weren't even talking about marriage. "We're kind of putting the cart before the horse about all this, aren't we?" They were, but she also had a decision to make about this particular baby, before someone else adopted him, and it became a moot point for Maddy. And she knew she wouldn't go out looking for any other baby. But this was different. He was the product of a life-altering event, and she wasn't entirely willing to ignore that. Andy's sudden arrival in her life felt like an act of fate.

"What do you want to do?" he asked her simply. "What would you do if I didn't exist?" That simplified it for her.

"Adopt him," she said without hesitation.

"Then do it. You can't live your life for someone else, Maddy. You've done that all your life. I could die tomorrow or next week. We could decide that we're both terrific people but we'd rather be friends than lovers, although I hope not. Follow your heart, Maddy. If it's right for us, we'll work it out eventually. And who knows, maybe I'd love having a kid to play baseball with in my dotage." She loved him all the more for the way he said it. And she didn't disagree with him. She didn't want to give something up that had perhaps been meant to be. She felt there was a reason why God had given her another chance, not only with Bill, but Lizzie, and this baby.

"Would you think I'm completely nuts if I adopt him? I don't know if I even have a job now. Jack threatened to fire me."

"That's not the issue here. You'll have a job in the next five minutes, if you don't now. The question is if you want to bring up someone else's child, and take on that responsibility for the rest of your life. That is something to consider."

"I am," she said seriously. He knew her well enough to know that she wouldn't make the decision lightly.

"To answer your question, no, I wouldn't think you're crazy. Brave. And young. And energetic. And incredibly honorable and decent and loving and giving. But not crazy." It was all she needed to know and it helped her with her decision.

She lay awake thinking about it all night, and in the morning, she called the social worker, and told her she wanted to adopt Andy. The social worker congratulated her, and told her she'd put the paperwork in motion. It was a heady moment in Maddy's life, and first she cried with joy and relief, and then she called first Bill and then Lizzie, and both of them sounded pleased for her, although she knew he had reservations. But if it was going to work with them, she couldn't give up her life's dreams for him either. And she knew he didn't want her to. He just didn't know if he wanted to be coaching Little League baseball at seventy, and she couldn't blame him for that. All she could hope for was that it would prove to be a blessing for everyone, not only for her and Bill, but especially for Andy.

When she left the hospital that day, she was wearing the clothes Bill had bought for her, and she went straight back to his house. She was amazed by how tired she still was, even though she hadn't gotten seriously hurt, the trauma of the explosion at the mall had taken a lot out of her. But she called her producer and promised to go back to work on Monday. And Elliott had called her several times, in awe of what had happened to her, and grateful that she had survived. It seemed like everyone she'd ever known had sent her flowers at the hospital. It was a relief to be peacefully at Bill's house. And the next day she was going to get her things in spite of Jack's threats that she could keep nothing. She had hired a security guard she knew to go with her. She hadn't heard a word from Jack since she told him she was leaving.

And that evening, she and Bill sat in front of the fireplace and talked for hours, while listening to music. He had cooked her dinner and served it by candlelight. She felt utterly spoiled and pampered. And neither of them could believe their good fortune. Suddenly, she was staying in his house, and she was free of Jack. They had a whole new world before them. Although it felt strange to Maddy. It was suddenly as though Jack didn't exist, and their entire life together had disappeared.

"I guess the abuse group really worked," she beamed at him. "I'm a big girl now," but she could still feel tremors of the past from time to time. She worried about Jack, and felt sorry for him, and feared he was depressed over what she'd said, and how ungrateful she appeared to be to him. She had no way of knowing that he had spent the weekend with a twenty-two-year-old girl he had met and slept with in Las Vegas. But there was a lot Maddy didn't know about him, and never would now.

"All it took," Bill teased, "was blowing up an entire shopping mall to bring you to your senses." But they both knew how seriously he took it. He had been devastated watching the tragedies all around him as he waited for them to rescue her. But it had been such a shocking thing that they both needed to lighten the moment a little. "When are you getting Andy, by the way?"

"I don't know yet. They're going to call me." And then she asked him something she had thought of from the moment she decided to adopt Andy. "Will you be his godfather, if you won't be anything else to him?" she asked him seriously and he took her in his arms and held her.

"I'd be honored," and then after he kissed her, he reminded her of something. "I haven't said I wouldn't be 'anything else to him.' We still have to figure that out. But if we're going to have a baby, Maddy, there are a few details we still need to attend to." She laughed, and understood instantly what he was saying.

They put the dishes in the dishwasher, and turned the lights off, and walked quietly upstairs together, with his arm around her, and she followed him cautiously into his bedroom. She had discreetly put her few possessions in the guest room, not wanting him to feel pressured. She knew from everything he had said to her that there had been no other woman in his life since Margaret's death, but it had been just over a year now. The anniversary of it had been excruciating for him, but he had seemed freer and a little more lighthearted ever since.

She sat on his bed and they talked for a while, about the mall, his kids, Jack, and everything she'd been through. They had no secrets from each other. And as he looked at her, with love in his eyes, he pulled her slowly closer to him.

"I feel like a kid again when I'm with you," he whispered, which was his way of telling her he was scared, but so was she, though only a little. She knew she had nothing to fear from him.

And when they kissed, all the ghosts of the past fell

away from both of them, or were at least put away for the moment, the good as well as the bad. It was like starting a new life with a man who had been her friend for so long she could no longer imagine a life without him.

It all happened naturally and easily, and they slid into his bed side by side, and lay in each other's arms as though they had always been together. It was as though it was meant to be. And afterward, he held her and smiled and told her how much he loved her.

"I love you too, Bill," she whispered as he held her. And as they fell asleep in each other's arms, they knew that they were blessed. It had been a long journey through two lives to find each other, but the trip, and the sorrows, and the pain, and even the losses they had both sustained, had been worth it to both of them.

Chapter 23

*T*HE SECURITY GUARD *MADDY HAD* hired met her at Bill's house the next day, and she explained to him that all she wanted to do was go to the house she had shared with Jack and pick up her clothes. She had enough empty suitcases there to pack them in, and she had rented a van to transport them. She was going to drop them off at the apartment she had rented for Lizzie, and that was all there was to it. The art, the furniture, the mementos, all the rest of it, she was leaving for Jack. She wanted nothing more than her clothes and personal items. It seemed straightforward and simple. Until they got to the house.

The guard was driving the van for her. And Bill had offered to come, but she didn't think it was right, and assured him he didn't need to worry. She figured it would only take her a few hours, and they went after she knew Jack would have left for work. But as soon as she got to the front door, and turned her key in the lock, she knew something was wrong. The door wouldn't open. The key seemed to fit perfectly, but when it turned, it opened nothing. She tried again, wondering if something was wrong with the lock, and the security guard tried it for her. And then he looked at her and told her the locks had been changed. Her key was useless.

She was still standing outside the house, when she used her cellular to call Jack, and his secretary put her through to him promptly. For a moment, she'd been afraid he wouldn't talk to her.

"I'm at the house, trying to pick up my stuff," she explained, "and my key doesn't work. I assume you changed the locks. Can we come by the office and pick up the key? I'll bring it back to you later." It was a reasonable request, and her voice was level and pleasant although her hands were shaking.

"What stuff?" he asked, sounding blank. "You don't have any 'stuff' at my house." It was an odd way to put it.

"I just want to pick up my clothes, Jack. I'm not taking anything else. You can have the rest." She also had to pick up the clothes she kept in Virginia. "And obviously I'm taking my jewelry. That's it. The rest is all yours."

"You don't own the clothes or the jewelry," he said in a voice that sounded frozen. "I do. You don't own anything, Mad, except whatever you're wearing right now. I paid for it. I own it." Just like he used to tell her he owned her. But she had seven years of wardrobe and jewelry in the house and there was no reason why she shouldn't have it, except if he wanted to be vindictive.

"What are you going to do with it?" she asked calmly.

"I sent the jewelry to Sotheby's two days ago, and I

had Goodwill pick your things up the day you told me you were leaving. I told them to destroy them."

"You didn't?"

"Of course I did. I didn't think you'd want anyone else wearing your things, Mad," he said as though he had done her a big favor. "There's absolutely nothing of yours in that house now." And even the jewelry didn't represent a big investment to him. He had never given her any really important jewelry, just some pretty things that she liked, and wouldn't bring him a fortune when he sold them.

"How could you do that?" He was such a bastard. She was standing outside the house, stunned by the meanness of what he'd done to her.

"I told you, Maddy. Don't fuck with me. If you want out, you'll pay for it."

"I have for all the years I've known you, Jack," she said evenly, but she was shaking from what he had just done to her. She felt as though she'd been robbed as she stood outside their house wearing the clothes Bill had bought for her.

"You ain't seen nothing yet," Jack warned her. And his tone sounded so sick it scared her.

"Fine," she said, and hung up and went back to Bill's house. He was there, working on some things, and looked startled that she had returned so quickly.

"What happened? Had he packed it all up for you before you got there?"

"You could say that. He says he destroyed everything. He changed the locks and I never even got in. I called him. He says he's selling the jewelry at Sotheby's, and he had Goodwill destroy all my clothes and personal things." It was like a fire that had taken everything with it. And she had nothing. It was so cruel and so petty.

"The bastard. Screw him, Maddy. You can buy new things."

"I guess so." But somehow she felt violated. And it would be expensive to buy a whole new wardrobe.

She felt shaken by what Jack had done, but in spite of it, they managed to have a nice weekend, and she was bracing herself for an inevitable encounter with Jack when she went back to work on Monday. She knew how difficult it was going to be working for him, but she loved her job, and didn't want to give it up.

"I think you should give them notice," Bill said sensibly. "There are lots of other networks that would love to have you."

"I'd rather keep the status quo for now," she said, though perhaps not sensibly, and he didn't argue with her. She had had enough trauma for one week, between the bombing, and losing everything she owned to her soon-to-be-ex-husband.

But she was totally unprepared for what happened when she went to work on Monday. Bill dropped her off on his way to a meeting with his publisher, and she walked into the lobby wearing her badge and a brave smile, as she prepared to walk through the metal detector. And she instantly saw, out of the corner of her eye, the head of security waiting for her. He took her aside, and explained that she couldn't go upstairs.

"Why not?" she asked, looking surprised. She wondered if they were having a fire drill or a bomb threat or even a threat against her.

"You're not allowed to," he said bluntly. "Mr. Hunter's orders. I'm sorry, ma'am, but you can't come into the building." She was not only fired. She was persona non grata. If the guard had hit her it wouldn't have stunned her more than what he had just said to her. The door had been slammed in her face. She was out of work, out of clothes, out of luck, and for an instant she felt the panic he had intended her to feel. All she needed was a ticket to Knoxville on a Greyhound bus.

She took a deep breath as she walked outside again and told herself that no matter what he did to her, he couldn't destroy her. She was being punished for leaving him. She hadn't done anything wrong, she reminded herself. After all he'd done to her, she had a right to her freedom. But what if she never found a job again, she asked herself, or if Bill got tired of her, or Jack was right and she was worthless? Without thinking, she started walking and walked all the way back to Bill's house, which took her an hour, and when she got there, she was exhausted.

He was already back by then, and when he saw her, she was sheet white, and she started to sob the moment she saw him, and told him what happened.

"Calm down," he said firmly, "calm down, Maddy. Everything's going to be okay. He can't do anything to hurt you."

"Yes, he can. I'll wind up in the gutter, just like he said. And I'll have to go back to Knoxville." It was totally irrational, but she had been through too much in a short time, and she was completely panicked. She had money in the bank, that she had saved from her salary without telling Jack, and she had Bill, but in spite of that, she felt like an orphan, and that was precisely what Jack had intended. He had known exactly how she would feel, how devastated, how terrified, and that was what he wanted. It was war now.

"You're not going to Knoxville. You're not going

anywhere, except to a lawyer. And not one on Jack's payroll." He called one for her when she calmed down, and they went to see him together that afternoon. There were some things he couldn't accomplish, like get her clothes back. But there was a lot he could do to get Jack to honor the contract. Jack was going to have to pay her for what he destroyed, he explained, and he was going to have to pay her a healthy severance, and damages, for barring her from the station. He was even talking about punitive damages in the millions for breach of contract, as Maddy listened in amazement. She was not, as she had feared at first, either helpless or his victim. He was going to have to pay dearly for what he was doing, and the bad publicity it would generate for him wasn't going to do him any good either.

"That's it, Ms. Hunter. He can't do any worse than he just has. He can annoy you. He can cause you some grief personally, but he can't get away with this. He's a walking target, and a very public figure. And we're going to get a healthy settlement from him, or get you punitive damages from a jury." Maddy beamed at him like a child with a new doll on Christmas, and when they left his offices, she looked up at Bill with a sheepish grin. She felt safer than ever with him.

"I'm sorry I freaked out this morning. I just got so scared, and it was so awful when the guard told me I had to leave the building."

"Of course it was," Bill said sympathetically. "It was a lousy thing for him to do, and that's why he did it. And don't kid yourself. He's not through yet. He's going to do every rotten thing he can think of to do to you, until the courts let him have it. And he might even try it after that. You have to brace yourself, Maddy."

"I know," she said, sounding depressed about it. It was one thing to talk about it, another to go through it.

And the next day, the war continued. She and Bill were having breakfast peacefully, and reading the newspaper when she gasped suddenly and Bill glanced at her quickly.

"What's wrong?" Her eyes filled with tears and she handed the paper to him. There was a small article on page twelve that said that she had had to give up her place as co-anchor on her show, as a result of a nervous breakdown she'd had after being trapped for fourteen hours in the mall bombing.

"Oh my God," she said, looking at Bill. "No one's going to hire me if they think I've gone crazy."

"Son of a bitch," Bill said, reading it carefully, and then put in a call to her lawyer. He told them, when he returned the call at noon, that they could sue Jack for slander. But it was clear now that Jack Hunter was playing for high stakes, and that his only goal in life was wreaking vengeance on Maddy.

She went back to the abuse group the next week, and told them what he was doing to her, and none of them was surprised. They warned her that it would get worse, and that she needed to watch out for him physically as well. The leader of the group described sociopathic behavior to her, and it fit Jack perfectly. He was a man with no morals and no conscience, who, when it suited him, turned things around and imagined himself to be the victim. The description fit Jack to perfection. She told Bill about it that night, and he entirely agreed with them.

"I want you to be careful when I'm gone, Maddy. I'm going to be worried sick about you. I wish you'd come with me." She had urged him to go to Vermont for Christmas, as planned, and he was leaving in a few days. She wanted to stay in town to settle Lizzie into her new apartment. She was arriving the day Bill left. And Maddy still thought she should move in with her. Although she loved staying with Bill, she didn't want him to feel pressured or cramped. And she was still waiting to hear about the baby. And that was the last thing he needed to disrupt his peaceful existence. She wanted to move slowly for him.

"I'll be fine," Maddy reassured him about Jack. She no longer thought he was going to attack her physically. He was too busy making trouble for her in ways that would ultimately do great damage to her.

Her lawyer had the paper print a correction of the story they'd run, and word got out quickly that she had been fired by her irate ex-husband, and within two days, she got calls from all three major networks, and the offers they made her were all tremendously appealing. But she wanted time to think about that too. She wanted to do the right thing, and not move too quickly. But at least she was reassured that she was not going to be unemployed forever. His allusions to trailer parks and winding up broke in the gutter were nothing more than yet another form of torture.

The day Bill left, she went to Lizzie's apartment to organize the things she'd bought for her, and by the time Lizzie arrived that night, the apartment looked cheery and bright, and everything was in perfect order. And she was thrilled that she would be sharing her apartment with her mother. She thought what Jack had done to her was awful. But trying to get rid of Lizzie before Maddy even knew about her had been the worst of his crimes against Maddy. There was an endless list of hideous things he had perpetrated on her, all of which were clearer to her now. It embarrassed her now to think about all the abuses she'd allowed him. But she had always secretly believed that she deserved it, and he knew that. She had given him all the weapons he needed to hurt her.

She and Lizzie spent long hours talking about it, and Bill called her from Vermont as soon as he got there. He already missed her.

"Why don't you just come up for Christmas?" he said, and sounded as though he meant it.

"I don't want to intrude on your children," she said fairly.

"They'd love to have you, Maddy."

"What about the day after Christmas?" It was a reasonable compromise, and Lizzie was dying to learn to ski. Bill was thrilled with the suggestion, and so was Lizzie when Maddy told her about it later.

He called her before he went to bed that night, to tell her how much he loved her.

"I think we need to renegotiate this living arrangement of yours. I don't think it's fair for you to live with Lizzie in a one-bedroom apartment. Besides, I'm going to miss you." She had actually thought of getting an apartment of her own, for the same reason she didn't want to go to Vermont for the holiday. She didn't want him to feel put upon. She was very sensitive to that. But he sounded almost insulted that she had moved out and moved in with Lizzie.

"Well, considering the size of my wardrobe at the moment," she laughed ruefully, "it's a decision I can change in about five minutes."

"Good. I want you to move back in when I come home. It's time, Maddy," he said gently. "We've both had enough rough, lonely times. Let's start a new life together." She wasn't sure exactly what that meant, and she was embarrassed to ask him. But they had plenty of time to figure it out. The next morning was Christmas Eve, and they all had a lot to do, although she no longer had a job to worry about, and she was planning to turn her full attention to Lizzie.

They went out and bought a tree the next day, and decorated it together. It was a far cry from her grim holidays with Jack, trapped in the house in Virginia, while he ignored the holiday and forced her to ignore it with him. If anything, this was the happiest Christmas in her life, although she still had a certain amount of regret about Jack, and how sour it had turned. But she reminded herself regularly that she was better off without him. And when the good memories washed over her, she canceled them out with the bad ones, of which there were far too many. But what she knew most of all was how lucky she was to have Bill in her life, and Lizzie.

And at two o'clock that afternoon, on Christmas Eve, she got the call she'd been waiting for, and had no idea when to expect. They had told her it could take weeks, or even as much as a month, so she had put it out of her mind, and was concentrating on enjoying Lizzie for the moment.

"He's ready, Mom," a familiar voice said over the phone. It was the social worker who was helping her with Andy's adoption. "You've got a little boy here who wants to come home to his mom for Christmas."

"Do you mean it? Can I have him now?" She looked

at Lizzie and waved frantically, but Lizzie had no idea
what she was doing and just laughed at her.

"He's all yours. The judge signed the papers this
morning. He thought it might mean a lot to you on
Christmas. It's a great way to spend the holiday, with a
new baby."

"Where is he?"

"Right here in my office. The foster parents just
dropped him off. You can pick him up anytime this afternoon, but I'd like to get home to my own kids."

"I'll be there in twenty minutes," Maddy said, and
hung up, and told Lizzie what had happened. "Will you
come with me?" she asked her, suddenly feeling very
nervous. She had never taken care of a baby. This was
all going to be new to her, and she hadn't bought anything for him. She hadn't wanted to count her chickens
before they hatched, so to speak, and she had somehow
thought they'd give her more notice than this.

"We'll go buy some stuff after we pick him up,"
Lizzie said sensibly. She had baby-sat for kids in all her
foster homes, and she knew a lot more than her mother
about babies and their needs.

"I don't even know what to get . . . diapers, formula, I
guess . . . rattles . . . toys . . . stuff like that, right?"
Maddy felt about fourteen, and so excited she could
hardly stand it, as she combed her hair and washed her
face, put on her coat, grabbed her bag, and ran down
the steps of their apartment with Lizzie.

And when they reached the social worker's office by
cab, Andy was waiting for them in a white sweater and
hat, and a pair of little blue terrycloth pajamas, and his
foster parents had given him a little teddy bear as a
Christmas present to take with him.

He was sleeping peacefully when Maddy looked down at him, and ever so gently she picked him up and held him. And there were tears in her eyes as she looked at Lizzie. She still had so much guilt and regret for never having been there for her. But Lizzie seemed to understand what she was feeling, and put an arm around her shoulders.

"It's okay, Mom . . . I love you."

"I love you too, sweetheart," Maddy said, and kissed her, just as the baby woke up and started to cry, and Maddy put him carefully on her shoulder, and he looked around as though looking for a familiar face and cried harder.

"I think he's hungry," Lizzie said with more confidence than her mother felt, and the social worker gave them his bag, his formula, and a list of instructions for him. She handed Maddy a thick envelope with his adoption papers. She still had to go to court one more time, but it was only a formality. The baby was hers. She was keeping his first name, and had decided to change his last name and her own to her maiden name of Beaumont. She didn't want anything more to do with Jack Hunter. Even if she went on another show again, she had decided to do so as Madeleine Beaumont. And he was Andrew William Beaumont now. She had given him his middle name in honor of his godfather. And as they left the social worker's office, she was wearing a look of awe as she carried her precious bundle.

They stopped at a baby shop and the drugstore on the way home, and bought everything Lizzie and the woman in the store told her she needed. It filled the taxi so full there was hardly room for them, and Maddy was beaming when they walked into the apartment, and the phone was ringing.

"I'll hold him for you, Mom," Lizzie volunteered and Maddy hated to give him up even for a minute. If she had ever wondered if it was the right thing, she knew for certain now that it was, and had been exactly what she needed and wanted.

"Where've you been?" the familiar voice asked. It was Bill, calling from Vermont. He had just come back from an afternoon of ice skating with his grandson. And he couldn't wait to tell her about it. "Where were you, Maddy?" he asked again, and she smiled as she answered.

"Picking up your godson," she said proudly. Lizzie had just turned the Christmas tree lights on, and the apartment looked cozy and warm, although she was sorry not to be with Bill on Christmas. Especially now that Andy had joined them.

For a moment, he didn't understand what she meant, and then he realized, and smiled. He could hear in her voice how happy she was. "That's a pretty major Christmas present. How is he?" He could hear how she was.

"He's so beautiful, Bill." And then she glanced at Lizzie and smiled at her as she held her new brother.

"Not as pretty as Lizzie was, but he's pretty cute. Wait till you see him."

"Are you bringing him to Vermont?" But he knew it was a silly question as soon as he said it. She had no other alternative, and he wasn't a newborn. He was a healthy two-and-a-half-month-old. He would be ten weeks old on Christmas morning.

"If it's all right with you, I'd love to."

"Bring him along. The kids will love him. And I guess he and I better get acquainted if I'm going to be his godfather." He didn't say more to her, but he called her again that night and the next morning. She and Lizzie went to midnight mass, and took the baby with them, and he never woke up once. Maddy put him in the elegant blue carrying basket she had just bought him, and he looked like a little prince as he lay there in a brand-new blue hat and sweater, beneath an enormous cozy blue blanket with his teddy bear tucked in next to him.

And on Christmas morning, she and Lizzie opened all their gifts for each other. There were bags and gloves and books and sweaters and perfume. But the best gift of all was Andy, as he lay in his basket and looked at them. And when Maddy leaned over and kissed him, he beamed at her. It was a moment she knew she would never forget. A gift she would eternally be grateful for. And as she took him in her arms, she said a silent prayer of thanks to his mother for her incredible gift.

Chapter 24

ON THE DAY AFTER CHRISTMAS, Maddy and Lizzie set out for Vermont in a rented car, and the car looked like a gypsy van with all the equipment for the baby. He slept most of the way, and Maddy and Lizzie talked and laughed. They stopped for a hamburger, and while they ate, Maddy gave Andy his bottle. She had never been as happy in her life, or as sure that she had done the right thing. It made her realize now what Jack had taken from her when he had forced her to have her tubes tied. He had taken a great many things from her, her confidence, her self-respect, her self-esteem, her trust, the power to make her own decisions and run her own life. It had been a poor exchange for the job and material things he gave her.

"What are you going to do about the offers you've had?" Lizzie asked with interest on the way to Bill's house in Sugarbush, and Maddy sighed.

"I don't know yet. I want to go back to work, but I want to enjoy you and Andy for a while. This is my first chance, and my last, to be a full-time mother. Once I go back to work, they'll crawl all over me again. I'm in no rush." And she had some legal things to work out. Her lawyer was organizing a major lawsuit against Jack and his network. He owed her a huge severance for kicking her out of her job, and there was the issue of slander, malicious intent, and a number of other things the lawyer wanted to incorporate in the lawsuit. But mostly, she wanted to stay home for a while and enjoy Lizzie and the baby. Lizzie was starting Georgetown in two weeks, and she was wildly excited about it.

They reached Sugarbush at six o'clock that night, just in time to meet all of Bill's children, and join them for dinner. And his grandchildren went crazy over the baby. He laughed and smiled at them, and the youngest one, who was two and half, played patty-cake with him, and he loved it.

Lizzie took him from her mother after they all ate, and said she'd put him to bed for her. And after Maddy helped Bill's daughter and daughters-in-law clean up the kitchen and put the dishes away, she settled down with him in front of the fire, and they talked for a while. And when everyone went upstairs, he suggested they go for a walk. It was freezing, but the stars were bright, and the snow crunched beneath their feet as they walked down the path his son had shoveled. It was a large, comfortable old house, and it was obvious that they all loved it. They were a nice family, and they enjoyed spending time together. And none of them seemed shocked by his relationship with Maddy. They had made a point of welcoming her, and they were even nice to Lizzie and the baby.

"You have a wonderful family," she complimented him, as they walked hand in hand, with their gloves on.

Everyone's skis were lined up outside, and she was looking forward to skiing with him the next day, if they could find someone to stay with the baby. It was a new aspect to her life, and she knew it would seem strange for a while, but she loved everything about it.

"Thank you," he smiled at Maddy, and then put an arm around her in her heavy coat. "He's a sweet baby," he said with a smile. And he could see easily how much she already loved him. It would have been wrong if she could never have experienced that. And she was able to give him a life he would never have had, even with his natural mother. God had known what he was doing in the rubble of the mall that night when he had put the three of them together. And who was he, Bill realized, to take that from her? "I've been thinking a lot," he said after a while, as they started to turn back toward the house, and he saw that she looked terrified when she looked at him. She thought she knew what was coming.

"I'm not sure I want to hear about it." Her old terrors shone in her eyes, as she looked away from him so he couldn't see the tears that were forming.

"Why not?" he asked gently, turning her around to face him as they stopped on the snow-covered track. "I figured some things out. I thought you might want to hear them."

"About us?" she asked in a choked voice, afraid that so soon after it started, it was already ending. It didn't seem fair, but nothing in her life had been so far, except what she had now. Bill and Lizzie and Andy. They were all that mattered to her. Her life with Jack seemed like a bad dream.

"Don't be afraid, Maddy," Bill said softly. He could feel her trembling as he held her.

"I am. I don't want to lose you."

"There are no guarantees against that," he said honestly. "You've got a lot more road ahead of you than I do. But I think I've figured out at this point in my life that it's not about when you get there, or how fast, it's about the journey. As long as you travel the road together and do it well, maybe that's all you can ask. None of us is ever sure of what's around the corner." He had learned that lesson the hard way, but so had Maddy. "It's kind of a trust walk." She still wasn't sure what he was saying to her. But he wanted more than anything to reassure her. "I'm not going to leave you, Maddy. I'm not going anywhere. And I don't ever want to hurt you." But they would from time to time, as long as there was no malice in it. They both understood that.

"I don't want to hurt you either," she said softly, clinging to him for dear life, but slightly reassured by what he was saying to her. She could sense that she had nothing to fear from him. This was a new life, a new day, a new dream they had found together, and carefully nurtured.

"What I'm trying to say to you," he said, as he looked down at her with a smile in the cold night air, "is that I've figured out that it might do me good to play baseball in my seventies. If all else fails, Andy can throw the ball at me in my wheelchair."

She looked at him with a funny smile, "I hardly think you'll be in a wheelchair by then," but she could see now that he was laughing.

"Who knows? You might wear me out. You've already tried. God knows, explosions in malls, babies, crazy ex-husbands . . . you certainly keep my life exciting. But I don't just want to be his godfather. He deserves more than that. We all do."

"You want to be his Little League coach?" she teased him. She felt as though her ship had just come in, and it was one she'd waited for for a long time, all her life in fact. But she knew that with Bill, she was finally safe and in good hands.

"I want to be your husband, that's what I'm trying to say to you. What do you think, Maddy?"

"What will your kids say?" She was worried about that, but they had been incredibly nice to her so far.

"They'll probably say I'm crazy, and they'll be right. But I think it's the right thing to do, for both of us . . . all of us. . . . I've known it for a long time. I just wasn't sure what you were going to do, or how long it would take you."

"It took me too long," she said. She was sorry about it now, but she also knew that she couldn't have done it any faster.

"I told you, Maddy, it's not about how fast you get there. It's about the journey. So what do you think?"

"I think I'm very lucky," she whispered.

"So am I," he said, as he put an arm around her shoulders and walked her back to the house, as Lizzie held the baby in her arms and watched them from an upstairs window. And as though Maddy sensed it, she looked up at her and smiled and waved, as Bill led her into the house, stopped her in the doorway, and kissed her. For them, it was not about a beginning or an end. It was about a life they shared, and the joy of knowing that the journey would continue for a long time to come.

About the Author

DANIELLE STEEL has been hailed as one of the world's most popular authors with over 430 million copies of her novels sold. Her many international bestsellers include: *The House on Hope Street, The Wedding, Irresistible Forces, Granny Dan, Bittersweet, Mirror Image, The Klone and I, The Long Road Home, The Ghost, Special Delivery, The Ranch,* and other highly acclaimed novels. She is also the author of *His Bright Light,* the story of her son Nick Traina's life and death.

DANIELLE STEEL

COMING OUT

COMING OUT

On sale now

Chapter 1

Olympia Crawford Rubinstein was whizzing around her kitchen on a sunny May morning, in the brownstone she shared with her family on Jane Street in New York, near the old meat-packing district of the West Village. It had long since become a fashionable neighborhood of mostly modern apartment buildings with doormen, and old renovated brownstones. Olympia was fixing lunch for her five-year-old son, Max. The school bus was due to drop him off in a few minutes. He was in kindergarten at Dalton, and Friday was a half day for him. She always took Fridays off to spend them with him. Although Olympia had three older children from her first marriage, Max was Olympia and Harry's only child.

Olympia and Harry had restored the house six

years before, when she was pregnant with Max. Before that, they had lived in her Park Avenue apartment, which she had previously shared with her three children after her divorce. And then Harry joined them. She had met Harry Rubinstein a year after her divorce. And now, she and Harry had been married for thirteen years. They had waited eight years to have Max, and his parents and siblings adored him. He was a loving, funny, happy child.

Olympia was a partner in a booming law practice, specializing in civil rights issues and class action lawsuits. Her favorite cases, and what she specialized in, were those that involved discrimination against or some form of abuse of children. She had made a name for herself in her field. She had gone to law school after her divorce, fifteen years before, and married Harry two years later. He had been one of her law professors at Columbia Law School, and was now a judge on the federal court of appeals. He had recently been considered for a seat on the Supreme Court. In the end, they hadn't appointed him, but he'd come close, and she and Harry both hoped that the next time a vacancy came up, he would get it.

She and Harry shared all the same beliefs, values, and passions—even though they came from very different backgrounds. He came from an Orthodox Jewish home, and both his parents had been Holocaust survivors as children. His mother had gone to Dachau from Munich at ten, and lost her entire family. His father had been one of the few survivors of Auschwitz, and they met in Israel later. They had married as teenagers, moved to London, and from there to the States. Both had lost their entire families, and their only son had become the focus of all their energies, dreams, and hopes. They had worked like slaves all their lives to give him an education, his father as a tailor and his mother as a seamstress, working in the sweatshops of the Lower East Side, and eventually on Seventh Avenue in what was later referred to as the garment district. His father had died just after Harry and Olympia married. Harry's greatest regret was that his father hadn't known Max. Harry's mother, Frieda, was a strong, intelligent, loving woman of seventy-six, who thought her son was a genius, and her grandson a prodigy.

Olympia had converted from her staunch Episcopalian background to Judaism when she married Harry. They attended a Reform synagogue, and Olympia said the prayers for Shabbat every Friday night, and lit the candles, which never failed to touch Harry. There was no doubt in Harry's mind, or even his mother's, that Olympia was a fantastic woman, a great mother to all her children, a terrific attorney, and a wonderful wife. Like Olympia, Harry had been married before, but he had no other children. Olympia was turning forty-five in July, and Harry was fifty-three. They were well matched in all ways, though their backgrounds couldn't have been more different. Even physically, they were an interesting and complementary combination. Her hair was blond, her eyes were blue; he was dark, with dark brown eyes; she was tiny; he was a huge teddy bear of a man, with a quick smile and an easygoing disposition. Olympia was shy and serious, though prone to easy laughter, especially when it was provoked by Harry or her children. She was a remarkably dutiful and loving daughter-in-law to Harry's mother, Frieda.

Olympia's background was entirely different from Harry's. The Crawfords were an illustrious and extremely social New York family, whose blue-blooded ancestors had intermarried with Astors and Vanderbilts for generations. Buildings and academic institutions were named after them, and theirs had been one of the largest "cottages" in

Newport, Rhode Island, where they spent the summers. The family fortune had dwindled to next to nothing by the time her parents died when she was in college, and she had been forced to sell the "cottage" and surrounding estate to pay their debts and taxes. Her father had never really worked, and as one of her distant relatives had said after he died, "he had a small fortune, he had made it from a large one." By the time she cleaned up all their debts and sold their property, there was simply no money, just rivers of blue blood and aristocratic connections. She had just enough left to pay for her education, and put a small nest egg away, which later paid for law school.

She married her college sweetheart, Chauncey Bedham Walker IV, six months after she graduated from Vassar, and he from Princeton. He had been charming, handsome, and fun-loving, the captain of the crew team, an expert horseman, played polo, and when they met, Olympia was understandably dazzled by him. Olympia was head over heels in love with him, and didn't give a damn about his family's enormous fortune. She was totally in love with Chauncey, enough so as not to notice that he drank too much, played constantly, had a roving eye, and spent far too much money. He went to work in his family's investment bank, and did anything he wanted, which eventually included going to work as seldom as possible, spending literally no time with her, and having random affairs with a multitude of women. By the time she knew what was happening, she and Chauncey had three children. Charlie came along two years after they were married, and his identical twin sisters, Virginia and Veronica, three years later. When she and Chauncey split up seven years after they married, Charlie was five, the twins two, and Olympia was twenty-nine years old. As soon as they separated, he quit his job at the bank, and went to live in Newport with his grandmother, the doyenne of Newport and Palm Beach society, and devoted himself to playing polo and chasing women.

A year later Chauncey married Felicia Weatherton, who was the perfect mate for him. They built a house on his grandmother's estate, which he ultimately inherited, filled her stables with new horses, and had three daughters in four years. A year after Chauncey married Felicia, Olympia married Harry Rubinstein, which Chauncey found not only ridiculous but appalling. He was rendered speechless when their son, Charlie, told him his mother had converted to the

Jewish faith. He had been equally shocked earlier when Olympia enrolled in law school, all of which proved to him, as Olympia had figured out long before, that despite the similarity of their ancestry, she and Chauncey had absolutely nothing in common, and never would. As she grew older, the ideas that had seemed normal to her in her youth appalled her. Almost all of Chauncey's values, or lack of them, were anathema to her.

The fifteen years since their divorce had been years of erratic truce, and occasional minor warfare, usually over money. He supported their three children decently, though not generously. Despite what he had inherited from his family, Chauncey was stingy with his first family, and far more generous with his second wife and their children. To add insult to injury, he had forced Olympia to agree that she would never urge their children to become Jewish. It wasn't an issue anyway. She had no intention of doing so. Olympia's conversion was a private, personal decision between her and Harry. Chauncey was unabashedly anti-Semitic. Harry thought Olympia's first husband was pompous, arrogant, and useless. Other than the fact that he was her children's father and she had loved him when she married him, for the past fifteen years, Olympia found it impossible to defend him. Prejudice was Chauncey's middle name. There was absolutely nothing politically correct about him or Felicia, and Harry loathed him. They represented everything he detested, and he could never understand how Olympia had tolerated him for ten minutes, let alone seven years of marriage. People like Chauncey and Felicia, and the whole hierarchy of Newport society, and all it stood for, were a mystery to Harry. He wanted to know nothing about it, and Olympia's occasional explanations were wasted on him.

Harry adored Olympia, her three children, and their son, Max. And in some ways, her daughter Veronica seemed more like Harry's daughter than Chauncey's. They shared all of the same extremely liberal, socially responsible ideas. Virginia, her twin, was much more of a throwback to their Newport ancestry, and was far more frivolous than her twin sister. Charlie, their older brother, was at Dartmouth, studying theology and threatening to become a minister. Max was a being unto himself, a wise old soul, who his grandmother swore was just like her own father, who had been a rabbi in Germany before being sent to Dachau, where he had helped as many people as he could before he was exterminated along with the rest of her family.

The stories of Frieda's childhood and lost loved ones always made Olympia weep. Frieda Rubinstein had a number tattooed on the inside of her left wrist, which was a sobering reminder of the childhood the Nazis had stolen from her. Because of it, she had worn long sleeves all her life, and still did. Olympia frequently bought beautiful silk blouses and long-sleeved sweaters for her. There was a powerful bond of love and respect between the two women, which continued to deepen over the years.

Olympia heard the mail being pushed through the slot in the front door, went to get it, and tossed it on the kitchen table as she finished making Max's lunch. With perfect timing, she heard the doorbell ring at almost precisely the same instant. Max was home from school, and she was looking forward to spending the afternoon with him. Their Fridays together were always special. Olympia knew she had the best of both worlds, a career she loved and that satisfied her, and a family that was the hub and core of her emotional existence. Each seemed to enhance and complement the other.

COMING THIS FALL

H.R.H.

BY

DANIELLE STEEL

On Sale in Hardcover
October 31, 2006

In a novel where ancient traditions conflict with
reality and the pressures of modern life, a young
European princess proves that simplicity,
courage, and dignity win the day and forever
alter her world.

Danielle
Steel

H.R.H.